REAL REGRETS

C.W. FARNSWORTH

REAL REGRETS

www.authorcwfarnsworth.com

To regret deeply is to live afresh.

HENRY DAVID THOREAU

CONTENTS

AUTHOR'S NOTE

Real Regrets can be read as a complete standalone, but it follows characters and storylines first introduced in *Fake Empire*. If you're planning to read both books, *Fake Empire* should be read first.

Happy reading!

Charlotte

REAL REGRETS

A bachelor party in Las Vegas is the last place Oliver Kensington wants to spend a long weekend. He likes controlling outcomes, not the uncertainty of gambling. For the most part, his reputation as the reliable, responsible Kensington brother is well-deserved. But for one of the few people he considers a friend, he'll show up in sin city.

Oliver's focus is on work—and on getting back into his father's good graces. But he's not expecting absolution for past mistakes; Arthur Kensington doesn't forgive.

So when an offer to forget is made as soon as Oliver returns to New York, it's shocking. And it's the same demand his father made years ago: to marry a woman as part of a business arrangement. This time, there's no chance his brother Crew will be the one waiting at the end of the aisle, which is how Oliver's last engagement ended.

The answer should be obvious. Most of Oliver's life has centered around earning his father's approval and becoming CEO, both of which he thought were lost opportunities. Learning they're not should be the best news he's received all year.

Problem is, there's a piece of paper in his pocket that says he's *already* married...to the blonde woman he met in the bar of a Vegas hotel.

REAL REGRETS

C.W. FARNSWORTH

PROLOGUE
OLIVER

"Don't answer."

I look away from the buzzing phone at my father's proud profile. Chin raised; shoulders squared. He's backlit by a single lamp that casts a golden glow over the study that's almost an exact replica of his office in New York. Oiled leather, dark wood, and expensive whiskey are the sights and smells I associate with my father. We're thousands of miles from Kensington Consolidated's headquarters, but it feels like we could be sitting in his corner office overlooking Manhattan.

"It's Crew."

"Don't answer," he repeats.

"Stock is in fucking freefall. Everyone will be panicking, and we're both out of the country."

My father sips his whiskey, appearing unbothered.

"Dad," I try again. "You can't just leave him on a sinking ship without telling him—"

"I'll do whatever I damn well want, Oliver." His voice is so soft, so low, that I automatically flinch. Loud, angry exclamations don't wound the same way quiet, intentional statements do. "And you're neither a current or future CEO, so your opinion is irrelevant." He sips from the glass tumbler he's holding, staring at the snow that glitters under the starry sky.

Words meant to maim.

Meant to sting.

Meant to hurt.

I swallow and nod, compartmentalizing the ache those words incite. Falling short has always been my biggest fear, and Arthur Kensington knows it. *Uses* it. Dangles his approval up ahead, part of a peak above a mountain he'll never let me reach the top of.

I'm the fool who keeps climbing anyway.

He tosses back the final inch of his drink and stands suddenly.

Glass doors lead out to the patio that's been coated with snow and ice every visit for the past decade but is probably pleasant in other seasons. My father stares at the endless stretch of white, his body language just as still and unmoving as the frozen water.

"Ethan Gorton will be accompanying me to Chicago next week."

My spine stiffens, the ice in his voice chilling my skin and spreading through my veins.

"I've worked on that offer for two months."

"You're needed in New York. Scarlett is expecting, and Crew's focus will be affected. Pregnant women are volatile and needy. Be glad you're not about to discover that for yourself."

I pull in a harsh breath of air as he carelessly brushes against the topic I'm terrified to raise.

My relationship with my father has always been centered around work. When I answered his summons, it was easy to pretend the company's insider trader investigation was the only current catastrophe.

Easy…and cowardly.

Suitcases line the front hall.

I step forward, sucking in another deep breath, as if oxygen equals courage. "Dad, I'm so sorr—"

I don't see it coming.

One second, I'm moving toward the tense figure facing the snow. The next, I'm nearly toppling backward as black dots explode across my vision, reeling from the impact and the shock of the physical blow.

I gape at him, stunned speechless and still.

My father has never, ever been the warm and coddling type of parent. He issues orders and makes demands. He doesn't ask questions or attempt small talk.

But he's never hit me.

Previous punishments were long silences or heavy stares. He's always preferred to let his disappointment do the talking, to smother me like a heavy blanket.

Pain trickles in slowly, as the shock ebbs away. I touch the raw skin of my cheek tentatively, tasting the metallic tang of copper on my tongue.

Fuck, that hurt. More than a punch from anyone else would have.

There's so much I could say to him. Justifications, explanations, admissions, excuses.

I could say I'm sick of being boiled down to my last name. I was born and raised to be a Kensington, and it's all I'm diminished to.

And I fucked up, trying to escape that for a minute.

I could shove my father's own shortcomings in his face. Tell him he was a terrible father and a worse husband and that plants wither without nourishment, but people become desperate. Become petty. Tell him that he's the reason his wife begged me to fuck her. That he shouldn't have married a woman younger than me and then ignored her existence, if her loyalty mattered to him.

"I've lost every iota of respect I ever had for you, Oliver," he hisses, pointing a finger in my face. His knuckles are red and raw, just as angry as his expression. "So don't you fucking say sorry, because *Kensingtons don't apologize.* And you be damn grateful for that name because it's the only reason you're not struggling to find a janitorial job. Outside of the company, you're no son of mine."

I knew my father wouldn't want an apology. Knew he sees admittance of mistakes to be weakness. But I needed an outlet. To expel the churning mass of regret in some way.

He wouldn't even let me get the damn word out.

Sorry, I say in my head.

But what comes out is, "I've *never* been your son outside the company."

A vein in my father's temple pulses. I focus on the rapid rise and fall, as rhythmic as a drum's beat.

He's used to deference from me. Crew was always the headache. The son who partied too much and snuck girls into the estate and was too easygoing for my father's ruthless tastes.

I was the reliable, predictable child. And while my father might not have always respected that obeisance, he appreciated it. Maybe more than he realized up until now.

My father walks over to the crystal tumbler I know is filled with his favorite whiskey. It costs five figures a bottle, and he downs it like water. I watch him pour himself a second glass, purposefully not offering me one. The minimal light is enough to show the platinum wedding band on his left hand is already gone.

Red eyes and soft pleas and a workaholic reputation. That's how I ended up here.

I ended a marriage.

A volatile, unhappy one I'm quite certain my father only entertained because having an attractive, young wife was convenient arm candy. Someone he could train and control, the same way he molded Crew and me.

But still…a marriage.

And despite spending most of my life being surrounded by—and half of—unhappy couples, that commitment still seems sacred to me.

Maybe because I saw it transform Crew firsthand. Watched my brother discover love as part of his marriage and learn to treat it as something precious.

My father and Candace never shared that bond, but knowing so isn't much of a relief. Not when my cheek stings, and I can hear Candace's desperate pleas begging me to make him reconsider.

Arthur Kensington doesn't listen to anyone.

Especially not me.

He turns, one eyebrow arching as he drains half a glass of amber liquid.

"Get the hell out of my sight."

I turn, knowing he'll think less of me for walking away on command, like a well-trained dog. But if I stay, he'll bemoan my inability to comply with a simple instruction. With him, I can never win.

"Oliver."

I stop, hand on the doorknob.

"Guard your secrets closely. If you ever fuck up again, I'll make sure every person in this country learns about it. I'm protecting *myself*, taking care of this. Not you. *Never* you. Understood?"

"Understood," I grit out.

I slam the study door behind me. It's childish and paltry, but the brief glimmer of satisfaction is the best I've felt all day.

CHAPTER ONE

OLIVER

When the door opens, my very drunk, very irritated brother is leaning heavily against the frame. All of his weight is supported on one hand while he aggressively yanks at his navy tie with the other.

He scowls when the knot refuses to give, like it's personally offended him by staying put. Belatedly realizing the door has opened, Crew shoves past me and stumbles into the penthouse, grumbling under his breath.

"Hello. Hi. Sure. Yeah. Come on in," I call after his disappearing back.

I'm still in my suit from work, but it doesn't smell like a distillery the way Crew's does. The woodsy, buttery aroma of whiskey lingers in the entryway longer than Crew does. It's the same scent I associate with my father. And what I usually drink.

I shut the door, sigh, and then follow my brother down the hall that leads to the living room.

When the doorbell rang, there were only two unread emails left to answer before I poured myself a stiff drink and changed into some sweatpants. I can feel that number ticking higher with each second that passes.

Kensington Consolidated does business with companies all over the world. Someone, somewhere, is always awake and replying. And when you're struggling to make it to the top—or struggling to accept you'll never *be* at the top, in my case—it means regular business hours don't exist.

Crew is sprawled out on the brown leather couch when I walk into the living room. One arm is flung dramatically over his eyes, black fabric blocking most of his face from sight.

"Guest rooms are upstairs."

He grunts. Doesn't move.

I rub my forehead, feeling a literal headache form, then drop into one of the matching leather armchairs. I hired an interior decorator to furnish this place, too busy to pick out anything myself. Since I always sit on the couch and rarely have company, this is the first time I'm sitting in one of the chairs. They're uncomfortable.

"So… What are you doing here?"

No response.

I clear my throat and cross my arms, worried I'll be stuck in this awkward purgatory where Crew sulks—or sleeps, I can't really tell what's happening under his arm—and I'm stuck sitting on what feels like a wooden board waiting for him to speak or shift.

Crew visiting me at home doesn't happen. He's been here once—twice, maybe—since I bought this penthouse a few years ago.

We're brothers who work together. Spending time together outside of the office or beyond the social events we're obligated to attend as part of our prominent roles at the company our great-grandfather founded is basically unheard of. It was rare back when Crew spent his free time at Manhattan's most elite clubs, and basically unheard of now that he has a wife, daughter, and dog.

"I got into it with Scarlett earlier." Crew finally speaks. "Went to a bar and then came here." He lifts his arm and fixes me with a serious, tired stare. "Don't get married, Oliver."

"Thanks for the unsolicited advice," I reply, eyeing the bar cart in the corner of the room with the same longing desperation someone stranded in a storm would seek shelter.

Marriage is an unappealing prospect, low on my priority list—if it's even on there at all. Aside from the phase in my life when I thought my wife was already chosen for me, I've given little thought to it. With each failed relationship, the possibility has drifted further away. If you ask any woman I dated in the past decade, I'm already married—to my job.

Ironically, Crew is the reason I have any favorable thoughts about the institution. All the marriages I've seen up close have fallen apart in some way, cracks cratering the surface until they collapse.

Except for Crew's.

I've witnessed his relationship take hits, but I've never seen a fissure form. Cynical as I am, that gives me a little hope.

I glance at my brother. He's silent. Still. I can't even hear him breathing.

A vein in my temple pounds as I study his unmoving form. I don't know what to say to him. Crew doesn't want to hear about how close I was to clearing my inbox before he arrived. I have no marital wisdom to offer. But I can't bring myself to leave him lying here, sulking and showing no signs of leaving, so I can return to my usual evening routine.

Even if that's what he was expecting—hoping—by coming

here. Crew probably showed up so he could sleep off the whiskey in silence, not for an amateur therapy session.

I focus my gaze on the windows, which boast a twenty-million-dollar view of Central Park. The lights of the city twinkle around the rectangle of greenery that's currently just brown grass and the skeletal outlines of trees, representing a hundred places I'd rather be than hearing my little brother complain about his happy life.

Ever since he fell for the heiress our father arranged for him to marry—because in our world, billionaires marry billionaires, or at the very least multi-millionaires—Crew has changed. He starts conversations about feelings and family. He mentions our mother, Elizabeth, who he named his one-year-old daughter after. And he talks about his relationship with his wife, Scarlett, as if I have insight to offer or will make restaurant recommendations for their weekly date night.

My romantic past is boring at best and scandalous at worst. Each "relationship" has ended with tears, yelling, or my father punching me in the face.

In a word, I'm *replaceable*. Usually by the guy who inherited the same genes yet somehow turned out better, currently half falling off of my sofa, grumbling something about being home by eight and unreasonable expectations. Since he's obviously not talking to me, I don't even pretend to be paying attention.

Saying my life has ever been hard is a stretch. I'm a Kensington. Everything has always been handed to me on a platinum platter.

In theory, the easy deliverance sounds wonderful.

In reality, it means I work twice as hard for everything I accomplish, and it's written off as nepotism or purchased achievements anyway.

That I'm always reaching for something while already having everything.

As the second son, Crew was supposed to be the spare. My supporting act. He's always been the relaxed, charming brother. Devil may care. Rather than resent all he's been handed already, everyone wants to pass him more.

More praise, more admiration, more attention, just *more*.

That's not to say he doesn't deserve recognition. Crew is smart and driven. People underestimated him as a cocky playboy and are lulled into a false sense of complacency now that he's the wholesome family man.

But it stings—being constantly upstaged by your *baby* brother. I tried to set a good example for him. I tried to show my father I was strong enough to survive losing my mother. And all those good intentions turned into expectations I can't seem to shake.

Crew's reputation has changed and shifted over the years. Mine has remained constant. I'm the serious, responsible oldest child. The Kensington you can always rely upon. The dependable brother who does exactly what's expected. The few times I've attempted to escape that predictability have ended horribly and have never managed to make me any happier. They've always turned into regrets.

So I've accepted my role, the same way I watched as Crew was handed the CEO position and the billionaire bride.

I didn't want to marry Scarlett Ellsworth. I *would* have, but I didn't *want* to.

I expected to be my father's successor at Kensington Consolidated.

Worse, *everyone else* expected it.

And the depressing kicker is, I *did* want the coveted title. Still do, even knowing it's forever out of my reach.

I don't really care what people think of me. It doesn't bother me that they whisper about why my father skipped over me. It's my own dissatisfaction that makes it burn, not what anyone else says or thinks. They're not the ones waking up every morning to work at a company they'll never lead.

"How long were you planning on staying?" I ask the sprawled figure that hasn't moved for the past few minutes.

Crew raises his arm again, this time to glare at me. "Am I inconveniencing you?"

Yes. "I figured you'd go to Asher's."

The arm drops. "He's busy tonight," Crew says.

I don't *want* Crew camped out in my living room, pouting. But it stings a little, knowing I was his second choice, even if it isn't surprising. His best friend would undoubtedly be better equipped to handle this situation.

Asher would have jokes ready or bring Crew to a club to get his mind off everything. I've been repeatedly told I have no sense of humor, and the last time I went clubbing was to celebrate graduating business school.

I stand and walk over to the metal bar cart, filling two glasses with the same expensive whiskey my father drinks. Even when he's not here, he is. And it's not just the alcohol that evokes his presence. He's also here in the awkwardness that always hovers between Crew and me, evidence we never learned how to act naturally around each other the way most siblings do.

I set one tumbler of whiskey on the coffee table in front of Crew and then retreat to my uncomfortable armchair, downing most of the smoky alcohol in one gulp.

"What happened with Scarlett?" I ask.

Crew and Scarlett arguing is nothing new. But Crew going out to a bar and then showing up here *is* new. And concerning.

For all the meticulous planning about merging their empires, my father and Hanson Ellsworth never considered their children might fall in love. They thought the allure of money and power would be enough to bind Scarlett and Crew together permanently —they're two logical, driven people who benefit more by being married than by not. And while love might have strengthened their marriage, it is also the one thing that could destroy it. My father understands that, even though I'm not sure he's capable of the emotion himself. It's why he didn't stop meddling once they were married.

After attending my brother's wedding, I would have bet five figures that he and his wife would be living in separate buildings two years later while one or both carried on discreet affairs. Last I saw them together, they looked nauseatingly happy.

Crew *finally* sits up and picks up the drink. He studies the amber liquid for a few seconds but doesn't take a sip. Instead he swishes the contents around like a connoisseur, watching the whiskey slosh up the sides and then drip down the inside of the glass. "She's pregnant," he states, then sucks the whole drink down in one go.

"Congratulations?" It comes out as more of a question than a celebration, since Crew is frowning instead of beaming. These are better circumstances than how he told me Scarlett was pregnant the first time, but not by much.

He nods once, studying the empty tumbler like it contains all of life's secrets. "Thanks. It wasn't planned…again."

"I hate to sound like a middle school health teacher, but there's this new thing called birth control. I can grab a banana from the kitchen if you need a demonstration."

Crew rolls his eyes and leans back with a sigh, the barest glimmer of a smile turning his lips up. "Not that it's *any* of your goddamn business, but Lili had strep last month. Scarlett came down with it too."

"Okay..." I have no idea what strep throat has to do with pregnancy.

His smile deepens a little in response to my obvious confusion. "Antibiotics mess with the pill's effectiveness."

"Oh." I study Crew's drooped posture. "Scarlett isn't happy about the pregnancy?"

"Lili is barely one. It's shitty timing; *rouge* is everywhere and Haute's distribution tripled last year. Scarlett wants to be flying around the world and pulling all-nighters at the office and modeling her designs...and she can't do any of that pregnant. It's already been a struggle balancing both of our schedules with one kid. *Two* kids under two?" He runs a hand through his hair, then exhales deeply.

I stay silent. I have no advice to offer him on this topic either. Kids are nothing I have experience with or have really considered, aside from the abstract knowledge that as the eldest child I'd probably need to have them so they could inherit my family's massive fortune.

Crew has taken care of that for me. Elizabeth Kensington—Lili, as she's called now—is currently the sole heir of an unfathomable amount of money. Not only the Kensington assets but also her mother's inheritance, which was massive to begin with and is constantly growing thanks to Scarlett's supercharged work ethic. In addition to owning a successful magazine, Scarlett started her own fashion line shortly after she and Crew got married.

Aside from the fact it's landed my brother on my couch, I'm happy to hear Scarlett and Crew are having another kid. It takes more of the pressure off me to settle down and do the same. Especially if this baby is a boy, since we live in a sexist society and the business world is no exception.

"I'm sure it will all work out," I say, emphasizing how terrible I am at offering useful advice.

I can't assure Crew of anything. I'm his older brother, yet in nearly every aspect of life, he's far ahead of me. He's a husband and father, weighed down by responsibilities his younger self laughed at. And they're responsibilities he *wants*, not obligations.

Crew is worried about how this baby will affect Scarlett. But he's juggling as much work at Kensington Consolidated as I am—a lot. Neither of us are great about delegating important tasks, partly to make it clear nepotism isn't the only reason we hold prominent roles at the company. Mostly because, for all his faults, Arthur Kensington did a remarkable job of instilling a solid work ethic into both of us, despite the immense privilege and wealth we inherited. Given the size of our trust funds, neither Crew nor I *needed* to work a day of our lives.

"Yeah." He holds up the empty glass. "Mind if I help myself?"

A snarky response forms at the tip of my tongue, about how he's already helped himself to plenty that was meant to be mine. But I swallow it the same way I compartmentalize everything else. I don't think Crew has any idea how much the CEO title matters to me, and I don't want him to. Who gets it has never been up to him—or to me. "Go ahead," is all I say.

Crew fills his glass and then slumps back down into the couch. His posture is defeated and exhausted. He alternates between glancing at his phone, which he set on the glass coffee table, and out the windows at the glittering city lights.

I yawn. I woke up at five a.m. to work out before heading into the office, and this is the first time I've sat with nothing to do all day. Exhaustion is spreading through my body, turning it sluggish and uncooperative.

If Crew was here wondering about stock options or wanting to discuss expense reports, I would know exactly how to respond. But a discussion of his marriage and a new baby has me at a loss.

He cares about his family in a way I've never witnessed up close. My mother died when I was seven. Long before then, I saw the cracks in my parents' marriage. Crew grew up in the same chilly circumstances I did, and now he's part of a family that laughs and hugs and loves and struggles openly. That doesn't pretend to be perfect and is infinitely closer to that standard because of it.

"Isn't the second kid supposed to be easier than the first?" I ask, taking another stab at reassurance. "I mean, you've done it all once before."

Crew laughs, but there's no humor in the sound. "Yep. Done it all once before. Went to the grocery store at two a.m. because Scarlett wanted strawberry ice cream and we had every flavor of ice cream *except* strawberry. Slept on a pile of dresses because she pulled everything out of her closet once her clothes stopped fitting. Once I put the toilet paper on the holder the wrong way, and she cried for twenty minutes. She will never let me forget how late I was to the hospital when she went into labor. And then there's diapers and crying and no sleeping *and* having to take care of Lili on top of all that. Does that sound *easier*?"

"No." Sounds terrible, honestly.

The last time I saw Lili was at Christmas, which Scarlett and Crew hosted. I attended the party at their penthouse, along with about forty other people. The highlight was that Lili had just started walking, wobbling around in a pair of toddler Mary Jane's, and a custom velvet dress Scarlett designed. Advanced for her age, according to the whispered conversation I overheard by the champagne tower, but hardly surprising considering who her parents are. None of the chaos Crew just described was visible.

The doorbell rings before I can come up with anything else to say.

Crew doesn't react to the sound. I stand, setting my empty

glass down on the coffee table before heading down the hall to the front door.

I'm surprised—and relieved—to see my sister-in-law standing in the hallway when I open the door.

My penthouse takes up the top two floors of the building, so it's the only door option in this hallway. But while Crew's visits have been rare, this is the first time Scarlett has *ever* been here. I wasn't even sure she knew where I lived.

"You included me on the approved list," she states, shoving both hands into the pockets of her down jacket. Scarlett is dressed more casually than I'm used to seeing her, in black leggings and snow boots. "I thought I'd have to bribe my way up here."

"I'll take some *rouge* clothes."

One dark eyebrow arches. "For…"

"What do you think?" The demand for Scarlett's designs is now infamous; what her brand is most associated with. When a woman learns my last name, I've grown accustomed to the first question being asked is if I can get her off *rouge*'s waiting list.

"We're sold out. You'll have to manage to get laid some other way." Scarlett smiles, but it fades fast. "Is Crew here?"

I step aside and tilt my chin toward the left. "Living room."

"Thanks." Rather than walk inside like I'm expecting, Scarlett reaches to the left. The next thing I know, a baby stroller and a golden retriever are filling what was once a clean, empty space.

Teddy's tail starts wagging as soon as he sees me, recognizing me from my second, occasional job as a pet sitter. Whenever they've both been out of town, Scarlett and Crew have asked me to watch their dog. I like animals, but considering I basically only come home to sleep, it doesn't seem fair to have one.

Scarlett scoops Lili out of the stroller while Teddy weaves around my legs, covering my once-pristine suit with golden hair.

"She woke up in the elevator," Scarlett says, holding her

daughter out to me. Lili's blue eyes—identical to Crew's—blink at me.

"Scarlett…" I'd take Crew showing up—alone—a hundred times over this. Teddy is one thing. But I've never babysat. I'm shocked Scarlett is even willing to entrust me with Lili.

"Five minutes."

Reluctantly, I take the toddler. Lili squirms in my arms, then grabs my tie and yanks. For a one-year-old, she's awfully strong.

"If she starts crying, feed her a banana," Scarlett tells me, then heads into the living room.

"Unbelievable," I mutter, looking down at my niece.

She pulls on my tie again.

I carry Lili into the kitchen, Teddy padding after us. He walks right over to the corner where I put his food bowl, sniffing around before curling up on the floor. Shifting Lili to one hip and hoping she can't reach my tie from this angle, I head into the pantry, sifting through boxes of pasta and cereal for the dog treats I bought last time Teddy stayed here. Finally finding them, I grab the treats before returning to the kitchen.

The first floor of the penthouse has an open layout. I can see Scarlett sitting on the couch next to Crew. Watch as she takes his hand and says something to him. Crew turns toward Scarlett and replies with something that has her leaning into him. He pulls her close, kisses her forehead, and I feel like a voyeur in my own space, witnessing a moment not meant for anyone except the two of them.

Teddy happily munches on the treat I toss him. Lili won't stop squirming, so I grab a banana out of the bowl and take a seat on one of the stools. I'm scared to set her down.

"Bnana." I glance down as Lili waves a little hand around, trying to grab at the yellow fruit.

"Wow, you can talk now, huh?"

Her reply is garbled nonsense before she shoves the first bite of banana in her mouth. Within a minute, she's eaten the entire thing.

Saving me from the dilemma of figuring out what to do next, Crew appears. He still looks tired but less stressed.

"Dada!" Lili calls as soon as she sees him.

"Hi, sweetheart." Crew takes Lili from me, wincing as she grabs at his hair. I guess I should be grateful all she got in her grip was my tie. "You talked Uncle Oliver into a banana after bedtime?"

"I didn't know she *could* talk," I say, standing and shoving my sticky hands into my pockets.

"She has a few words in her vocabulary now," Crew says, smiling proudly at his daughter. "She hasn't said Mama yet though, so Scarlett pretends it's all still gibberish."

"I heard that." Scarlett walks into the kitchen holding a red leash. Teddy stands and lumbers over to her, waiting patiently for her to clip it to his collar. "Thanks for watching her, Oliver."

"Yeah, thanks for…thanks," Crew adds. Our uncertainty about what to say to each other is mostly mutual.

I clear my throat and nod, not sure what else to say. The front door clicks shut a few seconds later, leaving silence behind. Annoyingly, I'm no longer looking forward to solitude and sweat-pants the way I was before Crew showed up unexpectedly.

I look at the browning banana peel on the counter, then at the tufts of golden fur on the kitchen floor. Instead of peaceful, the penthouse feels empty.

It's easier to be alone when it feels like a choice, instead of an inevitability.

CHAPTER TWO

HANNAH

Hockey rinks have a distinct smell. Different from the fresh air and earth scent of soccer fields or baseball diamonds.

My eyes close for a minute as I inhale deeply. The cool bite to the air burns my lungs, accompanied by the lingering odors of cooled sweat, chemical cleaner, rubber, and buttered popcorn. With my sight restricted, all the smells seem to sharpen. Something about the mix of them swirling in the chilled air is more relaxing than appalling. For a few seconds, I can pretend I'm somewhere else.

"Miss Garner."

I open my eyes, turning away from the bird's-eye view of the arena to watch Robert Damon approach. Balding, portly, and pushing sixty, the general manager of the Las Vegas Coyotes makes the predictable choice to check out my cleavage before his eyes migrate up to my face. I resist the urge to double check I didn't miss a button. I only had ten minutes to change between checking in to the hotel and heading here, so it's a definite possibility.

"Mr. Damon." I hold out a hand to shake and fix a polite smile on my face.

He chuckles as our palms connect, his hand warm and slightly damp. I suppress a grimace as the handshake lasts a few seconds longer than necessary, his beady gaze making another trip down to my chest in the extended length of time.

"Call me Robert, please." His voice is as repellant as the rest of him, high and reedy.

Robert waits, presumably for me to reciprocate the offer and tell him to call me Hannah. I don't. I'm happy to remain on professional terms with him.

"The facility is impressive," I say, pulling my palm free and gesturing toward the flawless ice I was just admiring. I focus on taking in the impressive view for a second time, instead of wiping my palm on my pants the way I want to. "This is only the team's second season, correct?"

I'm not actually asking; I *know* it is.

But allowing Robert to think he knows more about his team than I do serves a purpose, just like not commenting on his wandering gaze does. Pissing him off won't make this visit any more pleasant. I'm here to play a role, and I'll do a damned good job of it.

"That's correct." Robert smiles. "I appreciate when a woman does her homework."

My smile stays fixed. It tightens, freezing like poured concrete as he cements my initial assumption that he's a misogynistic asshole. Jerk or not, he's a bridge I can't burn.

Robert sighs, happily looking out at the ice rink. The frozen water reflects the bright lights of the arena, glimmering off the smooth surface.

It's an overwhelming sight, like standing in the center of an empty cathedral. Huge and majestic, to the point it shrinks everything else into perspective. Makes you feel tiny and inconsequential and awed.

"This was a bitch of a project to push through," Robert tells me, residual annoyance lingering in the words as he studies the finished product. "But worth it, in the end."

I nod, biting the inside of my cheek so nothing snarky about the questionable genius of building a massive hockey stadium in the middle of the desert can slip out. While dubious from an environmental and logical perspective, it's an architectural marvel. In keeping with the city's flashy reputation, the domed ceiling is designed to look like a mirrorball with thousands of reflective facets displaying a distorted image of the empty arena.

"Would you like a tour of behind the scenes?"

"That sounds great."

Robert nods, anticipating my answer the same way I was expecting the offer. When he looks away, I take the opportunity to check my shirt, relieved to see all the buttons are done up.

Today's visit to the Coyotes' facility is part of a tired, predictable routine.

Well, *I'm* tired of it. Robert looks like this is the highlight of his week as he summons over a petite redhead from the corner of the suite. She's dressed professionally, just like me, in a blazer, skirt, and heels. A lanyard emblazoned with the Coyotes' logo hangs around her neck.

"Lauren can show you around," Robert tells me. "She handles public relations for the team. Lauren, this is Hannah Garner. From *Garner* Sports Agency."

I don't miss the impressed look that appears on Lauren's face as Robert emphasizes my last name, immediately followed by understanding. The *that's why she's here* conclusion. The *nepotism look.*

I don't hate it because I worked my ass off to get here and am craving acknowledgment of that fact. I hate it because I *didn't* earn my spot at the business making a few hundred million in commissions annually.

My father is a big deal in the sports world. Since childhood—his, not mine—he's been involved in it somehow, some way. Player, coach, owner, manager, agent. When I graduated college and wasn't sure what to do next with my life, he suggested I give the "family business" a try.

So I did.

And now, five years later, I'm still stuck in place without really moving anywhere. I have a corner office and a generous salary, and an *Executive Vice President* nameplate on my door.

But it feels like I've accomplished next to nothing. Like I'm swimming, not just floating, but still headed nowhere certain. There's always more water ahead and no expected destination in sight. I just keep moving.

I shake Lauren's manicured hand when she holds it out to me. "Nice to meet you, Lauren."

"Nice to meet you, Miss Garner."

I open my mouth to tell her to call me Hannah, then shut it. Insulting Robert Damon would be a dumb decision. And that's exactly how he'll take me inviting an employee he undoubtedly considers inferior to call me by my first name when I didn't extend him the same courtesy.

A fake smile stays plastered on my face while I mentally count down the minutes until I can leave the Coyotes' facility and return to my hotel room.

This Vegas visit was a stop my father sprang on me. He called this morning, when I was already on my way to the airport from my best friend Rosie's apartment in Hyde Park, to ask if I'd be willing to meet with Robert this afternoon.

He said it made sense because I was already traveling but I know the real reason. I work for a sports agency, but I'm not a sports agent, which makes these sorts of interactions more casual. My father calls me his secret weapon, and it makes extricating myself from a career I never wanted infinitely more complicated.

"We can start by looking in the press office?" Lauren suggests.

"Sounds great," I reply, following her out of the executive suite that overlooks the rink.

Robert trails behind us, unfortunately. I was hoping he had something more important to do and wouldn't be tagging along on the tour.

This entire meeting is a sales pitch. Vegas is an expansion team in the middle of their second season. They're fighting for relevance among franchises that have existed for close to a century. Those teams have *history*. Dedicated fans and season ticket holders. Their jerseys are the ones PeeWee players dream of wearing, that carry a prestige earned through blood, sweat, and multiple championships.

Garner Sports Agency negotiates contracts for seasoned veterans and rising stars. Every team's money is worth the same amount, but that doesn't make them equal in other respects.

Vegas wants more established players who will bring relevance with them. Ones fans will turn on televisions and buy tickets to see play because of the name on the back of the jersey, regardless of the logo on the front.

Impressing me—by extension, my father, who represents and advises many current and future hockey stars—is what Robert Damon and the rest of the Coyotes management hope to accomplish this afternoon.

The rest of the building isn't nearly as impressive as the

ceiling was. Everything looks brand-new because it is. But the locker and equipment rooms otherwise appear the same as the ten other stadiums I've taken similar tours of in the past few years.

I keep nodding and smiling as we walk down a hallway lined with color photos of players on the ice, listening to Robert prattle on about the state-of-the-art, high-definition video boards.

Finally, we end up back in the executive suite where we started. Robert has me promise to return to Vegas for a home game sometime soon before I'm shown out of the stadium and into the waiting car that brought me here a couple of hours ago.

As soon as the car door shuts, I kick off my heels and sink back against the leather seat, wishing I could get on a flight back to Los Angeles right now, instead of waiting until the morning. Back when I first started working at Garner Sports Agency, the frequent travel sounded exciting. A chance to see more of the country after living my whole life in California. I no longer view it with the same excitement.

My younger sister Rachel texts me as the car turns onto the famous Strip. Neon lights flash on either side of the boulevard, the setting sun allowing the artificial brightness covering each building to start shining.

Rachel: *You're in Vegas???*

Neither Rachel nor my older brother Edward chose to become involved in the sports industry. Their athletic careers ended in elementary school. I was the one who stuck with soccer through high school, knowing my dad loved to coach. What's now a croquet course in my parents' backyard used to be a soccer field, complete with a regulation-sized goal.

Rachel is a high school English teacher. She's a bookworm who loves kids, so the job suits her perfectly.

Edward—Eddie—is an anesthesiologist married to his high

school sweetheart, April. Five months ago, they announced they're expecting a baby. My first niece or nephew will arrive in about a month.

And then there's me. The middle child outwardly successful and inwardly unsure.

I text Rachel back, knowing she'll blow up my phone if I don't respond quickly.

Hannah: *Yes.*

Predictably, Rachel replies immediately.

Rachel: *Yes????*

Rachel: *You're in VEGAS and you're only response is YES?*

Hannah: *I think you meant *your*

Bad grammar is one of Rachel's biggest pet peeves. If you ask her, she's unhappily single because the online dating world is chock full of the barely literate. Her words, not mine. Although I have seen some of the screenshots she's sent me and she has a point.

Rachel's name flashes across the screen with an incoming call a few seconds later. I answer it with a sigh, already knowing what she'll say.

"First off, it was autocorrect, not me. Secondly, when are you going to tell Dad that you're a grown woman, not an errand girl?"

"He's my boss, Rachel. It's my job."

"You took the day off. Dad will love you just as much, Hannah, if you set some boundaries."

"Wow. I can't believe you had time to get a psychology degree between teaching and reading those romance books you love."

I caught Rachel reading a paperback with a shirtless man on the cover on Thanksgiving, and I've made a point to tease her about it multiple times since.

"First off, I'm a Garner. *Obviously*, I can multitask. And second, you should read one. Your life could use a little romance."

Rachel isn't wrong, but I'm not about to admit it. Since breaking up with Declan, I've gone on plenty of dates. Partly to prove to my family I'm fine. But Declan's parting words echo in my head and make me wonder if there's any point. *No one wants a challenge that never ends*, he told me. I've heard some version of the same sentiment before. It's never felt easy with anyone, so it's always turned into a hard relationship until it ends.

"I'll keep that in mind, thanks."

"When will you be home? I was going to see if you wanted to go to that new sushi place tonight, and then Mom mentioned Dad sent you to the seminary of debauchery."

"My flight leaves at eleven a.m. tomorrow. I'll be back in LA early afternoon. And it's not that exciting here. Hardly a *seminary of debauchery*."

I got used to Rachel's wordsmithery back when she won the fifth-grade spelling bee. It doesn't even merit a sarcastic comment about memorizing the dictionary at this point.

"Then you're obviously doing it wrong."

I don't argue with that because she's probably right.

For someone who spends so much time in fictional worlds, Rachel has a zest for life I lack. She's always trying new hobbies. She spends her summers off traveling around the world. When I'm not working, I mostly just redecorate my house because I can't settle on a consistent theme.

"I'm here for work."

"You won't be working tonight," Rachel sings. "Put on a tight dress and go to one of those male stripper shows."

I roll my eyes as the car stops in front of the swanky hotel I'm staying at. "I have to go. I'll talk to you when I'm back in LA and we can go to the sushi spot soon."

"Fine. Love you, sis."

"Love you too."

I say goodbye to the driver and then climb out of the car, headed for the hotel's automatic doors.

CHAPTER THREE

OLIVER

Asher Cotes and Isabel Sterling jump apart as soon as I enter the executive floor's break room to grab a sparkling water from the fridge. Since they were only standing about a foot apart to begin with, I take their mutual jumpiness to mean they've spent time together in even closer proximity.

I couldn't care less if they're sleeping together. My father—and *Crew*—would be another story. Kensington Consolidated likely has a non-fraternization policy, but since dating an employee has never been so much as a passing thought in my mind, I don't actually know if we do or not. If it's not explicit, it's certainly implied.

"Morning, Oliver," Asher says easily, tucking a hand in his pocket and leaning back against the wall. His expression evens as he regains his usual, relaxed composure.

"Morning," I respond, striding over to the glass-fronted fridge to grab the chilled water I came in here for.

"Good Friday so far?" Asher asks, the casual smirk that's normally a permanent fixture on his face appearing.

Cool air chills my face as I grab a glass bottle from the neat line of waters before shutting the fridge door. "No major complaints."

"I'm hearing good things about Thompson & Thompson."

I nod before twisting the cap off my water and taking a long sip. Bubbles burn my throat as Asher attempts more small talk. I'm guessing he's trying to distract me from Isabel.

"Ready for the Henderson pitch this afternoon?" he asks me.

"I won't be there. I'm leaving for Las Vegas in a couple of hours."

Asher's eyebrows crawl up his forehead until they're nearly to his hairline. "*You're* going to *Vegas*?"

Irritation sparks in response to his incredulous tone, so I address Isabel in response. "That's what I *just* said, no?"

She nods and clears her throat, smoothing the unwrinkled fabric of her dress. Wisely opting to say nothing.

If she and Asher are actually involved, I'm surprised. Asher is competent in his role, but everyone knows he works here because of Crew. In contrast, Isabel is ruthless and motivated. Every project we've worked on together, she's impressed me. I wouldn't have guessed she'd be willing to possibly sacrifice her professional reputation for a fling with a colleague. And I wouldn't have guessed Asher was willing to overlook the obvious crush she had on Crew when she first started working here. I always figured he avoided women interested in Crew, the same way I do.

"Enjoy your…break." I cap my water and head for the door.

Employees scatter out of my way as I stride back down the carpeted hallway toward my office. I have a dozen tasks to take care of before leaving a long list I'm sure has grown in the past few minutes.

My hasty steps falter when a familiar voice calls out my name.

I look over at Scarlett, and so does everyone else in the immediate vicinity. My sister-in-law saunters toward me purposefully, ignoring the many stares she's attracting.

There's no trace of the casual attire she was wearing last night. Scarlett looks every inch the successful billionaire she is, dressed in a tailored wool coat. Her dark hair is pulled up in a high ponytail that swings with each confident stride, the red-bottomed heels she's wearing not slowing her down.

I pause in place, my grip on the glass bottle tightening as I experience a flicker of uncertainty.

I'm never quite sure how to act around Scarlett. She has an intimidating presence, but it's more than that. I spent years thinking I would marry her. She represents part of the future I expected to be living right now.

"Morning, Scarlett." I lean forward and kiss her cheek, hyper-aware of how this hallway is lined by glass offices.

"Good morning, Oliver."

In public, Scarlett and I are unfailingly polite around each other. In private, we don't have much of a relationship at all. Most of our interactions are performative.

"Crew's office is the other way."

Her humorless expression shifts, revealing a glimmer of amusement. "I know. I was headed toward yours."

"Oh?" I incline my head, masking my uneasiness. That's another thing about Scarlett. Her poker face is as good as—better than—mine. I rarely have any idea what she's thinking, and now is no exception.

"I wanted to thank you," Scarlett says. "For last night."

"Oh." I break eye contact and tug on my tie. The knot suddenly feels too tight and restrictive. Uneasiness has turned uncomfortable as we move into totally foreign territory. I'm from a *pretend it never happened* family, and my guess is the Ellsworths were like that too. "All I did was get him drunker."

Scarlett's signature red lips quirk upward. "You did more than that. You were there for Crew. That means a lot to him. And…to me."

The last two words are tacked on after a pause.

Another one follows them.

I have to clear my throat twice before speaking, and my response still comes out gruff. "Anytime."

"Don't you have a fashion empire to run, Mrs. Kensington?" Asher's teasing voice interrupts.

I startle, having completely forgotten we're standing in the middle of the hallway.

Scarlett tightens the belt on her coat before she glances over at Asher approaching us. It draws my attention down to her flat stomach. I wonder if she knows Crew mentioned the pregnancy to me.

He's the convoy for most information between us, the source of what I hear about Scarlett and what she knows about me, and it's belatedly occurring to me that our relationship could be more dimensional.

"Surprised to hear you mention hard work. I thought that was a foreign concept to you." Scarlett sends Asher a sweet smile.

He chuckles in response. "Just here to keep Crew company while he takes over the world. He's in a meeting with Arthur, at the moment."

Something ugly and unpleasant curdles in my stomach. I should be used to getting cut out by now, but it stings every single time.

"I know," Scarlett replies. But she's not looking at Asher. She's focused on me with an intensity that makes me think she noticed my reaction.

Crew has always tiptoed around unequivocally becoming our father's favorite. I know it's because he knows Candace is a touchy topic. Scarlett's piercing gaze seems to see deeper than that, down to the other reasons it bothers me so much.

"Did you hear that Oliver is headed to *Vegas*?" Asher chuckles, still finding the trip funny.

Scarlett nods, then glances at me. "Garrett Anderson's bachelor party, right?"

"Right." Crew is a more detailed messenger than I thought. I wasn't expecting her to know that.

"You're friends with Garrett Anderson?" Asher asks. He sounds surprised, and a little impressed.

"We went to college together," I say.

Friends is a term that's thrown around loosely among the elite. A way to signify alliances or hint at insider knowledge. Truly the personification of *keep your friends close and your enemies closer*.

Garrett Anderson is someone I actually consider a friend. Aside from Crew, he's the one person I would attend a bachelor party in Las Vegas for. Asher was in charge of planning Crew's bachelor party, and we ended up at a rock-climbing place. It was about as terrible as it sounds. Strippers and gambling aren't my scene either. But Garrett called to invite me personally, so I agreed to go.

"You guys must be pretty close, if you're flying to Vegas."

"Chase planned it."

"Wait. Chase…as in *Chase Anderson*? The hockey player?" Asher asks. "You're partying in Vegas with Chase Anderson?"

"Yep," I confirm. "I suggested we go to a rock gym instead, but he thought that sounded lame."

"Fucking hilarious, Oliver."

Scarlett's red lips twitch. I forgot she was at the start of Crew's bachelor party. After she stormed out shortly after we arrived, Crew sulked for the rest of the night. Saying the "party" was a disaster is an understatement.

The elevator doors we're standing next to *ding* and open. My father steps out, with Crew right behind him.

They're an intimidating pair. A king and his chosen heir. An emperor and his successor.

The only difference between them is that Crew's stoic mask drops when he sees our small group, and *Scarlett*, specifically.

My father's stoicism never wavers. He's never learned how to appreciate someone for more than how they benefit him. Not even a nod of acknowledgment is aimed our way. Probably because I'm part of the group.

"Get me updates on those projects by noon, Crew." That's all my father says before continuing down the hall toward the largest office on the floor.

"Okay," is Crew's reply to his retreating back.

He's fully focused on Scarlett, who's mouthing something to him that makes Crew grin and shake his head.

Crew looks to me next. My expression remains blank. I know exactly what he's testing me out for, and I have no interest in reacting.

"Hey."

"Hi," I reply.

Crew appears unsure what to say next.

"I've got a meeting. I'll see you at lunch," Asher says. He glances at me. "Have fun in Vegas, man."

"Thanks."

Crew is whispering something to Scarlett that makes her smile and shake her head.

They look like a happy, normal couple, with no trace of the stress that was on display last night.

Crew and I share the same parents and the same upbringing.

Yet Crew somehow managed to do what has always felt impossible for me.

He let someone in.

I always expect the worst from people. Often, they deliver. They try to use me for my money or my name. My connections or my favor. When you're always looking for duplicity, it's easy to spot.

But I don't think there's anything Scarlett could do that Crew wouldn't forgive. He fought for her even when evidence was damning. I've never been able to figure out where that confidence came from. I've never experienced that surety.

"I have to get to a meeting." Scarlett smiles, pats Crew's chest, then glances at me. "Have a good trip, Oliver."

I nod. "Thank you."

I'm expecting Crew to follow Scarlett over to the elevators, but he remains by my side after giving her a quick kiss goodbye.

"He wants a Thompson & Thompson update."

When I glance over, Crew is staring straight ahead. Everything about his body language is now uncomfortable—his tensed shoulders and tightened jaw and rigid arms. We both know where arguing with Arthur Kensington leads—nowhere.

"It'll go through."

"I told him to ask you himself."

"And here you are, asking." I sigh when Crew manages to look even stiffer. I wish he'd stop trying to bridge the divide between me and our father. The outcome never changes. "It's my shit, Crew. I'll deal with it. And I'll have someone from the team contact you if it's finalized while I'm out of town, so you can tell him."

I catch Crew's nod before I continue down the hallway toward my office. My secretary, Alicia, is missing from her desk, so I make a mental note to tell her to have Crew cc'd on all the

Thompson & Thompson emails going forward. He can break the happy news to dear old dad once the deal is done.

Predictably, emails piled up during what I planned on being a brief water break. I sift through everything unread. Approve three proposals and draft a memo. Answer two phone calls, and then realize I have to leave if I'm going to make my flight.

My luggage sits in the corner of my office, piled neatly next to the leather couch. I'm flying commercial to Vegas since my father has the company jet reserved. I have no idea where he's flying or why. He might have placed a permanent hold just to keep me from using it.

I'm sliding a few packets of papers that I'm planning to review on the plane into my briefcase when there's a firm knock on my door.

"Come in," I call.

I glance up, expecting Alicia, but Crew is the one who walks in. Twice in one day with no meetings together is practically a record. He shuts the door behind him and strolls toward my desk, hands deep in his pockets.

"Shouldn't you be on your way to sin city by now?" he asks, pausing to spin the giant metal globe that sits next to the bookcase before continuing toward my desk.

"I'm about to leave."

He glances at the papers I'm holding. "Don't forget to pack a few weeks' worth of work for your Vegas weekend."

"I'm not packing much," I lie, quickly shutting the briefcase.

Crew's grin is knowing. "Uh-huh. Celeste has been camped out in the copy room with Alicia all morning, making sure you have the latest Isaac Industries report along with everything else you requested."

"I didn't ask your secretary to help mine."

Crew shrugs, glancing out the windows behind my desk,

which offer an impressive view of the city's skyline. "I've been distracted this morning. Not much else for Celeste to do."

"I wasn't sure what I'd need to prioritize, so I figured I'd bring it all," I admit.

"Knowing you, you'll finish it all."

It's meant to be a compliment, but it also pricks. Despite knowing about my biggest mistake, Crew has complete confidence in my ability to accomplish everything. He knows Kensington Consolidated is my whole life. I have few friends. No girlfriend. No pets. No hobbies. Not even a plant to take care of.

I have no idea how to take time off from work. To be *not* thinking about the million and one tasks piling up whenever I'm doing anything else. I sleep, I work out, and I work. Everything else is handled for me. Groceries are delivered. A cleaning crew comes through my penthouse once a week. Alicia handles managing all my travel and appointments.

My life is both privileged and pathetic.

"Someone needs to review it."

"Someone *will* review it. It doesn't have to be you." Crew shakes his head, smiling a little. "You're doing the jobs of three people right now, Oliver."

I prod the inside of my cheek as I lock my computer and grab my briefcase off the desk. "You're putting in the same number of hours."

Crew shakes his head. "Not even close." His voice softens. "Look, I know you want to prove that you're—"

I interrupt. "I really need to get going."

"Yeah, of course. I just wanted to say…thanks. For last night. Sorry I was kind of a mess."

I don't tell him it was kind of…nice. That if he'd stayed longer, I wouldn't have hated it.

"Things are okay with Scarlett?"

A brief flash of surprise crosses Crew's face in response to the question. It makes me feel like total shit. Because, yeah, I don't usually ask. I listen to what he tells me about his family, but I don't usually participate or ask any questions.

"Yeah. We're good. We just both needed to freak out a little."

"Good."

Crew's smile turns boyish. He rocks back on his heels, hands back in his pockets. "I'm hoping it's a boy," he confesses. "I'm not sure I'll make it through Lili's teenage years as she is. She's a mini-Scarlett."

I smile. "Just don't name him Arthur Jr." Our father doesn't deserve the same honor our mother did.

Crew's eyebrows rise in surprise. "I wouldn't, Oliver."

I'm surprised by the steel in his tone.

I know he hates how the deterioration of my relationship with our father has come at the benefit of his own. Our father used to vacillate between favorites, constantly making us fight for his favor, but now Crew is firmly planted in the number one position.

But it's my own fucking fault. Because of one moment when I said *yes*, simply because I knew anyone I'd ever met would have bet I'd say *no*. Crew's sympathy—his solidarity—doesn't feel deserved.

I walk toward my luggage. I'm cutting it even closer on departure. "I need to get going."

"Yeah, sure. Fly safe."

"Thanks."

"And try to have a *little* bit of fun."

I force a smile in response. Aside from seeing Garrett, I'm already dreading everything about this trip. "I'll try."

Alicia is seated at her desk when I emerge from my office. Her graying hair is tucked away in a neat bun, but she smooths the strands as I approach anyway. "Have a safe trip, Mr. Kensington," she tells me. "I've already checked you into your flight and the ticket is in your email. Patrick is waiting downstairs and there's a car arranged for you at the Las Vegas airport as well. It will take you straight to your hotel."

"Thank you, Alicia. Head out soon, all right?"

"Sure."

We share an amused glance. She's about as likely to leave the office at this hour as I would be under normal circumstances.

"I mean it," I say, rapping my knuckles on the wooden ledge of her desk. "Or you're fired."

"Yes, Mr. Kensington."

I head down the hallway, pulling my luggage behind me. I should have left it in the car this morning like Patrick suggested, but I figured I'd need to pack work papers in the suitcase after filling my briefcase. And I was right.

As poor luck would have it, my father is leaving his office right as I pass it. "Oliver."

The acknowledgment is for show, so I'm forced to respond. "Dad."

"You're leaving?" He glances at his watch, as if to emphasize the time.

My molars grind. My office is the last one occupied most nights. After he's long gone, out with women half his age.

He didn't love Candace. The ink wasn't dry on their divorce papers when he started bringing a different date to each event. Instead of freezing me out, he should be *thanking* me for blowing up their unhappy marriage.

"Yes." My response is curt. If he wants to know where I'm going and why, he could ask.

He doesn't, of course. All he does is keep walking. My expression remains blank through all of it, before I continue down the hall toward the elevator. I press the button for the garage.

When the doors open, my driver Patrick is already waiting. He loads the suitcase into the trunk for me as I settle into the backseat, pulling out my phone and sighing at the number of emails that have already piled up.

Rather than read any of them, I toss my phone on the leather seat, opting to stare out the window as Patrick drives through the city toward the airport.

It's a gray, dreary day. Streaks of rain run down the outside of the tinted glass, blurring the sights and buildings we pass.

Once Patrick drops me off at the terminal, I head for security. Alicia handled all of the check-in logistics. She also set up the pre-check clearance. It takes me all of ten minutes to get through the metal detector before I head for the gate. There's commotion everywhere. Screaming children, rushing flight attendants, confused passengers milling about.

I make it to my gate right as the first zone is boarding. Since I'm in first class, I join the line and am on the plane a few minutes later. I stick my suitcase in the overhead compartment and then settle in the third row, resigning myself to a long wait as the other passengers trickle onto the plane one by one.

I busy myself by pulling up the email Chase sent a few weeks ago detailing the itinerary for the weekend. As long as my flight doesn't leave late—which I'm not confident *won't* happen, based on the pace of passengers boarding—I'll arrive at the hotel right around six. According to the email, dinner is at six thirty at a restaurant just down the street from the hotel. I should have plenty of time to check in and then make it to dinner.

"Well, *hello there*."

I glance up from my phone to watch a woman with a wild array of brown curls take the seat next to me. She's wearing a camel-colored coat and a bright pink sash that reads *Bridesmaid*.

"Hello," I respond, polite but not overly friendly.

"I'm Marie."

"Nice to meet you, Marie."

"And you are?"

"Oliver."

"It's *so* nice to meet you, Oliver." Marie beams at me, not bothering to be the least bit subtle about her appraisal as her eyes skim up and down the suit I'm wearing.

I glance at the front of the plane. It's still mostly empty, with no more passengers coming aboard. Across the aisle, two more women with pink sashes are now seated.

"Are you visiting Vegas for business or pleasure?" Marie asks me.

I start to get the sense that no matter how short my responses are, there will be a conversation taking place between us. Unless I want to be a total asshole, I'm stuck talking to her.

"Uh, pleasure, I guess."

Her beaming expression suggests that's the answer she was hoping for. "Oh my God! Me too! My best friend is getting married next month. We're having her bachelorette party this weekend."

"That explains the sash."

Marie glances down. "Oh! I totally forgot I was wearing this."

I'm not sure how. It's *neon*. Easier to spot than the reflective vests the workers down on the tarmac are sporting.

She leans closer to me, and I realized exactly why she forgot about the sash. Marie smells like wine. The sweet, fruity scent surrounds me, cloying the stagnant air. She's drunk, and I'm stuck sitting next to her for the next five and a half hours.

"What *pleasure* are you planning in Vegas?" Her elbow lands on the armrest between as she blatantly glances at my crotch.

"I'm going for a bachelor party," I admit, certain that's a tidbit Marie will latch right on to.

She doesn't disappoint. "Oh my God! Really? How perfect. Are the rest of the groomsmen on this plane?" Her gaze whips away from me, obviously hoping to spot them.

"No. I'm traveling alone."

Marie's undivided attention returns to me. "Do the rest of the groomsmen look like *you*?"

I'm tempted to laugh. She's tipsy and overly talkative, but her blunt interest is entertaining.

"I've never met most of them. The groom is an old friend from college."

"That sounds so fun!"

I manage a polite smile in response. *So fun* is not how I would have characterized it.

"Have you been to Vegas before?" Marie asks.

"No. You?"

"Yep. Lots of times. It's a really fun city."

"That's what people say."

My phone vibrates with an incoming call from Alicia.

"Excuse me. I need to take this."

Marie nods, leaning across the aisle to whisper something to her friends.

"Hello?" I answer.

Alicia's exhale is loud. "Mr. Kensington, I'm so glad that I caught you. I just realized the Isaac Industries report that was printed isn't the most up-to-date version. They sent new numbers late last night, and I didn't realize—"

"It's fine, Alicia. Thanks for letting me know."

"I checked, and your hotel has a business center. I can call them and coordinate a way to get it printed. Or overnight a copy—"

"Alicia, really, it's all right. It's fine. I have other work I can do."

"Okay." Her exhale is hesitant.

Alicia is a perfectionist. She's been my assistant ever since I finished business school and started at Kensington Consolidated full time. In that time, I could count the number of mistakes she's made on one hand.

"I told you to leave the office."

"There's still—"

"*Leave*, Alicia. I mean it."

"I'll be gone by four thirty," she tells me.

I smile. "Okay. Have a good weekend."

"You too, Mr. Kensington." No matter how many times I tell Alicia to dispatch with the formalities, she still insists on calling me Mr. Kensington.

The final passengers are finally boarding the plane. The overhead loudspeaker crackles to life, starting the pre-flight announcements. Marie shifts back into her seat, flashing me a bright smile.

I begin to wonder how much I'll regret going on this trip.

CHAPTER FOUR

HANNAH

I shut my laptop and lean back. Rosie arranged for us to get manicures while I was visiting her in Chicago. My pink-tipped fingers run across the smooth surface of the laptop, the shiny silver a sharp contrast to the dark wood of the hotel desk and the rose nail polish.

An exhale leaves me in a disbelieving huff.

Honestly, I never thought I would do it.

For months—years—I've been telling myself I would.

But it's not until this exact second, when I *did*, that I realize I truly believed I wouldn't.

That realization chips away at some of the excitement and anxiety. I feel hollow, knowing I've sent this dream out into the world and it will probably get rejected.

I had the possibility; the I *could* do this.

Now, it'll be I *can* do this. Or more likely, I *can't* do this.

I blame Vegas for this impulsive decision. After returning from my meeting with Robert Damon, I felt restless. I was more optimistic with Rachel on the phone than my true mood was.

Being at my father's beck and call wouldn't bother me as

much, if this was the job I really wanted. But there's nothing worse than working toward something you're indifferent to. And maybe I'll feel differently, after knowing whether or not this alternate path is a possibility. At least I'll have tried, and that's more than I've been able to say before.

My plan for the evening was to lounge around my hotel room, order room service, and possibly break into the overpriced minibar. But there's a new thrill humming beneath my skin. The energy of new possibilities, which my life has been lacking lately.

Architecture school has been an abstract dream of mine since undergrad. For months, I've had the forms filled out and ready, but I've never clicked *Submit*. Until tonight. And the woman who finally took that step wouldn't be spending a night in Vegas lounging in her hotel room.

I stand and stretch, glancing down at my phone next to my laptop. I have this giddy urge to tell someone what I just did.

But there's no one to call—not really. Rachel would be supportive but shocked. She, like everyone else in my life, thinks architecture was a passing phase in college. That I studied it because I always knew I'd have a place waiting for me at Garner Sports Agency no matter what I majored in. I know Rosie is going to a play with her boyfriend Jude tonight. I don't want to put my mom in the position of keeping this from my dad, and I don't want him to know yet. Maybe ever.

Beyond those three people, I come up blank.

I have lots of friends.

They just aren't the ones you call with life-altering news.

I abandon my phone and sort through the contents of my suitcase, deciding I'll at least go down to the hotel bar for a drink. Celebrate myself. If this is as far as this possibility ever goes, I'll know I did something.

None of what I packed is what I would have chosen to bring to Vegas, because I didn't know I *was* coming to Vegas.

Rosie warned me Chicago would be cold, and she was downplaying it, honestly. A bulky sweater and jeans were great for walking around Millennium Park. Not so great for a fancy hotel.

I end up slipping into the one dress I brought—a navy, sheath style that clings to my curves but isn't impossible to breathe in. After accessorizing the outfit with heels and a swipe of lipstick I grab my phone and room key, then take an elevator downstairs.

My heels tap against the marble floor of the lobby as I walk toward the bar. It's located toward the front of the hotel, overlooking the fountains spraying toward the sidewalk.

I slide onto one of the many empty stools, setting my clutch on the marble counter. A waterfall is sandwiched between two panes of glass behind the alcohol that's lined up in neat rows, the constant flow casting shifting shadows on the bottles.

I order a gin martini from the bartender. She's brunette and beautiful, probably about my age. Maybe a few years younger. Her eyeliner swoops up in the corners in the style I've never been able to manage, and I'm tempted to ask her for makeup tips when she delivers my drink.

My phone begins ringing before I can say anything except "Thank you."

I answer the call, stirring my drink with the olive.

"Hey, Dad."

"Hi, sweetheart. I'm just checking in. Did everything go okay with Robert Damon?"

I stamp out the sigh that wants to slip out. "It went well. He was very welcoming."

My father chuckles. "I figured he would be. Thanks again for changing your plans, sweetheart."

I exhale, my annoyance receding. "Of course."

This is why I'm still working at Garner Sports Agency despite my ambivalence toward the job.

I like hearing pride in my dad's voice. His approval is why I practiced penalty kicks after dinner every night on the goal he assembled himself. I'm twenty-seven. Not seventeen and chasing a state championship. But the same principle of pride remains. The worst part is, I know my dad would tell me to pursue a different career if he had any clue I wanted to. Just like he told me to quit soccer whenever I stopped enjoying it.

"I stopped by your house on my way home from the office today. The front yard looks good."

"Yeah, I hired a new company. They mulched all the flower beds on Tuesday."

"We're supposed to get a lot of rain this week. Make sure they're planning to mow soon."

I run a finger around the rim of the fluted glass. "Okay, I'll mention it."

"You had a package outside. I put it in the kitchen."

"Thanks, Dad." I suck down a sip of martini, grimacing as the uncut alcohol sears my throat.

"You'll be here tomorrow, right? For April's baby shower? Your mother told you?"

I down the remnants of my drink and gesture for another from the bartender. "She not only told me, she reminded me about twenty times. My flight leaves tomorrow morning. I'll be there."

He chuckles. "Okay, good. We'll see you then. I love you, Hannah."

A fresh drink is set in front of me. I mouth a *Thanks* to the bartender. "Love you too, Dad. Good night."

I hang up, dropping my phone onto the bar top and massaging my left temple. I roll the stem of the glass between my fingers and stare at the clear liquid mixed with the murkiness of the olive juice, my dad's cheerful voice echoing in my head.

Even if I *do* get into the program I applied for, I have no idea how I would tell him.

My dad keeps handing me more important clients and more responsibility—like this trip—and I know it's just a matter of time until he admits outright he wants me to take over when my mom finally talks him into retiring.

The second martini slides down as easily as the first one did. It leaves a pleasant trail of warmth behind that settles in my stomach and spreads through my veins.

"Whiskey. Neat."

Commanding, deep voices are common in the sports industry. Cocky athletes. Confident coaches. Certain announcers.

In my experience, they're always connected to men who think they have something especially meaningful to say. Who infuse their voice with an inflated importance that's never merited.

But none of those voices have ever infected me with any interest. They've never made me believe they actually have anything notable to say.

Until this one.

All he did was order a drink, and my every sense is on high alert, waiting to hear what else he might have to say.

When there's nothing but silence, I glance away from my empty glass toward my left, curious if the enticing baritone belongs to an equally appealing sight.

I'm not disappointed.

The formerly empty stool one down from mine is now occupied by a man watching as the bartender rushes to pour his drink. His light brown hair is ruffled, like he ran a hand through it recently. Even seated, I can tell he's tall and muscular, wearing a suit that fits him too perfectly not to be tailored.

He pulls a phone out of his pocket and glances at the screen.

His entire profile tenses as he frowns, then he tucks the phone away as the bartender sets a glass of light brown liquid down in front of him seconds later.

He thanks her.

It's a small detail. A common courtesy that's actually rare.

That's when you learn the most about someone—in the split seconds they're not expecting to give anything away.

The bartender hovers for a few seconds, like she's hoping he'll say something else. All he does is sip and stare at the waterfall. Eventually, she moves down to help another customer.

"It's a little early to be drinking by Vegas standards, don't you think?" I'm just buzzed enough voicing that question seems like a smart idea.

Sober, I'm not shy. But I'm calculated. I get a good sense of someone right away. I decide to approach them knowing how they'll react. With this stranger, I'm *waiting* to see how he'll react.

When I glance over, he's still looking ahead. Ignoring me.

I study his perfect profile. Every part of it is proportional, all the angles and ridges seamless. The stubble on his jaw is just a dusting, the unyielding line fully visible. It matches his straight nose and squared shoulders. Everything about his appearance and posture seems intentional, like he's projecting a certain image the world has no choice but to accept.

I've given up on a response by the time his head turns in my direction.

The motion is deliberately slow, like he has an endless supply of time to look over. Green eyes meet mine a second before he swipes a thumb across his lower lip, clearing a drop of whiskey.

Fire simmers, low in my stomach. His whole face is attractive, not just his profile. And the full force of his attention hits me like a crashing wave, overwhelming and thrilling and a little terrifying.

"It's a little hypocritical to be judging, don't you think?"

Deliberately, he glances at the empty martini glass. And then he looks away.

No flirty comment. No glance at my cleavage. None of the behavior I'd expect from a guy alone in a bar, and my interest in him grows.

"I've been called worse."

His eyes are back on me, just as devastating as the first glance was. One corner of his mouth curls up a centimeter, a blink-and-you'll-miss-it smile. "Me too."

"Pathetic?" I suggest. "You're sitting alone in a hotel bar while the sun is still out. A *Vegas* hotel bar."

He makes a show of looking at the empty seat between us. "Who are you here with, again?"

I roll my eyes but can't help the small smile that appears. Flattery from a stranger is often awkward. I'd rather experience this—someone I've never met before matching my sass. Avoiding politeness and diving right into honesty.

"Are you here on a business trip, or something? With a wife at home who doesn't like to go out past ten, so you forgot how?"

His chuckle is low and dark, and everything south of my naval clenches. "I'm here for a bachelor party," he answers.

"Yours?"

"Fuck no."

I've heard many watered-down versions of *I'm not looking for a relationship*. Usually it's *I'm waiting for the right woman* or *I'm not ready to settle down yet*.

None of those prepared responses have encompassed the same undercurrent of certainty as those two words.

"Bachelor party, huh? You bailed?"

"I got a work call. Needed a minute—and a drink—after it."

"Your boss is difficult?" Making assumptions seems to get more out of him.

"Understatement," he mutters into his glass of whiskey.

I spin my stool, drawn in by his broodiness for some inexplicable reason. I'm used to guys coveting my attention, as conceited as that sounds. Offering me drinks and compliments and interest. This genuine indifference is refreshing. Intriguing.

"I'll do you one better," I say. "My boss is demanding, overbearing, and he *also* happens to be my father. So I can't turn down a last-minute detour to Las Vegas, for example, on the way back to LA after visiting my best friend."

He glances at me, then, and a glimmer of interest interrupts the staid expression.

Detachment shifts into something else. I feel his eyes trace my features before they trail down to the cleavage my dress teases at.

One corner of his mouth rises. An inch this time. Closer to actual amusement. The improvement feels like a victory, and I'm not sure why. Maybe because he looks like someone unaccustomed to smiling for show. Like a man who doesn't laugh just to put others at ease.

"You work for your dad?" he asks.

"Yeah." I mean to add more to my response, but his eyes drop to my legs and it's hard to remember what I was going to say.

Attraction crackles between us, like lightning in a summer storm. The sparks feel raw and tangible. He's not shy or bashful about looking, the way some guys are. His appraisal is purposeful and methodical as his eyes trace up my bare legs, not lingering on a single spot but missing nothing.

My thighs squeeze together when our gazes collide again. He has piercing, shrewd eyes. Paired with messy brown hair, a hint of stubble, and a chiseled jaw, his appearance is as striking as his presence.

"Dumb decision," he says.

It takes me a few seconds to remember what we're discussing. "Yep."

The bartender sets a fresh martini down.

I thank her and grab the thin glass stem, tilting the glass toward him until the liquid *almost* spills over the rim. "Cheers."

When I glance over, he's still looking at me. I can't get any read on what he's thinking. There's no arrogance or irritation. No interest or dismissiveness. Just silent scrutiny.

Eventually, he holds out a hand. His fancy suit suggests he has an important office job, but his hand is calloused and tanned, like he does more than sit at a desk all day. "I'm Oliver."

I press my palm against his, suppressing a shiver when his grip closes around my hand. I'm imagining those long, sure fingers brushing my skin in other places. "Hannah."

Since he didn't share a last name, I don't either.

That's why people come to Vegas, right? To shed their inhibitions and be a different, wilder version of themselves.

I clutch back when his grip tightens. This feels more like an intimidation tactic than flirting, but my racing heart is reacting regardless. My insides are in a riot simply because this gorgeous, mysterious man is touching me.

Oliver continues studying me.

I stare back, feeling like I'm sitting beneath a spotlight.

I resist the urge to shift or blink. To say something and fracture this moment that feels important for some reason.

He drops my hand, then turns back to his drink like our conversation never happened. The words are a blur in my head. I was more focused on him than what he was saying. I exhale and scooch back onto my stool, trying to regain my composure.

"What do you do?"

"Huh?" I glance over, startled he's speaking to me.

There's a brief flash of entertainment on his face, so quick I barely catch it between blinks. Oliver's mouth barely twitches before returning to a straight line. "For work. What do you do?"

"Oh." So much for composed. "I, uh, I work for a sports agency. We negotiate contracts, network with teams, recruit new talent, handle marketing, brand deals. Stuff like that."

"So you're a sports agent?"

"Not exactly. I do whatever needs to be done." I already told him I work for my father, but admitting it's in a position that was created exclusively for me sounds pitiful.

"And you hate it," he surmises.

"I don't *hate* it. I just…it's not what I thought I'd be doing at twenty-seven."

"It gets worse, not better."

I grimace, then take a sip of martini. His voice says he means it.

When I look over, Oliver is looking at me. Still. Again. It's like I'm being tested, but I'm not sure how or why or on what.

"Do you hate your job?" I ask.

"No. I love it, actually." He exhales, sounding irritated about the sentiment for some reason, then reaches for the tumbler that's now close to empty.

I wish the bartender was refilling his drink as quickly as she's been supplying my martinis. I'm strangely worried he'll leave as soon as the amber liquid is all gone.

The sleeve of his suit jacket pulls back as he lifts the glass to sip, exposing the shiny watch on his wrist. The *very* expensive watch.

I already figured he was wealthy. Rooms here start at four figures and run into the high fives. But this hotel could have been the groom's choice. A watch with that price tag suggests a whole different amount of personal wealth.

"Even considering your boss?"

"Even then."

His phone rings. Oliver pulls it out and sighs before answering. "Hey."

I stare at him as he listens to whatever is being said on the other end. He rubs a long finger along the rim of the tumbler, nodding along.

"Yeah, okay. I'll meet you there."

A pause.

"No, I'm close. Uh-huh. Bye."

Oliver sets the phone down and drains the rest of his glass.

He's leaving, and I'm embarrassingly disappointed about it. I've known him for all of twenty minutes.

I watch as he pulls out his wallet and drops two hundred-dollar bills on the bar top.

The bartender appears, whisking away the empty tumbler. "Can I get you anything else, sir?"

Oliver shakes his head and pushes the money toward her. His gaze doesn't linger on the pretty brunette; he just gives her a polite smile before sliding his wallet back into his suit pocket. Considering I'll probably never see him again, the lack of flirtation pleases me a ridiculous amount.

"For my drink." He glances at me. "And hers. Keep the change."

"Thank you, sir."

Once the bartender is gone, Oliver turns back toward me. "I've gotta go."

I nod, like it makes no difference to me. "Don't go too wild tonight. What happens in Vegas doesn't always stay here."

There's a flicker of *something* in his eyes as he rests one arm on the counter. Something that makes me think Oliver isn't quite as buttoned-up and serious as he seems.

Most people project the opposite—they act more interesting and important than they really are. Maybe that's why I'm so drawn to his hidden depths.

"You planning to stay here all night?" he asks.

I raise one shoulder, then drop it. "We'll see."

That sounds better than saying I have no plan for the evening past stopping here. I should eat something besides olives. Then go to bed, probably.

The rest of the evening stretches out like the flat section after a hill. I know this will be the highlight of my night, no matter what I do next. Where I go or who I talk to.

Oliver leans closer. My inhale is quick and surprised at the sudden proximity.

Based on how much his watch must have cost, he likely wears some outrageously pricy cologne. Where I'm sitting, savoring the smell, it's worth every penny. Arousing and addictive and a little spicy.

"That doesn't sound very fun."

"This, coming from the guy dressed like he just left a conference call who's hiding out from his friend's bachelor party? I'm not taking any advice on having fun from you."

"You didn't even bother with a no offense?"

"You don't seem offended."

He shrugs. "I'm not."

An involuntary smile curls my lips up. I like talking to Oliver. It feels like we've known each other for longer than we have.

"I wasn't supposed to stop here," I say. "I had a direct flight back to LA. No time to plan an itinerary for Vegas. I'll probably get some food and then go to bed."

He glances away, out at the fountains.

The air between us feels like it's gaining substance. Thickening and filling with more than just a farewell. But Oliver's expression is a blank slate when he meets my gaze, giving me no indication what he's thinking or contemplating.

"According to the itinerary the best man sent, we're going to Champagne Cabaret at eleven."

"Okay… Have fun." I'm guessing that's a strip club.

Oliver smirks, and it's crippling. The sight is so sudden, so unexpected, so *consuming*, that I have to remind myself to breathe.

It's completely different from him staring straight ahead, only offering a glimpse of his profile. Oliver with dancing eyes and a dimple in one cheek, inches away, looks like a secret. A sight I don't want to share. A view I won't forget.

"Will you meet me there? I'll ditch the group. We can go wherever you want."

Not *at all* what I was expecting him to say.

"Won't they mind?" I ask.

"That I'm abandoning them while they're surrounded by booze and half-naked women?" He raises one eyebrow. "Doubt it."

Oliver's phone begins buzzing again. He glances at the screen but doesn't answer it.

His green gaze is back on me immediately, waiting for an answer. He's looking at me like he knows exactly what he's staring at, and no one has ever appraised me so confidently before.

"Isn't getting a lap dance in a strip club part of the Vegas bachelor party experience?"

I'm treated to a second glimpse of his smirk, and the effect is no less potent this time. "Are you offering?"

My heartbeat stutters when he takes another step closer, the stiff material of his suit pants brushing against my bare legs.

Heat crawls across my cheeks as my body temperature spikes. I'm picturing it. I'm imagining the thick fabric of his pants chafing against the inside of my thighs. His hands gripping my hips. His erection growing beneath me. Oliver's eyes flare, and I think he's imagining me in his lap too.

"You can't afford me." I take a fortifying sip of gin, attempting ignorance to his proximity and trying to regain a little control of the conversation. I'm in an unfamiliar city, talking to a strange man. I might be feeling a tad reckless and a lot tipsy, but I wasn't expecting this to go anywhere.

I don't get a whole smile. It's a half one, maybe even a quarter.

"Never been told that before." His words are dry, almost dismal. Hardly a boast.

"You do this a lot?"

He shakes his head. "No."

"Really?"

"Really. I work a lot. And…I'm usually terrible about going after what I want."

Me too. Until I hit that green button earlier.

"You saying you want me?"

"That's exactly what I'm saying, Hannah." His voice is all gravel, even lower than before, and I feel it directly between my legs. My name sounds like a dirty word, spoken in that indecent rumble. "Will you meet me?"

"Yes," I whisper, not sure what I'm agreeing to.

This feels like more than sex. More than continuing a conversation. I've been wading away from shore, and now I'm suddenly realizing how deep that water around me has gotten.

His lips curve up, and I think he's going to kiss me.

I'm expecting it. Anticipating it. I even swipe my tongue across my bottom lip.

Oliver catches the movement, and his eyes darken to pine. But he doesn't kiss me. He holds out his hand, again, like we just closed a business deal.

I take it with a bemused laugh that fades when his thumb brushes against my knuckles. A simple touch, and it infects my whole body.

He drops my hand, then walks away.

I glance over one shoulder to watch him leave.

Oliver doesn't strike me as the sort of man who looks back, though.

And I'm right.

He doesn't.

CHAPTER FIVE

OLIVER

Garrett stands and waves as soon as I walk into the steakhouse. I bypass the hostess with a polite nod, weaving around tables and past wine displays until I reach the far corner of the restaurant. The lighting in here is dim, a relief to my eyes after the few blocks from the hotel past the bright, flashing colors of the Strip.

I unbutton my suit jacket and take a seat in the open chair. "Sorry, I got caught—"

Garrett shakes his head. "Don't worry about it, man. We all get how it is."

"No, *we* don't. Don't lump me in with you boring businessmen," Chase comments, reaching out to grab the bottle of bourbon sitting in the center of the table and pouring himself another drink.

"How could any of us forget you skate after a rubber circle for a living?" Garrett replies, grinning at his younger brother.

Chase flips him off.

I glance between them. The Andersons are old money. But

Garrett is a self-made multi-millionaire, thanks to the tech company he founded after college. And Chase plays hockey professionally.

Maybe that's why they have such a different sibling dynamic than Crew and I do. We both went into the family business, working for a father who thrives on manipulation. We have too much common ground in some ways and absolutely none in others.

As Chase and Garrett continue to banter back and forth, it's noticeable to me in a way it never has been before. I'm comparing it to my conversation with Crew last night, bothered by the many differences.

"Your old man doesn't believe in a Friday night off?" Edmund Lee asks from my left.

When I glance over, he's smiling. It's the guarded, hesitant one I'm accustomed to seeing aimed my way.

Most people are either intimidated or intrigued by the Kensington name, and Edmund's expression says he's the former. He works at Garrett's tech company as a high-level executive, meaning he would be the wealthiest and most successful person at every table in here…except ours.

"Business doesn't sleep," I respond, opening up my menu and scanning the cuts of meat listed.

I took the work call for a couple of reasons. One, I was the only one who could answer the question since I've been handling that contract personally. Two, it was a reprieve from the chaotic debauchery that started as soon as I met up with the rest of the bachelor party attendees. Aside from Garrett, no one had much confidence I'd be here, based on the amount of surprise that greeted my arrival.

"That's true." Edmund chuckles. "Rumors are going around that you're negotiating with Thompson & Thompson."

I close the menu, having decided on the New York Strip with a peppercorn rub. That pharmaceutical company was partly what the call was about, so my expression is carefully blank as I look at Edmund. "Kensington Consolidated negotiates with a lot of companies."

Edmund studies me, clearly looking for some signal. My expression remains carefully blank. If Edmund is smart, he should buy some stock.

"Is your father still deliberating on the next CEO?"

"Yes."

If Edmund is trying to annoy me, he's doing a damn good job.

But his voice is all curiosity, not malice. The passing of power at companies like Kensington Consolidated is usually predetermined, like a line of succession in royal families. From the age I understood the concept of leadership, I should have been working toward taking on the CEO role. But even back when I was the firstborn son engaged to the billionaire bride, long before Candace, he never handed it over. That title was always dangled just out of reach. He wanted me to keep working for it. He wanted Crew prepared for the position too.

I reach forward and grab my water glass, hoping that will be the end of the conversation with Edmund. And that I won't need to answer that same question five more times tonight.

While my father might have fun teasing business associates about how he has too many good options to succeed him and how he hopes retirement is a long way off, everything was decided in his mind as soon as the agreement between him and Hanson Ellsworth changed from me and Scarlett to Crew and Scarlett.

Being born two years earlier was nothing in comparison to being half of *the* power couple. If America had royalty, they'd be crowned king and queen. That kind of interest and charisma is gold when you're asking people to do business with you.

And if I ever had any prayer of convincing my father that Crew could still be the face of the company while I claimed control, it disappeared the moment he found out about me and Candace. He might not have loved her, but my father is the proudest man alive. Trust is paramount, and betrayal is unforgiveable.

But officially announcing Crew as CEO isn't as much fun for him as vague comments, so the rumors about who will take charge of Kensington Consolidated next continue swirling. And there's another reason my father won't officially announce his successor: he loves watching me squirm when people ask about it.

"I like Crew. But it should be you. From what I hear, you've earned it five times over."

Edmund's reasoning is unexpected. I know it was *expected* I'd be CEO. But no one has ever told me it was *earned.* And there's a big difference between the two paths to success.

"Thanks." I force a smile and sip some water, trying to hide how uncomfortable his unexpected comment made me.

The waitress arrives then, ending all the side conversations as we place our orders. Once she leaves, Chase launches into another run-through of the weekend plans. It's obvious he spent a lot of time planning this trip. Chase knows the schedule without even looking at his phone, running through everything he has planned for the weekend in extensive detail.

Garrett laughs and shakes his head through most of it.

Service is fast. Chase reaches the end of his list right as our food arrives. My stomach grumbles as a plate of browned meat is set down in front of me, steam rising in curled ribbons. I skipped lunch to get as much done at the office as possible before leaving for the airport, so I'm starving.

Edmund strikes up a conversation with Levi Gamble while I dig into my dinner. Levi's great-grandfather started a department store chain that still exists today. But Levi isn't involved in the family business. He works for a media conglomerate, last I knew.

But Levi and Edmund aren't discussing business. They're talking about the model Levi is dating.

I continue cutting through the tender steak and listening to the babble of multiple conversations at the table.

I socialize and schmooze when I need to. When there's someone to impress or a deal to close. As pathetic as it sounds, I don't socialize just to be social. I'm more comfortable sitting back and observing, letting others be the center of attention.

"What about you, Oliver?" Levi asks, right after I've taken a bite of steak.

I chew and swallow. Sip some water. "What?"

"Are you dating anyone? I never see you out. Or Crew."

I cut another piece of meat, focused on the plate. I'm surprised by how I immediately think of blonde hair and blue eyes. After tonight—assuming she shows—I'll never see Hannah again. I'm definitely not dating her. But it's been a while—forever, maybe—since a woman captured my attention as effortlessly and entirely as she did.

"Crew is married," I reply, dodging the question.

Edmund chuckles before tossing back some whiskey. "We both know that doesn't mean anything. Couples have arrangements."

"They don't have an arrangement," I say, cutting my meat more aggressively.

"Of course not. He married *Scarlett Ellsworth*. Can you blame him?" Admiration fills Mason Jenkins's voice before he knocks his water glass over. He just laughs, tossing his cloth napkin on the table in a half-hearted attempt to clean up the mess. "She's a fucking—"

"Remember she's my fucking *sister*, before you finish that

sentence."

All the other conversations at the table die off as Mason leans back in his chair, lifting both of his hands in an overdone show of passivity. I've never called Scarlett my sister before. Never even referred to her as my sister-in-law to someone. My family is messy and lacking a matriarch. But I consider Scarlett a part of it.

"Wasn't she your fiancée first? Keeping it all in the family, Kensington?"

I flinch. The negotiations between my father and Hanson Ellsworth were never publicized, but plenty of people assumed Scarlett would be my bride, right up until her engagement to Crew was announced.

And Mason's question hits home in a different way than he intended. My father buried the affair with Candace so deep it can never be dug up. Any other married woman, and it would have been dangled over my head in a lifetime of blackmail. But it embarrasses him too, even more than me. A dent to his pride, knowing his much younger wife looked elsewhere.

"Shut up, Mason. You weren't invited to be a dick," Chase says.

A few of the guys chuckle in response, and it breaks the sudden tension around the table. Conversations about cars and sports pick up again.

After dinner, we duck into a magic show taking place across the street. It's mostly card tricks, and I focus on each flick of the magician's hands, noting each flip and shuffle to catch the clues.

We're all handed playing cards as we leave.

One side has the magician's contact information, for marketing purposes. I smile to myself, imagining how my father and Crew would react if I hired Blaine Burke Magic to entertain at our next company event.

The other side looks like a normal playing card. I end up with a six of spades.

I slip the card into my pocket, playing with the thin edge as we walk along the sidewalk. Our destination looms up ahead, a giant, green champagne bottle with *Cabaret* written inside of it above the entrance. Yellow lights frame the windows, doors, and beige stucco siding.

Champagne Cabaret has a modest exterior in comparison to its immediate neighbors. To the left is a bar with pink panels attached to the siding, creating a rippling waterfall effect. To the right is a wedding chapel, white with a miniature imitation of Vegas's iconic welcome sign out front.

A line has already formed to enter the club but we're waved past it after Chase says something to the bouncer.

"City law says clubs can have full nudity or serve alcohol," he tells us, beaming like a little kid on Christmas morning. "This is the only place that has both."

"What's the point of the law, then?" Garrett whispers to me.

I shake my head and smile, glancing around the interior of the club as we walk deeper inside. It's even darker in here than the steakhouse was, all the furnishings in various shades of black that create a mysterious, sultry atmosphere. It feels like you could do anything in here and it would remain a secret in the shadows, which is the exact point.

"Whoa," Mason breathes, looking upward.

I'm still annoyed with him, but I follow his gaze.

The ceiling is high, the interior not two stories like the outside suggests. Swings are suspended twenty feet overhead, the shiny metal flashing in the lights then rotate slowly around. There are women in lingerie perched on each swing, the wandering lights illuminating a glimpse of skin here and a peek of lace there. They move in perfect sync with the slow, sensual beat sliding out of the speakers, a rhythmic pulse that sounds like sex.

"*That* should be illegal," Garrett says. But there's an admiring note in his voice as he watches the hypnotic sight, which is reflected on every guy's face here. "What if one of them falls?"

"They wear harnesses," Chase says. "Don, the manager, told me all about their safety measures when I called to reserve everything. I'm not about to get suspended right before playoffs, just because I was in a club where a stripper died."

Mason guffaws. Garrett rolls his eyes. "So glad you've got your priorities straight, little brother."

"Hey, I still asked. Come on, this corner is us."

We all follow Chase deeper into the club. Long leather booths section off large areas of the club, the black glimmering strings hanging above them almost translucent but not quite.

Chase leads us into one of the private areas. There's a stage with a pole in the center of the room, and a bar set up in the corner with a bartender ready to mix drinks.

I sink down onto the leather booth that encircles the stage. It's surprisingly comfortable, much plusher than the leather furniture in my living room. I lean back, trying not to think about the amount of bodily fluids the surface is likely coated with.

Garrett sinks down beside me a few minutes later, while most of the other guys linger around the bar waiting to be served. He got first drink as the groom, it looks like.

"Having fun?"

"Yeah, actually," he replies. "Nice to get away. I'm glad you came."

"Me, too."

"Just wait," Garrett says. "According to Chase, there's…and yep."

I follow his gaze. Five women are strutting toward the center stage. Five *naked* women. All they're wearing are stilettos.

Chase whoops, from his spot by the bar. The beat quickens and changes as the women fall into a choreographed routine, each movement purposeful and erotic.

"Fuck. I thought Chase was kidding about half of this," Garrett tells me, taking a sip of what smells like straight vodka. His gaze is fixed on the brunette spinning around the pole. "Which one should I bring back to the hotel?"

I glance over at him, startled.

Garrett's head rolls to the left to look at me, a lazy grin appearing. I'm pretty sure I'm the only semi-sober one in the group. Aside from the whiskey I had at the hotel bar, I haven't had a drop to drink. But I didn't realize how drunk Garrett is, until right now.

"That's your plan?" I scrub all judgment from my voice, but I'm surprised. Garrett met his fiancée after we graduated. I've only met Sienna a few times, and one of them was Scarlett and Crew's wedding. She was the wedding planner.

None of those times did I get the impression they have an open relationship.

"If she's sleeping with other people, why shouldn't I?"

I blink at him, even more shocked. "Sienna cheated on you?"

"Yep."

"Are you…sure?" Not the most sympathetic response, but it's the first question that pops into my head.

He laughs, darkly. "Yeah. I'm sure. Hard to mistake seeing another man balls deep in your fiancée on your bed."

I'm starting to wish I *was* drunk. "I'm sorry, man."

Garrett nods. "Yeah." He pauses. "You didn't ask why I'm still marrying her."

"I… Not really any of my business."

He slouches lower, eyes back on the women dancing. His expression droops as well, weighted down by alcohol and sadness. "You're the only person I've told. Figured that was the first question someone would ask."

"You love her, right?"

Garrett takes a long drink. "I don't know, anymore. She says she loves me. That I'm always working, and it was a mistake. But can you cheat on someone you love?"

"I don't know. I've never been in love."

But I *have* slept with a woman who was committed to another man. I have more in common with Sienna's lover than Garrett in this situation, and that's a bitter realization to have.

"You always were smarter than me, Oliver." Garrett drains the rest of his drink. "Let's go up on stage."

I glance at my watch. "Would you hate me if I ducked out?"

Garrett laughs. Heartily. Uncontrollably. "Are you kidding me, Kensington? This is the view—" He waves an arm toward the stage. "And you're ready to go?"

I stare at the women. Objectively, they're all gorgeous. But I appreciate their beauty like I'm watching the scene on a television screen. Nice to look at, but not evoking any deeper emotion. One-dimensional.

I should tell him about Hannah, so my departure makes more sense. But I want to keep her to myself, to avoid having to answer any questions tomorrow. And honestly, I'm not sure if she'll be waiting outside. I've never invited a woman to meet me at a strip club before, and I never thought I would.

"It's been a long day. There's all this shit with my dad…"

My voice trails, knowing Garrett will fill in the blanks. His relationship with his father is more detached than contentious, but he gets the dynamic. Aside from Crew, he has the closest sense of what my interactions with my father are really like.

"See you in the morning, yeah?"

I nod. "Yeah."

Garrett claps my shoulder and then stands, headed straight toward the stage. The brunette he was eyeing earlier breaks away; her steps so smooth it looks like she's gliding over. She leans down and whispers something to Garrett that has him nodding eagerly, her breasts right in his face. He helps her off stage and then follows her to a dark corner, where she mounts his lap. I have no idea if they're going to have sex here, and I don't stick around to find out. I pass Edmund, who's approaching the stage now that Garrett has demonstrated you can look *and* touch, exit our private section, and then head toward the red *Exit* sign.

Cool smoke blows around me as I walk past other groups similar to ours. There's an excess of everything here; alcohol, lust, and enticement cloying the air with the scent of sin.

I take a deep breath of cool desert air once I'm outside the club, cleansing my lungs from everything inside. The line to enter Champagne Cabaret has grown, snaking along the sidewalk and around the corner into the alley.

The city is so bright it looks like daylight, a network of lights snaking up and down the block in a dazzling array. The cacophony of color is a contrast to New York's monochrome skyline. It feels like the sun rising in reverse. Like the city is coming alive slowly, while the rest of the country is going to sleep. Each flash of blue or red or pink is an enticement, a call away from the dark sky that suggests sleep.

I shove my hands in my pockets as I start to walk down the street, almost slicing my finger on the playing card that's still in my pocket. I glance around, looking for blonde among the people passing by me on the sidewalk.

A large group of laughing women pass by, and then I see her.

Hannah is leaning against one of the palm trees planted along the sidewalk, studying the flashing sign in front of the wedding chapel. The red and blue flashes on her face like the sirens of a police car.

Somehow I forgot how beautiful she is, in the few hours since I last saw her. The dress she's wearing clings to every curve, the modest cut somehow sexy. Wind plays with the loose strands of her blonde hair as she stares at the sign.

I slow my steps as I approach, since she hasn't spotted me yet. The foreign sensation of nerves settles in my stomach.

I was nervous she wouldn't show, and the relief that she did is a heady, confusing feeling.

But I'm also nervous she *did* come. It's been a long time since I was interested in a woman who had no idea who I am. More than interested, I'm intrigued by her. It's why I made the risky request she meet me here, instead of giving her my room number.

I want to talk to her, not just fuck her.

Although attraction is definitely warring with fascination, as my eyes sweep over her body a second time.

An electric jolt races through my body, when her head suddenly turns, blue eyes meeting mine. My body temperature heats as her gaze moves lower, appraising me the same way I just looked at her.

I barely feel the chill in the night air anymore. When we make eye contact again, I see everything I'm experiencing reflected in hers.

"You're late. Get a little distracted?" she says, once I'm only a couple of feet away. Hannah doesn't straighten, letting the palm tree continue to hold her upright.

"Yes, but not in the way you think." I exhale, kicking the edge of one of the concrete slabs that make up the sidewalk. Garrett's confession lingers in my head, right along with the image of the stripper in his lap. It felt wrong, watching him make that decision. But that's exactly what it was—his decision. None of my business. And I'm not exactly in a position to be looking down from the moral high ground. "The groom told me he walked in on his fiancée with another guy."

Hannah's eyebrows rise. "And he's still marrying her?"

"He loves her. He thinks she still loves him, despite making a mistake."

"Big mistake."

"Yeah."

What would she think of me, if she knew what mistakes *I've* made?

I've never told a single person what happened between me and Candace. She told my father. Crew guessed; I essentially confirmed. I assume Crew told Scarlett, since they don't seem to keep any secrets from each other. But I've never willingly offered the information up to anyone before.

"You okay?"

I blink, refocusing on Hannah instead of the past and shaking the strange concern she wouldn't like me all that much, if she really knew me. Shoving away the realization I want her to *like* me, not just be attracted to me.

"I wasn't sure you'd be waiting out here."

The small admission is a large one, for me. Doubt is a weakness, and everyone prefers a strong leader. Certainty has been drilled into me since the age I learned to walk. *You only mess up when you admit it*, my father likes to say. Maybe that's what I should have said about Candace, instead of apologizing. He'd still hate me but would probably respect me more.

"I got a couple of better offers, but you asked first," she says.

I can't tell if she's joking or not. Hannah is stunning. Beauty that's impossible to miss or ignore.

I take a step closer, resting a hand on the bark above her head. She's close enough to touch. Close enough to kiss. Close enough I hear the tiny hitch in her breathing when our proximity registers.

She bites her bottom lip, and we're standing close enough I can see the tiny indentations left behind in the plump skin. Blood rushes south when she soothes the spot with a swipe of her tongue, the sight affecting me more than anything I saw inside.

"Can I kiss you?" I don't realize I said the words out loud until they're out, hovering between us.

"I thought you were going after what you wanted tonight?" she asks.

"I'm making sure you want it too."

"I wouldn't be here if I didn't."

Before I can respond, before I can kiss her, *she's* kissing *me.*

Hannah tastes like gin and mint.

Her tongue slides into my mouth, rubbing mine in an erotic rhythm. Rough bark scrapes my palm as I press against her, my free hand falling to her waist and wishing there wasn't a layer of fabric separating our skin.

She moans into my mouth when she feels my erection, rocking her hips against mine and making it impossible to think straight. Her fingers fist in my hair, the spark of pain when she tugs only enhancing the pleasure.

I haven't been this affected by a woman in a long time. Maybe ever. And I've definitely never made out with a woman on a busy street, in full view of anyone who looks over here.

We're both breathing heavily when we separate. I suck in deep lungfuls of cool air, trying to calm my racing heart. Trying to rationalize why kissing Hannah feels like skydiving instead of an easy, expected glide.

“You can kiss me anytime you want,” she whispers.

I smile, and it’s unexpected. My smiles are usually planned. Part of a farewell or in response to someone else’s. Around Hannah, they’re natural. Just like I don’t think before grabbing her hand and tugging her toward the sidewalk. “Deal.”

CHAPTER SIX

OLIVER

Waking up with a hangover is the worst. And as soon as consciousness filters in, I know I drank too much last night.

My head is pounding. My tongue is dry. My stomach is churning.

I'm not just hungover. This feels like a step away from death.

When I roll over, I'm expecting white sheets.

Instead, all I see is blonde hair.

This isn't the first time I've woken up in bed with a woman, but it's one of a few times. My romantic relationships can be boiled down to one word: short.

And lately, all of my sexual encounters have been unattached and uncomplicated. Where numbers aren't exchanged and preferably names aren't either. When I don't wake up in the same bed as a stranger. No awkward morning of picking crumpled clothes off the floor and exchanging forced small talk.

Based on how hungover I am, I'm not surprised I was drunk enough not to ask her to leave. If I asked for her name, I can't remember it. I rub my right temple in an unsuccessful attempt to ease the pounding headache. I don't want to move but am too uncomfortable to fall back asleep.

As I'm deliberating that quandary, the blonde beside me stirs. She rolls on her side, facing me. Her face is still partially obscured by her hair, but I see her eyes scrunch shut like she's trying to chase sleep.

Our legs brush beneath the covers, the touch of her soft, bare skin instantly affecting me. Regardless of how much I had to drink last night—and how much is still lingering in my system—I'm completely capable of getting hard.

I shift onto my back, staring up at the plaster ceiling. My brain feels like sludge, soggy and uncooperative. This is my hotel room. I have no idea who the woman next to me is or what happened between us last night.

I try to recall yesterday. I remember leaving the office and driving to the airport to come to Vegas. After that, it's disorganized flashes. Talking to Garrett. Eating steak. Women on swings. Flashes that slip away like water in cupped hands whenever I try to expand my memory.

What the fuck did you do?

I'm distracted by a tug. The sheet slips off my chest, as the woman beside me sits up. She yawns, rubbing her eyes and then tucking her hair behind one ear. The white sheet pools around her waist, offering a spectacular view I'm in no position to resist. Literally. Looking over, lying down while she's sitting, all I can see are round, perky tits.

My dick reacts, stiffening further. As annoyed as I am with myself for getting so drunk, I can't recall how I ended up here, I'm also applauding him. Because I've never had a specific type when it comes to women, but she's somehow exactly what I'd look for.

She glances over at me and freezes, appearing just as shocked to be in bed with me as I was to look over and see her. I'm not sure if that's a good or a bad thing.

The blonde woman clears her throat, sweeping her blonde hair over one shoulder. "My eyes are up here."

I focus on her blue irises and say the first thing that pops into my head. "Your boobs are closer."

She surprises me by laughing. Since she hasn't lifted the sheet yet, I watch her tits bounce with the movement. There's something oddly mesmerizing about it. I'm still drunk, obviously. She looks beautiful, even with flecks of mascara below her eyes and blonde hair in a wild tangle.

Then she's suddenly a whirl of movement, tripping over the hem of the comforter that's haphazardly hanging off her side of the bed. "Shit!"

"What's wrong?" I sit up, wincing when the movement rachets the pounding in my head up to a whole new level.

"I was supposed to be at the airport ten minutes ago," she replies, shimmying into a wrinkled navy dress that looks vaguely familiar. She picks up her phone and frowns at it. "Dammit. Dead."

I watch as she rushes over toward the couch, grabbing the back for balance as she slips into her heels.

"Airport?" I ask, my voice a sleepy rasp.

She glances over. "I'm flying back to LA this morning."

"Oh." I'm weirdly…disappointed by that revelation.

"Are you still drunk?"

"Probably. I feel like roadkill. How much did I drink last night?"

"I don't know. A lot?"

I groan, dropping my hands in my palms and massaging my forehead. A few seconds later, I hear the tap of heels against hardwood.

"Here." Something damp and cold brushes my right arm.

I raise my head to find her holding a chilled water from the minifridge out to me. "Thanks."

She shrugs. "You're the one paying for it."

A smirk tilts her lips upward. I trace the curve with my eyes, then focus on the rest of her features.

Hannah, I suddenly remember. Her name is Hannah.

"I've gotta head—"

She abruptly stops talking, grabbing a piece of paper off the bedside table and staring at it.

"What?"

No response.

"Hannah? What is it?"

She stumbles back a few steps, until her back collides with the wall.

I clamber out of bed, urgency hastening my movements. Naked with no sign of my clothes, I yank the white sheet off the bed and wrap it around my waist.

"Your last name is *Kensington*?"

I freeze, registering the tone of the question.

Surprise about my last name isn't anything new from a woman. But the scorn—the horror—in Hannah's voice is new. My back is to her, so I can't see Hannah's expression to tell if I'm reading that right or my headache is warping it.

"Yes."

"Fuck. Fuck. Fuck. *Fuck*." Hannah is no longer standing. She's sliding down the wall and sitting on the floor, her long legs stretched out and exposed as her dress rides up her thighs. "This cannot be happening."

"You know, most women are *excited* when they find out my family is worth billions," I say, taking a few hesitant steps forward.

And it's never a reaction I've enjoyed. It always makes me feel cheap. But I would rather Hannah was looking at me with dollar signs in her eyes than dread.

"Or they ask me if I can get them *rouge* clothes."

Hannah closes her eyes, leaning her head back against the wall. "Scarlett Kensington would rather set one of her designs on fire than see me wear it."

"I..."

Weird response, but it explains some of her reaction. She and Scarlett have a past? Maybe they went to school together?

"You know Scarlett?"

Hannah's head shakes, her eyes still closed. "Crew."

His name drops between us like a lead weight.

"Oh."

I should be less shocked than I am.

Hannah is stunning and Crew spent plenty of nights out partying before he got married. I met many of the women he spent time with, either when they'd sneak out of his room in Kensington Manor back when we both lived there, or at society events. Some of them would flirt with me, especially when it was generally assumed I'd be the next CEO.

None of them sparked the slightest interest, most of them coming off as meek or manipulative.

I never expected I *would* be interested in a woman Crew has history with. And it bothers me, honestly, knowing that she's been with him. It feels like another thing Crew has taken away from me. Which is ridiculous; I barely know Hannah.

I clear my throat in an attempt to break the long silence. "How did you meet him?"

Hannah plays with the edge of the paper she's still holding. I can't tell what's written on it from this angle. Maybe it's a receipt? Or a bill from the hotel? Something with my full name on it.

"At a bar, in New York. The sports agency has an office there, and I was in the city a fair amount for work. Some girl spilled her drink on me, he brought me napkins." She shifts, uncomfortable in a way I doubt has anything to do with the hardwood floor. "It went on for a few months. Random nights, here and there. And then, I heard he got married. He'd mentioned Scarlett, but made it sound like an arrangement."

"I think that's all he thought it'd be, at first."

Hannah nods. "I was in a bad place. Mostly about stuff that had nothing to do with Crew, but that was an easy target. I said some shit to him—and to Scarlett."

I take a seat beside her on the floor. "Were you in love with him?" A question that I have no right to ask but one that's been stuck in my head since she said his name.

She shakes her head, and the relief is intense. Immediate. Inexplicable. "No. I felt stuck. In my job. In other relationships. Crew was an escape from all that. Something different and exciting. I hated losing that distraction, way more than I hated losing him."

"He'll never know about this, if that's what you're worried about. Crew and I don't have that kind of relationship."

Hannah's lips purse, none of the anxiety leaving her expression. That spikes mine. "Do you have any regrets, Oliver?"

My throat feels thick. "Yeah. A lot of them, actually."

"You can add this to the list." Her hand lifts, holding the piece of paper out to me.

I take it, glancing at her questioningly. Her eyes close again. I can't figure out her behavior. She doesn't strike me as someone who tends to be overly dramatic.

But I know hardly anything about her. Maybe she is, and it just wasn't obvious last night.

I glance down.

My stomach falls the fifty or so stories we're suspended in the air.

I barely know anything about Hannah, except she used to have sex with my brother and that, according to the state of Nevada, she's my *wife*.

For a few seconds, it feels like everything around me is frozen. There's a part of my brain that's chanting *fuck, fuck, fuck* on repeat. Another section that's desperately flipping through a list of everyone I know who could help this go away. And the rest of me is too stunned by the realization *I got married in Vegas* to so much as twitch.

I drop the paper and blink at it. My eyes feel gritty from sleep deprivation and too much alcohol. "How the fuck—is this *real*?"

Hannah sighs. "I've never seen a marriage certificate before. But it looks legit to me."

I exhale, shakily. "I…"

Honestly, I'm at a complete loss for what to say. Marriage has never struck me as an appealing prospect. It was always a possible inevitability, outside of my control.

Even drunk, I can't believe the thought crossed my mind. More than crossed it, obviously, according to the paper I'm holding. Just a simple, unassuming sheet that made me a *husband*.

What.

The.

Fuck.

"We got married."

"Apparently. I thought *Fuck no* summed up your thoughts about marriage."

"It does. You must be awfully convincing."

I can't believe I'm *joking* about this. I rarely joke about anything.

"Aside from a brief phase in fourth grade when I told complete strangers I was going to have my wedding in the same church as my parents, I've never wanted to get married," Hannah informs me. "So I doubt I was very convincing."

"I never even had a brief phase."

"Weren't you going to marry Scarlett?"

When I don't answer, she glances over.

"Drunk New Yorkers are chatty. Especially about Kensingtons."

"My dad decides a lot more than my travel schedule," I reply.

She nods.

"How much of last night do you remember?"

"After the High Roller, not much."

"We went on the High Roller?"

Hannah studies me. "How much do *you* remember?"

"Not much." I clear my throat, glancing at the clothes scattered on the floor and then back at her. "Did we have sex?"

"I don't think so."

I raise an eyebrow. "Based on what?"

"Based on the size of your dick. There would be… aftereffects. I'm not sore."

I smile as soon as she says *aftereffects*. "You looked."

"You stared at my boobs for several minutes, so I think we're even."

"They're great boobs."

"Thanks. I grew them myself."

If anyone had told me I'd be on the floor laughing after discovering I'd married a stranger who's been with my brother, my response would have been, *You're insane*. But here I am, doing exactly that.

Hannah stands. "I have to go, or I'm going to miss my flight."

I stand too, wincing when my head protests the movement. "You can't *leave.* We have to—"

"I'm well aware we're in a fucking mess, Oliver," she says, picking her phone up. "But I have to go. I have to be back in LA by tonight. We'll both need to hire attorneys and figure out how to get divorced or an annulment or just light that thing on fire and pretend this never happened."

"Fine." She's right. There's nothing we can do to fix this imminently. "Give me your number."

Hannah rubs a palm across her face. "I don't know it."

"What? How do you not know your phone number?"

"I just got a new phone, and the company screwed it up and gave me a new number too and I suck at memorizing…" She exhales. "It doesn't matter. Just give me your number and I'll call you."

I hold a hand out for her phone, and she waves the black screen in my face. "My phone is *dead.* Write your number on something." I glance at the piece of paper I'm still holding. "You can't write your number on that!"

"I don't have anything else!" There's a pen with the hotel logo on the desk next to the couch, but no pad of paper.

I find my pants on the floor and pull my wallet out, hoping to find a receipt.

A playing card advertising a magician falls out. As soon as I see it flutter to the floor, I remember attending the show last night. Hopefully the rest of my memories aren't far behind. I hate being caught off guard, and that's basically all that's happened this morning.

I grab the playing card and scribble my number on it, then hold it out to Hannah. "Seriously?" she asks.

"It's that or the marriage certificate."

She rolls her eyes and takes the card. "I'll call you on Monday."

"Okay." I feel awkward all of a sudden. Waking up with a woman is a strange experience in itself. Discovering I'm also legally linked to her isn't simplifying anything.

I go to stick my hands in my pockets and discover I'm still wearing a sheet. So much for a casual pose.

Hannah bites her bottom lip. Suddenly, I remember kissing her beneath a palm tree. Desire heats my body, and I wish she wasn't leaving for reasons entirely unrelated to our surprise marriage.

"Fly safe."

"Yeah, thanks." She waves the card at me. "I'll call you."

I nod.

With one final, unsure smile, Hannah walks out.

I don't move, long after the door has clicked shut. I'm still in a state of shock. Still hungover and tired. Still…married.

Eventually, I toss the white sheet back on the bed and head into the bathroom. Under the pounding spray of hot water, I try to think rationally.

But my mind is too busy spinning in answerless circles. Now that Hannah is gone and I'm alone in my room, I can almost fool myself into thinking it was all just a dream. Part fantasy, part nightmare.

But as soon as I'm back in the room getting dressed, the piece of paper is just sitting there, taunting me.

I don't even know *how* you get married in Las Vegas. Did my drunk self really figure it out? If I had time, I'd go chapel to chapel until I figured out where this took place and could demand some concrete answers.

There's no time, though. I'm due downstairs in ten minutes for the start of day two of Garrett's bachelor party.

The last thing I want is for anyone here to find out what happened last night. Based on nothing but the Kensington net worth, I'm considered the most eligible bachelor in the country. Any tabloid would leap on the story, and Garrett is the only person here I would trust not to sell it.

I read articles about alcohol use and memory on my phone in between getting dressed. According to one study, heavy drinking can affect the transfer of memories between short- and long-term storage in the hippocampus. Still, I can't figure out how I was cognizant enough to get *married* but drunk enough to forget the entire experience.

Maybe my brain is repressing it in an attempt to pretend it didn't happen.

Unfortunately, life isn't that easy to edit.

There's a reason people view marriage as a massive commitment. That they think long and hard about whether to take that step and when and with whom.

And I just…went for it.

I finish getting dressed and leave the hotel room, resolving to push the avalanche of issues away until I have the time and wherewithal to deal with them. I sip the water Hannah handed me as I walk down the carpeted hallway, and then press the *Down* arrow when I reach the elevator.

The doors open a few seconds later, revealing a familiar face. "Oliver!"

I blink a few times, her cheerfulness more grating this morning than it was on the plane yesterday. Anything I was stressed about then seems mild in comparison to my current predicament. "Good morning, Marie."

Marie beams as I step inside the elevator with her. "You remembered."

"I'm good with names." I force myself to return her smile as the doors glide shut.

"You're staying *here*?"

"Yeah. You?"

"Uh, no. Just visiting."

I glance over, belatedly noticing her wrinkled dress and smudged makeup. "Are you okay?"

"I'm great. Do I not look great?"

I don't know how to respond to that. "You do. Just a little…rumpled."

Marie giggles, then leans against the wall. "I had a *great* night."

I nod. "Good."

The elevator chimes, then the doors slide open, revealing the lobby. Marie walks out first, glancing back and winking at me. "Enjoy the rest of your trip, Oliver."

"You too," I call back.

I continue into the hotel's dining area, spotting Garrett immediately. He's slumped over a mug of coffee at a table in the center of the room, looking about how I feel.

When the chair legs scrape the floor and announce my arrival he leans back, rubbing at both eyes with the palm of his hand. "Hey, man."

"Hey."

Garrett looks me up and down. "How was the rest of your night?"

"Uh, fine. Yours?"

"Still processing it, honestly." I nod, because *boy* do I get that. Garrett swallows some coffee, then glances at me. "Sorry about unloading on you last night."

"Don't apologize. I'm always happy to listen."

He sips more coffee. "I think this weekend was just what I needed. Evened things out, so to speak."

"You slept with her?"

"Yeah." Garrett exhales. "I needed to prove I could, I guess. And part of me feels guilty, but at least I got some good sex out of it. Sienna and I haven't since… I forgot what fucking someone new was like." He clears his throat. "Anyway, I feel better. I think she stole my watch though, because I can't find it. At least Sienna's not with me for the money. Her family has plenty, and we have an ironclad prenup."

My hand freezes halfway to my water bottle. The rest of the guys are beginning to join us, chairs scraping on both sides, most of them wearing sunglasses and pained expressions.

I return the greetings aimed my way on autopilot.

My entire life, I've been wary of anyone wanting me for my money. I saw the rounds of negotiations between my father and Hanson Ellsworth as the details of Crew and Scarlett's engagement were hammered out. The gossip rags reported extensively on how little Candace received after her marriage with my father ended, and how, of course, Arthur Kensington protected his assets. Of course, *little* to a Kensington is a lot to anyone else. Last I knew, Candace was living in France, set up for life.

In my world, prenups are more important than how many carats the ring is. The reality is, most marriages end. It's smart and responsible to prepare for that outcome, no matter what.

Smart and responsible are two adjectives most people would use to describe me. Also rich. I'm very, very rich.

And what did I do?

I got married without a prenup.

CHAPTER SEVEN

HANNAH

A sixth onesie gets unwrapped, prompting excited chatter all around me.

I take a sip of my mimosa, which is mostly orange juice. My body is still recovering from Friday night. From the amount of alcohol I drank and the shocking revelation I *married Oliver Kensington.*

Every romantic relationship I've ever been in, there's always been something missing. Something holding me back. A lack of trust or a lack of passion or a lack of interest, who knows.

And then I get married in Vegas to a man I'd known for less than twelve hours. It'd be funny…if it wasn't a serious commitment that could have disastrous implications.

Sitting and watching my sister-in-law open different versions of the same gift I got her—because I know onesies are a popular baby shower gift but didn't think they'd be *this* popular—feels a long way away from that Vegas hotel room.

But as Sunday afternoon creeps closer to Sunday night, it's impossible to totally ignore what happened. I promised Oliver I would call him tomorrow, and I've never dreaded anything more.

I don't understand how it happened. Me and him…married. Parts of that night are so clear and then others are a complete blur.

I remember talking to him in the hotel bar. The moment when I thought he was going to kiss me. And the moment he *did* kiss me is permanently seared into my brain. We did shots in a bar. Rode the High Roller and marveled at the view of the city. After that, it starts to get fuzzier. But nowhere in my recollection is there anything wedding-related. No chapel or Elvis impersonator.

We had to get a *license*.

Exchange *vows*.

I can't figure out how two people opposed to marriage end up married at all, let alone to each other. I didn't think there was enough alcohol in the world to make me say *I do* to a guy I hardly knew.

But for some reason, I did.

And he's Crew's brother, which makes it all even worse. I'm embarrassed—and ashamed—about how everything ended between me and Crew.

Crew never mentioned his older brother to me. I could have guessed they're not close based on that alone, but Oliver confirmed it yesterday, with his matter of fact *We don't have that kind of relationship*.

I wonder if that separation is by choice or default. Nothing I know about Crew offers any insight into who he is as a brother. And I know nothing about Oliver, period.

"Tell me you didn't get them a *onesie*," Rachel says, leaning in from my left.

I glance at April, who's unwrapping a box covered with familiar pink paper.

"The woman at the store recommended it," I whisper back. "It's cute! It has ducklings on it!"

My sister laughs and then shifts back into her seat.

"Thank you, Hannah! It's adorable." April hands the little yellow outfit over to a waiting Eddie, who folds it up neatly and adds it to the bags of gifts they've already received. My mom, sitting next to him, dutifully writes down the gift for thank you notes.

I stand and meet my sister-in-law in the middle of the room for a hug. "You're welcome. I can't wait to meet him or her."

"I can't wait to not be pregnant," she comments, rubbing her swollen belly.

I smile, ignoring the strange pang in my chest. Suddenly, it feels like everyone I know is settling down. Getting engaged or announcing pregnancies. Every time I go onto social media, every other post is an announcement. Even Rosie, who spent years dating casually, is in a serious relationship now.

April waddles back over to the front of the room, while I return to my seat next to Rachel.

"It is cute," she whispers to me.

I roll my eyes and drink more orange juice.

Opening the rest of the gifts takes April and Eddie another half an hour. Three more onesies get added to the large stack by the time the last of the wrapping paper has been ripped. I'm going to have to buy them a better gift.

By the time the final guests leave, I'm yawning. Between the jet lag, time change, and stress, I'm exhausted.

My mom shoos us out into the backyard, declining all offers to help clean up. She always insists her favorite part of hosting is putting everything back together at the end. Since I rarely have anyone over, I've never put that theory to the test.

My dad's behavior is even more predictable than my mom's. He beelines for the mallets as soon as we're outside. Croquet could challenge his family or company as his first love.

Eddie, Rachel, and I got him a custom set for his fiftieth

birthday a few years ago, and it's become his most prized possession. He buffs it and everything.

"Who's playing?" he calls over one shoulder.

"I'm in." Rachel trudges toward the blue mallet, her usual choice.

"I'll just watch," April says, sinking down into one of the patio chairs.

In the many years she and Eddie have been together, she's only participated in croquet a few times. Her sweet, forgiving personality doesn't mesh well with our cutthroat competitiveness.

"Eddie?" Dad calls.

After glancing at April, my brother nods. "Yeah. I call yellow."

I roll my eyes as I kick off my wedges and pad across the springy grass. "Don't call the same color every damn time. Or there's no point."

I pick up the orange mallet and hit my ball toward the starting stake.

My parents' backyard is my favorite part of this property. Its square footage is rare for Los Angeles, especially considering they bought this property before my dad's career really took off.

Spring's approach means the air is perfumed with the scent of eucalyptus and lilac. Prickly pear and poppies and irises and succulents spill out of the flowerbeds, stopping when the mulch turns to lush grass.

My dad hits first, which has always impacted his color choice. He makes it through the first two wickets, which is a typical start for him.

Rachel sinks down in the grass with an exaggerated sigh.

First rounds tend to take a while. Once, he made it all the way to the opposite stake before the rest of us even touched our balls.

This time, he only makes it through five wickets before it's

Rachel's turn to hit. She manages three, then Eddie is up. He only gets the yellow ball through the first two, bouncing off the edge of the white metal when he attempts the third.

"How embarrassing, Ed," I tease, leaning down and using my mallet to measure the starting distance.

I'm pretty sure Eddie replies with a rude gesture, because I hear my dad say "Edward" in the stern tone that he's used to chastise us since we were little kids. Rachel laughs.

I tune them all out as I focus on my first hit. The orange ball sails through the first two wickets, rolling to a stop in the exact spot I was aiming for. Eddie groans when I hit right past his yellow ball, easily clearing the third wicket as well. Then I pass Rachel's blue ball, rolling through the fourth. I overtake my dad at the fifth hoop, then barely miss the sixth.

"Thank God," Rachel says, dramatically.

My dad gives me a subtle thumbs up.

My whole family is tight knit. But I'm closer with my parents than my siblings, especially my dad.

Rachel is relaxed and independent. During her summer trips, we won't hear from her for weeks. Eddie is busy with work and his growing family.

I'm the one who lived at home after college and who comes over for dinner once a week.

That extra time has translated into my croquet game. I've logged many more hours in this backyard than either Rachel or Eddie have.

Eddie and Rachel give up on making it through the course themselves and settle for sending wild swings toward the orange and black balls heading toward home. Fortunately for me and my dad, their aim is terrible. Eddie comes close to hitting me once but never manages to.

Hits are allowed but unsportsmanlike, according to my dad.

Since our first family game, he's maintained a motto of *win with your own skill, not by bringing others down.*

Considering how ruthless he can be at work, I think it was more a rule he made when we were younger and more likely to whack each other with mallets. And now that we're adults, he still feels like he needs to stick with it.

It only takes two more turns for me to complete the course and return to the first stake. Once my dad manages to hit the final mallet as well, he walks over to me, leaving Eddie and Rachel to finish the game.

"Excellent game, Hannah."

I smile. "Thanks, Dad."

His proud expression prompts a guilty twinge in my chest. I've never withheld anything important from my father. And I think my *marriage* qualifies.

I know nothing about the process of divorce. I'm sure Oliver has realized the same thing that occurred to me mid-flight to LA: we didn't sign a prenuptial agreement. He'll undoubtedly hire the best divorce attorney money can buy to protect himself. I should do the same, and my dad knows a lot of powerful, important people.

But I can't force the words out, no matter how terrifying it is to be tied to a stranger. Can't bear to see pride turn to disappointment.

"I have a meeting with Logan Cassidy and his coach set up for tomorrow night," my father says, oblivious to my inner turmoil.

"You finally hooked him, huh?"

"He's smart to play hard to get. Sets him apart from Donovan."

"There are already plenty of differences there."

Trey Donovan is widely expected to go first in next year's

draft. I know nothing about Logan Cassidy except my father has a keen interest in him.

But this is typical for my father. Not only is he already looking ahead toward next year, he's looking past the player every agency wants to sign. He always has a master plan that means playing the long game.

"Donovan thinks he's entitled to play," my father says, rubbing some dirt off his mallet. "Cassidy *wants* to play."

"All the best players are confident."

"So are all the best sport agents," he replies. "Which is why I'd like for you to come with me tomorrow night. And why I think you should get licensed…and sign him."

My grip tightens around the wooden handle of the mallet.

This is a topic that comes up every once in a while. I started at Garner Sports Agency as a glorified assistant. Worked my way up to more substantive tasks than filing and scheduling travel. But I've never gotten licensed as an agent, meaning I'd be able to represent athletes. It's felt like a permanent step in a way accepting a job there didn't.

"This guy is the real deal, Hannah. If you sign him as your first client, you're setting yourself up for one hell of a career."

Rachel approaches, her blue mallet swung over one shoulder like a polo player. "I thought you guys were over here *celebrating*. You're talking about *work*?"

"Not anymore," my father replies, patting me on the back and starting toward the patio. "Let's head inside and see if your mother will accept any help."

Rachel hooks her elbow through mine as we walk across the lawn. "You okay, Han?"

"I just kicked all your asses at croquet. I'm *amazing*."

"You just seem… I don't know. Distracted, I guess."

I force a smile. Part of me wants to blurt out *I applied to architecture school. And then married a billionaire in Vegas!*

Just to have this weight off my chest. This crushing uncertainty of handling problems alone.

I squeeze Rachel's forearm. "I'm fine. Thanks for checking. Just tired. I didn't sleep well last night. Everything is fine."

Rachel nods, believing me.

And I hope I didn't just lie to my sister.

CHAPTER EIGHT

OLIVER

Pierre, my doorman, nods as I walk past him. "Good morning, Mr. Kensington. Have a wonderful day."

"Thanks, Pierre." I inject some warmth into my tone, knowing my voice will come out flat otherwise. The glass front of my building's lobby reveals a gray morning. The flinty sky matches my mood.

I landed back in New York late yesterday afternoon. The rest of my trip to Vegas was far less eventful than the first night.

I mostly gambled, wishing I could throw an unwanted marriage into the pot. Annoyingly, I won almost every game, so none of the guys understood why I was scowling.

And I spent last night perusing law firm websites and reading blogs about how to obtain a quick divorce.

I know plenty of lawyers. Kensington Consolidated has a veritable army of them. Half my college classmates continued on to law school.

The problem is, I have no idea who to trust. People will care I'm married, even—especially—that it's a short-lived one. And realistically, not only do I need to proceed carefully, I also need to go on the offensive.

I looked the Garners up last night, too. Hannah's family is wealthy. Her father represents some of the biggest names in sports, and he even held shares in a professional team at one point. She probably has a trust fund and isn't desperate for money.

But her personal wealth can't come close to representing a fraction of my net worth. In addition to my trust fund and sizable salary, the stock I own in Kensington Consolidated is worth a hundred million, easily.

I hate negotiating from an inferior position. And that's exactly where I am with Hannah. Based on my basic research last night, she has a legal claim to half of my financial assets. In addition to that, her involvement with Crew obviously didn't end well. I've just handed her a golden opportunity for revenge.

I hate thinking that way. I like Hannah. Under very different circumstances, I could see myself dating her. I saw her reaction to the license, and it was legitimate distress. But my cynicism has gotten me as far in the business world as my last name has. I would be a fool to bank on her expecting nothing when she has the opportunity to become a billionaire because I signed above her signature.

That's the main reason I'm leaving for the office even earlier than usual. I've slept terribly ever since I woke up married. Tossing and turning and thinking.

Unsurprisingly, traffic is light at this hour. My twenty-minute commute to the office only takes fifteen.

When I enter the lobby, the security guard is yawning. It's still the night attendant, waiting to be relieved for the day shift. He gives me a respectful nod that I return before scanning my access key and stepping into the elevator.

There's no front desk on the executive floor. All the desks are empty and offices dark as I walk down the carpeted hallway.

I stop in the kitchen to brew a second cappuccino, the first one doing little to combat my exhaustion. The fancy machine whistles to life as soon as I hit the button, grinding and brewing and frothing until the cup is filled.

I continue down the hall, enjoying how quiet the floor is. I avoid leaving my office unless it's necessary for this exact reason. People act oddly when I do. They react the same way around my father and Crew, but they both handle it better than I do. My father revels in how his employees find him intimidating. Crew is excellent at pretending not to notice. I'm just uncomfortable.

Walking into my office after days away is strange. Normally, I'm here on Saturday or Sunday. Sometimes both.

I'm reminded why when I unlock my computer and discover I have fifteen hundred unread emails.

Most of them are threads I was cc'd on that don't require any direct attention. But some of them do. By the time the number of unread emails has dwindled down to a reasonable number, I can hear activity out in the hall as everyone else arrives.

At five of ten I stand, button my suit jacket, and open my door.

Alicia glances up from her computer and smiles. "Good morning, Mr. Kensington."

"Good morning, Alicia."

"Did you have a good weekend?"

It's the same question she asks me every Monday, but I know I'm not imagining the extra scrutiny in the question. For once, she knows I wasn't here. So it's a little harder to force out a "Fine" than it usually is. "How about you?"

"It was good. Thanks for asking, sir."

I nod and continue down the hallway, keeping my gaze aimed

straight ahead. I dread these meetings for many reasons, but the worst part is everyone knows about them. They're all wondering what Crew, my father, and I are discussing. Who we're promoting or firing or hiring.

There's no sign of Crew when I step inside the main conference room. But my father is already sitting at the table, tapping a pen against the dark wood impatiently.

My dread grows. No buffer, and he's irritated I kept him waiting. If I'd beaten him here, he would have commented I must be having a slow morning.

With my father, there's no winning. Only varying degrees of defeat.

"Dad."

"Oliver."

I take a seat across from him, wishing I'd brought the mug with an inch of coffee remaining. Varnished mahogany stretches between us, as sparse and depressing as our relationship. There's no paper record of these meetings. They exist without notes and never include anyone besides the three of us.

A long time ago, I thought they were my father's way of connecting family and company in some small way. He guided Crew and I toward working here with all the subtlety of a shove, yet rarely acknowledges we're his sons within the walls of this building.

Now, I see these meetings as having little to do with me or Crew.

They're a power play.

My father is all about perception. He wants it to appear as if we're a tight unit, whatever the truth might be. Wants his employees to spread word the Kensington leadership is united and infallible.

Tap. Tap. Tap.

I lean back in my chair and hold my father's gaze.

I'm expecting him to look away. Ever since he found out what happened between me and Candace, he's alternated between ignoring me in private and heaping adulations on Crew in public.

There's petty, and then there's my father. He's never met a grudge he hasn't held.

But he holds my gaze now, something simmering in eyes the same color as mine. Crew looks more like our mom. I resemble him.

Surprising me further, he speaks first. "Thompson & Thompson should go through today."

"I know." That's what half the emails I just sorted through were about.

"That deal closed faster than expected."

"I know," I repeat, knowing that comment is the closest to *good job* I'll get.

"Crew isn't coming."

I hide my surprise. Crew has never missed a Monday meeting.

"I told him I wanted to talk to you alone."

Automatically, I tense.

"While you were away on *vacation*…"

I grind my molars at the characterization of a *weekend* but don't otherwise react.

"I met with Leonardo Branson."

I nod once, familiar with the name. Leonardo Branson founded an investment management fund a couple of decades ago that catapulted his own wealth and made him a lot of powerful friends, including my father.

"His daughter Quinn just moved back to New York. She was living in London, where her mother is from. She works in public relations." My father waves a dismissive hand. "More of a hobby than a career, based on what Leonardo says. She's twenty-five. Ready to settle down and start a family."

My shoulders stiffen. Dread uncoils in my gut.

I can see *exactly* where this is going.

Years.

I spent *years* expecting to marry a woman of my father's choosing. To be used as a bargaining chip that ensured some deal or aided an important merger.

Then my father told me Crew would be marrying Scarlett Ellsworth, not me. That I should focus on the company, while Crew would be the all-important link to the Ellsworth empire.

It took me weeks to adjust to the idea. Not because of any attachment to Scarlett—I barely knew her. But because I knew what other implications it would have.

"She's amenable to the match," my father continues. His tone is relaxed. We might as well be discussing the weather. "Recalled you as a perfect gentleman." He scoffs. "Although we both know that's hardly the case, that's the impression Miss Branson will keep. You'll get married this summer. I'll leave the proposal to you. Surely, you can manage that much."

It takes effort to hold in the incredulous laugh that wants to escape.

Years of waiting and wondering about how my father will dictate my future, and he chooses to do so right after I drunkenly married a woman my father would never approve of.

There's no hesitance in his expression. He thinks I'll do this. He's expecting me to fall right into line, the way I've done every single time he's asked me to do something.

I've always carried that same confidence. I've known I *would* do exactly what he asked.

But this time is different. That blind allegiance to my father has shifted right along with our frosty relationship.

Do I regret what happened between me and Candace? Yes.

Do I resent my father for how he's treated me since? Also yes.

And this time is different for another reason.

I *can't* do what he's asking.

Literally can't. I'm legally married to someone else.

"I'll think about it."

Not much surprises my father. But that response did. I catch it in his stilted blinks. The flex of his jaw. There's a weighted pause, as he adjusts whatever he was planning to say next.

"The Bransons are coming over for dinner tomorrow night. I'll expect you at six sharp."

"I'm busy."

It's immensely satisfying to watch my father struggle not to react to that response. To keep emotion from breaking through his stoic expression. He thought I'd agree without hesitating, and I can't decide if that's more sad or infuriating.

Evidently, me not agreeing never occurred to him. And I suddenly resent my marriage to Hannah a little less, knowing it's the source of my sudden stubbornness. It's freeing. Like I took one step away from expectations and now it's easier to take a second.

"Leonardo is expecting you to be there. So is Quinn."

"I didn't make them any promises. Enjoy your evening, Dad."

I stand and turn my back to my father.

"It's the least you owe me, Oliver," he calls after me.

My nails dig into my palms. I bite the inside of my cheek until I taste the metallic tang of blood. "Kensingtons collect debts. They don't acknowledge them. Isn't that what you taught me? You'll never forgive me for what happened."

"If you marry Quinn Branson, I will."

I turn to look at him. "What?"

"If you marry Quinn Branson, Candace will be completely forgotten. Gone for good."

"You think I'm *that* desperate for your approval?" I shake my head. "I fucked up, Dad. I apologized. I'm not going to marry a total stranger in some twisted penance."

"I'm not inflicting you with some hardship, Oliver. Quinn is bright, wealthy, and beautiful. She'll make a perfect Kensington."

"Then why don't *you* marry her?" I snap.

A cruel smile spreads across my father's face. I have a good idea of exactly what he'll say before the words leave his lips. "You'd be interested in her then?"

I shake my head. "Thirty seconds ago, you said Candace would be forgotten."

"Agree, and she will be."

"No."

I keep walking. I'm almost out the door when he speaks again. "I'll name you the next CEO of Kensington Consolidated. Effective in five years."

I freeze, my instant reaction giving too much away. I should keep walking, but my muscles won't cooperate. Those words run on a relentless loop in my head.

I'll name you the next CEO of Kensington Consolidated.

I'll name you the next CEO of Kensington Consolidated.

I'll name you the next CEO of Kensington Consolidated.

A sentence I never, ever thought I'd hear my father say to me. My goal. My birthright. My dream.

I turn again, not missing the triumphant smirk on my father's face. He knows what this means to me. Knows what he's dangling. It's what has separated me and Crew when it comes to this company. Crew would make an excellent CEO. He'd step into the role and thrive under the pressure. But he's never *wanted* it, the way I did. Do.

"What about Crew?"

"He'll understand. You're the oldest. You've given a lot more to this company than he has. And he has other responsibilities."

"You're asking me to take those same responsibilities on."

"A family man is good optics, Oliver. Leonardo doesn't offer the same assets Hanson did. But Quinn doesn't share in Scarlett's ambitions either. You won't have to worry about *her* jetting off to Paris instead of on a honeymoon."

I understand exactly what he's saying.

Quinn will take on the traditional wife role that Scarlett shuns, allowing me to focus on business. I can picture the image he's painting perfectly. A separate life from my spouse. Playing the happy couple only when we're in public.

It's what I always expected my marriage would look like, and for some reason all I can think about is sitting with Hannah on a hard floor wearing a sheet, laughing. My life already has plenty of cold, pretend relationships, and I hate the idea of adding another. For *optics*.

"Why would you step down in five years?"

"The board—and company—deserve fresh blood. New ideas. It was always my intention to hand CEO over to you or Crew as soon as you were ready to take over. I'll still have a role on the board, of course. But I'll also explore other opportunities I can't as CEO. Start a foundation, perhaps. Or look into politics."

I don't believe a word he's saying. He's pivoting the same way he taught me to do, homing in on exactly what it will take to close the deal. And he has the advantage of knowing me better than a business associate. CEO of Kensington Consolidated in five years is an incredible offer.

He's waving the one thing I want—the one thing I've always wanted—right in front of me.

And he's pairing it with the elusive allure of forgiveness.

Something I'm not sure he is capable of. But at least I'll have this to throw back in his face whenever he brings Candace up.

And for all his many faults, my father is a man of his word. He's never reneged on a deal. Our relationship will never be the same, and that's a regret I'll have to live with. But it could be *better*, and that sparks a hope I thought I'd given up on.

But I can't say yes. Not only because there's no way I'm committing to marrying a woman I've never met but because I've never reneged on a deal, either. I'm currently married, and I have to sort that mess out first.

I exhale. "I'm not agreeing to anything. But I'll be at dinner."

My father nods. "Fine." Then he leaves the conference room without another word, leaving me reeling.

Instead of returning to my own office, I head to Asher's.

"Come in," he calls out, after I knock.

His usual grin is replaced by confusion as I walk into his office. I've been here once before, and it was when I couldn't find Crew and was trying to hunt down a signature.

"Do you have a minute?" I ask.

"I—yeah, sure." Asher clears his throat and closes the open folder on his desk.

I close the door behind me and walk deeper into his office, glancing at the leopard-print armchair and potted plant in the corner of the office before I take a seat in one of the standard leather chairs opposite his desk.

"Joke?"

"Huh?"

"The leopard print chair. Is that a joke?"

Asher grins. "Nah. I just like it."

"Oh."

He leans back in his desk chair, folding his hands behind his head. "How was Vegas?" he asks.

Instead of answering, I ask, “Does Kensington Consolidated have a nonfraternization policy between employees?”

Confusion, then excitement cross his face. The first I’m expecting. The second, not so much.

“Damn, Oliver. You’re hooking up with an employee?”

“Not me. You.”

Asher’s expression freezes. “I don’t know what you’re talking about.”

“I’m not going to tell anyone about Isabel.”

I lean back in my chair, then look out the window. The sky is still a foreboding shade of gray, dark and menacing against the outline of the skyscrapers that make up New York’s distinctive skyline. Asher is silent, but I can feel his eyes on me.

“What do you know about Hannah Garner?” I ask.

Silence.

When I glance at him, Asher’s eyebrows are furrowed together. “Hannah Garner? Crew’s ex-fuck buddy?”

If Hannah hadn’t said anything about Crew, this would have been a hell of a way to find out. “Yes.”

Asher is obviously waiting for more of a response from me. When it never comes, he shrugs. “Not much. She’s hot. Blonde. Her father owns Garner Sports Agency. They’re bigtime. She’s worked there for a while, doing what I’m not exactly sure…”

“All you know about her is she works for her father?”

Asher shrugs as he picks up a pen and spins it around his finger. “Basically. I only met her a couple of times and both times were at a bar. We weren’t exactly discussing her political positions and credit score.”

I exhale and stand. Talk about a waste of time.

“Wait.” Asher flies to his feet and hurries around his desk. “Why are you asking about her?”

I smooth the front of my suit jacket. “Because I married her.”

It's the first time I've said the words out loud. They linger in the air with an uncomfortable presence.

"You—married—what?" Asher shakes his head back and forth wildly.

"I hired a private investigator who's running a background check on her." It was the one action I took from Vegas, even if making the call made me feel like my father. "I thought you might be useful in the interim, but obviously, I was wrong."

"You *married* Hannah Garner?" Asher still looks comically stunned.

"That's what I just said, yes."

"I—you—how—does Crew know?"

"No."

"Christ, Oliver." Asher runs a hand through his hair, the motion jerky and uneven. "When are you going to tell him? I'd like to be out of town."

"Hopefully, never."

"Never?"

"Again, that's what I just said."

"You can't expect me to keep this a *secret*!"

"Why not?"

"Because you're asking me to lie to him!"

"If you have a problem lying to Crew, you must have told him you're sleeping with Isabel?"

The remaining color drains from Asher's face.

"Look, I don't care what you do with your dick, Asher. But we both know Crew will. You're putting him in a hell of a position."

Asher groans. "I know. It was only supposed to be one time. And then—"

"I don't want any details. Just keep your mouth shut and I will too."

Asher nods once.

I nod back, then turn to leave.

"Hey, Oliver. I'm assuming this was a drunk in Vegas thing?"

"Yes."

"So, no prenup."

I don't answer, which is one.

Asher whistles, long and low. "Things didn't end well between her and Crew."

"I know."

"Get a good attorney."

I nod again, then walk out of his office.

CHAPTER NINE

HANNAH

I scroll through the notifications on the screen, pocketing my phone again when I see there's nothing from Oliver. I called him earlier, as promised, and got his voicemail. And the dread I carried around all weekend has only grown with each minute that passes without a response, as I wonder why he didn't answer and worry about what he'll say when we talk.

My name gets called, so I walk up to the counter to pick up my sandwich. I grab the paper bag, turn toward the door, and freeze.

I haven't seen Crew Kensington in nearly two years. And now he's standing in my favorite lunch spot three days after I accidentally married his brother. Considering we parted under incredibly poor terms, awkward doesn't even begin to cover it.

Before I can decide how to react, Crew glances over and spots me. We stare at each other for a few stunned seconds, before Crew says something to the man he's with and heads in my direction.

My palms start to sweat as he approaches. He looks the same, as assured and attractive as the first time I met him. But it's different. There's no draw, no excitement. Just dread.

"Hi, Hannah."

"Hi, Crew." I'm grateful my voice sounds normal, at least.

He's studying me cautiously. I'm probably looking at him the same way. I doubt Oliver told him what happened between us in Vegas, but I don't know that for certain.

"Wasn't expecting to see you here." Crew chuckles uncomfortably, but there's still an easiness to the sound. He has an innate confidence to him, which is part of what drew me in. It's relaxing to be around, like coasting. And I can't help but compare it to Oliver's sharp edges. Everything he said at the bar reads differently now, in the context of knowing his last name.

"I live here."

"Yeah, I know." He clears his throat. "How've you been?"

"Fi-Good," I reply. "I'm good."

"That's good."

"You?"

He smiles. "I'm good too. Sleep-deprived, but good."

I'm starting to lose circulation in my hand, with how tightly I'm clutching the bag's handle. "I, uh, congratulations on the baby."

Crew nods. "Thanks."

I inhale. "I'm sorry, Crew. For what I said to you…and for what I said to Scarlett. It was way, way over the line."

He nods again, this time slower. "I'm not going to lie; it pissed me off at the time. But, I'm sorry too. I know I said my life wouldn't change after I got married. If it makes any difference, I thought me and Scarlett would just be on paper. Things changed."

"You don't have to explain anything to me. You never owed me any explanation."

Crew studies me, but there's nothing sexual about his appraisal. It feels more like he's checking me over, making sure I'm okay. "Jeff and I just stopped here because it was on the way. Glad to know it's endorsed by a local." He nods toward the bag I'm holding.

"Yeah, the food here is great."

I'm not sure what else to say to Crew now that I've apologized. There was never much substance between us. I don't even know what kind of sandwich he'd order from a place like this.

"You're here for work?"

The question has nothing to do with Crew. I'm fishing for information about Kensington Consolidated because of Oliver, curious about the company he's so devoted to.

"Uh, yeah." Suddenly, he looks a little uncomfortable. "Speaking of which, I'd better get back to Jeff. We're on a tight timetable." Crew pauses. "Take care, Hannah."

"You too."

We share a smile, and then Crew walks back over toward the man he walked in with.

I head out the door, turning the interaction over in my mind as I walk down the sidewalk toward the baby store down the street. It's where I got the duckling onesie for Eddie and April's baby, and where I'll hopefully be able to find them a more original gift.

Seeing Crew was strange, and not just because of Oliver. It was a relief to apologize, although Scarlett is really who I owe one to. I've changed since the last time I saw him, and so has he. Any familiarity that existed between us was erased a long time ago.

It's a relief to fully realize that, but impossible to forget everything that's happened. I'm married to his brother, which tangles the past with the present.

I check my phone again. Still nothing from Oliver.

Both of the saleswomen in the baby store are busy helping

other customers when I walk in, so I start browsing in the front. There's a large selection of strollers. That wasn't a shower gift, and I realize why when I check the price tag on one.

I move on to the toys section. There's a plush duckling that would match the onesie I already gave them. And then practically every other animal is piled on the shelves as well. It's an overwhelming selection.

I'm petting a stuffed pig when my phone rings. I lean against the display of pacifiers and pull it out of my pocket.

My stomach twists itself into a knot as *Oliver Kensington* flashes across the screen.

"Hi," I answer. "Can I give you a call back in like fifteen minutes? I'm shopping for baby stuff."

"Baby stuff?"

My body reacts to the sound of his deep voice in a way I resent. I know I'm attracted to Oliver. But it wasn't supposed to be this lasting, overwhelming interest that fills my stomach with butterflies.

"Yeah. My sister-in-law is pregnant, and my shower gift was lame. I'm trying to find something better for when the baby is actually born."

There's a long pause. Then, "Do they have any nursery rockers?"

"What?"

"An elephant or a giraffe. Maybe a hippo?"

I spin in a circle, scanning the store. "Um, they have a lamb? Or a unicorn."

"Do they know what they're having?"

It takes me too long to answer, totally thrown by the direction of our conversation. "No."

"I'd get the lamb, then. Not all boys love unicorns."

"But all babies like rockers?"

Another pause. "Lili did. She still tries to sit on it, even though she's getting too big."

"Oh." That's my brilliant response to learning Oliver bought his niece a rocker. Based on everything that's been said and I surmised, I thought he had no relationship with Scarlett and Crew's daughter.

"Call me back when you can," he says, then hangs up.

I stand and listen to dead air until the sales associate approaches me. "Can I help you with anything, miss?"

"Yes. I'll take the lamb rocker."

She blinks at me, appearing taken aback by my surety. "All right. I'll get it packed up for you."

"Great. Thank you."

I pay for the rocker, load the oversized box into the back of my SUV, and then call Oliver back.

He answers on the second ring this time. "Hi, Hannah."

"Hi."

Hearing him say my name twists my stomach into knots. It's so unexpected. Unfamiliar. We know too much about each other…and nothing at all.

Oliver clears his throat. "How have you been?"

I smile. "We can skip the small talk, you know. I called you because I said I would. I haven't had time to find an attorney."

"Just to go shopping for baby gifts?"

I'm silent, not sure if he's judging or joking.

"I haven't gotten an attorney yet, either" he says, after a beat of strained silence.

"Really?" I'm surprised, and it fills my voice. I was certain he'd be on the phone with a hotshot lawyer before my plane left Las Vegas.

"Really," he confirms, but there's a note of hesitance in his voice. Like he's unsure if that's an admission he should have made.

"I'm planning to make some calls this afternoon."

"Good luck. I've heard divorce attorneys are hard to find in Los Angeles."

A joke, I realize. He just made a joke.

Too late, I laugh.

"Um, yeah. I'll send you the name of my attorney in the next few days," I say. "Once you've decided who's representing you, it will probably be best to let them handle all the communication going forward."

Oliver doesn't reply right away. I'm not sure how, but I can *feel* the surprise in his silence. Did he think I'd ask for money? Expect daily calls?

"You're right," he finally responds. "That will probably be best."

"Great. Goodbye, Oliver."

"Goodbye, Hannah."

There's another awkward moment when neither of us hang up right away. But there's nothing else to say, so I do, dropping my phone in the cupholder.

I know I'll probably have to talk to Oliver again. But the chances of it being face to face are low. You can sign and mail anything these days.

I'll be divorced before I'm thirty, and it feels anticlimactic. I don't remember my wedding and I'll be divorced as soon as possible, likely without ever seeing the man I'm married to again.

All of it is just…weird.

I shift into drive and pull out of the parking lot. In addition to a regular workday, I have the dinner with my dad and Logan Cassidy tonight.

And now, I also have to find an attorney in the next couple of days.

"I'm so sorry, ma'am. The table isn't quite ready yet. If you'd like to take a seat at the bar, one of the wait staff will let you know when it's ready."

The maître de eyes me warily, like a ticking bomb. The last time I was here, I saw a man make a scene about the size of his ice cubes, so I understand her apprehension. Perch wouldn't be my first choice of restaurant, but I'm not surprised it's where my father chose. It has a formal, sleek atmosphere that works well for an evening business meeting.

"That's fine," I say. The maître de's shoulders visibly relax before I head toward the bar.

Several stools are open. Not only is it on the early side for dinner, but not many people come here to eat at the bar.

I slide onto one of the stools, the cool metal uncomfortable against my bare legs. I cross them, suppressing a shiver, as I set my clutch down on the quartz counter. One finger traces a darker vein in the rock, marveling at the sleek finish. Maybe I should renovate my kitchen again.

"Can I get you anything, miss?"

I glance up at the bartender. He's smiling, and it's an interested one that should elicit some reaction in me. But I feel empty instead of giddy.

"Just a sparkling water, please. With lime."

He nods, his friendly smile turning forced. I watch as he fills a glass with ice and then opens a green bottle. The contents hiss as he pours the bubbly liquid over the ice, then flips open a container and adds a wedge of lime. It's served with a napkin emblazoned with the restaurant's logo.

"Thank you."

"You're welcome." Then he's gone, moving down the line of few customers.

I stare down at the bubbles rising to the surface of my water. The last time I was in a bar setting was the night I met Oliver, and it's an uncomfortable memory to revisit.

I didn't feel empty when he looked at me. I felt like my drink —fizzy and sparkling and effervescent.

With a scoff, I shake my head and take a sip. I pull my phone out of my clutch and glance at the screen. I'm early, but my father usually is too. He must have hit some of LA's infamous traffic. It never bends to anyone's schedule.

I don't have any new texts or missed calls. Just five emails, all follow-ups from attorneys I contacted earlier.

"You know, I swore off blondes, but for you I'd make an exception."

The dark-haired man smirks when I look over at him, sliding a step closer. He's attractive—tall, built, and muscular. Obviously practiced at picking up women. But I'm more fascinated by the agitated energy emanating from him. His fingers tap against the stone surface restlessly, even as his eyes focus on my face.

"How romantic," I say, picking up my water and taking another sip. "Unfortunately, I like my men principled. If you swear something off, you should follow through."

"I'm *plenty* principled," he replies, then grins.

I half-smile in response to his boyish one. He's charming, I'll give him that. And not easily dissuaded, unlike the bartender. Immediately interested, unlike Oliver.

But comparing other guys to Oliver is not something I should be doing. And neither is flirting. I'm here for work. As a possible momentous step into a career I haven't fully decided I want.

My phone buzzes with an incoming message. I grab it immediately, expecting it to be my father.

It's not.

Oliver Kensington: *Text me the name of your attorney once you've settled on one.*

I make a face, sourness swirling in my stomach. I already told him I would let him know as soon as I decided. He doesn't need to remind me like I'm a child. I'm not going to *forget* about needing a divorce.

And what bothers me even more is the detached tone. He didn't even bother with a *Hi.* I stare at the message, debating how to respond.

"Everything okay?"

I shut off my phone. "Great."

"Ex?"

"Husband," I mutter, glaring at the glass of water.

"You're married?"

I glance up, almost wanting to smile at the guy's crestfallen expression. It's flattering. And also the perfect out.

"Yes."

"Dammit."

I do smile this time. "On the bright side, you didn't break your rule."

"Miss? Your table is ready."

I glance over at the uniformed waitress and nod, grabbing my clutch and water. "Have a good night," I tell him before following the waitress toward the back of the restaurant.

The table is empty, and I experience a trickle of worry. It's not like my dad to be late. He's lived in LA for four decades; he knows what a realistic driving time is. And for this meeting in particular, I would have expected him to plan ahead.

I butter a piece of bread while looking over the menu, hoping it'll appease my growling stomach. I only picked at my sandwich at lunchtime, still processing my conversations with both Kensington men.

Five minutes later, I'm still sitting alone. A few of the other diners are casting me pitying looks. At least this isn't a table for two. It looks like I was stood up by a group, not on a date. Which is slightly better. I think.

Finally, I spot my father. Hastily, I swallow the last bite of the bread. Take a sip of water and wipe my mouth, careful not to smudge my lipstick.

"Sorry, Hannah," he says, straightening his tie. "There was an accident on the 405. And I was on the phone with Tracy, talking through a contract issue, so I couldn't call."

"It's fine, Dad."

"David, this is my daughter, Hannah. Hannah, this is David McKenna, who coaches the Bobcats."

I shake the hand David offers. He's about a decade younger than my father, gray creeping from his temples and wrinkles webbing from his eyes, probably from squinting at a field. "Nice to meet you, David."

"Likewise." He's no-nonsense and respectful. I like him immediately.

"And this is Logan Cassidy."

I turn toward the other man with my father, surprise and dread warring for space.

Logan looks just as shocked. He didn't know who I was at the bar. He's probably worried hitting on me might affect his chances of representation.

And I…I've told exactly one person about my marriage since

I woke up in Vegas. One stupid, offhand comment to a man I thought I'd never see again.

Logan looks away from me, at my father. "I just want to clear the air, sir."

My stomach sinks as blood whooshes in my ears. It feels like everything is sped up and slowing down at the same time. Like I'm watching a vase fall from across the room, knowing I'll never be able to reach it in time and that it's going to break.

I know exactly what is about to happen and have no clue how to stop it.

"I had no idea who Hannah was when I approached her at the bar, and I just want to make it clear that I would never flirt with a married woman. I know your company is known for valuing character, and I just—"

"I think there's been a misunderstanding, son," my father says. He chuckles, and my eyes drift shut slowly, wishing I could shut the rest of the world out for good. "Hannah isn't married."

When I blink, Logan's confused expression comes into focus. He's staring at me expectantly, waiting for me to correct my father. Then my father is looking at me too, waiting for me to correct Logan. The only unbothered person in our group is David McKenna.

"Could I talk to you outside for a moment, Dad?" I ask, standing and walking toward the door before he has a chance to answer.

Whether or not he follows, I desperately need some fresh air.

He *does* follow, appearing on the sidewalk just a few seconds after I've inhaled my first lungful of clean oxygen. As soon as I get a glimpse of his expression, I start to wish he stayed inside.

"What is going on, Hannah? Did Cassidy say or do something inappropriate? I'll make sure—"

"No. This has nothing to do with Logan." I cross my arms,

rubbing my bare skin. The sun is sinking, taking warmth with it. "I, um..."

It's hard to force the words out. I've done plenty of stupid things, but I've never admitted most of them to my parents. And marrying Oliver is *the* stupidest thing I've ever done.

Concern creases my father's forehead. "Hannah—"

"I *am* married. I did get married. In Vegas, last weekend."

My father's expression literally freezes, nothing but shock visible. "I... I didn't even know you were dating anyone."

"I wasn't dating him."

His face manages to look more stunned. And worse, there's a flash of disappointment.

"For very long," I add hastily. "I wasn't dating him for very long. He was there for a bachelor party. We had too much to drink, and it was a stupid mistake. We're getting divorced. I didn't want you and mom to know."

My father exhales, long and rattled. "I...wow. I don't know quite what to say, Hannah."

"Logan was flirting with me, which is why I told him about the marriage. But he was completely respectful. We should go back inside."

My dad is blinking rapidly, still looking shocked. Eddie dated April for eight years before proposing to her. They were engaged for two years before they got married.

In contrast, my marriage and divorce are a whirlwind.

I can only imagine how fast he would be blinking if he knew I'd only known Oliver for a few hours before marrying him. A vague *we hadn't been dating for long* isn't much of an improvement, but it's something.

"Do you need an attorney?"

"I contacted some today. I have calls lined up for tomorrow morning."

He nods. "Send me the names. I might have some insight."

"Okay."

As much as I hate that my father knows—especially *how* he found out—it's a relief that he does. For the first time since I saw that piece of paper next to the bed, it feels like I can see past this mistake. Like it's a manageable one.

"You're okay, Hannah?"

"Yeah." I nod, twice. "I'm good."

"I can handle the meeting, if you want."

"I want to stay."

A proud smile spreads across my dad's face, and the rush of relief is forceful. I was worried he'd want me to leave after making a mess of things with Logan. And I was terrified he'd think less of me for using such horrible judgment.

"Then let's go," he says.

And we head back inside.

CHAPTER TEN

OLIVER

I hate this house.

If I had any positive memories of the mansion where I grew up, they're long gone.

One finger taps against the side of the glass set next to me. I haven't taken a sip of the cognac handed to me when I arrived. The nutty, fruity aftertaste has never been my favorite. And I also want to keep a clear head.

I don't know how long it will take until I'm declared legally single. I've been purposefully vague with all the attorneys I've talked to, not wanting to provide any specific or damning details until I've decided on one. Hannah hasn't sent me the name of who is representing her. She never responded to my text, either.

The one I wrote and deleted dozens of follow-ups to. Which is stupid in and of itself. I never second-guess myself this much. But I think the complete silence means I offended her, which wasn't what I meant to do at all.

I'm fumbling through the dark on how to navigate this situation. And the only person who knows about this mess is Asher, and I'm not sure he'll be of any help in drafting texts.

"Wow, what a party."

I glance up at the sound of Scarlett's voice, surprised to see her and Crew walking into the sitting room where I'm seated, alone.

The Bransons haven't arrived yet. The butler showed me in when I arrived, handed me a glass of cognac, and informed me my father was on the phone.

They make a striking pair, Crew in a tuxedo and Scarlett in a floor-length black dress that has silver threaded into hidden folds, flashing with every step she takes. I'm sure she designed it herself.

I stand, offering a hand to Crew and then kissing Scarlett's cheek. She smiles at me. This is how we typically greet each other in public, not private. I wasn't sure if it would be welcome, and Scarlett's response is reassuring.

Crew is looking around the sitting room. A massive stone fireplace takes up most of one wall, a portrait of our great-grandfather, Charles Kensington, who founded Kensington Consolidated, hangs above the mantle. Even though it's almost spring, a lit log crackles in the fireplace. All the furnishings in here are unchanged from when we were young. The velvet rolled arm sofa I was just sitting on is the same one nannies chided me for jumping on as a kid.

"I didn't know you guys were coming tonight," I state, sitting back down.

An intentional decision on my father's part. He could have told me he had or was planning to invite Crew and Scarlett to dinner tonight.

And a reminder Crew and I don't talk. Not regularly. I haven't seen or spoken to him since I returned from Vegas.

"Dad said it was an important night," Crew says, taking a seat on the matching sofa across from me. Scarlett sinks down beside him.

I know exactly why my father invited them. He wants to show off for Leonardo Branson. Make it obvious what he's marrying into and why he would be a fool not to encourage this arrangement.

"Can I get you a glass of cognac, Mr. Kensington?" The same butler who served me reappears.

"Sure," Crew replies.

"Can I get you anything to drink, Mrs. Kensington?"

Scarlett shakes her head. "I'm fine. Thanks."

Voices filter in from the hallway, low and polite.

My father appears in the doorway first, nodding approvingly when he sees Scarlett and Crew seated. No glance is spared in my direction.

Mr. and Mrs. Branson follow him. Nothing about either of them is especially remarkable, but I must have met them both before. In her heels, Mrs. Branson is a couple of inches taller than her husband. He's an agreeable, serious-looking man dressed in a navy suit that matches the blue shade of his wife's dress. Surprisingly, Leonardo's second wife looks close in age to him. It's much more common for men to remarry younger versions like my father did with Candace.

Quinn walks in behind them. Even before she speaks, remarking on the size of the house in a crisp British accent, I'm reminded that was her upbringing. Her posture is straight and proper, her expression polite and alert. The pale pink dress she's wearing stands out against the darker colors of the room.

When she turns toward me, there's a flicker of warmth—of interest—on her face. "Hello, Oliver."

"Hello, Quinn." I take her offered hand, fingers long and delicate.

Her small smile grows as our eyes connect. Hers are a darker shade of brown than her hair, which is almost copper.

I like that she greeted me first without waiting for our fathers to arrange the introductions. It suggests a confidence I wouldn't have guessed at, based on her pastel outfit and demure demeanor.

I don't know if I can picture a life with this woman. I can't imagine her walking down the aisle toward me or kids with the same unusual hue of hair.

But I'm intrigued by her, and it's honestly expected. I may want what my father is offering, but I don't want to get married—again—to a stranger. I thought that distaste would color meeting Quinn. Make it impossible to like her. But there's no resentment as our hands shake.

"Oliver, you remember Leonardo? And his wife, Zara?"

I drop Quinn's hand and take her father's, nodding respectfully. "Of course. Wonderful to see you, Leonardo."

"You too, Oliver."

"I was disappointed you weren't able to join us at dinner on Saturday. I'm glad we were able to set this up."

I nod. "Me too."

"Did you have a nice time in Vegas?"

My smile doesn't falter. "I did."

I'm not surprised my father mentioned where I was last weekend. He would have wanted to brag about my friendship with Garrett.

"Must have been quite the trip."

I keep smiling and nod before shaking Zara's hand. A butler enters the room to serve everyone drinks, followed by a couple of maids with trays of appetizers: fancy cheese served with toasted bread, freshly shucked oysters, and caviar with crackers.

Leonardo takes the seat next to me, immediately striking up a conversation about business. The Thompson & Thompson deal was announced today, so I field mostly questions about that, straining to listen to what Quinn is saying to Crew during the pauses.

It sounds like she's telling Crew about an English soccer team her company worked for.

Crew has always been more interested in sports than I am. He even owns part of an Italian team, which I hear him telling Quinn about.

I wonder if he and Hannah talked about sports.

The thought is sudden and unwelcome. The phone in my pocket feels heavier, like the message with no response is adding to its weight.

I excuse myself about twenty minutes later to use the restroom but end up on the back patio instead. The chill in the air feels like winter, the flicker of outside lights almost ghostlike on the grass and stone pavers. The pool is covered, not that it gets much use in the summer months either. Aside from the staff, my dad lives here alone.

I take a seat on the metal bench that faces a row of bushes that will bloom into blue hydrangeas, tipping my head back and staring at the dark sky. I finally sip at my cognac, the warm alcohol a little more palatable in the evening air.

"Spent part of my engagement party hiding away too."

Scarlett lifts the hem of her dress as she walks across the stones toward me, her approach nearly silent, even in heels.

She takes a seat on the bench beside me, kicking off her shoes.

My gaze returns to the bushes. "This isn't my engagement party."

I wondered how much about this evening my father shared

with Crew. It sounds like he didn't withhold details, which surprises me. He hates to tip his hand early. Make a move before all the pieces are in place. I'm the same way.

Scarlett hums. "I thought you'd do anything to snag CEO. Quinn is pretty, and she seems nice. You could do worse. You *have* done worse, actually."

I look over at her, ignoring the dig about Candace. "I don't care about being CEO," I lie.

Scarlett smiles. "I told my father I wouldn't marry you, you know."

I shake my head. I hadn't known that. My father was the one who told me; I assumed he was the one who'd made the decision to swap grooms.

"I made him amend the agreement with Arthur so it was between me and Crew. We would have been miserable together. We're too alike, Oliver. CEO is your birthright, as the oldest. *Of course* you want it. You were born and raised and trained to want it."

"It's not up to me or Crew who becomes CEO. It's my father's decision."

"I know. And Arthur is giving you the chance to have it. Maybe it's his way of admitting he made a mistake, taking it from you in the first place. If he asks for something in exchange, he can preserve his pride."

"It shouldn't have to be a trade."

Scarlett laughs. "Of course it does. That's how the world—our world—works. You were going to marry me to be CEO, right? How is this any different? It's all about how you look at it."

"It's more complicated than that."

"It doesn't have to be. I've been the person convinced an arranged marriage will just be a business relationship. I wish I'd opened up to Crew sooner. Been less cynical from the start. If he hadn't been so…stubborn—" She smiles. "—my life would look very different. Would be worse. You don't have to force anything. Just be open to it and start tonight. If you brood out here all night, Quinn will feel like she has to ignore you next time you see each other. Next thing you know, you'll be making up affairs and spying on each other through security footage."

I frown at the random examples, then exhale. "I can't marry her, Scarlett."

She nods and leans down to pull her heels back on. "Okay. I tried."

I swallow the rest of my cognac in one massive gulp. "You don't understand. I literally *can't*."

Scarlett frowns as she looks over at me. "What? Why?"

"I went to Vegas last weekend for Garrett Anderson's bachelor party."

She nods. "Yeah, I know."

"Well, while I was there, I got married."

Scarlett's expression doesn't even twitch. I'm suddenly overwhelmingly grateful she's who Crew married. She's the person you want when there's a crisis. I've never seen her composure rattled.

She leans back and slips her heels back off. "God, I wish I could drink."

A surprised laugh leaves me.

"Does Crew know?"

I shake my head. "No. But he knows *her*. My, um, wife."

Scarlett's head tilts, eyebrows rising. "Knows her how?"

"Her name is Hannah Garner."

Her lips tighten into a thin, straight line. "*Dammit*, Oliver."

"She mentioned you two were…acquainted."

"We ran into her a few times, shortly after we got married. They were…unpleasant. I don't know exactly what happened between them, and I've never asked Crew. At the company party that year, Hannah told me Crew was cheating. Described their liaisons rather graphically."

I'm surprised Hannah was at a Kensington Consolidated party, that she attended society events on her trips here. Hundreds of people are invited, but it's still an exclusive list.

"She was lying," I tell her. "He's never cheated on you."

Scarlett half-smiles. "I know."

"I believe she regrets it, if it makes any difference. But if I'd known she'd said that to you, I never would have touched her. Let alone married her."

Scarlett's lips twist wryly. "You aren't the first guy to get distracted by a pretty face, Oliver."

I scoff, staring at my empty glass. "I didn't marry her just because she got my dick hard, Scarlett. I was drunk, and don't remember most of it. But there was something… I don't know. She was different than any other woman I'd met."

"By *different*, do you mean bitchier?"

I glance over at her.

Scarlett rolls her eyes. "Sorry. I'm a grudge holder. And, I'm hormonal." She touches her flat stomach.

"Congratulations, by the way. Crew mentioned it when he…"

"Showed up drunk to your apartment?"

I chuckle. "Yeah. I'm happy for you guys."

"Thanks. The best baby gift you could give me is taking CEO. I'm sick of Crew getting home a minute before eight just to hole up in his home office all night."

I sigh. "Look, aside from the fact pissing my dad off by not agreeing to it has been fun, I would consider marrying Quinn. The problem is…"

"Hannah."

"Yeah."

"What are your options?"

"What do you mean?"

"From a legal perspective. Didn't you go to law school?"

I laugh. "What? No."

"Oh." We're both silent, realizing how little we really know each other. My fault. Hers. Crew's. This world's. "Then, do you have a divorce attorney?"

"Not yet. And...we don't have a prenup."

Scarlett shakes her head. "*Jesus*, Oliver. When you decide to fuck up, you don't fool around."

"She won't fight me on this. She wants it over and done as much as I do."

"Are you sure about that? Hannah could have planned this entire thing."

"How?"

"Plenty of people knew you'd be in Vegas for Garrett's bachelor party. She could have shown up and seduced you."

I shake my head. "No. She didn't plan it."

"How do you know?"

"I was...after we met at a bar, I was the one who asked her to meet me later."

Scarlett rolls her eyes. "If she got your interest, of course you'd try to meet up with her later. That means nothing, Oliver."

Logically, I know what Scarlett is saying makes sense. But I'm certain she's wrong, that marrying me was nothing Hannah planned. I can't explain it beyond that—I'm certain.

Scarlett sighs when I don't budge. "Who knows?"

"Just you. And...Asher."

"You told *Asher*?"

I shrug. "I was trying to learn more about Hannah. I thought he might know something."

"Did he?"

"No."

Scarlett stands. I watch as she holds the side of the bench, stepping into her heels. "We should get back."

Before I can say anything else, she's gone in a swish of skirts. I stand reluctantly, and then follow her inside.

CHAPTER ELEVEN

HANNAH

My phone rings at three fifteen exactly. I chew on my bottom lip, knowing who is calling without even looking at the screen. Westbrook High, where Rachel works, lets out at three fifteen.

I send the email I just finished proofreading and answer.

"Hi, Rachel."

"*You got married?*" The question comes out in a shriek, running through a couple of octaves. "You got *actually married*—in *Las Vegas*, to a guy I've never heard you *mention*, let alone met—and I find out about it because you told Dad and Dad told Mom and Mom told me?"

I pause. "Yes."

"Hannah! What the *fuck*?"

"I didn't know how to tell you." That's true, at least. I've never lied to my sister, not about anything like this.

"How did you even meet this guy?"

"At a bar, in New York." I lean back in my chair, staring at the black and white prints I have framed on my wall. Palm trees, the silhouette of a surfer, the Santa Monica Pier. "He came over to me and said all the perfect things. We both travel a lot for work, so we've met up in different places the past few months."

It's not a total lie.

But it's not how I met the guy I'm married to. And it feels wrong to swap one Kensington in for the other. I might have met them both in bars, but that's where the similarities in the stories end.

Crew pursued me. I made the first move with Oliver.

"He happened to be in Vegas for a friend's bachelor party. Dad sent me there about the Coyotes, you know. We met up for drinks, one thing led to another, and…"

"And you *married* him. You, who said marriage was for fools with unrealistic expectations after Declan proposed."

"We're getting divorced, Rachel. Proving my point."

"Yeah, that's what Dad said. He's disappointed, Han. He thought he'd *finally* have another son."

I rest my cheek on my palm so I can massage my temple. "Don't guilt trip me. I made a drunken mistake. If I'd gotten a tattoo, wouldn't you support me getting it removed?"

"It would depend on what the tattoo was."

I sigh. "Look, I'm really sorry I didn't tell you. But it's because I was hoping there would be nothing to tell. I just want to pretend it never happened."

"Yeah…good luck with that."

"What do you mean?"

"I mean, Mom is hell bent on meeting the guy who got you down the aisle."

"What do you mean, she's hell bent on meeting him?"

"Exactly that. You *married him*, sis. Drunken or not, that means something."

"It really doesn't."

"More than Declan managed."

"If Declan had asked me while I was drunk, I probably would have married him too."

Rachel laughs. "Yeah, right."

"Okay, well, this has been fun. But I actually have a meeting to get to..."

Another lie. All of a sudden, they're really piling up.

"Fiiinnneee. Bye."

"Bye."

I toss the phone on my desk, rubbing my temple faster.

I've avoided my father ever since dumping the news of my marriage on him. We finished the meeting with Logan Cassidy, and thankfully, most of the awkwardness faded by the time we ordered our meals.

Of course my father told my mother. They've always had that fairytale sort of relationship I've secretly been in awe of. The type that endures hardships and lows with the stability of a steamship at sea.

And considering my family leans toward oversharing, I shouldn't be surprised Rachel found out. If she knows, Eddie and April must too.

The only upside of my historically harsh view on marriage is that my father and Rachel were both too shocked by the revelation I am married to ask any questions about who I'm married to. None of my family members know about my history with Crew, and I don't think anyone besides my father will recognize the Kensington name. But still, it's more than I ever wanted them to know.

I rush through the rest of my work and head home right at five. Traffic is worse than usual, but at least it means I finish the latest episode of my favorite podcast before reaching my street. It always bothers me, stopping with only a few minutes left.

I park in the driveway, grab my bag from the passenger seat

and walk toward my house. California real estate is insane, especially in the southern part of the state.

I lucked out by finding a ranch that needed major renovations and was even luckier that I was able to live with my parents while they were taking place.

I've always loved interior design and decoration. It's part of what drew me to architecture. It's like a complicated puzzle, where you get to choose all the pieces and then also decide how to fit them together.

My steps up the front walk slow when I spot the figure sitting in the swing beside the door.

"Hi, Mom." My grip on the keys tightens as I force a casual tone, climbing the two steps that lead to the porch and making a show of flipping through the two magazines that were delivered to my mailbox.

She stands. "You got *married* and didn't tell me?"

It's the guilt trip from Rachel all over again. Except worse, because it's in person. And because she's my mother, not my sister.

"I'm sorry if you're upset—"

"Upset? Honey, I'm so happy for you!"

Not the response I was expecting. Or hoping for. It never occurred to me my Vegas marriage is anything my family might be *excited* about. "Mom…"

"When can I meet him?" she asks.

Dammit. Rachel wasn't exaggerating. "Mom…didn't Dad tell you I'm not *staying* married?"

She waves a hand in the air dismissively. "Yes, your father told me everything. And I still can't believe *you* didn't, Hannah! How do you think it makes me feel to know that you told a potential client of your father's you were married before informing your own mother?!"

I'm starting to really reconsider whether telling my father was the right decision. If Logan Cassidy wasn't involved, I never would have.

I was worried my lie would blow back on him somehow. That either he wouldn't want to work with Garner Sports Agency, thinking I was unhinged or overdramatic, going around telling men I'm married when I'm not. Or that my father would make too many assumptions about why I'd felt the need to lie in the first place.

Telling the truth seemed like the only option at the time. Staring at my mom's hurt, confused expression, I'm second-guessing.

I look down at my keys, running a fingertip along the edge of the rough metal. "I wasn't planning to tell *anyone*."

"You really thought we would judge you, sweetheart? Everyone makes impulsive decisions sometimes. That doesn't make them mistakes."

I huff a laugh. "Well, my impulsive decision was definitely a mistake."

"I wouldn't be so sure."

"*I'm* sure, Mom."

"Hannah, you've never jumped impulsively into anything in your life. That you did means something."

"I think you're seriously underestimating the effect of a few martinis."

She shakes her head. "Your father and I will always support you, sweetheart. If ending this marriage is what you really want, then that's what you should do. But at least let us *meet* him! He's your husband!"

"Mom, he lives in New York. He's busy. I can't just ask him to drop everything and fly here in a few days."

"Not even to meet his *in-laws*?"

"I'm not—it's not—we don't have that kind of relationship. We're getting divorced!"

"Your father said you've been dating this man for a few months. He's never asked to meet your family?"

The dig of metal into my skin is painful at this point. I force my fingers to unclench the keys before I draw blood.

This is why you don't lie. Because the twist of the truth complicates it. When I saw my father's stunned, worried expression, all I could think about was getting rid of it as soon as possible. Marrying a guy I was dating sounded a little bit better than marrying a guy I'd known for a matter of hours. But now, I can see where that was a massive mistake.

"We were dating casually."

She tucks a piece of hair back into her blonde bob. "You've always been an excellent judge of character. I trust anyone you chose to get involved with is someone special."

Maybe it was a mistake, not allowing my parents to see the messiness in my life up until now.

I've shielded my parents from my disastrous love life, in particular, because their marriage is such an aspirational one. As most of my friend's parents got divorced, I heard over and over again how lucky I was my parents were steady and solid.

"Rachel, April, and Eddie are all coming over for dinner on Saturday night. Hopefully you'll be able to join us too. With a special guest."

I don't need to ask who I'm supposed to be bringing. "I'll ask him, Mom. No promises."

The last time I saw my mother look this thrilled was when she found out her first grandchild was on its way. "Wonderful." She beams. "The weather this weekend is supposed to be gorgeous. Hopefully, we'll be able to barbeque."

"He has an important job, and it's last minute and a long way to come for just a weekend."

I call out as many excuses as I can think of after my mom's retreating back. Her car is parked along the curb, almost to my neighbor's hedge.

Her only response is a wave. "See you Saturday, sweetheart!"

I swear under my breath before stomping into the house.

She's certain Oliver will show up, and I share none of that confidence.

I can't even imagine asking him. I went into this divorce intent on not asking *anything* of him. To make it quick and painless and cordial, like snipping a string.

That's all that's tying me and Oliver together: a piece of paper we both signed during an alcohol-induced bout of insanity.

It's bad enough he sent me a text reminding me to get an attorney, which I still haven't responded to. Now I'm going to have to be the one to renege on my *let the lawyers talk* suggestion, call him, and ask for a favor.

Once inside, I change out of my work clothes into a pair of leggings and a t-shirt. Hair up in a messy ponytail, I pad into the kitchen to survey the contents of my fridge. I'm an experimental cook, the kind who buys random ingredients at the store based on what sounds good at the time and then has to cobble them together into some semblance of a meal.

Tonight, it's leftover chicken and an assortment of vegetables over lettuce. I drizzle the creation with dressing and skip over the bottle of white wine that's chilling in favor of the grapefruit infused vodka in the freezer.

I don't even bother with a glass. Just carry the plate and the bottle over to the couch and plop down to call Rosie.

She picks up on the fourth ring with a cheery tone that indicates her day is going way better than mine. "Hey! How was Vegas? How was the baby shower? Did—"

"I fucked up, Rosie."

There's a pause. I steel myself, taking a pull from the frosted bottle and resisting the strong urge to spit it out. It's like drinking frozen fire. "Worse than the time you—"

"I'm drinking flavored vodka straight out of the bottle as we speak."

"Okay, so you're not pregnant. It can't be *that* bad."

"I married Oliver Kensington."

Silence. A long, incredulous silence.

"I'm sorry, there must be wires down between Chicago and LA. Because you couldn't have possibly said you *married* Oliver *Kensington*."

I groan and take another sip. Her shocked horror isn't helping. I was kind of hoping she'd be blasé about the whole thing and tell me I'm overreacting. But not only does my best friend tend to be dramatic, she's the one person who knows about my fling with Crew Kensington.

"How, Hannah? Why? I swear, if this is a joke and you're fucking with me—"

"It's not a joke. I met him in a bar—"

"What is it with you and billionaires in bars?"

I ignore her commentary. "I didn't know who he was. He was just a hot guy, and we got drunk and somehow married. I don't remember much of it."

"Not even if he's the *bigger* brother?" she teases.

"We didn't have sex."

"I thought you don't remember anything."

"I don't. But I got a look at his dick the next morning. I would have been sore."

"Excellent work, Detective."

I scoff and take another pull from the bottle, contorting my face when the artificial taste of grapefruit burns my throat. "I'm less concerned about the size of his dick and more with how I'm *married to him*, Rosie."

"Does Crew know?"

"I don't think so. I actually ran into him a few days ago, at the sandwich shop on Melbourne."

"You *did*?"

"Yeah. It was…I don't know. Fine. Weird. We cleared the air a little. He didn't say anything about Oliver. They're not that close."

"Holy shit. I just realized…you married a Kensington. You're a *multi-billionaire*, Han."

Rosie grew up with money, same as me. But there's rich, and then there's the generations of wealth the Kensingtons have accumulated.

"Not for long. I'm divorcing him as soon as possible."

"After getting half, right?" she teases. "You can buy me a yacht."

"I just want this over with as quickly as possible."

She sobers, her voice growing serious again. "I can't believe you got married before me. Never would have expected that."

I take another sip of vodka and then lie back, staring up at the white plaster ceiling. "Me neither. My family knows."

"Wow. You didn't tell them about you and Declan for a month."

"It was an accident. I said something to a client of my dad's. It was either come clean or possibly ruin this guy's career."

"Are you sure you chose right?"

"Haha," I intone. "And now, they want to meet him."

"Of course they do. The only downside of being part of a wholesome, supportive family."

"I don't want to ask him to come. But I have to, I guess? And I don't think there's any way he'll agree—"

"Holy *shit*." Rosie exclaims, suddenly.

"What?"

Her urgent tone would probably make me sit up, in other circumstances. But vodka is starting to swim through me in lazy warmth, making moving sound really unappealing.

"I just looked up a photo of your *husband*. I've never actually seen what Oliver looks like. Crew is always the one who was out getting photographed."

Rosie grew up in New York City. She even went to school with Scarlett Ellsworth for a couple of years before Crew's future wife left for some fancy boarding school. The stories she told me are part of what spawned my instant dislike of the stunning brunette.

Keys tap. "Wow, does he *ever* smile? I mean, the tall, dark, and broody thing works for him, but really, what does he have to complain about? He's hot, rich, and married to my beautiful best friend."

"I think that last part is probably *why* he's scowling," I reply.

Rosie laughs. "Oh, Jude's here."

"Okay. I'll talk to you later."

"I just need to buzz him in. We don't have to hang up. If I park him in front of the television with a beer and something sporty, he'll probably thank you for keeping me occupied."

I smile, then stare at my sad salad. I should have stopped for takeout on the drive home. "No, it's fine. I need to go make dinner anyway."

The lies keep piling up.

"Okay. We'll talk soon." There's a pause. "Is *Congratulations* the wrong sentiment to end with here?"

I huff a laugh. "Probably. But thanks."

Rosie laughs too. "Bye, Han."

"Bye."

I drop my phone onto the couch, then grab the remote to turn on the television. The next hour is spent picking at my salad while half-watching a comedy I've seen a dozen times before. Occasionally, I sip more vodka.

When I pick up my phone again, it's after ten. There's a chance he's still at work, but it seems unlikely. And the less serious version of Oliver is who I want to talk to.

Oliver answers the call with a groggy, "Hannah?"

Belatedly, I realize he's on east coast time. It's after one in the morning in New York.

"Shit. I'm so sorry. I forgot about the time difference."

There's a sigh. Sheets rustle. *He's in bed,* I realize. "I thought you were apologizing about not texting me back. Nice to know your phone works."

"Sorry, I forgot to text you back."

His exhale almost sounds like a laugh, but I can't tell for sure.

There's a pause where we're both silent. I stare up at my ceiling, picturing him doing the same. He must live in some big, fancy building.

It should feel strange, lying here listening to him breathe, but it's not. It's surprisingly…nice.

"You called me," Oliver says eventually. He doesn't sound mad about it, more curious.

"My family knows we're married."

Another long pause, this one neither peaceful nor comfortable.

"You told them?"

"Not exactly. My dad accidentally found out. He told my mom; my mom told my siblings."

"You have siblings?"

"Uh, yeah." I clear my throat. "Two. A brother and a sister."

"Huh. I figured you were an only child."

"Is that an insult?"

"No. Just an observation." He pauses. "I have a brother."

I laugh, caught off guard by his dry comment. Oliver's sense of humor is…unexpected, I guess.

"Sorry for waking you up. I'll, uh, good night."

I'm a coward. I should just ask him about this weekend and listen to his *No*, like tearing a Band-Aid off.

But that will ruin this conversation, this quiet moment where it just feels like I'm a girl talking to a guy who gives me butterflies. I can feel them fluttering in my stomach, probably vodka-soaked.

"Is everything okay, Hannah?" His voice has changed. It dips, so it's a little softer. Almost caring.

"Everything's fine. Bye."

I hang up before he can say anything else, rolling over and burying my face in the couch cushions.

CHAPTER TWELVE

OLIVER

I'm expecting my office to be empty when I walk in, like it is every morning. There weren't lights on in a single office I just passed.

But my office is *not* empty.

"*Finally*." Scarlett rolls her eyes, crossing her legs. She's tilted one of the chairs that normally faces my desk so it's aimed at the window instead, turned toward the sunrise.

I blink at her, wondering if I walked into the wrong office somehow. Last night was the worst sleep I've had in a while, so it's possible I turned right instead of left. But a quick glance at my desk confirms I'm in the right place.

I walk over to my chair and set my briefcase on the desk.

"What are you doing here?"

She ignores my question, standing and walking over to my bookcase. Her nails are painted the same crimson shade as her lips, contrasted against the black leather spines as she skims them. "I couldn't find any legal pads. Do you have a secret office supplies stash somewhere?"

"I—"

There's a knock on the door. Scarlett turns away from the books and walks right over to it like she's expecting someone. "Morning, Jeremy."

"Morning, Scarlett." Jeremy Brennan walks into the office, and Scarlett closes the door behind him. "Hi, Oliver."

I nod at Jeremy. "What is going on, Scarlett?"

"You need a lawyer." She points at Jeremy. "Lawyer."

"*Kensington Consolidated* lawyer. No offense to Jeremy, but this has nothing to do with the company."

"He's the only attorney we should trust to keep this quiet."

"There's something called attorney-client privilege, Scarlett."

She shakes her head. "All it would take is a legal secretary whispering to a friend about a new client, and every journalist in this city will be combing through the Nevada marriage certificates, Oliver."

Another knock on the door. This time Asher enters, holding two cups of coffee. "Morning, gang." He hands one cup to Scarlett. "Boss."

Jeremy laughs as I sink down into my desk chair.

"Scarlett didn't mention you guys would be here, or I would have grabbed you all coffee," Asher says.

"Scarlett didn't mention *any* of you would be here. I came in early to work on the Cushings report."

Asher takes a seat on the couch and spreads an arm across the back of the cushions. "Have to say, I didn't see you telling Scarlett about this."

"Anyone feel like cluing me in on what *this* is?" Jeremy asks.

Scarlett sips her coffee. "Oliver's a newlywed. He married a woman in Vegas last weekend. No prenup."

Something about the matter-of-fact way she summarizes the situation makes it sound way worse. I adjusted to the state of things in my head, I guess. Spoken out loud sounds dire.

Asher's expression doesn't change since it's not news to him. But a flash of shock crosses Jeremy's face before he shuts it down and glances at me. "You're wanting to end the marriage, I presume?"

I nod. "Yes."

"And she feels the same way?"

"*She* is *Hannah Garner*," Asher tells Jeremy, emphasizing the name in a way that makes it obvious it should mean something to him.

Crew and Jeremy are good friends, so I probably shouldn't be surprised. But I am. I had no idea who she was, and that emphasizes how wide the chasm between me and my brother is.

It's also strange to realize everyone in this room has met Hannah. Since I returned from Vegas, it's felt like the short amount of time I spent with her was a mirage, almost. Being here, in my familiar office, discussing her, a wife I barely know, is an unexpected collision of worlds.

"I don't need to ask if she's aware of your net worth, then," Jeremy states.

Asher snorts. I start to question why Scarlett invited him.

"How long will a divorce take?" I ask Jeremy.

"I can't give you an exact answer. Aside from one seminar when I was a 2L and studying for the bar, I don't know much about family law. But marriage is a legal commitment, not just a romantic notion. Until a judge signs the divorce decree, you're married in the eyes of the law. And every state is different. Some have separation waiting periods. Ideally, the petition will be for a no-fault divorce on the grounds of irreconcilable differences. Once it's filed, your spouse is served with the papers. She'll have a set amount of time to respond. If she raises no objections, there's just the divorce settlement. Ideally, you'd present one to the court to sign off on."

"Is there a way to keep it quiet? Out of the press?"

To my relief, Jeremy nods. "If the divorce is uncontested and you settle without going to trial, no one besides you, Hannah, and any attorneys involved will have any details. If you can't agree on the terms of the divorce, it will go to trial. Family court trials are public, so court reporters are allowed in the proceedings. That could get very messy, very fast. You can also add a confidentiality clause, which would bar Hannah from discussing the divorce with anyone—even family. If she violated it, she would owe you punitive damages. In this circumstance, she could make millions off talking, so we could set that number high as a deterrent."

I nod. "What about an annulment? That means the marriage never happened, right?"

"Technically, yes. But I wouldn't recommend an annulment. Grounds for annulment are very specific, and you have to prove they apply."

"What are the grounds?" Scarlett asks.

"Fraud or misrepresentation, coercion, under the age of consent, incest, bigamy or polygamy, force or threat of force, mental incapacity—"

"He was so drunk he doesn't remember marrying her," Scarlett says. "Doesn't that count as mental incapacity?"

"It's better for Oliver if he's the one petitioning. If he is, that means to file for an annulment on the grounds of mental incapacity because of alcohol, he'll have to prove *she* meets the definition of mental incapacity set by state law in the jurisdiction where he files."

Asher lets out a long, overdone snore.

Jeremy rolls his eyes. "That will most likely require a hearing. And frankly, it's hard to prove. Divorce will be quicker and easier, in my estimation." He glances at me. "If you want me to represent you, I'm happy to. And you have my word it'll stay private on our side. I don't even have to involve a paralegal. But you could have any attorney you want. There are plenty of sharks out there who have decades of experience with high-profile divorces. You might be better off with one of them. Especially if Hannah decides to make anything difficult."

"Which she probably will," Asher comments.

I don't realize I'm glaring until he shrugs and grabs his coffee cup from the table next to the couch. Of course, he's not using one of the coasters.

"Fine." Asher sighs. "I'll be optimistic. She probably won't try to get a few hundred million out of this, knowing you're worth ten times that, and she has a good chance of getting half if she puts any effort into it."

I'm not annoyed with Asher's pessimism. I'm irritated he's insulting Hannah. If she has a devious, underhanded side, I've never seen it.

And it feels wrong, listening to someone disparage the woman I'm married to. It doesn't feel like we're on adverse sides. It's felt like we're figuring this out together.

"The marriage was never…consummated," I tell Jeremy. "Does that make any difference?"

"Legally, no. Not unless we wade into certain grounds or canon law, and it will be much cleaner to just file for divorce. You have the marriage license?"

I nod. "Not on me," I lie.

It's in my wallet, but revealing I've carried it around with me feels personal, somehow.

"You really don't remember the wedding?" Jeremy asks.

"The whole night is hazy."

"Probably drugs," Asher says. "Vegas is wild. People put all sorts of shit in drinks."

I'm not sure if the possibility should make me feel better or worse. It's not a comforting explanation, but at least it's one.

Asher's phone buzzes. "It's Crew," he says, squinting at the screen. Then he laughs. "He wants to know if I'll get him coffee on the way into work. His fridge is full of plant liquid."

Scarlett shrugs. "If he forgot to put cow milk on the grocery list, that's his fault."

"Where does he think you are?" Asher asks, typing a response to Crew.

"A textiles meeting in SoHo. It's his morning with Lili."

Jeremy stands. "I've got to go finish drafting a contract." He glances at me. "Think it over and let me know how I can help, Oliver."

"I will." I stand too, walking over and shaking his hand. "Thanks, Jeremy. I really appreciate it."

Jeremy nods and leaves. Asher heads out right after him, still on his phone, tossing a "Good luck" over one shoulder. Scarlett picks up her handbag and prepares to leave as well.

"Have you spoken to Hannah since you left Vegas?"

"Just once, about our attorneys."

I lie again, and I'm not sure why.

Maybe because I know Scarlett wouldn't be nodding approvingly if I'd told her we talked last night, and I proceeded to lie in bed for hours after she hung up, replaying our short conversation over and over again.

This is more interest than Scarlett has ever shown in my life. I thought she would want Crew to become CEO. Instead, she's encouraging—helping—me possibly take the role.

Or maybe this has nothing to do with me and everything to do with Hannah. If I'd married someone who has no history with Crew, she probably wouldn't care this much.

"Once you decide who's representing you, you should cut off all contact. Have everything go through the lawyers."

I nod as Scarlett strides toward the door, not bothering to mention Hannah already suggested that. Because while that's what we both agreed to, she hasn't given me an attorney's name. I haven't given her an attorney's name.

And now her family knows, which shouldn't matter. Unless they're planning to contact the *Los Angeles Gazette* and offer up an exclusive, it'll have no impact on our divorce. But it feels… odd, knowing they know. Wondering what they think of it. Of me.

"Oh, and don't tell her about Arthur's offer. If she knows you have a reason to hasten the divorce, she might try to drag it out."

I nod again.

She nods back, grabbing the door handle.

"Thank you, Scarlett."

Whatever her motivations, this is more than I expected. And even if she's focused on helping because she's worried about the Kensington fortune or hates Hannah, it deserves acknowledgment.

Scarlett nods. "Family is supposed to support you no matter what, right?"

I raise a brow. "Not mine."

She laughs. "Yeah. Not mine, either."

"Change is good."

"It is. Bye, Oliver."

"Bye, Scarlett."

I stare at the closed door for a minute after she's gone, then shake my head and sit down at my desk. I get through the Cushings report that I came in to finish, send it, and then start sifting through unread emails.

Once I'm caught up, I decide I need another cup of coffee.

When I open my office door, my father is standing next to

Alicia's desk. She glances at me nervously as I stand in the doorway, studying my dad.

I could count on one hand the number of times he's come to my office. He always summons me to his, the largest on the floor, with its own conference room and eating area. It even has a private bathroom. I think it used to be aspirational, a *Look what could be yours if you work hard enough* enticement. Now, I see it as a taunt. *Look what will never be yours, no matter how hard you work.*

But never is no longer as solid as I thought. I'm sure he's here for an update regarding Quinn, and I don't have an answer for him.

My father follows Alicia's gaze over to me.

"Dad," I greet.

"Oliver." He mirrors my blank tone. "Do you have a minute?"

I nod and step to the side, letting him walk in first and then closing the door behind him.

"You're in early."

I nod again, not mentioning I've been here for hours, same as most mornings.

"We haven't had a chance to speak since dinner. Leonardo is anxious to know—"

"We both know you're the one impatient for an answer, Dad. And I don't have one for you. Not yet."

"Did you find Quinn objectionable?"

He knows as well as I do that Quinn is a perfect candidate to become a Kensington. Wealthy, educated, beautiful. Well-mannered but not boring. We didn't spend any time alone together all night. But unless it's an impeccable act, she's exactly what is expected for a CEO's wife.

If this conversation was taking place before I left for Las Vegas, I probably would have already agreed to propose.

"Quinn seems wonderful. But it's a big decision to make, and I'm not ready to make it."

A vein throbs in my father's forehead. He wants me to take his deal; that much is obvious.

But I'm not sure why. Because he's second-guessing Crew's commitment? Because he regrets not leaving it to me all along, like Scarlett suggested?

"Fine," he says, in a tone that suggests the opposite. Because my father hates nothing more than being in a situation where he's not making the decisions. "But I'll need an answer soon, Oliver."

I don't miss the vague deadline. He wants me to be constantly on edge, waiting for soon to become now. Knowing at any moment the offer could expire, and I'll be left with no chance.

"Understood."

He studies me for a minute before he eventually nods. "I was hoping for an update on the Cushings—"

"Already in your inbox."

Something that *almost* looks like pride appears on his face. But he says nothing else before leaving my office.

I exhale once the door shuts behind him, sitting back down at my desk and staring out the window.

A couple of minutes later, there's a knock on the door.

"Come in," I call.

Alicia pokes her head in, a mug of steaming coffee in one hand. "I figured you were headed toward the kitchen earlier."

"Thank you," I tell her, as she sets the coffee down and then heads back toward the door.

"Hi, Mr. Kensington."

I glance up as Crew returns the greeting. I usually have one visitor in my office a day. Sometimes two. Today, it feels like I'm working in the middle of Grand Central.

Alicia closes the door behind her, leaving the two of us alone.

I start to stand, but Crew waves me back down as he takes the seat across from me. Ironically, it's the same spot Scarlett was sitting in earlier. It's still tipped toward the windows. "Passed Dad on the way here."

"Yeah. He wanted a report on dinner."

"And an answer?"

"Yes." I already knew Crew was aware of the potential deal, thanks to Scarlett. But discussing it with Crew directly is different. More awkward.

"Is that the one you gave him?"

I shake my head. "I haven't decided."

"Why not?" There's no judgment in Crew's voice, just curiosity.

"I don't know what to do."

"You take the damn deal, Oliver, and become the next CEO of Kensington Consolidated."

I look out the windows. "I'm sick of Dad pulling the strings. He told you marriage came with CEO and look how that's turned out."

"I would have married Scarlett even if it meant I'd *never* became CEO," Crew tells me. "And that's why I think you should give Quinn a chance. Allow yourself to have more than work. I promise you Candace isn't sitting around punishing herself."

"You can't just shove two people together and expect they'll fall in love, Crew."

He shrugs. Grins. "It worked for me."

I roll my eyes. "And I'm happy for you and Scarlett. It's just not the reality for most people."

"Are you going to ask Quinn out?"

I exhale. "Yes. It'd be nice to have a conversation without both of our families within earshot."

Crew smirks. "So…you got her number?"

"No," I admit. I spent most of dinner worrying whether Scarlett was going to tell Crew about Hannah, and what his response might be if she did. Aside from some basic questions, I barely spoke to Quinn.

Crew reaches into his pocket and pulls out a piece of paper. When he unfolds it, I realize it's a cocktail napkin. He balls it up and tosses it to me. "There you go."

"*You* asked for her number?"

He nods. "It was Scarlett's idea. I told Quinn you asked me to get it discreetly, so you guys could set up a meeting without the pressure from your parents. Quinn called it a 'brilliant idea,' then gave me that." Crew grins, and it's a boyish one. He looks less like a work colleague and a lot more like my *little* brother, for the first time in a while.

I flatten the napkin, staring at the neat digits. "Thanks."

I'm surprised—touched—he made the effort. And I feel extra guilty for keeping Hannah from him, especially as the list of people who know about our marriage grows.

"Well, I'll get out of here. Unless you need help with how to ask her out?"

I probably do, but there's no way I'm asking my younger brother for dating tips. "I'm good, thanks."

He smiles and stands. "Assuming you came in early and already finished the Cushings report?"

"Yeah. I sent it to Dad. You were on the email too."

"This company would be fine without me, Oliver. You? Not so much."

Before I can formulate a response—or really register his words—my phone rings.

"See you later," Crew says, then leaves.

"Bye," I call after him, then answer the call. "Hello?"

"Hey, Oliver! How are you?" Garrett's baritone booms across

the line. I haven't talked to him since we parted ways in the New York airport after returning from Vegas.

"I'm good, thanks." Not entirely accurate, but the expected response. "How are you?"

He sighs, some of the cheerfulness leaving his voice. "Wedding is still on, if that's what you're asking. I told Sienna about Vegas. She threw my phone at a wall, which is why I'm calling you on your work line. Some of my contacts got erased when they transferred the data to my new phone."

"Oh." I'm not sure how else to respond to that.

Garrett chuckles. "Sorry. Too much information. Anyway, I wanted to see if you might want to grab a drink this weekend. Or dinner. All the craziness in Vegas, we hardly got to catch up."

I look at the napkin Crew left on my desk. "You want to double?"

It's been a while since I went on a proper date. I'm apprehensive about the prospect for a whole host of reasons. Going out with another couple sounds like lower stakes. And if Quinn and I do enter an arrangement, it will be a common occurrence.

"Double? You're seeing someone?"

"Sort of. It's new."

"Yeah, that sounds fun. I'd like for you to get to know Sienna better. Setting aside…everything."

"None of my business, Garrett."

"I appreciate it. Hey, give me your cell and I'll get a reservation, then text you the details. Sound good?"

After I've rattled off my cell number, we say our goodbyes and hang up.

By the time I've reviewed everything that's urgent in my inbox, it's almost one. Lunch is always catered in the executive floor's eating area. That's the worst part of working on the weekends, honestly. It's hard to beat the convenience of quickly grabbing a hot meal right down the hall instead of having to pack something or order it to the lobby.

Instead of sitting down at one of the tables, I carry a plate of roasted chicken and vegetables back to my office. Despite coming in early, this morning's distractions mean I'm running behind on what I'd planned to accomplish today.

Right as I've sat down at my desk with lunch, my phone rings. My personal cell, not my work line.

I glance at the screen, an unexpected jolt of excitement immediately affecting me. There's no dread or annoyance when I see her name.

I rub my palms together and clear my throat twice before I answer Hannah's call.

"Good afternoon," she greets.

I smile, then glance at the clock. "Good morning."

"Thought you might be at lunch."

"It's a working one today," I answer. "You were hoping for my voicemail?"

"Honestly…yes."

I make a beeping sound and instantly feel like an idiot.

Hannah's laughter catches me off guard. It's bright and warm and ends too soon. "I called to ask you this last night, then chickened out," she admits.

My mind begins racing with different possibilities. What could she possibly be nervous about asking me? Were Asher and Scarlett right? Is this going to become about money?

"My parents are hosting a family dinner on Saturday night. And they wanted me to invite you. They…want to meet you."

"Why?"

She mumbles something unintelligible. Then exhales. "They met other guys I've dated, and I didn't marry any of them.

They're curious. Overbearing. I don't know. I tried to talk my mom out of it, but she insisted I ask you. So I'm just…asking."

My work phone starts ringing. It's an extension few people have, so it's probably important.

I ignore it. "They know we're getting divorced, right?"

"Yes. But they also think our marriage means you're important to me, so you're important to them."

"I can't this weekend, Hannah." I pinch the bridge of my nose. Surprisingly, I'm not having to feign the note of regret in my voice. I'm curious about her family. And part of me wants to see her again, away from the neon lights of Vegas. "We just closed a deal with a pharmaceutical company, and I—"

"Yeah, I saw. Thompson & Thompson. Congrats."

"Right." I'm surprised she knows the details, and it resonates in my response. It was a nice deal, but not exactly front-page news. The only people I'd expect to take note are those ensconced in the business world.

There's a knock on the door.

"Not now!" I call out, right as the phone on my desk begins ringing again. "I'm sorry, Hannah." I'm not even sure what I'm apologizing for. I hate apologizing. Usually avoid it at all costs.

"It's fine, Oliver." There's not even the barest hint of anger or disappointment in her voice.

No is the answer she was expecting, I realize. She was reluctant to ask and fully expecting me not to accept. Neither of those sit well with me.

"I settled on an attorney this morning," Hannah says. "I'll send you her information."

"Okay."

"Okay. Have a good day, Oliver."

She doesn't continue with our time zone game and wish me a good afternoon.

That bothers me just as much as the way she immediately sends me the name and number of her attorney once we've hung up. She's selected representation, and I still haven't. Of the two of us, I'm the one holding up our divorce.

I don't know what to make of that. Of any of this.

CHAPTER THIRTEEN

HANNAH

I shouldn't be here.

I should be reading through the latest contract the Los Angeles Titans sent over. Since my father used to be involved with the organization, he passes off anything related to that team to other employees. And if I wasn't reviewing that contract before the legal team takes a look, there are dozens of other things I should be doing, instead of sitting outside the automatic doors of Los Angeles' international airport.

Waiting for my *husband.*

I'm under no illusions about why Oliver changed his mind about coming here. He has a lot more to lose in our divorce. Since we didn't sign a prenup, I could fight him for a massive amount of money. And likely win.

Maybe he took me choosing an attorney as a warning.

Maybe he thinks this favor will keep me amenable.

He's coming to protect himself.

But still, he's coming. So I felt some misguided obligation to take the afternoon off work and pick him up at the airport.

A new wave of arrivals walks out from the baggage claim. I

scan the faces quickly, a mixture of disappointment and relief filling me when I realize Oliver isn't among them.

"Miss, you can't park here."

I stop chewing on the inside of my cheek and glance at the airport security agent from my spot leaning against the hood of the car. "I'm not parked. I just got here, and I climbed out of the car to greet my husband. He'll be here any second."

The older agent scratches at his grizzled jaw. I'm sure he's heard it all. "If he's not here in five minutes, you'll need to move the vehicle, ma'am."

I nod. "Of course."

The agent keeps moving onto the next illegally parked vehicle. My gaze returns to the exit, my heart leaping as soon as I see the tall figure walking toward me. Part of me wasn't certain he would actually come.

Oliver doesn't break stride once he's past the automatic doors and through the thickest part of the crowd.

His expression is carefully blank, giving no indication of what he's thinking or feeling. He's dressed in a navy suit, looking like he just exited a boardroom instead of disembarking a five-hour flight.

The only similarity I can find between this polished man and the guy I left in a Vegas hotel room with bed head and a sheet wrapped around his waist is that Oliver wears both looks well.

Too well. My body's reaction isn't just anxiety.

"Hello, Hannah."

Something about the way he says my name makes it hard to form words in response.

"I told you I'd order a car."

He did. That was about *all* he told me, aside from what time his flight was landing. No explanation for what swayed his firm *No* into a *Yes*, although I could make a good guess. No questions about what a weekend with my family would entail. He's just *here*, all cool confidence and inscrutable features.

I raise a shoulder, then let it drop. "You flew all this way."

The motion draws Oliver's attention to my clothes. I worked from home until I left to drive here, so I never bothered putting on anything professional. I'm in ripped jeans and a cotton t-shirt. No makeup and messy, unstraightened hair. It's a more casual look than I'd normally wear around anyone except my family.

I didn't want Oliver thinking I dressed up for him or care what he thinks of me. Now, I'm realizing I might have taken it too far to one extreme.

"Thanks for coming."

Three simple, *unexpected* words. It wouldn't have shocked me if Oliver told me the limo pulled next to the curb two cars up is here for him and he's headed to a five-star hotel.

"Um, you're welcome." I shift awkwardly, not sure what to say or do next.

Spotting the same security guard spurs me into movement. I straighten and pull my keys out of my pocket. He passes us by, glancing between me and Oliver.

Unexpectedly, he smiles at Oliver. "Glad you arrived safely, sir. Your wife was very excited to see you."

My cheeks blaze as he continues down the sidewalk.

Oliver glances to me, one eyebrow raised.

"I was worried he was going to give me a ticket for parking here," I tell him, hastily rounding the front of my car and climbing into the driver's seat.

Oliver stows his suitcase in the back and then climbs into the passenger seat.

"Controls are on the right," I mutter as I start the car. His legs are shoved up against the glove compartment, too long for the current settings.

Oliver adjusts them and then leans back. “Nice car,” he comments, clicking his seatbelt into place.

I pull away from the curb, undecided if he’s messing with me. I bought this SUV new when I graduated college, and it was a splurge that took years to pay off. My parents paid for school, and that was it. Neither of them came from money, and they were careful to never “spoil” us. After graduation, I was on my own financially.

“What kind of car do you drive?”

Crew’s car was worth more than my house.

“I don’t have a car.”

I glance over at him. Oliver is looking out the window, at the line of palm trees that line the airport exit. “What?”

“I have a driver who takes me between the office and my apartment. That town car belongs to the company.”

“What about when you need to go somewhere besides work?”

“Doesn’t happen very often. If it’s a work event, I’ll use the company car. Otherwise, I’ll take public transit.”

“*You* ride the *subway*?”

“I have, yes. Like I said, it doesn’t happen very often.” He half-smiles at my shocked expression. “It’s faster. Better for the environment.”

“How green of you.”

“Nah. I’ve just taken a lot of private jets. Need to balance that somehow.”

“You should talk about how much you love the subway, at dinner. LA doesn’t have good public transit. Also, mention you have a fear of earthquakes. Make sure to talk about how much time your job takes up. If you get a work call, take it. My dad—”

“I’m here to make your family hate me?”

“Not hate. Just recognize getting divorced is the best thing for both of us.”

Oliver makes an annoying humming sound that gives me no insight into what he's thinking.

I take a deep breath, deciding now is as good a moment as any to come clean about why my parents are attached to the idea of us together.

"So I, um, when I accidentally told my dad I got married—"

"You still haven't told me how that happened."

"What do you mean?"

"How did you *accidentally* tell your dad?"

"Oh." I merge onto the 405, glad I have the distraction of driving to justify my long pause. Once we're sitting in traffic, not moving, it's harder to avoid. "I was meeting my dad and a potential client for dinner. I was early, so I waited at the bar. A guy came over to me, and we were—he was—flirting with me. So I mentioned I was married, and I thought that was that. But then it turned out he *was* the potential client. He apologized to my dad, thinking he'd hit on his married daughter. It was come clean to my dad or risk this guy's career with all the subsequent awkwardness."

"What did he say?"

"Well, he was shocked, obviously. I didn't—"

"Not your dad. The guy at the bar. What did *he* say when you told him you were married?"

I risk a glance at him since we're at a predictable crawl along the freeway. Oliver's looking straight ahead, giving no indication of what he's thinking.

"He was…disappointed, I guess?" I've never discussed another man with the guy I'm married to but never even dated, and it's a weird dynamic to navigate.

No response. But it looks like a muscle in Oliver's jaw jumps as he stares out at the unmoving line of cars.

I still need to clue him in on the lie I told my family, so he knows we're supposed to be friendlier than strangers. But this doesn't feel like the right moment, so I say nothing.

It takes another twenty minutes of crawling through traffic until we're off the highway.

"Is it always this bad?" Oliver asks.

"Pretty much," I answer, as our surroundings turn residential. It's rained more lately than usual, so lush grass is visible on both sides of the street.

"You like living here?"

I side-eye him. Still, all I can see is his profile, just like the night we met. "New York doesn't have wide-open streets."

"I wasn't talking about the traffic. I just meant generally."

"My family lives here," I answer, as I pull into my driveway.

I rub my sweaty palms on my jeans once we're out of the car, watching Oliver out of the corner of my eye as he grabs his suitcase and walks toward the house. I could make a pretty good guess what his place in New York looks like. Nothing like the single-level bungalow I live in.

Oliver says nothing as he climbs the stairs, glancing at the porch swing and the row of bushes I planted last spring before glancing over the white siding. The blossoms in the window boxes dance in the slight breeze.

Awareness crawls over my skin as I pass Oliver to unlock the front door. He shakes his head when I gesture for him to walk in first, so I head inside before him.

Unlike my personal appearance, I made sure the house was spotless. Vacuumed and dusted. I even mopped the kitchen. A vase of pink peonies sits on the kitchen counter next to a bowl of limes.

Oliver sets his suitcase down and looks around. There's interest and curiosity on his face as he wanders toward the kitchen.

It's way too intimate, having him in my home. In my space. I assumed he'd stay at a hotel, but he asked for my address when he was ordering a car. Since he came all this way, hosting him is the least I can do. But it also feels like broaching a boundary that used to be set firmly in place.

"You got the lamb."

Oliver is looking at the corner of the living room, where the rocker I got for Eddie and April's baby is sitting, waiting to be delivered once my niece or nephew arrives.

"Yeah." I watch him look around for a minute longer before I step forward. "Guest room is down here."

Without waiting to see if he's following, I head down the hallway, past the living room and my bedroom.

Footsteps follow behind me, into the second bedroom. This room has the better view of the backyard, which is a square of grass and a stone patio, but my bedroom is slightly bigger.

"I use this as an office, sometimes. So it didn't make sense to put a bed in here…" I clear my throat and glance at the sleeper sofa that I unfolded and made up with fresh sheets this morning. It's a queen, but it seems smaller in Oliver's presence. This whole room does, actually. "I won't be offended if you want to stay at a hotel."

"This is great, Hannah. Thank you."

I wish he'd stop using my name. Something about the way Oliver says it unsettles me. Makes my heart race and stomach twist.

I take a step toward the door, striving for nonchalance as I shuffle past him. "Okay. I'll be in the kitchen. Bathroom is down the hall if you need it."

And it's been meticulously scrubbed and emptied. I'm going to have to haul the toiletries that usually cover the counter down the hallway in a caddy, like I did in college.

Once I'm in the kitchen—alone—I exhale a sigh of relief. We're supposed to show up at my parents' house in an hour and a half. If I budget forty-five minutes for what is usually a half-hour drive, that still leaves forty-five minutes.

Less than an hour suddenly sounds like an endless stretch of time.

I fill the tea kettle and set it on the stove, simply for something to do. I already did all the dishes and wiped the counters, so I rearrange the limes and then lean against the counter and stare into space.

"How long have you lived here?"

I jump before glancing over a shoulder at Oliver, who's standing in the doorway.

His grin is brief, but it appears. "Forgot I was here?"

I rub my chest, trying to calm my racing heart. "No."

But I was expecting him to remain in his room. To work or to pretend to be busy or something that didn't involve standing in my kitchen a couple of feet away.

"So?" He walks closer, and I resist the urge to take a step back.

"Three years."

Oliver nods, glancing around the room again. Even though I'm not much of a chef, I do love my kitchen. The wallpaper is a cheerful pattern of lemons and bees, and I spent an afternoon agonizing over different slabs of marble for the countertops.

The kettle begins to whistle on the stove. I shut the burner off and grab a mug. "Do you want any tea?"

Instead of declining, he nods. "Sure." Then he rounds the island and takes a seat on one of the stools, obviously planning to stay.

Maybe I should stop making assumptions about what Oliver

will do or say. I might feel less off-kilter when he chooses the opposite.

I pour two mugs of peppermint tea, not bothering to ask him what kind he wants since it's all I have.

I set the steaming cup down in front of him. "My family thinks we dated for months before we got married."

"How'd they get that idea?" Instead of mad, he sounds amused. Another surprise.

I rephrase. "I *told* my family we dated for months before we got married."

He nods, and that's it. His whole reaction. "Tell me about your family."

I blow on my tea. "My older brother is Eddie. He's an anesthesiologist. His wife April is expecting their first baby in a month."

"How did they meet?"

"Uh, they were high school sweethearts. Met in elementary school, started dating freshman year, and that was it."

"You're a cynic, though?"

"Aren't you?"

"Yeah." He nods. "I am. Not as much as I used to be, though."

"Now that you're a married man?" I tease.

Oliver smirks. Not a full smile, but close. "My father had Scarlett followed, after she and Crew got married. He claimed it was because of a business deal. But it was because Scarlett was too bold. She had too much power over Crew. My father showed Crew photos of her at a hotel with another man. They weren't kissing or touching, but it looked bad. He—I—expected Crew would turn his back on her. But Crew did the opposite, and I realized…he loved her. Really loved her. That was the first time I'd ever seen a relationship like that. So now, I know it exists. Just not for everyone."

I hesitate before asking my next question. Both because I don't want Oliver to think I'm fishing for information, and because I realize I'm asking it because I want to know more about Oliver. To understand him. "Were you and Crew ever close?"

"Not really. My father loved—*loves*—pitting us against each other. Crew made more of an effort after getting married. Especially after Lili was born. I never really did, I'm realizing."

"What about you and your dad?"

"We had highs and lows. Things were better between us when I was younger. I did well in school, exactly what he expected. When I was nineteen, I found out the agreement between my father and Hanson Ellsworth had changed. Not marrying Scarlett was fine with me. But I knew what that would mean for CEO, and that bothered me. It was supposed to be mine. I had the rest of college and then business school to decide how I was going to handle it. My dad was thrilled when I started working at the company. Crew was still in school, so it was just the two of us. Then…things went downhill."

"Because Crew came back?"

"No. Because he found out I had sex with his wife."

At first, I think it's one of his deadpan jokes. When I realize he's serious, I start coughing. "Your *stepmother*?"

Oliver nods, looking down at the mug. "She was younger than me. It wasn't quite as weird as it sounds. But still fucked up, I know." He glances up at me, and there's something in his expression that tells me this is a crossroads. That how I react will impact a lot. We'll end up in the same place—divorced—but the way we get there is being decided right now. He's trusting me, and I want to be worthy of that.

So I swallow the million questions I have and say, "We all have regrets, right?"

Because I don't need to ask if he does. It's obvious in the

subtle shift in his expression, the darkening in his eyes and the shadows that line his face.

"Right."

There's an awkward beat where we hold eye contact for too long.

Oliver breaks the silence by asking me another question about my family. After we've covered Rachel and my parents, I excuse myself to get ready for dinner.

Standing in my kitchen any longer started to feel dangerous. Oliver is here to prove how incompatible he is with my life. Not for me to imagine him fitting in.

CHAPTER FOURTEEN

OLIVER

Hannah appears in the living room while I'm scanning her bookshelf. If these are all hers, she has eclectic taste. It matches the rest of her house, in an odd way. I expected her space to be sleek and polished. Instead, it looks like every room is decorated in a slightly different style.

She hasn't changed, like I thought she left to do. Still in worn jeans that show off a few spots of tan skin and a cotton t-shirt. She braided her hair, so part of it is pulled away from her face, but that's the only change in her appearance. I hadn't even realized I'd memorized every detail of what she was wearing until right now.

Her eyebrows rise as she glances at my clothes. "You're changing, right?"

I look down at the navy suit I'm wearing. It's not that wrinkled, which is impressive after a five-hour flight and lots of sitting in traffic. "Uh, no."

"You're wearing a suit to dinner?" Hannah raises her eyebrows at me, and I raise mine right back.

I wear a suit every day. Everywhere, unless I'm home. And sometimes even then.

I didn't go into the office this morning. I put on this suit to fly here, expecting I'd wear it to dinner.

"We got married in Vegas, Hannah. I'm trying to make a good impression."

Her mouth twitches. Almost a smile. "It's a backyard barbeque. The only impression you're giving is overdressed."

"Well, suits are all I have."

She glances at my suitcase, which is still sitting by the front door. "May I?" She nods toward my luggage.

"Sure."

I watch her look through the contents of my suitcase. Two suits—one gray, another navy—socks, boxer briefs, undershirts, and a pair of flannel pajamas that was all I could find in the way of sleepwear. Hannah hones in on the last item.

"What are these?"

"Pajamas."

"You sleep in these?" she sounds amused.

"I've never worn them," I admit.

"What do you usually wear?"

I'm not sure if the truth is an appropriate answer to give a woman I hardly know, but I've basically left caution back in New York. Since I landed in Los Angeles, I've shed my careful, restrained inclinations.

"Nothing. I sleep naked."

At least the truth has the satisfying outcome of realizing I can affect Hannah. She hasn't looked at me with anything close to desire since she found that piece of paper in the hotel room. And since I'm wildly attracted to *her*, it's nice to see a flush spreading across the small section of her cheek I can see.

She clears her throat—twice—which I've noticed is a nervous

tell of hers. After zipping my suitcase up, she stands, glancing at me with her former mask back in place. "You should lose the tie and jacket, at least."

I loosen my tie and then shrug my jacket off, holding eye contact with Hannah the whole time. This time, I can see the changes to her whole face. The way she bites her bottom lip and how her eyes look even bluer when they're totally focused on me.

After tossing my jacket and tie over the arm of her couch, I take off my cufflinks and roll up the sleeves of my white button-down. Her throat bobs with a swallow before she looks away, walking toward the dish by the door where she left her keys without saying anything else. I take that to mean she approves.

It feels domestic, leaving her house together. My dating history has never included anything like this. All of the women I've dated were part of families I already knew. A big, official introduction like this never took place. And this is especially strange, since I'm going into it expecting to never see these people again. Intentionally striving for an imperfect impression.

"Anything else I should know?" I ask Hannah as we drive.

"Nope, I think we covered everything."

"What about your job?"

She's focused on the road, but her hands tighten on the steering wheel, the knuckles paling in contrast to her skin. "*What* about my job?"

"Well, that's basically the one thing we *did* discuss before we got married."

"They don't know how I feel."

There's a warning note in her voice, so I don't push. We ride in silence, until she pulls into a circular driveway and parks.

The house we pull up in front of a half an hour later isn't as large as I'm expecting. It's a beautiful home, welcoming and well-maintained. But after reading the report I received from the private investigator I hired—which included a rough estimate of Hannah's father's wealth—I know they could be living in a place five times this size.

"This is where you grew up?" I ask, already knowing the answer.

I've already known the answers to most of the questions I've asked her today, which is probably why I told her about Candace. It felt fair to bare something of myself after secretly invading her privacy that way.

Hannah's fingers tap the steering wheel.

"Yep." That's all she says before climbing out of the car.

Silently, we walk up the path of gray stones that leads to a porch covered by a trellis dripping with verdure.

The front door opens before we've even reached it, revealing a smiling blonde woman.

Hannah shakes her head. "Were you seriously watching out the window, Mom?"

"Rachel was," Hannah's mom replies.

There's a "Hey!" that echoes from somewhere inside the house. I don't hide my smile, relaxing some despite my apprehension about this dinner.

The mother-daughter resemblance is obvious. Both women are blonde and slender. But Mrs. Garner's hair is trimmed in a short bob and her eyes are a warm brown, not blue. She's wearing a brightly patterned sundress, which helps me feel a little less overdressed.

Hannah glances to me. "Mom, this is Oliver. Oliver, this is my mom."

"It's very nice to meet you, Mrs. Garner." My manners kick in automatically, years of socializing at important events ingrained in me. *No impression is irrelevant*, my father always said. My grandfather said the same thing, so I know where he got it from.

"Cynthia, please." Hannah's mother shakes my offered hand. Her smile is friendly and open, but her eyes are curious, scanning me over with an unexpected intensity.

I have no idea what Hannah has told her family about me, and her mom's expression gives nothing away. There's only curiosity on her face, no approval or animosity.

"Come on in."

I follow Hannah inside, glancing around the entryway. A staircase curves up ahead, leading upstairs. There's an opening to the left that reveals the living room. Window seats run around two sides of the room, the panes of glass above the cushions showing off all the greenery surrounding the house. There's a fireplace that looks like it's never been used, the bricks beneath the grate spotless. The walls are plaster, painted in neutral, soothing shades.

We pass the living room and enter the kitchen. It's long and rectangular, centered around the French doors on the far wall. Everything else is constructed of tile or wood. It reminds me of a winery.

Cynthia keeps walking through the open doors and outside. Wooden floors transition into terra-cotta tiles. The outdoor seating area is huge, the yard past it much larger than the front of the house suggests.

I'm distracted by the view of the sprawling yard by the woman who leaps up and approaches us. Her hair is the color of dark honey, a few shades darker than Hannah's. And the wide, unguarded smile she aims my way is nothing I've seen from Hannah, either. But I'm certain this is her sister, Rachel.

"You came!"

"I was invited," I answer, smiling at her exuberance. It's refreshing, since I'm usually surrounded by people who hide their emotions. Including Hannah, who's a rigid statue next to me. "Nice to meet you, Rachel."

"I don't know which is more surprising: that Hannah mentioned me to the guy she claimed to barely know or that you remembered my name."

Rachel's eyes bounce between us. I glance at Hannah in time to catch the wide eyes aimed at her younger sister. The universal *stop talking* look.

"I'm good with names," I say. "Comes in handy at work."

"What do you do? Hannah didn't mention that either."

"You didn't ask!" Hannah says. There's a note of exasperation in her voice. And also maybe a hint of embarrassment.

"I work for my family's company."

"*With* your family?"

I nod. "We're not the only employees, but my brother and father both work there as well."

"You and Hannah both went into the family business, then," Rachel comments.

"We did."

"Hey, sis."

Hannah turns toward the dark-haired man lumbering toward us, clearly welcoming the distraction. "Hey, Eddie."

Hannah's brother has brown hair and a deep tan. Laugh lines crinkle the corners of his eyes as he hugs his little sister. I assumed Hannah was closer with her sister, but she beams up at her brother with a hero-worship I'm a little envious of.

He turns to me next and holds out a hand. "Hey, I'm Eddie. Nice to meet you."

"You, too. Oliver." Once our hands drop, I say, "You're awfully tan for a doctor. I didn't think operating rooms get much sunlight."

Eddie chuckles, completely at ease. "They don't. I go out surfing most mornings. Can't get enough of it. You surf?"

I shake my head. "Never been."

"Well, you should—" Eddie breaks off abruptly, hurrying over to a petite redhead who's hugely pregnant and walking outside carrying a platter of cheese, tomato, and lettuce. "What are you doing? You shouldn't be carrying that!"

"I can't see the ground anyway. Might as well make myself useful."

Eddie takes the platter from his wife and sets it on the table before guiding her over to me. Her expression is a mixture of apprehension and admiration as she approaches, glancing between Hannah and me the same way Rachel did.

I smile at her. "Nice to meet you, April."

She smiles back. "You did your homework, huh?"

"Oliver is good with names," Rachel comments, cracking open a can of soda and taking a seat at the table.

"Well, it's nice to meet you too, Oliver."

"There you are!" Cynthia calls. "Where have you been, Dean?"

"I had to get more charcoal from the garage," is the gruff response.

I turn to greet the one family member I haven't yet met.

Dean Garner is hugging Hannah with one arm, while balancing a plate piled high with freshly cooked burgers in the other.

For a man who must be in his mid-fifties, he's in excellent shape. He could easily pass for a decade younger. Eddie is a younger version of him, the same way Hannah favors her mother. Rachel has more of a mix of her parents' features.

I'm not a parent, so I don't know if you have favorites. My father has vacillated between me and Crew too many times for me to tell if he genuinely prefers one of us to the other. But it's obvious Hannah and her father have an especially close bond. It's clear in the way he squeezes her, then turns a stern gaze on me.

I make the first move, holding a hand out to Hannah's father.

His grip is firm, his expression steely.

"Nice to meet you, Mr. Garner."

Unlike his wife, he doesn't offer a less formal address.

"Dad, this is Oliver," Hannah says, as the silence of us staring at each other stretches and stretches.

I hold Dean's gaze the whole time. I'm no stranger to intimidation tactics. I've used plenty of them myself. And despite how this meeting won't mean anything in the grand scheme of my life—not to mention, Hannah's intention it goes poorly—I want Dean Garner to like me. Respect me, at the very least.

He finally speaks. "Oliver..."

"Kensington."

Hannah didn't mention my last name. It's obvious in the upward creep of his eyebrows, a reaction he doesn't fully manage to control. Coming from a man who has made a career of being successful at bluffing and negotiating, the tiny motion says a lot.

Dean glances at Hannah, who avoids her father's gaze, looking at Rachel instead. She's eating a piece of cheese and watching us, same as everyone else.

I'm realizing I read this situation wrong.

I thought Hannah was inviting me to save face with her family, to show them I'm the reason our pretend relationship and real marriage will never work, not her. Now I'm realizing she would have rather I never met them at all. The concept of parents taking a genuine interest in their child's life is a foreign one to me. My father only cares about what serves his interests. What benefits him. What he can control.

"Well," Mr. Garner finally says, after another *long* pause. "You hungry?"

"Yes, sir."

He nods and continues toward the table with the burgers.

Everyone else follows him toward the table, grabbing plates and taking seats.

Sir? Hannah mouths at me.

I shrug before walking toward the table.

"Can I get you anything to drink, Oliver?" Cynthia asks.

"I'm good with water, Cynthia. Thanks."

All of the glasses at the table have already been filled. I take a sip as soon as I'm seated in one of the wooden chairs.

"You live in New York?" Hannah's mother asks, before I've had a chance to set down my glass.

"That's right. I grew up there and returned after college. It's a great city. Wonderful place to live." I glance at Hannah, hoping I've accurately conveyed my love of the east coast. She rolls her eyes and takes a bite of her burger. I hide a smile before refocusing on Cynthia.

"Where in the city do you live? I haven't been to New York in years."

"I live in the Upper East Side. Carnegie Hill."

"Oh, that's a lovely area. Right by Central Park, right?"

"Yes."

"Do you have roommates? Pets?"

I shake my head. "No. I live alone. I travel a lot for work, so it would be hard to leave a pet. My brother has a dog, so I watch him sometimes."

"What kind of dog?" Cynthia asks eagerly.

"He's mostly golden, I think. They're not entirely sure. He was a rescue."

"Is your brother married?"

I nod. "Yes. He got married a couple of years ago."

"And is he your only sibling?"

"Mom!" Hannah cuts in. "Really, with the twenty questions?"

"I'm simply trying to get to know your husband, Hannah."

There's a sincerity and a hurt in Cynthia's voice that reminds me—again—how different Hannah's family is to mine. The last two times I was alone with my father, he told me to marry a stranger. The time before that, he punched me in the face. I can't even remember the last time my dad, Crew, and I ate a meal together, just the three of us. Our version of family dinner is our weekly meetings that are totally focused around work and my father's agenda.

"I don't mind the questions," I say, breaking the awkward silence that's fallen.

It's the first time anyone has acknowledged the real reason I'm here. That legally speaking, I'm a part of this family I've never met until now.

"You work at Kensington Consolidated?" Surprisingly, Mr. Garner is the one who speaks first.

"Yes."

"That sounds fancy," Rachel says. "What does your family's company do?"

I shift in my seat. I was expecting this to come up, but I'm not thrilled now that it has. Too often, it feels like that's all I boil down to: my family's company. My last name.

"It's a multinational conglomerate holding company. We have a broad portfolio of subsidiaries in several different industries."

"They just bought part of Thompson & Thompson," Hannah contributes, dipping her burger in a pile of ketchup without looking up.

"You handled that deal?" Mr. Garner asks.

"I had a team working with me," I reply.

"You got thirty percent?"

"Twenty-six point five."

"That must have cost you a pretty penny."

I nod but don't disclose the figure. I'm certain everyone here has figured out my family is wealthy, but specifics seem unnecessary.

Maybe Dean senses that. Or maybe he's testing me, trying to figure out whether I'm just a figurehead who does nothing but expects everything.

"You cleared two hundred billion in revenue last year, right?"

Across from me, Rachel's eyes grow huge.

"We ended up just over two fifty," I answer, not looking at Hannah. Thanks to Crew, I'm sure she has an idea about how much my family is worth. But concrete numbers are different.

"Holy shit," Rachel comments. "So you're *very* rich."

"I work for a profitable business," I reply, then take a bite of my burger.

"Do you follow baseball, Oliver?" Mr. Garner asks.

After hastily swallowing, I shake my head. "Not really, sir."

"I have a box available at the Condors' afternoon game tomorrow, if you're interested."

"Sure, that sounds great." I don't hesitate in my response, even realizing it will require changing my flight back to New York. I was supposed to leave at two-thirty, and one thing I do know about baseball is the games are long.

Mr. Garner nods. "Good."

"Is this a guy thing or…" Rachel says.

Hannah's father smiles. "You're always invited. The whole box is available."

"You hate baseball," Eddie comments.

"Hate is a strong word," Rachel replies. "And Dad *invited* Oliver. No way am I missing it."

Eddie shakes his head twice, but then quickly glances at his father. "Okay if we come too?"

Hannah's father looks amused. "Yes."

Hannah is the only one at the table who looks less than

enthused about the baseball game. Her eyes remain on her plate as the conversation shifts to a discussion of April's pregnancy and Rachel's stories about her high school students.

As soon as everyone is finished eating, Hannah suggests croquet. It elicits a stronger reaction that I would have guessed. Dean looks thrilled. Rachel grumbles loudly. Eddie appears resigned. Cynthia and April carry their drinks over to the lawn chairs just past the edge of the patio overlooking the yard.

"I'll play," I volunteer.

Hannah meets my eyes. She avoided looking at me for most of dinner, and I didn't realize how much it bothered me until we make eye contact again. It feels like that first breath of oxygen after swimming underwater.

There's a challenge in the blue. "In your *suit*?"

"You think jeans are an advantage?" I reply.

My expression stays serious, but I'm tempted to smile.

The last time I played croquet was years ago, in the Hamptons. I avoided the Kensington house whenever I was there, since it holds the strongest memories of my mother, ones I'm not willing to risk overwriting. But there are always certain society events that take place there in the summer which are impossible to avoid, like the Ellsworth's Fourth of July party. And while it's been a while since I played croquet, I've had a lot of practice at golf.

I get last pick on color, meaning I go last in the order.

Everyone watches me as I line my mallet up with the starting stake. There's a shift in the air when the green ball flies through the first two wickets. I sink it through a third, passing Eddie. A fourth, passing Rachel. And then I aim straight for Hannah's ball, glancing it with a satisfying tap.

All the side commentary that filled other turns dies away, as I walk over and line my ball up next to hers. I hold mine down with my shoe, then swing.

I grin as Hannah's ball flies away with a satisfying *thump.*

Hannah gapes at me, her mouth literally open. Everyone else looks surprised, but Hannah's expression is the only one frozen with horror. "You did *not* just do that."

I just continue grinning at her. "Better start walking."

"Cheater," she hisses, then heads for her ball.

"It's in the rules, Hannah!" I call after her.

"Hannah is kind of competitive," Rachel tells me conspiratorially, stopping beside me.

"Really? I hadn't noticed."

Rachel laughs before walking to take her hit.

Hannah manages to knock her ball back into play faster than I'm expecting, and then becomes hell-bent on revenge. Fortunately for me, her annoyance affects her accuracy, so I'm spared from her ire for two turns before she taps me. With a triumphant smirk, she sends me flying into the bushes.

"Oops." Hannah feigns a regretful expression, and I want to kiss her. I probably *would* if we were alone right now. Her blue eyes are full of laughter, sparkling mischievously.

I shake my head before trekking into the flowerbeds to find my ball.

Mr. Garner ends up winning the game. Hannah and I vote for continuing and seeing who takes second and third, but we're overruled by everyone else. They're probably worried how long it will take, considering Hannah and I have volleyed between knocking each other off course ever since the first hit, and Rachel and Eddie's balls have both been collateral damage.

"Let's go to Canyon!" Rachel suggests. She glances at Eddie and April. "You guys in?"

Eddie looks apprehensive. "I don't know if that's—"

"Absolutely!" April says.

Rachel looks to Hannah next. "How about you guys?"

It's strange to realize she's grouping me and Hannah together the same way. Even weirder to comprehend we're *married*, same as Eddie and April, so it makes sense to couple us.

"Um..." Hannah looks to me.

I'm exhausted. I got up at five a.m. and it's now ten here, which is one a.m. my time. In a few hours, I'll have been up for twenty-four straight. But I nod because I'll go along with whatever Hannah wants to do.

"We could get one drink, I guess," she says.

Rachel claps her hands. "Yay! Let's go!"

After saying goodbye to Mr. and Mrs. Garner, we climb into cars. Eddie and April drove here too, but Rachel took a rideshare, so she comes with us. I climb into the backseat, letting the sisters sit up front. Rachel chatters away as we turn out of the residential area into a more commercial stretch of street.

About five minutes into the drive, my phone rings.

I recognize the number. It's from a Kensington Consolidated work line. I sigh and answer. "Oliver Kensington."

"Hi, Oliver. It's Scott. Do you have a minute?"

"What the hell are you doing at the office this late?"

He chuckles. "What the hell are you doing answering your phone at this hour?"

"I'm on the west coast. It's only ten here."

"That's not much better."

"I'm not at the office. You are."

"Acquisitions wants a recommendation on the Porter account Monday morning. So I'm researching the stock options and reviewing the last proposal we received from them."

"You have copies of their quarterly statements?"

"Not the most recent ones. We requested them, but they haven't been sent yet."

"That's unacceptable. Tell them to get them to us by tomorrow, or any offer is off the table."

"I don't have the clearance to issue that kind of ultimatum."

"I do. Draft an email, send it to me, and I'll get it to their chairman."

Scott's exhale is loud and relieved. "Thank you, Oliver."

"And then *leave*, okay?"

"Don't have to tell me twice. Thanks again."

Scott hangs up. Seconds later, my phone rings again. This time, it's Garrett.

"Hey, man," I answer.

"Hey. I just realized I never sent you the restaurant name for tomorrow night. I'm driving so I thought I'd just—"

Fuck. "I totally forgot about dinner. I can't make it."

"No worries. Is everything okay?"

"Yeah. All good. I just...something came up this weekend. I'm sorry I forgot to tell you. Work's been so hectic, and—"

"It's fine, Oliver. No problem. I'll move it to next weekend?"

"Sure. I'll have to check with—yeah, that should be fine. I'll let you know if not, okay?"

"Sounds good. Bye."

"Bye."

I shut off my phone and lean my head back, mentally berating myself. I can't believe I forgot about dinner with Garrett. If I'd ever gotten around to inviting Quinn, I probably would have forgotten to let her know I couldn't make it too, which is a terrible first impression. Or second, technically.

Work is always hectic, and I've stayed on top of the rest of my life just fine.

It's Hannah—our marriage, our divorce, just us—that's been

occupying most of my time. I spent an entire day obsessing over a text message I sent her.

I'm distracted enough that it's a surprise when we're suddenly parked and climbing out of the car. I trail behind Hannah and Rachel, exhaustion and worry surrounding me like a haze.

The walls inside of Canyon are decorated by earthen murals. Meant to look like its namesake, I guess. The booths are brown leather, just a few shades darker than the paint. A long bar top runs along one wall, with tables scattered across the floor.

April heads for the bathroom as soon as we're inside. Eddie and I take seats at an open booth, but Hannah and Rachel stay standing.

"We're going to grab drinks," Rachel says. "Usual, Eddie?"

"Yeah, thanks. And a ginger ale for April."

Hannah glances to me. "What do you want?"

"A beer?"

My usual surety comes out like a question, confused by her shift in attitude. When we left her parents', Hannah was smiling and teasing. Since we arrived at Canyon, she's been stiff and unamused. Did she not want to come? She's the only reason we're here.

"What kind of beer?"

"Uh…" My mind goes blank, every brand name slipping away like water through a sieve. I haven't ordered anything except whiskey in years. "Whatever."

Hannah snorts, then spins and walks away. Rachel follows her, after shooting a confused look my way. Good to know I'm not the only one taken aback by Hannah's attitude shift.

Eddie notices it too. "Everything okay there?"

I shrug.

"Yeah, that sounds about right." He chuckles. "I couldn't believe it, when my mom told me Hannah had gotten married."

"It was a surprise to me too. It's a weird situation."

"What's weird about it?"

I glance at him, and he grins.

"Kidding. I get what you mean. But I doubt you guys are the first Vegas marriage to not go the distance."

"I didn't mean that. I meant this part. Honestly, I thought you'd all hate me."

Eddie shakes his head, grinning. "We all know Hannah. She's never done a single thing she didn't want to. If she married you, she had some reason."

"Neither of us were thinking straight."

"Well, you're doing fine, Oliver. Dad never invited Declan to do anything."

"Who's Declan?"

Eddie huffs a laugh, scratching the side of his jaw. "Uh, Hannah's last ex. They were together for about a year."

"What happened?"

"He proposed. And she said no."

"Oh." There's an uncomfortable twist in my stomach. Hannah has always sounded resolute in her anti-marriage views, so it's not a total surprise she rejected a proposal. I'm more thrown she was in a serious enough relationship to get to that stage—and how much that bothers me.

The foreign feeling—jealousy, I guess—is amplified when I glance toward the bar and see Hannah talking to a random guy.

I can't see her expression from this angle, and there's no sign of Rachel.

"I'll be right back," I tell Eddie, barely catching his nod before I'm cutting through the crowd toward the blonde head standing at one end of the bar.

It's crowded in here but not packed. It takes me a couple of minutes maneuvering around tables and patrons before I'm stepping into the empty space behind Hannah. My hand slides around her waist automatically, like it's a move I've made a thousand times before.

Hannah's body tenses as she looks over one shoulder. Her blue eyes are confused at first. But then her body relaxes, leaning into me. My thumb rubs back and forth over her stomach, savoring the way her lips part and her throat bobs with a swallow. My blood heats, reacting to the sudden shift in energy between us. Instead of annoyance, Hannah is looking at me with heat.

"Nice talking with ya." The guy who was talking with Hannah grabs his glass and makes a quick exit.

Hannah turns so she's facing me. I should drop my hand, which is now resting on her back, but I don't. I like the way it feels, the soft fabric of her tee and the blazing heat of her skin soaking through the cotton.

"Did you need something?"

If she were anyone but my *wife*, I'd kiss her. I'm tempted to kiss her despite that. This is a better location than her parents' backyard was.

But I don't have the excuse of too much alcohol or letting loose in Vegas tonight. I'm here to clean up those consequences, not complicate everything.

And *coming here* complicated everything, I'm realizing. It was supposed to be stilted and uncomfortable, two strangers who are polite and distant. It wasn't supposed to be the best night I've had in a long time. And this moment—the staring into her eyes and thinking about how she looked naked—was never supposed to happen.

It's here, though, and I have to decide how to react.

"No." I finally answer her question.

"So…you just came over here to chase him off?"

Two fingers slip beneath the hem of her t-shirt, grazing her lower back. It's the barest of brushes, but Hannah shivers, goosebumps raising on her skin.

I'm playing with fire, but I don't want to stop.

"You left me with your brother so you could flirt with some guy?"

She tilts her chin. Even in sandals, she's tall, easily meeting my eyes. "If you'd taken a little longer to come over here, we'd probably be fucking in the bathroom by now."

My inhale is sharp, like she just landed a blow.

"You could watch, if you want."

She's pushing me, and I can't figure out why. I shouldn't care. The whole point of this visit was to show off our incompatibility to her family. And instead, we're ignoring her siblings, ensconced in what feels a lot like sexual tension.

I drop my hand and step away, immediately missing the warmth of her skin. I stuff my hands in my pockets, so I'm not tempted to touch her again.

"What? Infidelity bothers you?" There's an exaggerated note of surprise in her voice, so I know exactly what she's referring to.

It's like a bucket of ice water. I've heard enough about my sins from my father, and sharing one of them with Hannah was clearly a massive mistake.

I swallow the hurt, the same way I stuff away everything else. Shake my head—stiffly—until it turns natural. "Doesn't bother me at all. If you really hit it off with someone, just text me and I'll go to a hotel."

I force an indifferent smile, then turn and walk back toward the table.

CHAPTER FIFTEEN

HANNAH

"So six a.m.?" Eddie says, as we walk through the parking lot.

Oliver winces, but it's infinitesimal. I don't think anyone else notices. Or has registered that it's already the middle of the night for him. "Yep," he replies. "See you then."

"Awesome. Night, man." As an afterthought, Eddie calls out a goodbye to me too. April and Rachel wave before heading for the car. Since Rachel lives closer to them than to me, they're driving her home.

My brother has tons of friends. One of the bonuses of growing up in southern California is people tend to stay here. Most of my friends from elementary, middle, and high school still live locally, and the same is true for Eddie. He's not desperate for male company. And he's never made an effort to hang out with any guy I've dated beyond polite chitchat before.

I assumed my mom and Rachel would be friendly toward Oliver. April too. But I thought my dad and Eddie would be reticent. Instead, my brother is making private plans and my dad invited Oliver to a baseball game. In the year I dated

Declan, he didn't get a single invite outside the events I brought him to.

"What's happening at six?" I ask.

"He invited me surfing." Oliver doesn't look at me as he responds. He *hasn't* looked at me since I suggested he watch me have sex with someone else and then shoved a secret he trusted me with back in his face.

"You surf?"

"No."

"Eddie's a good teacher. He taught me."

"Great." His tone is flat as he climbs into the passenger seat.

I click my seatbelt into place, gnawing the inside of my cheek.

Earlier, I wished Oliver would act exactly how he is right now —distant and cold.

He was too charming at dinner, patiently answering my mom's questions. Too daring at croquet, making me enjoy it more than if I'd won. And then his phone had to keep ringing on the drive to Canyon, reminding me that he's busy and important and had plans for this weekend that didn't involve entertaining my family.

But now that he's staring out the window like he'd love to be anywhere else, I'm hit with the persistent ache of regret.

I clear my throat. "My family liked you."

"Sorry." His voice is dry, no trace of apology.

I exhale. "I'm sorry, Oliver."

"For what?"

"Earlier. I shouldn't have brought up…that."

"If exhibitionism is your thing—"

An unexpected laugh spills out. "It's not."

"If it is, though…" There's a teasing note to his tone, and the rush of relief is dizzying. I didn't realize how worried I was the harm I did was irreparable until there's a sign it wasn't.

I bite my bottom lip to hold in another laugh. "I won't tell anyone. I promise. You can trust me. And that probably means nothing to you, after what I said earlier. But you can."

When I glance over, any amusement in Oliver's expression is gone. He's back to looking stoic.

Once he realizes my eyes are on him, he nods. "Okay."

I swallow, nod back, and then tighten my hands around the steering wheel. It's not the icy chill from the start of the trip, but it's not warmth either.

"I applied to architecture school the night we met."

My eyes are back on the road, but I catch the motion out of the corner of them as he looks my way.

"That's why I went down to the bar, instead of ordering room service. A mini celebration, since I didn't tell anyone I was applying."

"Including me."

"I just told you."

"I mean that night," he replies.

"I didn't know you. You just wanted me to blurt that out, first thing? I had a hard enough time getting your attention."

Oliver says nothing, for long enough I think he won't. And when he does speak, it renders *me* speechless. "You've always had my attention, Hannah."

I'd think it was a line, a sweet sentiment that means nothing. Except there's a sincerity to the words that's almost angry. Like the admission is being dragged from him. Or that it's something he'd love to change but can't. Rather than being romantic, the words sound painfully honest.

Since I'm not sure what to say in response, I say nothing.

The silence is a charged one. Not uncomfortable, but noticeable. It feels like those six words—*You've always had my atten-*

tion, Hannah—are lingering and growing between us with each mile we drive.

The same pulsing awareness that keeps resulting in stupid decisions—like marrying or insulting him—appears, making me restless and uncomfortable.

It's been too long for me to respond to his last comment, and not long enough to broach a different topic.

Finally, I pull into the driveway.

Oliver says nothing as we climb out of the car and walk up the porch steps to the front door. I unlock the door and flip on the hall lights before kicking off my shoes and continuing into the kitchen.

I grab a bottle of sparkling water out of the fridge and twist off the top, taking a long, fortifying sip.

The footsteps that enter the kitchen are unexpected. I'm used to living alone to the soundtrack of nothing but my own movements. And I thought Oliver would head straight to bed.

I turn to face him, leaning back against the counter as I take another long sip of fizzy water. The bubbles scratch my throat, reminding me this moment is real.

"You struck out at the bar, huh?"

I raise both eyebrows. I was back at the table about five minutes after Oliver walked away. Aside from the one guy who approached me at the bar, I didn't talk to anyone besides him and my family all night. Which he already knows.

"You can't *strike out* if you don't play."

He walks closer, leaning against the island and crossing his arms. I've spent way too much time admiring his forearms tonight. The map of veins and the lean lines of muscle. "Do you remember anything about that night?"

His voice is low. *So* low and so deep. Sexy.

I find too much about Oliver to be sexy, including that he's still wearing a suit because he didn't pack anything more casual. That he looks buttoned up but spent the night playing croquet with my dad and sitting in a bar with sticky floors listening to my sister-in-law debate baby names.

I pull my hair over one shoulder, watching him track the movement. His eyes on me feel like the fall of silk over skin. The slightest, barest tease that squeezes my chest and speeds up each beat of my heart.

"Parts," I choke out.

"Which parts?"

"The bar. Meeting you at the club. Watching the fountains. Being up in the sky. Drinking. After that…not much."

"The—our—wedding?"

I swallow. Shake my head. "No."

"After?"

"Passing out in bed? Not really." There's a subtle reaction. Not much, but his cheek shifts. It boldens me to add, "Not much of a wedding night."

"Is that what you wanted, Hannah?" His voice is all gravel. And there's an added rasp to my name, like he's well aware of how him saying it affects me. "A real wedding night?"

A throbbing starts between my legs, keeping pace with my racing thoughts.

What is it about Oliver Kensington that makes me lose all sight of logic? *He's* logic. Solid, smart, and serious. But for the first time, I get how we ended up married.

I'm completely in control of my decision-making, and so, so tempted to make another stupid decision where he's concerned.

Sex is messy. Lust is confusing. Desire is dangerous.

But as we stare at each other, I can't find the willpower to care.

I buried what it was like to touch him—kiss him—beneath the

stress and anxiety of our unexpected marriage. But the knowledge is still there, playing out in technicolor in my mind.

I nod.

There's a flicker of heat in his gaze. "Can I fuck you, Hannah?"

The edge of the quartz countertop digs into the small of my back. Distantly, a siren sounds. But I'm barely cognizant of my surroundings. I'm focused on him, swimming in that intense green.

He's really asking, just like he did before kissing me.

This isn't foreplay or dirty talk. Part of him probably wants me to say no, to shut down this possibility between us that will complicate everything between us even more.

I take a step forward. The hardwood is cool and smooth against my bare feet as I push away from the counter and approach him.

Oliver doesn't move. Doesn't reach. He watches me walk, until I'm so close I can see the flutter of his pulse beneath his jawline. Keeping my gaze fixed on him the whole time, I start unbuttoning his shirt. One by one, they pop open, exposing bare chest.

Working at Garner Sports Agency means I spend a lot of time around professional athletes who stay in shape for a paycheck. Oliver could choose to never work a day of his life. But not only does he work, he *works out.*

His body is a masterpiece. Firm skin and sculpted muscles. I take my time with each button, my fingers brushing and lingering over each new inch.

Once I reach the final button, I run my hands all the way back to the top, spreading my right palm over his left pectoral until I find the steady thud of his heart.

"Yes." I whisper my answer.

His hand splays on the center of my back the same way it did at the bar. Just like then, I want to sigh at the contact. It's not sexual, it's support. I stumble into him, and then he's kissing me.

And *fuck*, can Oliver kiss. I'm swept into it, like a wave leaving shore.

He hasn't shaved since he arrived. There's a slight rasp as his stubble abrades my skin, the roughness of his scruff contrasting the soft brush of his lips.

I fall into it, into him. Wonder why I didn't kiss him as soon as he walked out of the airport earlier, because embarrassment and uncertainty don't seem like monumental enough barriers to justify resisting this sensation.

I whimper when his lips leave mine, and I'm too turned on to care how pathetic it sounds.

"Couch or bed?"

I deliberate for half a second. Couch is closer, bed is bigger. "Bed."

In a move that I'm not expecting at all, I'm suddenly airborne. Breath leaves my lungs in a surprised *whoosh* as Oliver begins walking, leaving me with an upside-down view of my kitchen.

"What the hell?" I sputter. It sounds much less indignant than I was hoping for.

Oliver's hand runs up my left calf and lands on my thigh, holding me more securely against his shoulder. Even through the denim I can feel the heat searing through the fabric and branding my skin.

"It's my turn."

"Your turn to…what?" The last word comes out breathlessly, as the world reorients again. I'm on my back, spread out in the middle of my mattress, with a smirking Oliver hovering above me.

"To touch *you*."

His head dips, finding a sensitive spot right above my collarbone. He presses his lips right on the curve where my neck meets my shoulder. I didn't even *know* that was a sensitive spot. Not until right now, when he gently sucks before swiping it with his tongue, and my nerve endings respond like a lash of lightning finding metal.

Oliver's mouth journeys up my neck.

Sometimes licking, sometimes sucking, sometimes nibbling.

Always touching.

By the time he reaches my jawline, I'm a panting mess. A puddle of need. So wet I can *feel* it gathered between my thighs.

I thought this would be a quick encounter. Sexy and satisfying, but not slow. It was supposed to be instant gratification. Mutual relief.

Not this growing, glowing sensation that makes me never want to move. To sink into the way it feels like he's worshipping me.

When he kisses me, it feels like falling.

But in the best way. When you know you'll land safely so you can enjoy the rush.

I'm not sure if I should feel so safe around Oliver. We both have the means to hurt the other. We're a precarious stack; one stumble away from destruction.

But I sink into it anyway.

His tongue slips into my mouth, the slide practiced and sensual. My hips lift, desperately trying to relieve the building pressure. The only sound I can hear is my heavy breathing, the desperate pull of oxygen loud and desperate.

Oliver's hand slides across my stomach, deftly unbuttoning and unzipping my jeans. Anticipation arcs through me as the pulse between my legs becomes more insistent.

I'm about to have sex with my husband, I realize.

There are too many emotions associated with that statement that I'm too overwhelmed to name, so I just close my eyes and *feel*.

Denim is tugged away efficiently, cool air caressing my bare skin as my jeans get tossed to the floor. I sit up and pull off my t-shirt, sitting on my bed in just a bra and underwear.

At least I chose a lacy, matching set this morning. I didn't want Oliver to think I made an effort, but I wanted to feel good today. When I got dressed this morning, I didn't think he'd see me like this.

The only light in here is what's spilling in from the hallway. I only catch a quick glimpse of Oliver's shadowed expression before his head ducks, teeth grazing my nipple through the lace of my bra.

I gasp, my back arching and my chest lifting like an offering as the inferno inside me sparks.

"*Fuck*, Hannah."

He sounds tortured. Overwhelmed. Wild.

"Fuck *me*," I tell him.

Oliver chuckles, the sound dark and decadent. It slides across my skin like a hint of smoke or a drop of whiskey.

I lift my pelvis, seeking out more contact. Begging without the words. My fingers dig into his shoulders, feeling the muscles bunch beneath my touch. His tongue is tracing circles on my chest, and my entire body thrums with each lick.

"Please."

His hand slides up my bare leg, setting my nerves off in a frenzy. The texture of his skin running over mine and the rub against his suit is too much—and not enough.

"*Please*, Oliver."

He rolls away, and for one horrible second, I think it was all a tease. That he was wondering how much I wanted him, and just got his answer. But then I hear the rustle of fabric and the crinkle of a wrapper, and I realize what's happening. I reach behind and unsnap the band of my bra, letting the heavy weight of my breasts fall free.

Then Oliver's hand is there, managing to make the discomfort better and worse as he rubs my nipple into a hard point. His other hand takes a slow journey down my chest and stomach until it's between my legs, tugging off my underwear and leaving me totally naked.

I feel him *there*, sparks of electricity racing through me as the head of his cock grazes my clit before he pushes inside of me. It's a relief to feel the length of him filling me. And a stretch to accommodate his size. He presses deeper and deeper, until I'm certain I can't take any more. When he withdraws, there's an immediate ache as I clench around nothing. And then he's spreading me again, inciting a delicious ache.

"Faster." I breathe the word, my hands moving lower, fingernails scraping his back. I need *more*.

I'm stripped down to the basest of instincts. Nothing but need. Right now, none of what got us here matters. It just matters that we're here. That the thick drag of Oliver's dick is pushing me higher and higher, a perfect pressure that will end in euphoria. I can feel it building in my center, the heat and pleasure so close I could cry. I angle my hips, desperately trying to take him deeper. To climb the peak faster.

"You're so tight. So wet." He murmurs the words right next to my ear, low and gruff, and my breathing becomes so fast that it's embarrassing. "Feel so fucking good."

I clench my inner muscles, smiling when he groans.

A heady rush of power courses through me, mixing with the lust and the desperation.

I love that I'm affecting him. That he's *admitting* I affect him.

"You take me so well. Even better than I imagined." His tone is low and uneven, a rasp that warms my skin like the lick of a flame and washes over me in waves of arousal.

He's thought about this.

It feels like this moment has been building ever since I heard his voice in that bar. I remember how it felt when he looked over at me, the rush that accompanied his attention. How it amplified to an almost unbearable intensity, reverberating throughout my entire body.

He's possessing me in a way I've never experienced. I usually guide guys during sex, telling them what I like and what I want. Some get off on it, some get offended by it, but none of them have escaped it.

Except Oliver. Since he kissed me, I've barely managed more than moans.

I don't have to make a single decision. He's controlling everything, the same way he seems to manage each aspect of his life.

I never want him to stop. But my body is also desperate for release, the pleasure I'm chasing hovering just out of reach.

My hands explore up and down his back, feeling muscle and tendon shift beneath my fingers as he moves above me. His mouth drops to mine and we're kissing again, his tongue taking my mouth with the same skilled assault as his cock fills my pussy.

His pelvis grinds against mine, stimulating every sensitive spot. Pleasure crashes through me, sudden and consuming and incredible, as I spasm around him.

I lose all sense of time or place or self, catapulted into a personal nirvana.

I'm still floating in clouds of bliss when Oliver flips me over, his hands lifting my hips up and back before I'm spread open by his hard cock again. I gasp, readjusting to the new position and realizing he didn't come during my explosive orgasm.

Everything is ultra-sensitive, the pleasure of him stretching me again even sharper and more intense. The angle is different and deeper, and Oliver takes full advantage. With each stroke he almost totally withdraws, a slow drag that feels like I can feel every ridge and vein even through the barrier of the condom. Then he fills me all over again, stretching me until I take every inch.

My body is beginning to build toward another peak faster than I would have thought possible. My breathing is ragged, heat trickling through me in endless streams. Sweat dampens my skin.

"You're close to coming again." Oliver groans the words, arousal deepening them to a low growl. "I can feel it."

I moan, my hands fisting the soft fabric of my comforter as he pulls out completely, sliding around my opening and gliding against my clit. Teasing me with the promise of more pleasure.

I don't know how he hasn't come yet. His dick is so rigid it barely moves as I arch my back and rub against him, trying to force more friction. Trying to get him back inside of me.

Oliver's hands leave my hips and run up the sides of my abdomen, leaving trails of goosebumps in their wake as he explores my body. One hand grazes the hard point of my nipple and I jolt at the fresh rush of pleasure.

Then his hands are back on my hips, sliding down to spread my legs open wider for him. Cool air brushes the wetness that's gathered there, feeding the relentless ache. A second orgasm no longer sounds impossible. It feels inevitable.

He slams into me again, suddenly and forcefully enough it feels like taking him for the first time all over again.

"The only way I'll ever see you getting fucked is if *I'm* the one fucking you, Hannah."

There's a dark possessiveness in the words, an undercurrent of intensity I'm not expecting. I picture what he sees, me spread and desperate for him. The complete opposite of taunting him about bathroom bar sex with another man.

I moan and whimper as he sets a punishing pace, pounding into me over and over again until I'm careening over a cliff into blissful oblivion. I come again, clenching around the hard length of his cock as he continues to rock inside of me.

Tremors quake through me as mindless pleasure washes over me with the force of a tsunami, pulling me under in endless waves. I'm barely aware enough to feel the jerk inside as he ejaculates, finally finding his own release.

I collapse onto the soft cotton of my bedspread, feeling like a towel that was just wrung out. There's a satisfied hum running through my body as I roll onto my back, luxuriating in a completely relaxed state.

I run a hand through my hair, brushing blonde strands out of my eyes and away from my face. My breathing begins to slow, desperate pants turning rhythmic and easy, as I watch Oliver lean over and grab a tissue off the bedside table.

He removes the condom, wraps it, and then tosses it into the trash. Even flaccid, his dick is impressive. My pussy is swollen and satisfied, but there's a fresh pulse between my legs, remembering how that long, thick length felt inside of me.

I can tell he's unsure what to say or do. That he's preparing to leave and walk down the hall to the guest room.

It's what he should do. What I should *want* him to do.

But before my eyes flutter closed, I whisper, "You can stay."

It's not really an invitation. Because invitations serve a purpose, and I'm not sure what the point of him staying is. I'm exhausted, and I'm not the one who flew five hours and is three hours ahead. All we'll do is sleep. And I should want the bed to myself. I like my space; it's why I live alone.

So I'm surprised when the dip of the mattress sends a small

thrill through me. When the sound of his breath is soothing instead of annoying.

Even with my eyes closed, I can sense him moving. A few seconds later, the cashmere blanket I keep at the bottom of my bed is draped over my body, the soft fibers lightly brushing my bare skin.

There's a delicate, fragile flicker in my chest. Waking up married to a stranger is one of the scarier things that's ever happened to me. But right now, I feel safer than I ever have.

And it's all Oliver Kensington's fault.

CHAPTER SIXTEEN

OLIVER

The best sex of my life wasn't supposed to be with my *wife*. And it wasn't purely physical, either. I always put effort into making sure a woman enjoys herself, but it was more than that last night. I was completely focused on Hannah, consumed with making sure her pleasure was the priority.

I rationalized it as the one-night stand we never got to have, the night we ended up *married* instead. But it felt like more than that. It felt meaningful.

So did waking up next to her again.

I shouldn't have stayed in her bed. I was stunned she offered, but I shouldn't have stayed. It muddied everything more. And now I'm dreading returning to her house.

"You ready to head in?" Eddie calls.

"Sure," I shout back, then lean forward on the board to begin paddling in. My hands cut through the chilly, salty water, the occasional wave helping to propel me toward shore.

This is about the only move Eddie taught me that I'm any good at. I tried to catch a few waves when we first got out here.

After three unsuccessful attempts, I opted just to bob on my board and stare at the brightening horizon.

The Pacific Ocean is peaceful and calm this morning, which isn't ideal surfing conditions. But it's good for self-reflection.

I always wake up early, but I never reflect. I drink coffee and eat oatmeal. Work out. Shower and put on a suit. Then go into the office.

This is the first morning in a while that's felt leisurely. Ironic, since I got about three hours of sleep. My eyes should be barely staying open. But I don't feel sluggish.

Sunbeams filter down from the blue sky, sparkling off the textured surface of the sea. The beach is a sandy strip ahead, dotted with the green leaves of palm trees. And I woke up beside a gorgeous blonde who made me come harder than I ever have in my life.

And that's the problem.

I wasn't supposed to *enjoy* this trip.

"Too bad we didn't have better waves this morning," Eddie says, paddling up beside me.

"I don't think I would have gotten up no matter what the waves looked like," I reply.

He laughs. "Nah, you just need a little more practice."

"I'm not much of an athlete."

"Me neither," Eddie responds. "Bit of a letdown to *the* Dean Garner."

The words are light, but I catch the undercurrent. Because while this might be my first time surfing, I have decades of experience when it comes to disappointing fathers. "He seemed happy enough not to have any competition last night."

A wide grin stretches Eddie's face. "Hannah usually wins. Dad was thrilled to have her out of the way." He glances at me. "She's his favorite. Deservedly so. Rachel and I never took much interest in croquet or the sports agency. That was all Hannah. She's his protegee."

I say nothing.

"He'll test you, but he wants her to be happy."

I'm not sure if I'm understanding right. Because it almost sounds like Hannah's brother is suggesting I'm the person who can make that happen. "We're getting *divorced*, Eddie."

"Yeah, that's what Hannah said."

I nod, glad we're on the same page.

"Except I've seen her with other guys, and she never looked at a single one of them the way she looks at you." Eddie drops *that* declaration on me, then glances toward shore. "Race you!"

He wins.

And it's mostly because this is the first time I've ever tried surfing.

But also because the mess in my head is becoming more snarled, instead of untangling.

When I walk into the kitchen, Hannah is standing at the stove wearing a light blue dress and cooking eggs. Her hair is loose and messy, and all I can think about is how it looked spread across her comforter.

Suddenly, startingly, scarily, I can *see* it. I can imagine walking into this kitchen every morning to this sight.

She glances up as I approach the island.

"Hey." Her smile is guarded, and the dread in my stomach turns to lead. "Sleep well?"

"I got a few hours."

"I didn't hear an alarm."

I guess we're not pretending we didn't spend the night in the same bed. "I was trying not to wake you."

She nods, sucking in her bottom lip as she continues pushing eggs around the pan. "I can tell my dad you needed to leave, if you want. You don't have to go to the game."

"I want to come, as long as that's okay."

Hannah's expression shows surprise, but she doesn't try to talk me out of going. "Okay. Yeah. Of course that's okay."

I rest a hip against the edge of the counter. "I've never been to one," I admit.

"A baseball game?"

I nod.

"You've *never* been to a baseball game?"

I shrug. "My dad was more into golf and polo. And my mom…" My voice trails, obviously, since I can't come up with any way to finish that sentence.

Since I don't talk about my mom.

"Is it okay if I take a shower?"

Hannah nods, jerky and fast. "Yeah, of course."

I continue through the kitchen and down the hall, trying to get my head on straight. I need to stay focused on the point of this trip: one step closer to being divorced. As soon as that's taken care of, I can decide what to do about Quinn. How to handle everything with my father.

Hannah has plans too. She might not have a second marriage breathing down her neck, but she's intending to start school in the fall. Her whole life is in California: her family and her careers, both present and planned.

After I've rinsed all the stickiness off and gotten dressed in a clean suit, I return to the kitchen.

Hannah is sitting at the island, eating eggs and reading something on her computer.

When she spots me, she coughs.

I wait for a suit comment, but it doesn't come. If I had something more casual to wear, I would. But I don't. It's just become easier to make it my default uniform no matter what else I'm doing. Even at home, ever since I had to stand to get a paper during a video call and revealed I was wearing sweatpants with my button-down.

"If you're hungry…" Hannah nods toward the skillet on the stovetop. "Plates are in the cabinet to the left of the sink."

"Thanks."

I pull a plate out of the cabinet and heap it with eggs, which are still steaming.

I can't recall the last time someone made me breakfast. Based on the size of the pile in the pan, Hannah made a lot more than she was planning to eat herself.

"Do you want coffee? I can make—"

I shake my head. "Eddie and I stopped."

"He took you to Pacific Beans?"

"Yeah."

"Wow. I had to catch two waves in a row before he brought me there. Took me five sessions."

"Well, that definitely didn't happen."

"You couldn't get up?"

I glance up, and there's a pause where pink crawls across her cheeks.

"On the board, I mean. You couldn't get up on the board?"

I smirk, my gaze dropping to the plate as I finish heaping eggs on it. "Maybe if you'd been there." I'm flirting, and it's a fucking terrible idea. But letting last night fester between us doesn't seem smart, either.

The dynamic between us changed the second I kissed her last night. Grown-up actions should come with grown-up behavior.

We've handled being married as maturely as possible. Acting like two hormonal teenagers who fooled around for the first time and then pass each other in the hallway, pretending not to know each other doesn't seem like the right way to handle this.

Hannah says nothing as I take the stool beside her. But she doesn't move away when my knee accidentally brushes hers.

I shovel a bite of eggs into my mouth, suddenly starving. They're cooked perfectly, light and fluffy and not over-salted.

"What are you working on?" I ask, nodding toward the screen.

"Just reviewing a contract."

"When are you going to tell your dad about architecture school?"

"If I don't get in, never."

"And when you get in?"

There's a lot I don't know about Hannah.

But I *do* know she's one of the smartest, most dedicated people I've ever met. That was driven home over and over again during the croquet game last night. If I was a gambler, I'd put all my money on her. If she wants to be an architect, I can't picture a world in which she won't become one.

"I don't know. I don't want to…disappoint him."

"He'll be happy for you, Hannah." I'm equally certain of that. Because I've seen a father who only views his child in terms of the value they bring to the family business. And that man isn't Dean Garner.

"What about you?" she asks, turning on her stool so she's facing me.

I swallow another bite of egg. "What about me?"

"Do you want to work at Kensington Consolidated?"

Oddly enough, it's a question I've never been asked before. It's always been expected I would, like my life was a highway without exits ending at a single destination. I guess the logic is, why *wouldn't* I? My family founded one of the most powerful, successful companies to ever exist. New employees walk into the building with wide eyes and awed expressions, disbelieving they'll be working within the legendary four walls. Walking away from that legacy would be a shocking betrayal.

"I'm good at it. I like it."

"That wasn't what I asked."

My fork plows through the yellow pile on my plate. I take another bite. Swallow. "Say you had a client come to you. His grandfather was the general manager for this underdog team. Built it up from nothing, made it into something. His father played for them, setting all the records. And they make him an offer. Give him a chance to contribute to the legacy. To add his name to the history books. If he signed, would you ask him why he wanted to play?"

"So it's pride?"

I exhale. "It's complicated, is what it is."

My father's offer is on the tip of my tongue.

Hannah has joined a short list of people whose opinions I value. I'm not sure when or why or *how* it happened, but she's on there. I barely know her. But it feels like I know *enough*, and for some reason I can't make sense of, the brief amount of time I've spent around her has been enough to make me certain of that.

And I'd like to hear her perspective, what she thinks about the proposal. She already knows about Candace, even. She has some sense of why my relationship with my father is even messier than most people think.

But she's also my wife.

And she's also the woman who I had sex with last night. Who I woke up next to this morning.

Telling her that part of the urgency behind our divorce is so

I'm free to potentially propose to someone else sounds like a terrible idea for different reasons than before.

I'm not worried she'll drag the proceedings out to spite me, the way Scarlett suggested. I'm worried how she'll react, period.

If she doesn't care, it will sting.

If she does care, it will hurt.

So I keep my mouth shut, aside from finishing my breakfast.

"You done?" I ask Hannah, once my plate is clean.

She looks away from her laptop screen, where she's been focused for the past few minutes. It must be something important. Or she's avoiding talking to me, after how I shut the last topic down.

"Yeah."

I grab her plate and pile it on top of mine, carrying both over to the sink and start to rinse them.

"You don't have to do that."

"I know."

"If you want to, uh, do something, we can go…do something."

I raise both eyebrows. "As heartfelt as that invitation sounded, I'm good staying here until the game. I have work to do too." I never sent Scott's email requesting the updated quarterly statements, and I'm sure lots of other questions have piled up in my inbox by now.

Hannah slides off her stool. "That doesn't mean you have to do dishes. You're a guest."

"You cooked. And I'm your husband."

Never, ever did I imagine I'd be saying those words standing in a tiny bungalow a few blocks from the beach. Life has a funny way of spiraling from one small decision.

"That doesn't count as a reason. We're not really married."

"We're not?" I squirt some soap on the sponge and start scrubbing the plates. "Been consummated and everything."

"So…we're discussing that?"

"Nothing to discuss. I'm just not pretending it didn't happen."

"It was a judgment lapse."

"Probably," I agree. I would have called it a mistake, but I don't say that. And standing in the kitchen with her watching me wash dishes, I'm not so sure it's an accurate descriptor. Because mistakes are choices you'd go back and change, and I definitely don't feel that way about last night.

"Are you sure you don't mind if I work?"

"I'm sure." I finish the dishes and dry my hands, Hannah watching me the whole time.

"The last guy who saw me do work on a Sunday told me my dad wouldn't fire me."

"The last woman who cooked for me was my mom. Thanks for breakfast."

I leave her standing in the kitchen and walk down the hallway to the work that's always waiting for me.

Hannah's family picks us up just after noon. Her *entire* family. Dean is driving, with Cynthia in the passenger seat. April, Eddie, and Rachel are taking up the middle row. Rachel climbs out so that Hannah and I can crawl into the third row.

Cynthia offers her seat to me, but I politely decline.

It takes some maneuvering to get into the seat, much less get comfortable. The stiff fabric of my suit isn't meant for twisting and contorting, and there's little space to work with.

Hannah's lips twitch as she glances over at me, my knees folded in front of me so high they nearly reach my chin.

It's cramped and warm in the rear of the car. The sun is on full blast, turning the temperature up to the mid-seventies. It's a shock to my system since New York hasn't passed sixty in months.

I've never ridden in the way back of a car before. Just like with breakfast, it's a realization that occurs to me randomly. It's usually just me and a driver in a vehicle, the same way the people who cook for me are always paid to do so.

Once we're moving, Hannah pulls her feet out of the footwell and taps my knee, tugging it toward her. I accept the silent invitation, stretching my legs out so they cross the center seat and taking advantage of the full length of the car. It's still tight but not quite as cramped. Hannah is the one huddled up now, her long legs mostly hidden beneath the skirt of her dress.

I lean over and grab her foot, pulling it toward me until her leg is in my lap. After a second of hesitation, her second leg slides over too.

Neither of us say anything.

Music is on, and the windows are down. Rachel and Eddie are arguing about something in the middle, while Cynthia is telling Dean what route he's supposed to be taking to the stadium. He's insisting he knows a better way.

There's a lot of noise and activity around us, and somehow that makes this feel more intimate. My right elbow is resting on the cupholder beneath the window, but I place my left on her calf because I'm not sure where else to put that hand.

This could certainly be defined as another judgment lapse. But I shove those thoughts away and focus on the scenery flying by. I've only been to Los Angeles a few times before, and the most recent time was years ago. All those trips were centered around work, the same as most of my travel.

These are all new parts of the city to me: the residential streets, the glimpses of the beach and boardwalks, the huge stadium we park outside.

April is the one who pulls a seat forward this time. She smiles when she sees me and Hannah tangled together, and we quickly separate. I climb out first, since I'm essentially blocking Hannah in. And then turn, offering her a hand. She tumbles out of the car, her foot getting caught up in the hem of her dress. I half-catch her, stumbling back a step as her body collides with mine.

"Sorry." She pulls away immediately, grabbing the side of the car for support instead.

"It's fine. You good?"

"Yeah. Thanks."

Her tone is casual, but her cheeks are red, obviously aware of her entire family staring at us. I nod and step away, putting more distance between us.

We join the streams of people crossing the parking lot, heading into the stadium. Then we split off to a private entrance that leads to an elevator, which takes us to the top of the field.

The view from the box seats is impressive. The contrasting stripes of green neatly mowed, the tan dirt immaculately raked, and the four white bases blinding in the sunlight. An array of food and drinks is spread out behind the indoor seating, and a door leads out into an uncovered section of seats that are closer to the field. A group much larger than ours could comfortably fit in here.

Everyone gravitates toward the food first. There's multiple kinds of salad, pizza, chicken tenders, grilled hot dogs, and pretty much every kind of food considered quintessentially American.

"Oliver."

I stop in my tracks as soon as I hear Mr. Garner say my name.

Rachel, who's right ahead of me, pauses, glances back, and then continues walking.

"Yes?"

Hannah's father's expression is impassive as he studies me, and I resist the urge to fidget. He may not know what happened between me and his daughter last night, but I sure as hell do. And it's all I can think about right now, unfortunately.

"Hannah mentioned you've never been to a game before?"

I nod, relaxing a little. Might as well set the bar on my baseball knowledge as low as possible. "That's right."

"I can safely assume you're not a San Francisco fan, then?" There's a new gleam in his eyes, what looks a little like amusement.

"Up until right now, I had no idea San Francisco had a baseball team, sir."

Shockingly, he cracks a smile before reaching into the canvas tote bag he's carrying and handing me a baseball glove. "In case anyone hits up here."

I take the glove, running a finger over the smooth, oiled leather. "Thank you, sir."

"Dean is fine, Oliver."

Then he walks away, leaving me with the sinking suspicion Hannah's father might actually approve of me.

After the game, Hannah and I get dropped off first. I changed my flight after breakfast, so I'm departing LA at five thirty. With the time difference, I won't be back in New York until after two a.m. But it was worth it, I decide, as I say goodbye to Hannah's family and the black SUV pulls away from the curb.

As we walk up toward her porch, Hannah hides a yawn. My baseball knowledge hasn't expanded very much from what I knew before the game—the team with the most runs wins and three strikes before you're out—but Dean did his best to explain it to me. As far as fathers-in-law go, I could have done a lot worse. I met Dean yesterday, and have had more civil, non-work-related conversations with him in these two days than I have with my father in years.

But from a broad perspective, I think it's fair to say this weekend was a total failure. I don't think I'm unlikeable, but I wasn't expecting to be embraced by Hannah's family the way I was. Based on how silent she's been this afternoon, I don't think she expected it either. Our marriage feels more real than ever, instead of an arbitrary, alcohol-influenced decision.

I set out my suitcase in the entryway before we left for the game, expecting it to be a tight turnaround to get to the airport following the game. I left my phone charging on top of my bag, since I forgot to plug it in overnight the way I ordinarily do. Not having it with me was nice, actually. I *couldn't* check emails or answer calls.

"The car should be here in a few minutes," I say, breaking the silence hovering between us. Hannah nods. I already told her I ordered one.

I kneel down and unzip my suitcase so I can add the baseball glove her dad insisted I keep. When I straighten, Hannah is staring at the luggage.

Her attention snaps to me with a jerk of her head, and then she's walking toward me, closer and closer until I realize she's planning to hug me.

I wrap my arms around her waist, tugging her closer. She smells like grapefruit and salt, a scent I recognize from the perfume bottle in her medicine cabinet. I snooped while looking for more hand soap in the bathroom. Her hair is tied back in a ponytail with a pink-patterned scarf, and the soft silk grazes my neck as we stand like that.

There's no compulsion to pull away, even long after the appropriate length of time for a hug to last has passed. Her body is warm and pliant against mine, and all I can think about is how easy it would be to pull her dress up.

My hand drifts higher and higher, until I reach the exposed skin of her upper back. We're close enough I can hear the change in her breathing, the way that deep and even quickens.

Her head turns so her lips are against my neck. And then with a deliberate, measured swipe, her tongue traces a small circle right next to my Adam's apple.

Fuck it, I decide. We already had sex once.

I pull back just far enough to kiss her, groaning when she responds immediately. Moving into me like she was waiting for this. *Hoping* for it.

I start gathering the skirt of her dress in my hands, tugging the fabric up, and she steps away, breaking all contact.

I drop my hands immediately, swallowing my disappointment, even though I know it's for the best. I'm not thinking rationally, so it's good to know she is.

Except her hands are suddenly on my belt buckle, her fingers unzipping my fly and tracing my growing erection through the fabric. And I realize she *isn't* acting as a voice of reason.

My boxer briefs get tugged down and then her fingers close around me. Hannah watches her hand stroke over the tip of my dick, and I watch her. Register the way her lips curve and her blue eyes heat with desire as my cock swells under her touch.

I've been battling an erection around her all day. It's a sweet relief to succumb to the lust, to let it build in the base of my spine.

My head hits the wall with a soft *thud*, an involuntary groan spilling out when her hand moves lower, gently squeezing my balls before she strokes my taint. My dick jumps, a powerful burst of need rushing through me as she grips me again, pumping and gripping and teasing.

I grunt, thrusting in her hand as my release rises. My gaze falls to her hand, the sight of her jerking me off just as arousing as the sensation.

My phone rings, sharp and insistent, from its spot on my suit-case. Without looking over, I know it's my driver.

Hannah stills, her grip tight but unmoving. "You have to go."

"Yeah." But I'm not leaving like this.

Her hold loosens until it falls away, color rising in her cheeks before she looks down at the ground and I lose sight of her expression. She's embarrassed, and I'm more amused than sympathetic. I like that she got caught up in this, same as me.

I set a hand on her waist and spin her around, so she's the one against the wall. Her inhale is surprised and fast, becoming labored breaths as I slide a hand under her dress and between her legs. She's fucking soaked.

"Take off your underwear," I tell her, pulling a condom out of my pocket and rolling it on. Earlier I felt stupid for stashing one there. Right now, I've never been more grateful for anything.

Hannah only hesitates for a second before reaching under her dress and tossing away what looks like a scrap of lace. I'm very glad I didn't know that's all she was wearing while we were at the baseball game. It probably would have shredded my self-control down to nothing.

"You might miss your plane," she warns.

"Worth it."

Hannah laughs. It quickly turns into a moan, as I lift one of her legs and enter her in one hard thrust, groaning as I feel her inner walls clench around me.

I fuck her with frantic strokes, and it has nothing to do with the ticking clock to get to the airport. It's that I can't get enough, that the split-second when I'm not inside of her feels too long. I'm addicted to the feel of her, to the ways she gasps and moans and begs, my name mingling between *yes* and *fuck* and *more*.

There's a primal element to the roughness too. Something I don't understand and can't control. I *need* to be deep in her. I want her to feel me for days. The next time a guy approaches her at a bar, I want Hannah to doubt whether he'll be able to make her feel this good.

She writhes against me, and I wish we were both naked. Wish this was happening in a bed, so I could explore her body with my hands and my tongue, then fuck her for a second time.

Distantly, I'm aware of my phone beginning to ring again. But we both ignore it.

Hannah is close to coming. I can feel the clutch of her cunt fluttering around me. As soon as I reach above the spot where I'm entering her and rub the nub of nerves there, they turn into powerful spasms.

It sets off my own release. I can't talk myself out of coming. I've been hovering on the precipice for too long, a slow burn that's been simmering ever since I woke up next to her and sparked the second she unbuckled my belt.

Bolts of heat race down my spine as my balls tighten and my cock twitches. She's tight and hot and wet, and I come inside of her until I can hardly see straight.

The pleasure fades slowly, the harsh sting of reality replacing it.

Reluctantly, I pull out of her and step away, tucking myself back into my pants and then walking into the kitchen to throw away the condom and wash my hands.

Hannah hasn't moved when I return to the entryway. She's slumped against the wall, her chest still heaving from the high.

My phone rings again, and this time I answer it. "Oliver Kensington."

"Hello, Mr. Kensington," a male voice says. "I'm at the address you requested a car to…"

"I'll be right out," I tell the driver.

"Very good, sir."

I hang up and slip my phone in my pocket. All my other belongings are neatly packed in my suitcase, ready to go.

I'm not, though.

I glance at Hannah, who's straightened. Aside from a few wrinkles, her dress looks the same. She gnaws on her bottom lip, playing with the hem.

"Well, thanks for coming."

I huff a laugh, and a small smile creeps across her face.

"That's not what I meant."

"I know."

Still, I don't move. I've never experienced this obsession with someone before. I just had her, and I'm already desperate to start all over again. It's an addiction, growing worse with each hit.

"Um, text me when you land, okay? So I know you made it."

I nod.

It's a sweet sentiment, and it also freaks me out. Because there's more than obligation in her question. There's a sincerity that's meaningful and noticeable. Mainly because it's been glaringly absent in my life up until now.

If I died in a plane crash, my dad's only concern would be how it would impact the company. Crew would view it as more than a corporate loss, but I know he would move on too. His daily life wouldn't look all that different without me in it.

It's a relief to know I'm not the only one caught up in this craziness between us.

But mostly?

I'm worried. I don't want to know that this matters to her. That *I* matter to her.

Maybe I don't. Maybe I'm just projecting my own feelings, getting caught up in the hot sex and how her family welcomed me.

And since this has already become messy and confusing, I don't resist the urge to kiss her one final time. It's gentle and sweet, the total opposite of how I was just touching her.

"Bye, Hannah."

"Bye, Oliver."

I don't look at her as I grab the handle of my suitcase and walk out the door, knowing this will probably be the last time we're in the same room.

From here until we're divorced, all of our communication should go through our attorneys. It will be simplest, fastest, and *safest*.

The driver is waiting on the sidewalk just past Hannah's front yard. I apologize for the delay and climb into the backseat. The air conditioning is on, countering the rays of warm sunshine coming through the windows.

"Did you have a good trip, sir?" the driver asks, as we pull away from the curb.

"Yes, thanks," I reply.

But good isn't the right adjective.

I don't know how to summarize my trip to California.

I don't know why I decided to come to begin with, and now I'm even more confused about this entire visit.

CHAPTER SEVENTEEN

HANNAH

The conference room is full when I wedge my way inside. Garner Sports Agency employs about two thousand people. A hundred of them work out of this office, and they're all present for our monthly update meeting.

An open seat is waiting for me at the center table. The first few meetings I ignored it, knowing the reserved chair was because of my last name, not my place in the company. But the times I haven't taken the seat, it's just sat empty. So I've accepted it, just like every other part of my role here.

Seconds after I've sat down, the chair beside me moves. I glance up into Tyler Sullivan's blinding smile. He's a few years older than me, a former athlete and forever sports buff who considers being an agent his calling. He's excellent at his job too, representing several of the agency's best-known athletes. Including Declan, which has always contributed an awkward element between us. Well that, and the fact he's asked me out a few times. Each time, I've told him I don't date coworkers.

"Hey, Hannah."

"Hi, Tyler."

"Happy Friday."

"Yeah, you too."

He leans back in his chair, spinning a pen around one finger. "Any exciting plans?"

"Not really." I have a meeting with my divorce attorney to discuss the upcoming process. And Rachel has been bugging me to join her book club, which meets tonight, but I doubt I will. I've been in a funk ever since Oliver left. In about thirty-six hours, he managed to leave a permanent mark on my life. My car, my house, my family, they're all associated with memories of him now.

"Well..." Tyler glances toward the front of the room, where my dad is talking to Albert Langley, one of the more experienced agents who's been with Garner Sports Agency since its inception. No one will dare interrupt them with a reminder that the meeting should have started two minutes ago. "I don't have much of a weekend planned, either. But I'm heading to New York on Monday for some meetings, and I'd love to have a second opinion at the discussions."

I nod, only half-listening.

"Dean suggested I ask you to go."

That gets my attention. "Da—Dean told you to ask me to go with you...to *New York*?"

Tyler nods. "You don't have to, obviously. It's short notice. I'm sure he'd agree it's your call." He chuckles.

And...there's the main reason I'll never date anyone I work with. Because there's always that undertone of nepotism, of the jokes how I'll never have to do this or will get a free pass out of that.

I wonder how Oliver handles it at Kensington Consolidated.

Maybe he doesn't have to, since he's a man.

"I'll go."

A wide smile splits Tyler's face. "Awesome. I'll have Marjorie send you all the flight details. I know she already booked the Carlyle."

"Great."

My father finally starts the meeting, and I open my notebook to take notes. But I'm not registering a word of what's being said, even as my hand moves across the paper.

When Oliver left, I was certain we'd never be in the same city again. And this trip might be for work, but the main reason I just agreed to go is…him.

I'm close to leaving for the day when my phone buzzes with a new email. It's to my personal account, not my work one.

And…it's from the Los Angeles School of Architecture.

I almost upend the watery remnants of my iced coffee as I grab my phone and open the email. I don't have to scan past the first line. The *Congratulations* is bold and big, the response to my application summarized in one word.

I stare at the email in shock.

I got in.

I'm stunned, both by the news and by my reaction. When I applied, I had no one to tell. No one I wanted or was ready to tell, rather. But the first thought that flickers through my head now is that I want to call Oliver.

The realization stills a little of the happiness bubbling inside of me. Instead of gaining a dream, it feels like I'm letting something slip away. And I'm not sure what to make of that. How to fix it. Especially since I'll be in New York starting Monday and am conflicted about whether to tell Oliver.

Practically speaking, there's no reason at all why I should contact him. Our attorneys are working out what mine has assured me will be the simplest divorce she's ever worked on.

We don't have children or joint property. We're not dividing assets or deciding alimony. We don't share *anything*.

Our divorce is a clean break.

But it feels a little jagged.

I turn off my phone and focus back on my computer screen, rushing through the remainder of the work I need to get finished.

Marjorie, one of the assistants, forwarded me the New York itinerary. I scan through it quickly—Monday morning flight, Wednesday afternoon return—and then shut off my computer.

The weather has been drab and dreary the past few days, a stark contrast to the past weekend, which felt like an early summer. Maybe that's what I should blame for my melancholy mood. I grab my umbrella and walk out into the hall, almost colliding with my father.

"Hannah! Perfect timing. Your mother just called, and she wanted me to see if you're free for dinner. Susan dropped off fresh tomatoes and cucumbers from her garden, so she's planning to make your favorite."

I'm not sure I'm in the mood for company but heading home to sulk doesn't sound all that appealing either. "Yeah, sure."

"Wonderful. Tell your mom I'll be home soon. I just need to check in with Albert on one quick thing."

"Okay," I agree, knowing one quick thing will probably turn into a *half an hour*.

Rosie calls, right as I'm pulling out of the building's private garage.

"Hey," I greet, turning left instead of my usual right as I head in the direction of my parents' house.

"*Hey?* The last we talked, you told me you married Oliver Kensington, and when you finally answer, all I get is *Hey?*"

I laugh. We've been playing phone tag this week, and part of me was relieved, since I haven't felt like talking to anyone. But Rosie's familiar voice pulls me out of my own head a little, which is welcome. "I'm sorry. Work has been crazy."

Work *has* been busy, but not in comparison to my personal life. To Oliver coming here and staying with me and ensuring that anytime I think about sex, he's the one thrusting into me. None of that is information I want to share with my best friend, and that's highly concerning.

Rosie knows all the details of my past relationships. But Oliver is different. It feels too personal to share, which I've never thought before. Especially the details I've been obsessing over: how he pulled a blanket over me and his promise before he came inside of me. *"The only way I'll ever see you getting fucked is if* I'm *the one fucking you, Hannah."*

I really wish I could forget those words. Wish I'd never made the stupid joke about him watching to begin with.

"So you haven't talked to your *husband*?"

I shake my head, then remember she can't see me. "No. We both have attorneys. They're handling the divorce."

"Have you changed your mind about asking him for money?"

I roll my eyes as I take a turn. "No."

"I'm not saying demand *half*. You could just request like…ten million?"

"Seriously, Rosie?"

"What? He can afford it! And then you can buy a penthouse in Lakeview and visit me all the time. Not to mention, quit working for your dad."

"I got into architecture school," I blurt.

Rosie shrieks. "Shut up! Are you serious?"

"Yep."

"I can't believe you applied. You talked yourself in and out of it for weeks senior year."

"It was an…impulsive decision." I made a few of those that night, as it turns out.

"Where did you apply?"

"Just Los Angeles School of Design."

"Nowhere in Chicago?"

"You could always move back here," I suggest.

Rosie makes a *pffttt* sound. "I like having seasons. And I'm not surprised you didn't apply to anywhere here, but why didn't you apply to any schools in New York? You wanted to live there for a while."

I did. I saw New York as a needed change, a way to experience something new and different. And it *was* new and different. But I also got swept up in the status and the toxicity of that city. It's been nearly two years since I visited. I retreated into the known, among family and familiarity.

"No. New York isn't for me."

I pull into my parents' driveway for the first time since I came here with Oliver. I'm prepared for the stab of sentimentality that's been a constant companion this past week.

"I'm at my parents' for dinner. I'll call you this weekend so we can catch up more, okay?"

"Okay. Say hi to Dean and Cynthia for me."

"I will. Bye, Rosie."

"Bye!"

We hang up and I climb out of the car. Despite the cooler temperatures, the greenery around my childhood home is flourishing thanks to the rain. The lemon tree to the left of the front path is starting to flower, the very beginnings of citrus appearing on the branches.

The front door is unlocked, so I walk right inside, heading toward the kitchen.

My mom is standing at the counter, chopping tomatoes. "Hi, sweetheart."

"Hey, Mom." I walk over and kiss her cheek, stealing a slice of red fruit off the cutting board. "Dad said he'll be home soon."

"I'm sure he believed that when he said it. Wine?"

"Sure, thanks."

My mom pulls a bottle of white out of the fridge and pours me a glass.

"Eddie or Rachel coming over?"

"No, Eddie and April are at her parents' for dinner and Rachel has her book club tonight."

"Oh, that's right."

"She was at a planning session for this summer's trip when I called her earlier."

"Is it still between China or Argentina?"

"I think Greece is in the mix now."

"Wow." I swirl the wine in my glass, then take a sip. It's dry, tasting subtly of floral and citrus. "Wine is good."

"Isn't it? Susan brought it over with the vegetables. It's from a vineyard in Napa."

I nod, then take another sip. "I'm going to New York on Monday. With an agent from the office."

"Really? That's nice." My mom continues chopping, periodically tossing tomatoes into a mixing bowl. I wait. "Do you think you'll see Oliver?"

I steal another bite from the bowl. "Doubt it. He's very busy."

"He wasn't too busy to fly across the country."

"You *made* me ask him, Mom. He felt obligated."

She shakes her head, a small smile appearing. "In my experience, men do nothing they don't want to do. He came here for *you*, Hannah."

"Can I help chop?"

She judges the topic change with another head shake but goes and grabs a second cutting board and knife. She slides both toward me, along with two cucumbers.

This dish has been a favorite of mine since I was a kid. It's relatively simple, just tomatoes, cucumbers, and roasted chicken seasoned with olive oil, thyme, salt, pepper, and vinegar, then topped with olives and feta. But no matter how many times I try to make it myself, it never tastes the same as when I eat it here beneath the trellis.

By the time my father gets home, we've chopped everything, and the chicken is in the oven. He kisses my mom and then grabs a beer out of the fridge, a domestic display I used to always cringe at.

Partly because they're my parents, but also because the placid predictability struck me as boring. It's the complete opposite of the uncertainty of a first kiss. That moment of anticipation when you're not sure what it will be like. Years of kissing the same person sounded dull and rote. But there's a comfort in it too, I'm noticing, as my mom hip checks my dad out of the way so she can finish seasoning the vegetables.

"Up for a game?" he asks, turning toward me.

"Always," I reply, following him out of the French doors and into the backyard.

Croquet is set up and ready, just like usual.

"Tyler said you decided to go with him," my dad says as he lines up his first hit.

"He asked me to go, and there was no reason I couldn't," I

reply, watching his ball sail through the first two wickets. Surprisingly, he misses the third.

"Tyler has got quite the line-up of prospective clients. Should be a good experience."

"Yeah. He mentioned you recommended me."

My ball goes through the first wicket but then bounces off one side of the second, stalling in place.

My dad doesn't take his turn. He studies me. "This trip is optional, Hannah. If Tyler indicated otherwise—"

"He didn't. It's fine. I'll go."

I'm looking forward to it. And dreading it. Just one of many things I have complicated feelings toward at the moment.

"Have you talked to Oliver recently?"

"Dad," I warn.

"What, I can't ask about my son-in-law?"

My grip tightens around the handle of the mallet. "*Ex*-son-in-law."

"I've seen enough couples get divorced to know it doesn't happen quite that fast, sweetheart."

"Just because it isn't official doesn't mean it's not happening."

"The answer to an impulsive decision isn't another one, Hannah. We have a New York office."

I look away from the course, at the plantings filling the flowerbeds instead. "I thought you'd hate him. Mom insisted I ask him. I never thought he'd come, and I was certain you'd agree divorce was best."

"Whether you stay married is entirely your decision, Hannah. Oliver wasn't who I was expecting. And once I found out he was a Kensington…well, Arthur Kensington has a reputation in the business world. He's ruthless. I wasn't sure how that would transfer to his son."

"You like him," I surmise. It comes out sounding like an accusation.

My father nods. "Yeah. I do. But it doesn't matter how I feel about him, Hannah. It matters how *you* do."

And then he turns back to the game, leaving me to contemplate *that*.

CHAPTER EIGHTEEN

OLIVER

There's a knock on my door, right as I'm getting ready to leave. I sigh and call out "Come in," expecting to see Scott with an update or Alicia with a question.

Instead, Scarlett walks in.

I straighten automatically, forgetting about the papers I was slipping in my briefcase to bring home for the weekend. My goal is to not come into the office until Monday, which will be three weekends in a row. A record for me.

"Hey," she greets, strolling into my office with all the confidence in the world.

"Hi." I watch as she walks over to the bookcase, running a finger over the titles the same way she did the last time she visited.

"Do you read?" I ask.

"I used to," Scarlett answers, still stroking the spines. "Reading by the pool at my parents' place in the Hamptons used to be my favorite way to spend the summer. Now, if I get a minute to myself, I just want to nap." Her hand falls to her stomach.

Maybe it's because I know about the pregnancy, but from the side it looks like a slight curve is beginning to appear.

"Parenting sounds like a blast."

Scarlett smiles, turning toward my desk. "Quinn *loves* kids."

"Subtle, Scarlett."

"I didn't know if I wanted kids, either. Then Lili was born, and I couldn't imagine my life without her in it."

"Just because you and Crew turned an arrangement into a fairytale, doesn't mean that's how Quinn and I will turn out. If we turn into anything. There's still a lot I have to figure out."

"Speaking of…how goes the divorce?"

I tense. Barely, but Scarlett's sharp eyes don't miss much. "Fine."

Or it *would* be going fine if I'd done anything about it. Instead, I've dragged my feet on having Jeremy file the petition for divorce.

I don't want to be married to Hannah. But I don't *not* want to be married to her, either.

I've become accustomed to the idea, I guess. Not marriage in general. But being attached to her, specifically? I don't hate it.

This week I've been back in New York, I've battled the urge to call her dozens of times. I've started eating scrambled eggs in the morning, instead of oatmeal. The second I get home I change out of my suit. And every morning I've woken up with a painful erection that's required me to use my hand and my imagination.

"She's not causing problems?"

I shake my head. "No. Ha—" Her name gets caught in my throat. "Hannah's cooperating."

Scarlett nods once, quick and direct. "Good."

There's another knock on my door. Instead of telling them to enter, I walk over and open it. People love to gossip. And while plenty probably saw Scarlett walk here, I'm not interested in fanning the flames.

"Hey." Crew's hand is still raised when I open the door, his expression surprised by my sudden appearance.

He holds up a packet of papers. "Final contract on NetLife came in. It got sent to me…by accident?"

"Or Dad told them to send it to you."

Crew's brow crinkles. "Have you talked to him this week?"

"No. Not since he got back from Miami."

Our usual Monday meeting was canceled, which was probably for the best. I was exhausted and confused, tangled up over the trip to Los Angeles.

I open the door wider. "Want to come in?"

"Yeah. Sure."

Crew walks past me into my office. "Red?"

Scarlett turns from the window, where she was standing and staring at the skyline.

She smiles, and it's one meant only for Crew as he walks over and kisses her soundly on the mouth. Tangible emotions swarm the air around them: love and happiness and a lightness that's hard to explain. It's nauseating to be around. And also kind of nice.

"What are you doing here?" Crew asks.

"I finished early, so I came to surprise you. I stopped to say hi to Oliver."

Crew glances between me and Scarlett. He seems surprised—happy—to find me and his wife together, and it feeds the feeling of guilt in my stomach. Not only am I lying to Crew about Hannah, I also dragged Scarlett, Asher, and Jeremy into it. Not to mention, I'm blackmailing Asher with a secret Crew should know. Brother of the Year, I am not.

His gaze lands on my half-packed briefcase. "You were *leaving*?"

"It's after five. Technically, that's when the workday ends."

"I know that. I just didn't think *you* did."

I roll my eyes as I approach my desk, finish shoving papers in my briefcase and then snapping it shut. "I have a date tonight. Trying to get home early so I have time to shower and change."

"With Quinn?" Scarlett asks. Her voice is high and excited. I thought her interest in my marriage was connected to her dislike of Hannah, but her reaction suggests a deeper interest in my love life.

I nod. "We're going out with Garrett and Sienna."

"Are you bringing her to their wedding next weekend?"

"I'm not sure. We'll see how tonight goes."

Truthfully, I don't want to, no matter how tonight goes. And it has nothing to do with Quinn. She was charming and sweet when I finally called her about getting dinner. Graceful, when I mentioned Garrett and Sienna would be joining us.

But Garrett and Sienna's wedding will be packed with New York's elite. If I show up with Quinn, there will be engagement rumors swirling by midnight. That's a pressure I don't need or want.

I have to decide how badly I want it. What I'm willing to sacrifice. I don't want to be forced into a marriage I'm not sure I want, just to gain something I'm entitled to. I was born expected to be the next CEO of Kensington Consolidated, the way crowns pass through monarchies.

It would be one thing if I wasn't capable of handling the pressure. If I was lazy or incompetent. Instead, I got knocked down the hierarchy by Scarlett's preference for my brother and Candace's unhappiness in her marriage. And while I certainly have culpability in one instance, it shouldn't have anything to do with my job.

I grab the briefcase off my desk and the umbrella from the corner of my office. It was spitting rain this morning, but the skies have since cleared.

"Don't forget the rest of your homework," Crew teases, holding the NetLife papers out to me. "If your date gets boring."

I take them. "My dates don't get bored."

Scarlett laughs, then grabs Crew's hand and pulls him toward the door. "Have fun tonight, Oliver!"

"Yeah, thanks," I reply.

I make sure I have everything, wish Alicia a happy weekend, and then head toward the elevators.

Traffic is worse than usual, probably because I'm leaving at a reasonable hour. It takes over thirty minutes before I'm back at my building.

After showering and shaving, I get dressed in slacks and an olive-green sweater instead of a suit. Casual for me.

I've never paid much attention to fashion, beyond making sure my suits are clean and tailored. Maybe it's the lack of a mother or a serious girlfriend in my life.

Impulsively, I snap a photo of myself in the mirror and send it to Scarlett. Not only is she my sister, technically, but she's also a world-famous designer.

When she likes the photo a few minutes later, I feel a little better about my choice.

Pierre is in his usual position beside the door when I step out of the elevator. "Have a good night, Mr. Kensington."

"You too," I reply, before stepping aside.

The nearest Metro stop is only a block away. I walk along the sidewalk at a more leisurely pace than usual, enjoying the hint of warmth in the air that signals spring's approach.

Really, I should be beaming ear to ear. I didn't have to deal with my father at all this week. Quinn eagerly accepted the invitation for tonight, suggesting she's interested in the union our fathers are already viewing as a sure thing. My relationship with Crew is in a better place than it's been in a while.

But there's still a restlessness and an uncertainty that I can't seem to shake.

I reach the stop and descend underground. Despite cleaning attempts, the unpleasant odors of urine and garbage swirl in the cooler air as I swipe my card and push through the turnstile.

After only a couple of minutes of waiting on the platform, a southbound train arrives. I step on board, choosing to stand and grab a pole instead of taking one of the open seats. Other passengers step on and off, all of them rushing and most in work attire.

I smile, remembering Hannah's shock when I told her I take public transit.

I'm tempted to snap a photo and send it to her as proof. But I don't, because the last message I sent her was when I landed at JFK early Monday morning. My flight was delayed, so I didn't get in until after three. She replied right away, even though it was past midnight for her too. Like she'd been waiting for the message.

If she was, I don't want to know that. I want to pretend last weekend meant nothing to her, the same way I've spent all week trying to convince myself it meant nothing to me.

The walk from the Midtown stop to the restaurant is another short one. Garrett booked one of the city's most exclusive restaurants, a seafood spot that usually has a waiting list months long.

Quinn is waiting outside. She spots me and spins, her navy dress picking up in the breeze.

"Oliver! Hi!" Her excitement sounds genuine, reflected in her animated expression as she smiles at me.

And I will myself to feel something. Feel *anything*, aside from a detached friendliness. My life would be a lot easier if I developed feelings for Quinn.

But my thoughts are stubbornly centered on blonde hair and blue eyes.

"You look beautiful," I tell Quinn. Honestly, because she does. But my appreciation is disconnected, the way you look at a rare artifact or a famous painting. You know there's relevance attached to it, but none of it is yours. It was already there, just lingering as something you know but didn't discover.

"Thanks. You look nice too." Quinn's answering smile is shy and sweet as we step inside the restaurant.

Wave murals cover the walls, setting the oceanic theme. I give Garrett's name to the maître de, and we're led to a table toward the center of the room where Garrett and Sienna are already seated.

Garrett stands and grins widely when he sees me, giving me a hug and slapping me on the back. I hug Sienna as well, but it's a much briefer one. After I've introduced Quinn, we all settle at the table. A waiter immediately appears, taking drink orders. Garrett orders a bottle of wine for the table, along with caviar, oysters, and tuna tartare. My stomach growls, but not because any of it sounds good. I'd kill for a burger and fries right now.

Sienna and Quinn exchange small talk while Garrett and I mainly discuss business. He just secured a massive government contract, which he's understandably thrilled about. He congratulates me on Thompson & Thompson, now that it's become public.

And then, unfortunately, Vegas comes up. Quinn is the one who mentions it, surprisingly. One of her former clients in London had a wild night there recently, and it was leaked to the press. And Sienna is the one who reminds her that Garrett and I were just there for his bachelor party.

"You guys had an amazing time, didn't you?" she asks. She's focused on me, not Garrett.

And I'm thrust into a dynamic I don't want to navigate, knowing way too many personal details about their relationship.

"We sure did." I have to force the affable tone in my voice.

I'm judging Sienna, and maybe that makes me a hypocrite. But my father and Candace were a train wreck disguised as a marriage long before anything happened between me and her. I know for a fact my dad had affairs. But as far as I know, Garrett was faithful to Sienna until she cheated first. So yeah, I resent her for not valuing that. And I can't understand Garrett's perspective either. Why he would forgive her. Stay with her.

This dinner was probably a mistake.

I'm relieved when my phone buzzes in my pocket. I shift in my seat, so I can pull it out. Garrett will understand work interrupting. Quinn will have to understand, if there's going to be any future between us. And I simply don't care what Sienna thinks.

But it's not work. *Hannah* is flashing across the screen.

I stand suddenly, almost toppling the table. I mumble a hasty "I'll be right back," before rushing out of the restaurant.

Worry ripples through me in debilitating waves as I step out onto the sidewalk. "Hello?" I answer.

"Hey." Surprisingly, there's no distraught note in her voice. I was expecting the worst about her calling me unexpectedly. "I didn't wake you up, did I?" More than normal, her voice sounds light. Happy. Teasing.

I turn and look at the glass window. I can see through the entire restaurant, straight back to the table where Garrett, Quinn, and Sienna are sitting. Sienna is saying something, gesticulating with her arms, and Quinn is nodding along. Garrett is talking to a waiter. "You didn't wake me up."

There's a pause. "Well…I got in."

"Got in?" I echo, turning back toward the street.

"To architecture school. I *got in*. They accepted me!"

I was so sure the only reason Hannah would be calling was with bad news. It didn't even occur to me she might be reaching out to me about *good* news. To celebrate. It takes me a second to recalibrate and respond. "Wow. I—wow. That's amazing, Hannah." I inject as much enthusiasm into my voice as I can muster, but she sees right through it.

"What's wrong?"

"Nothing, Han." I freeze as soon as the endearment slips out, then hurry to fill the silence that follows. "I'm sorry. I just…long day at work."

I glance inside again.

I'm happy for Hannah. But I also resent her for the way she's invaded my thoughts and made me rethink my future while she's forging ahead with hers like we never got married. Which isn't fair.

"I'm sorry," she says. "I shouldn't have bothered you."

Fuck. Now I feel even worse. I rub my forehead. "Don't apologize. I'm glad you called. I—"

"Oliver?"

I spin around to see Quinn standing on the sidewalk, rubbing her hands on her bare arms to ward off the evening chill.

"Arlo Hathaway is at our table. Garrett thought you might want to talk to him before he leaves?"

I nod. "Thanks. I'll be right there."

"Okay," Quinn says, then heads back inside.

Complete and total silence is all I can hear.

I clear my throat. "Hannah…" I'm not sure what else to say.

I wasn't expecting her to call. I thought that everything going forward would run through our attorneys, the way she suggested. And I never would have guessed she'd call while I was out on a date with another woman, which is a rare occurrence.

"You shouldn't have answered, Oliver."

Before I have a chance to respond, she hangs up.

I stand there, phone against my ear, staring at the lights of the passing traffic.

I'm on autopilot for the rest of the evening, witnessing but not really participating.

I'm not sure anyone notices. Garrett grows more gregarious with each glass of wine he consumes, and Sienna is always outgoing. They carry most of the conversation, peppering Quinn with questions about her life in London and her plans in New York, with several suggestive glances aimed my way.

I pick at the halibut that was served with braised leeks and picked rhubarb, washing each bite down with wine.

Rather than buoy my mood, the alcohol sinks it further.

I think of a thousand things I wish I had said when Hannah called. I'm not even sure if I congratulated her. I definitely didn't ask if she told her father or the rest of her family. If she didn't, is she celebrating alone?

A cold coil of dread appears in my stomach and spreads, imagining her and some other guy. I don't even have to imagine it —I witnessed it. And I lived it. I've been the guy in the bar, faced with the blonde mystery that is Hannah Garner. She's hard to resist, and most guys wouldn't bother trying.

I shove my plate away with a few bites of fish left, my appetite totally gone.

"Do you know where the restroom is?" I ask Garrett.

"Down in the basement," he tells me. "Head to the back and then take the stairs."

"Thanks." I glance at Quinn. "I'll be right back."

She nods and smiles. Her composure hasn't faltered all night, not even when I spent long enough standing on the sidewalk that I missed Arlo Hathaway at our table. We had a brief conversation as he was leaving, but not the prime networking that might have resulted inside. And I don't even care.

Garrett's instructions are accurate. The men's room is the first door past the kitchens.

But I don't walk inside. I lean against the wall just past the entrance and close my eyes, trying to calm my thoughts and regain some equilibrium. Tonight was supposed to be about Quinn. About getting to know her and determining how we might work as a couple.

But my head is full of Hannah. And I wish I could blame it all on her call, but she was there long before my phone rang. I thought that the more time that passed since seeing her, talking to her, *fucking* her, the easier it would be. Instead, it's an ache that's grown in intensity, like ignoring it has only made it worse.

I pull my phone out of my pocket and tap her name, staring up at the fluorescent lights as I listen to it ring.

And ring.

And ring.

"Hi, you've reached Hannah Garner. I'm not available..."

With a muttered curse, I end the call. Who the hell knows what I would leave in a voicemail. And there's no one I can ask for advice on how to navigate this situation. Garrett thinks I'm dating Quinn. Crew has no idea I've ever met Hannah. Scarlett is focused on helping me get a divorce. Beyond that, the list of people I communicate with on a regular basis are mostly business associates. They could either not care less about my personal life or would sell me out to the tabloids.

After a few frustrated exhales, I head back upstairs. Thankfully, dinner is wrapping up. Garrett insists on splitting the bill, and then Sienna and Quinn grab their jackets from the coat check.

I breathe deeply once we're outside.

It's one flash, at first. Then two, four, *ten*.

Garrett claps a hand on my back, then leans closer. "Sorry about this, man. Sienna wants to drum up some interest before the wedding. Come on, we'll drop you guys off."

I immediately understand, and it plummets my already low opinion of Sienna. She's the daughter of a newscaster and a socialite, who's worked as a wedding planner since graduating college. Not irrelevant, but nothing paparazzi would show up for. Me, on the other hand? I rarely go out, and I never advertise when I do.

Questions are thrown our way, asking Quinn her name. Wondering whether we're dating. Shouting if I'm single.

I grit my teeth and place a hand on Quinn's lower back, guiding her through the chaos and into the car.

I'm expecting some disbelief or uncertainty once we're inside the vehicle, the tinted windows blocking the flashing bulbs. Quinn looks just as composed as she has the entire evening. And it should be reassuring. A sign of someone well-suited to take on the pressures of being a Kensington. But it bothers me that I can't see past her mask. That I can't tell whether anything is genuine or feigned. If she's an excellent actress or just less cynical than I am.

There are still spots flashing in my eyes as the car pulls away from the curb.

"This is what New York is like?" Quinn asks, glancing between the three of us.

Sienna laughs.

"Sometimes," I say.

But all I can think is, *I hope Hannah doesn't see those.*

And that freaks me out more than anything else that's taken place tonight. That's nothing I should be concerned with and all I seem to care about.

CHAPTER NINETEEN

HANNAH

"What do you think, Hannah?" Tyler asks.

I glance away from the white lines and numbers painted on the grass. "Sounds great," I reply, with no idea what I'm agreeing to.

I've taken this whole tour on autopilot, letting Tyler ask questions and drive the conversation. I've regretted coming at all, knowing it was to please my father and some attempt to prove I changed from the last time I was here. And mostly, because of Oliver. Avoiding a difficult conversation with my dad about architecture school and being anywhere near my husband are terrible reasons to be here, though. It will only blindside my dad more, and after my disastrous call with Oliver, I shouldn't even be chancing running into him on the street.

Tyler is all business as we return to the side entrance of the stadium. "Thanks for meeting with us, David."

"Of course. It was a pleasure."

Tyler shakes hands with David Prescott, the general manager of the New York Eagles. So do I. David is more professional than Robert Damon, offering me a polite nod and nothing else.

Finally, we're leaving. The fake smile I've worn all day drops as soon as we're inside the car. I kick off my heels and reach down to rub my feet as the car rolls through the massive, empty parking lot. The stadium was built to accommodate seventy-thousand people and is surrounded by asphalt. It takes the driver twenty minutes to get on the highway and head back toward Manhattan.

"Want to grab dinner?" Tyler asks me, shutting his laptop and stowing it away as the skyline of skyscrapers comes into view.

I chew on the inside of my cheek. I can't tell if it's a coworker request or if it could be construed as a date. And either way, I'm too drained and distracted for dinner to sound appealing. I'd rather order takeout and lounge around in my pajamas. But I don't want to offend Tyler, either.

"I'm not feeling great. I think I'm just going to turn in early."

He nods, thankfully not looking upset. "It's been a long day. Do you want me to pick you up some food?"

"No, thanks. I'll order something."

Tyler nods, then focuses on his phone for the rest of the drive. I stare out at the familiar sights of New York City.

The landscape is familiar, but it also looks different.

It's not just a city. It's *Oliver's* city.

This is where he works. Lives. Dates. And while that shouldn't make any difference to me, it's a thought I can't shake as we sit in traffic.

I don't know exactly where Kensington Consolidated has its offices—no doubt some prime, downtown location—but I imagine Oliver making a similar drive to this one when he heads to and from work each day, past soaring skyscrapers and food trucks and yellow cabs.

Tyler and I split up once we arrive back at the lobby of the

Carlyle. He goes up to the hotel's front desk to request a car for later. I head toward the elevators, eager to get up to my room.

Even though we already said our goodbyes, Tyler waves before the doors close. He seems genuinely unbothered by me not wanting to spend extra time with him, and it's a relief.

I'll get through the next couple of days of meetings, and then I'll be back in LA. Maybe I'll host both of my parents for dinner this weekend, and I can tell them about architecture school then. It's not like it will be a massive surprise—I hope. They know it's an interest of mine, or *was*.

And then I remember how ecstatic my dad was on my first day as an official employee, and my stomach twists into an uncomfortable knot.

As soon as I'm inside my room, I strip out of the dress and blazer I've been wearing all day. We only stopped here for a few minutes between the airport and leaving for the first meeting, and it's a relief to finally be free of the constricting clothes. It feels even more amazing to step under a stream of warm water. New York is at least fifteen degrees cooler than LA was this morning, which I was expecting but didn't really dress for.

My phone rings right as I step out of the shower. Most likely my father, calling to check in.

I rush into the bedroom with dripping hair and a haphazardly wrapped towel, sending droplets of water flying everywhere. My phone is charging on the bedside table. I stub my toe as I skid to a stop, swearing as the stab of pain makes my knee buckle. I hop one-legged, checking my foot for permanent damage, as I answer the phone.

"Hello?" I answer, breathless.

"Hannah?" Icy heat works its way down my spine as I experience a flood of dread and excitement. My toe no longer throbs. I say nothing, cursing myself for not checking who was calling before I answered.

I didn't think he'd call me again. Didn't think I'd be in this situation.

"Hannah?" Oliver repeats.

I clear my throat and grip the towel tighter. "Hi, Oliver."

"Is this an okay time?" he asks hesitantly.

I'm panting like I've run a marathon. And the last time we spoke, I hung up on him. So I understand his apprehension. "Yes."

An opportunity to end this conversation before it's begun, and that's all I say: *Yes*. The surprise and panic are ebbing away, replaced by more pleasant sensations. Like…happiness. Relief.

He called, and I didn't think he would. Thought calling me back after I hung up was the end of our communication.

"The petition was filed today."

"I know."

The reminder dampens my mood a little, but not by much. Because that's not something he needed to call me about.

My attorney texted me this morning. The message from her delivered as soon as I landed in New York, which wasn't the best start to this trip. I was expecting it. It was a bit of a mystery why he hadn't filed already.

Even though it's silent on his end, I can practically hear his thoughts turning, wondering what to say next.

"Did you tell your dad about school?" he asks.

Rivulets of water continue to stream down my arms and legs, leaving tiny puddles on the floor. "We don't need to do this," I whisper.

"Do what?"

"I'm sorry I called you on Friday, okay? I shouldn't have. It was…unprofessional."

"Unprofessional? What are we *working on* together, Hannah?"

"Our divorce."

Oliver snorts.

I glance at the clock, the longer hand ticking the minutes away. "I don't want to argue. It's been a long day. My attorney is keeping me updated, so you don't need to. This will be over…soon."

That last sentence is harder to say than I thought. Not because I'm suddenly enamored by the institution of marriage or think marrying a stranger in Vegas is a recommended experience. But I associate both with Oliver now, and he's the component I've formed some attachment to. I've never put on an act with him, the way I do with most people. Especially men. I wanted to tell him about my acceptance before Rosie, who I've known for over a decade.

It feels like a loss to let that go. But I have to. He filed. He was possibly out on a date. There's nothing to hold on to.

Oliver says nothing. The silence is ominous and uncomfortable, stretching a shorter distance than he knows. I wonder if he's still at work or whether he's at home. Work, I'm guessing.

I tighten my towel like armor. "Well, I should go order dinner, so…"

"Dinner? It's only three thirty there."

A phone begins ringing in the background.

He's at the office. But he doesn't ask me to wait. Doesn't even acknowledge the sound as it continues blaring four more times before falling silent. He just waits for me to respond.

So I rule out lying, saying I skipped lunch and am eating early. And it's not just because I somehow sense he'll know it's a fib. It's because it was a secret hope of this trip, seeing him. "I, uh, I'm in New York," I admit.

"You're in New York." Oliver's voice is flat, and I wish I

could see his face. Based on his tone alone, I have no clue what he's thinking. It's not indifference; it's controlled. The way I imagine him lording over deals worth hundreds of millions of dollars. He exposes what he wants to be seen, nothing more, nothing less.

"It's a work trip."

Silence.

"An agent I've worked with before asked me to come with him, so I…did." I clear my throat. "Anyway, um—"

"Were you going to tell me?"

Honesty kicks in again. "Maybe. When I called Friday, I was… Maybe."

More silence. Awkwardness expands in my chest, heavy and uncomfortable, as I try to figure out how to navigate out of this mess.

"I shouldn't have gone out with her," he says, quietly.

My chest contracts in response to the confirmation but my voice manages to remain casual. "You don't have to explain—"

"I wanted a distraction, and it didn't work." Oliver exhales. "There's not going to be a second date. I didn't—I *haven't* been dating."

I'm not sure how to respond. He doesn't need my permission, and he doesn't owe me any explanation.

"Are you free for dinner?"

The offer is unexpected. *So* unexpected, I'm too shocked to speak. Barely able to think. "You don't have to…"

"I know I don't have to, Hannah. It was a yes or no question."

I want to say *yes*, which probably means I should say *no*.

"I'm free."

I really wish I could see his face now. There's no response right away. Then, "I'll pick you up at seven?"

Less than half an hour to get ready. That shouldn't matter. I shouldn't care about my appearance. But I'm already plotting in my head. Running through the clothes I brought.

"Sure." I strive for a casual tone. "I'm staying at the Carlyle. I'll meet you in the lobby."

"Okay. See you soon."

"See you soon," I repeat.

I hang up, drop my phone on the bed, and then turn into a flurry of activity. I upend my entire suitcase on the mattress, sorting through blouses and blazers and sleep sets. I packed *one pair* of jeans, and I'm tempted to wear them. But I have no idea what Oliver has in mind for dinner. Based on what he wore for dinner with my family, I should dress up. I pull on the navy dress I was planning to wear tomorrow and then rush into the bathroom. I blow dry my hair while also attempting to apply mascara, glancing anxiously at the clock the whole time.

At least the tight timeframe means I have less time to worry about what dinner will be like. I highly doubt Oliver is inviting me out to discuss divorce proceedings.

There's nothing *to* discuss. Everything is being handled by the court process and our attorneys.

This is...something different. And that's scary. Because I knew there was attraction between us, but I thought that's *all* that was there, besides our legal bindings. Oliver didn't need to ask me to dinner. He's a billionaire, he's attractive, and he can be charming when he wants to be. He's amazing in bed.

He has options. I'm not a last resort.

And he's not mine, either. I could have gone out with Tyler. Or with other acquaintances from past trips to the city.

This is intentional.

Real.

I step into the lobby with only one minute to spare, hoping Oliver is running late. But he's facing the wall just to the left of the elevators, studying the abstract piece of art hanging on the wall.

He's in a suit, one that's barely wrinkled even though I'm assuming it's the one he's been wearing all day. His hands are shoved in his pockets and his hair is slightly ruffled, like he ran a hand through it recently.

There's an unwelcome flip in my stomach as soon as I see him. A collision of nerves and eagerness, witnessing Oliver waiting for me. Everyone—the hotel staff and the other guests walking in and out of the building—are glancing at him. I'm not sure if it's because they recognize him or because he has that aura of power and importance.

My heels announce my approach, tapping against the buffed marble of the lobby floor.

Oliver glances my way, ignoring the other attention aimed in his direction. He smiles when he sees me, and the genuine reaction wreaks havoc on my heart.

There's nothing cursory or forced in his expression. It almost looks like he relaxes as I approach. Like he was worried I wouldn't show or wouldn't be smiling back. And there's a twinge in my chest, realizing he wouldn't be looking at me at all if my dad hadn't sent me to Las Vegas. If I hadn't gone down to that hotel bar exactly when I did. It makes me wonder whether destiny or fate actually exist, and if they can supersede consequences. How believing in something larger than yourself can make you feel bigger, instead of smaller.

"Hi." His eyes flick down, over the trench coat I'm wearing, my bare legs, and heels.

I'll be cold and the balls of my feet already ache. But I want to look good for him.

"Hi," I echo, unsure how else to greet him. Most of the familiarity from his trip to LA has vanished, so hugging or kissing him feels far too forward.

Oliver holds out a hand. And in the simplest of gestures, I take it. Our fingers weave together naturally, like a tapestry that's meant to be.

"Ready?" he asks.

I nod, following him across the lobby. Oliver drops my hand when we reach the revolving door, but only to guide me inside one of the glass sections. Rather than take his own, he crowds in behind me. For a few seconds, we're cordoned in our own tiny world, his smell and presence overwhelming. And then we're spit out on the street, the city coming alive despite the dipping sun signaling the end of a day.

He takes my hand again once we're on the street, and I hate how much that small act matters to me. Especially since it's a logical move, considering how crowded the streets are. There's an energy to New York that simply doesn't exist in other cities. A constant pulse that fills the city like a live presence.

Oliver says nothing about me not telling him I was here. About our last conversation, our marriage, or our divorce.

We walk down the street together, holding hands, looking like a normal, uncomplicated couple to any outside observer.

"You up for taking the Metro?" he asks me after we've walked a block.

I nod, despite the fact I've never ridden New York's subway system before and have never had any interest in doing so.

After another block, we descend stairs into a brightly lit, bustling station. The breezy night air turns stagnant and stale. Oliver buys a card at one of the kiosks, *laughs* at me when I try to pay for it, and then demonstrates how to swipe through the turn-stile in order to reach the tracks.

Every move is practiced and efficient, displaying the calm

confidence I'm used to witnessing from Oliver. He wasn't lying about taking public transit before, obviously. Oliver navigates the crowds and commotion with ease, waiting for one train to pass and then guiding me into the next one once the doors open.

The car we step into is already packed with people. All the plastic seats are taken, the nearest one by an elderly woman holding a paper bag filled with groceries.

I move quickly through the mass of bored and urgent faces, grabbing onto the nearest metal pole as soon as I reach it. Still, I'm unprepared for the sudden lurch once the doors close. I stumble back a step as the subway starts to move, colliding with a warm, muscular body. Expensive cologne replaces the scent of mustiness and sweat.

Oliver's arm snakes around my waist to steady me, absorbing every stagger and stumble as the train races along the underground tracks. I wobble when the brakes unexpectedly engage, leaning more solidly against Oliver as the doors open at the next stop.

His chuckle is low and amused as bodies shift around us, so close it sends a shiver down my spine. "You should have worn your flip-flops."

My face flames. I don't like that he's seen me so relaxed. That he knows me well enough to say that. It's a reminder of how much else he knows. How much else he's seen. "They didn't go with my dress."

"Then you should have worn jeans."

"I figured you'd be wearing a suit."

I tug at the sleeve of his jacket to prove a point, but since his hand is splayed across my stomach, I end up brushing his skin with more of a caress than an emphasis. A breath catches in my throat when his hold on me tightens.

"And I was right," I add.

The doors shut and we begin moving again.

"It's a busy week at work," he says.

I'm certain a busy week at work is a normal week for Oliver, but I don't say that. How many hours he spends at the office is none of my business. And if he really does have even more than usual going on, I can't believe he's taking the time to bring me wherever we're going.

After two more stops, Oliver drops his hand. My abdomen feels bereft without the weight and warmth of it. "This is us."

I follow two teenage girls off the subway. They're giggling, glancing over one shoulder every few steps. They're looking at Oliver, I realize, as we reach the stairs. I hope I was more subtle checking guys out when I was their age, but probably not.

I'm so focused on the high schoolers that I stumble again, this time with no excuse but my own clumsiness.

Once again, Oliver is there to steady me.

Don't get used to it, I tell myself.

I thought I craved independence too much. That my failure to follow through on a committed relationship was tied to me, not something missing. But something was: trust. Not the logical, quantifiable type that can be defined by reliability stacking up over time. The raw, instinctual kind, that is simply there, or it isn't. The catch after a fall.

"Maybe you should go barefoot," Oliver suggests.

I glance at the cement steps, stained with spilled drinks and dirt and who knows what else. "No thanks."

He lets go of my arm. But his fingers weave with mine, intertwining until there's no mistaking we're holding hands.

"You're stubborn."

"You're the billionaire with no car."

Oliver huffs a laugh, faintly amused. "Is that what you look for in a guy? A fancy car to take you out in?"

There's a lot lurking beneath the question. Enough for me to hear he took my words as a judgment. As a shortcoming.

I was just trying to distract myself from how it feels to have his hand gripping mine.

I react to the simmering ire, something dark and ugly and unexpected twisting in my stomach. "*I* haven't been dating. I'm married, remember?"

Oliver says nothing as we reach the top of the stairs, and I wish I'd kept my mouth shut.

The crowds are thinner in this section of the city, more people leaving than arriving.

We walk past a long, warehouse-looking building, under a pedestrian bridge, and cross a street. Flat, dark water stretches ahead, a walking path running alongside it. And then Oliver pulls me left, and I see it.

"Whoa." I stumble again on a crack in the sidewalk, more focused on looking ahead than what's right in front of me. For a third time, Oliver steadies me.

When I look over, his grin is bright and wide. He looks thrilled by my reaction. "Cool, right?"

I nod, my gaze returning to the structure we're walking toward. It's like nothing I've ever seen. A floating island, constructed from dozens of massive, attached funnels that are pressed together to form a park hovering above the surface of the Hudson. Boardwalks lead from solid land to the raised topiaries, filled with the flow of foot traffic.

"How long has this been here?"

"About a year," Oliver answers. "There was a company event here, right after it opened. Better venue than most of our parties. And I thought you might like it, from an architectural perspective."

My throat tightens. No one in my life, the few who know I

have any interest in architecture and the many who don't, has ever made the effort to engage in it with me. To bring me somewhere simply for me to marvel over its construction. Due to my own secrecy and insecurity, I know. But still, the fact Oliver chose to do so means more than words can express.

"You thought right."

We continue walking along the wooden board until we reach the edge of the park. Oliver says nothing, just lets me take everything in. He doesn't drop my hand either. We stroll along the paved paths in silence, passing chattering tourists and brown plants waiting for warmer weather to blossom with new growth.

The funnels aren't all the same height, so we have to walk up and down flights of stairs in order to explore the whole space. My toes pinch inside my heels, but I'm more focused on the scenery around us. Not just the park itself, but the Hudson River and the towering buildings lining both sides of its shores. Dusk has fallen, creeping toward night. Lights flicker on everywhere, bringing the city to life even as the day draws to a close.

There's an observation deck at the top of the tallest funnel, overlooking all the winding paths we just walked. Oliver leans against the railing, looking up instead of at any of our immediate surroundings. The final strokes of sunset are fading, dimming like a dying bulb.

"I always thought it would be cool to be an astronaut," he says, studying the sky.

"You're not claustrophobic?" I tilt my head back too, so I'm witnessing the same sight.

He laughs. "Something about space…it's mysterious. Dangerous. Massive. What you do doesn't seem as important. I bet it all looks really tiny down here."

"I can't picture you as an astronaut. They don't wear suits." I tug on his jacket with my free hand. "Not this kind, at least."

Oliver smiles. "My dad couldn't either. He shot that idea down fast. But my mom took me to the Space Center in Houston."

"That sounds nice." I bite the inside of my cheek to stop the flood of questions that want to spill out. Oliver doesn't talk about his mother, I've noticed.

"It was. But it was also kind of pointless. She and I both knew I'd go to business school and then end up at Kensington Consolidated."

I nod, still looking at the sky. "In college, I majored in architecture along with business. Another three years of school to get my master's didn't sound very appealing when I was graduating. It was easier to start working for my dad, so that's what I did. And I've thought about going back on and off over the years, but it was always easier just to stay put."

"I'm glad you applied. Not surprised you got in."

I smile, absorbing his faith. It feels good. Rare. "I haven't told my dad yet. Just you...and my best friend, Rosie."

"Did she tell you to go?"

"In a way. She mostly wanted to talk about you."

"You told her about us?"

"I told her we got married. Not...anything else."

He says nothing.

"She won't tell anyone."

I think that's what he's worried about, until he asks, "Why didn't you tell her anything else?"

The easy—understandable—answer would be that I didn't want to explain why I was spending time with my soon-to-be-ex-husband. I don't *have* an explanation. "I didn't want to."

"Did you tell her about Crew?"

I nod.

Oliver looks away, the dimming light illuminating his strong profile. And I realize he misunderstood.

I step closer, savoring his body heat. Any warmth from the sun is rapidly fading. "That's not what I—"

"We should get to dinner."

Oliver starts walking toward the exit. After a brief pause, I follow.

I should be relieved he didn't give me a chance to explain. To bare myself more than I already have. To admit he means something to me.

But I'm not.

CHAPTER TWENTY

OLIVER

I've seen enough photos of the interior of Blackbird plastered on social media to know what to expect when we step inside. This is the hottest restaurant in the city right now. You have to plan months in advance to get a reservation. Or have the right last name.

Hannah's eyes are wide as she looks around the narrow space. It's dimly lit and romantic, the brick walls covered with dripping greenery and wire baskets filled with wine.

"Good evening. What name is your reservation under?" the hostess asks once we reach her.

"Kensington."

Shock flashes across her face before she looks down. I don't have a reservation, and I watch the woman realize it.

I don't relish throwing my last name around. Requesting special treatment makes me uncomfortable. Makes others act awed. Most people *only* know me as a Kensington, and I've tried to carve out a separate identity. The difference tonight is, I want to impress Hannah.

"Let me get your table ready," the hostess says, then scurries off.

Hannah turns toward me, tightening the belt on her coat. We dropped hands when we got in the cab to come here, and I miss touching her.

"You don't have a reservation."

I raise one eyebrow at her. "I don't need one."

Her head tilts, studying me. "Are you trying to impress me?"

Yes, is the accurate answer. "I know it's not a car, but..."

She laughs a little, then looks away to survey the restaurant. "Have you been here before?"

"No, but it's—"

"Oliver!"

I squint toward the back of the restaurant, where the light is even scarcer.

Asher appears suddenly, stepping around the hostess stand and smiling widely. "I thought that was you! But I didn't think this is where you'd—" He stops talking abruptly, as soon as he sees Hannah.

"Hello, Asher."

I glance between the two of them. Asher appears stunned. Hannah looks composed but slightly uncertain. She has no idea Asher knows we're acquainted—married—so I'm guessing she's waiting for him to ask what we're doing here together. I'm waiting for the same question, just in a different context.

"Hannah." Asher recovers. "This is a surprise."

"I can't say the same," she replies. "This seems like *exactly* the kind of place you'd come to eat."

Asher grins. "It was Aida's request."

"Aida?" I ask, not recognizing the name. "What happened with Isabel?"

He shrugs a shoulder. "Eh. It fizzled."

"Easy come, easy go," Hannah comments.

"Worked well for Crew," Asher says.

I glare at him.

"Up until he got married," Asher continues. "And all that *nothing will change* turned out to be bullshit. Of course, you already know that."

I don't know exactly what went down between Hannah and my brother, and I'd like the details to remain fuzzy. My relationship with Crew is messy enough already. But I'd be lying if I said it didn't bother me. Not only that they were together in some way, but that Hannah possibly got hurt as part of it.

"Mr. Kensington, your table is ready." The hostess reappears, holding two menus.

"Great, thank you."

"Can I have a word, Oliver?" Asher asks. "About work," he adds, glancing at Hannah. His expression is almost apologetic.

I shake my head. "Now isn't—"

"It's fine, Oliver," Hannah says. "I'll meet you at the table." She turns and follows the hostess deeper into the restaurant.

I turn to Asher with a scowl. "What?"

"Continuing the Kensington tradition of not sleeping with your wife, huh? You seem awfully tense."

"Watch it," I snap.

Asher shakes his head. Sighs. "I can't keep you from wrecking this train, huh?"

"Are you going to tell him?" If Asher isn't with Isabel any longer, I lost any leverage to entice him to keep his mouth shut.

He laughs. "Are you kidding me? *No way* am I stepping a foot into this clusterfuck. Especially since I saw the photos of you with Quinn Branson. You looked like you were leaving a business meeting. And this is not where you have a business meeting. If you're not fucking her, you want to be. And that is not going to lead to a happy divorce."

"My marriage is none of your business."

"You came to me, Oliver, remember? I saw Crew go through this same thing, pretending he didn't give a shit about Scarlett. Look at him now. Except Hannah has none of the reasons to stick around that Scarlett did. She could walk away with a fortune, on to the next guy."

"I know her better than you do."

"I hope you're right." Asher shrugs. "Anyway, I really did want to talk about work. You sent the Isaac Industries documents before you left the office, right?"

Fuck. "Yes," I lie.

I was waiting for them to be finalized when I called Hannah. Learning she was in the same city overtook everything else.

As long as they're sent by midnight, it'll be fine. But it means I'll have to go back into the office tonight. Which is possibly for the best, because I know Asher is making valid points. If I'm wanting to get laid or take a woman out to dinner, there are much better candidates unrelated to the papers pending in state court. And if I'm wanting Hannah, that's a much bigger problem.

Asher claps my shoulder. "Enjoy dinner. I'd recommend the scallops."

He disappears as quickly as he appeared.

I walk over to the table where Hannah is seated. The muted lights make her blonde hair glow, turning it the color of spun gold.

She glances up as I take the chair across from her, grabbing her water glass and taking a delicate sip. "That was fast. I figured he'd have a longer list of reasons on why you shouldn't be out to dinner with me."

I huff a laugh before picking up my menu. "It *was* work. You like scallops?"

"Do you ever feel guilty about being rich?"

I raise one brow, caught off guard by the question. Something that happens a lot around Hannah. She has a tendency to ask me questions no one else has. Most people just whisper about my net worth with jealousy in their voice and dollar signs in their eyes.

"Asks the girl who grew up in a mansion in Montecito."

Hannah rolls her eyes. "That was my parents' money. And they both grew up middle-class. They paid for college, but then I was on my own."

"I feel *unworthy* of it," I say. "I'm just capitalizing on what was already built by someone else."

"Is that why you're always working? Trying to feel worthy?"

"That's part of it, probably. The rest is, I don't have anything else. I don't enjoy going to parties. I go to them with a plan on who I need to approach and do days of research so I know exactly what to say to them. When I travel, it's for work." I force a smile, hating the way my skin crawls from the vulnerability. "My life is pretty boring. Might as well work."

"What about women?"

I raise one eyebrow. "Asks my wife."

Even in the low light, her cheeks are clearly red. I'm not sure if I should mention Quinn again or leave the topic alone. I meant what I told Hannah earlier, I shouldn't have gone out with her.

"Have you ever been in love?" she asks.

I shake my head, but the motion is less confident than it would have been a couple of weeks ago. "For a while, I thought that part of my life was all planned out. I fooled around a lot in high school and the first year of college, rebelling against it the only way I could. After graduation there were a few women who lasted more than a couple of weeks, but not many. According to most of them, I worked too much."

Hannah half-smiles. “Imagine that.”

“Good evening.” A waiter appears, setting a basket of bread on the table along with a tray of olive oil dusted with colorful spices. “I’m Steve, and I’ll be your server tonight. Can I get you two anything to drink?”

Hannah orders a cocktail and I ask for a whiskey. Our waiter says he’ll be back shortly, then disappears.

“What about you?” I ask as soon as he’s gone.

She grabs a piece of bread and rips a section off, before dunking it in the oil. “I’ve never been in love. My last relationship was kind of an experiment, to see what would happen if I put the effort in. He lived in San Diego, and between the distance and his schedule with the team, I didn’t see him all that often. Didn’t bother me, which should have been my first clue. I think I’m just defective when it comes to that stuff.” Hannah raises a shoulder, drops it, and then pops the bread in her mouth.

“You’re not defective.”

“You’re not boring.”

I half-smile, hiding how much those words mean to me. Because I feel it, a lot of the time.

“How did it end?”

I assume she’s talking about Declan, the guy Eddie mentioned at the bar. When she shifts in her seat, I know I’m right. “He, uh, proposed.”

“Wow.”

“Yep.” She sighs. “He called me a never-ending challenge.”

“So, exciting?”

Hannah smiles. “I think the implication was more that I was exhausting. Not worth it. Things didn’t end well between us, obviously.”

“He was *wrong*, Hannah.”

She nods, dropping eye contact.

Our drinks appear a second later, the waiter setting them down quickly and rushing off with a promise to be back shortly to take our dinner orders.

I grab the tumbler of whiskey, raise it, and tilt it toward her. "To getting into architecture school."

Hannah bites her bottom lip before lifting her own glass. The blood orange garnish wobbles before settling back on the rim. "To Thompson & Thompson." She pauses. "Or did you already close another deal I missed?"

"That was the latest one. Do you have stock or something?"

She shakes her head. Swallows. Shrugs. "I looked you up, after." Her glass tilts closer. "Cheers."

"Cheers."

Our glasses tap.

Hannah sips her drink, then smiles. "Wow. This is really good." She holds it toward me. "Try it."

I can't recall the last time I had a mixed drink. But I take it, mostly because I don't want her animated expression to disappear. Sip it, making a face at the sweetness. "Delicious."

Her laugh warms my chest more than the alcohol. "You're not going to offer me some of yours?"

"I thought you knew what whiskey tastes like."

But I hand it over anyway, realizing I'm handing her a lot more than this glass.

And recognizing I'm screwed.

Holding a losing hand in a game I desperately want to win.

Married to a woman I'm falling for when I'm supposed to be dating someone else. A woman who is about to embark on a new chapter of her life on the opposite side of the country from where I live and work.

Asher calling the situation a clusterfuck suddenly seems tame. And he didn't even know the half of it.

CHAPTER TWENTY-ONE

HANNAH

Kensington Consolidated's offices are just as massive and imposing as I expected. The path up to the entrance of the building is immaculately landscaped, a fountain located just outside doors that require a keycard to enter.

Oliver's hand falls to my lower back, guiding me through the door in front of him.

A middle-aged man is seated at the desk that sits in the center of the massive glass lobby, decorated by couches and plants.

"Evening, Mr. Kensington."

Oliver nods at the man, who eyes me curiously. He has to swipe a keycard to get to the elevators, and again when we're inside.

I lean against the wall, watching the digital numbers above the buttons tick higher and higher as we ascend.

Oliver is typing on his phone, a furrow formed between his eyes.

Coming here was probably a bad call. When Oliver said he had to come back to the office after dinner, I should have asked him to drop me off at my hotel. Instead, I said I didn't mind stopping.

I'm curious about this central component of his life. This building that he spends so much time at, and this piece of his identity that's tied up with his family's company.

And I also don't want tonight to end. Not yet.

I don't know if I consider tonight a date. I don't know if Oliver does.

But I do know it's the best one I've ever been on. Even with the detour to a skyscraper.

The doors ding open. Oliver slides his phone back into his pocket, waiting for me to walk out first. Automatic lights flicker to life, bouncing off the glass fronts of the offices that line this hall. Everything is immaculate and expensive looking.

"I'm at the end."

I follow Oliver, walking past the long line of dark offices. It's eerie how quiet and still our surroundings are. Like we're the only two people in the world right now.

There's an open cubicle just outside the door that leads into Oliver's office. "That's where my assistant, Alicia, sits," he tells me. "She's been with me since I started here."

I glance at the two photos on the desk. One is a wedding portrait of a smiling couple. The other is of two kids sitting on a rock formation. Some petty part of me is relieved to know his assistant is married with children instead of single.

Oliver keeps walking into his office. No lights turn on; the only brightness is what's spilling in from the hallway. And from the floor-to-ceiling windows that make up the far wall of the office, displaying a dazzling view of New York's iconic skyline.

I head straight for the windows, pressing a hand against the cold glass. From this height, it feels like I could fall forward right into the skyscrapers.

Fingers tap against keys.

I turn to see Oliver leaning over his computer, focused on whatever he came back to work on. There aren't any framed photographs on his desk. I stroll past it, over toward the leather couch. I sink onto the soft surface, shrugging off my trench coat. It's much warmer in here than it was outside.

My phone screen is covered with messages. From my father, from Rachel, from Rosie.

I toss my phone away and stand, strolling over to the tall bookcase and skimming the spines. They're all business or law books, with long names. Ornamental more than functional, I'd guess.

"All set."

I spin, watching Oliver stand and shut off the computer.

"That was fast."

"I just had to send something. Forgot to earlier."

I reach the side of his desk, skimming my fingers across the flawless surface. My heart thuds out a steady rhythm in my chest as I inch backward, resting against the imposing, massive desk.

Oliver stills, his eyes tracking my every movement like a predator eyeing prey. The difference is, I *want* him to pounce. I crave seeing that leashed control shatter.

More of the desk supports my weight as my thighs part. Barely, but enough to catch his notice. Tension coils in the still air between us, the tangible tang of uncertainty and desperation humming between us. The acknowledgment we want to do this but shouldn't.

I decide to push, spreading my legs a little further. My dress inches higher. "You wanted to see me, Mr. Kensington?"

Oliver's lips quirk, but he shakes his head, not moving. "Hannah..."

"You called me Ms. Garner when you asked for this report." I bite my bottom lip, then bat my eyelashes. "Did I mess up the deliverables? Or the quarterly statements? Are you calling me Hannah because you're about to fire me?"

Oliver's jaw tightens as he studies me, deliberating.

The twinkling lights of the city mix with the soft glow of the moon streaming in through the windows. I can't make out his whole expression, but I can see the taut line of his jaw. The broad spread of his shoulders.

"Is this a fantasy?" I whisper. "In your office, where you give orders and decide big, important things? You're here late at night with a secretary or a coworker and she keeps leaning forward, teasing you until…"

I grip the edge of the desk and slide back, the smooth material of my dress easily gliding against the varnished wood. My knees part until I'm exposed, and I moan when cool air brushes against the wetness between my legs. Deliberately, I tug the hem of my dress an inch higher.

Finally, Oliver moves. He takes a step. Only one, and my body reacts with a jolt. "You want to know my fantasy, Hannah?" Another step. "My fantasy isn't fucking a woman in my office, Hannah. It's fucking *you*."

He moves closer, but he doesn't touch me where I'm hoping. He winds a piece of my hair around his finger, tugging gently. There's nothing sexual about it. It's sweet. Affectionate. Familiar.

I swallow, lust trickling back into my bloodstream in response. But it's not the wild, wanton urge that landed me on this desk. It's focused and intentional, thrumming an insistent pulse between my legs.

I want *him*, specifically. The intensity of it scares me a little.

Oliver releases the piece of my hair, only to wrap all of it around his hand, pulling my entire head back. His other hand lands on my thigh, the heat of it searing into my skin like a brand. "Tell me no."

I suck in a deep breath. But no words escape. I can feel him thickening against me, hot and huge and hard.

"Tell me no, Hannah." His voice is deeper now. Darker. Too easy to fall into.

I *should* say no. We both know it. Just like we both know that he shouldn't have called me. That we shouldn't have gone to dinner. That I should've asked him to drop me off at my hotel.

We've both toppled dominos, then looked away as they've fallen. Pretended we weren't the ones who pushed them over.

And even if we don't admit it, this is more than amicable strangers seeking a divorce. More than staying on civil terms. More than attraction or lust.

I acknowledge that truth to myself, at least, as the firm ridge of his desk digs into my skin. There's a flash of déjà vu as we face each other, this moment so similar to the charged one in my kitchen.

"Have you been here before?"

There's a tiny jolt of surprise. Oliver has never brought Crew up.

He's revealing a tiny flicker of insecurity, one I didn't realize existed. In order to care about my history with his brother, he'd have to care, period.

"No." I swallow, choosing my next words carefully. "He was *easy* to explain to Rosie, Oliver. You're…not."

"I keep having this dream," Oliver says, his grip tightening on my leg the same way it clasped around my hand. "Where you're standing across from me in a church and your lips are moving, but I have no idea what you're saying."

"I'm probably promising to love and cherish you in sickness

and health, for richer or for poorer …" My voice trails, dampened by the burning intensity in his gaze.

"I wish I remembered," he confesses. His hold on me tightens, and I know the fuse is lit. Can practically see it burning, racing toward explosion.

"Drunk people do things they want to, not things they don't."

"What the fuck does that say about us?" Oliver asks.

"I don't know," I say.

But what I do know is it's no longer a mystery to me, why I married him. My hazy memories from the night we got married are still incorporeal. *This* isn't, though. Feeling this lust and comfort and intensity every day isn't a fate I'd shy away from. Some part of me recognized that first night we met.

He exhales as we teeter on a knife's edge.

For tonight, at least, I know where I want to fall.

My hands press against his stomach, the ridges of his abdomen prominent even through the cotton shirt he's wearing. I move lower, gripping the firm leather of his belt.

"Tell me *to*," I whisper.

His exhale is ragged and rough, as my hand drifts lower to drag across his crotch. It's a rush, feeling him respond. Knowing his body can't lie, even if his mouth does.

"If you think I'll deny you anything, you haven't been paying close attention." The words are low and gruff. And then his hands are brushing against mine, unbuckling his belt.

I clench against nothing, desperate to have him inside of me.

"You sure you want this, Hannah?"

"I'm sure."

He tugs his pants down just low enough to free his cock. I reach forward, gripping his erection tightly, memorizing the shape and weight. Savoring every stroke as I draw the anticipation out.

"Lean back and close your eyes."

Breath catches in my throat as I comply. The wood of his desk is hard and unyielding against my spine.

The callouses on his hands rasp against my skin as they shove my dress higher and tug my soaked thong down.

I know what's coming, when his palm presses against my inner thigh until I feel the burn of my muscles stretching fully spread. But I'm in no way prepared for the slick heat of his tongue exploring tracing circles around my clit, sparking electricity everywhere.

His touch is teasing, a kiss on the inside of my knee or just above my hipbone before he's back between my legs. There's a dull roar in my ears as my body arches, my instinct to push closer to the pressure no matter how desperate it makes me look.

I'm lost to lust, desire eradicating every logical, nuanced instinct.

"More," I moan, lifting my hips.

Oliver chuckles, and I feel it reverberate against the sensitive flesh. "I'm never going to be able to work at this fucking desk again without picturing you like this."

Good, I think.

Because he's infiltrated my life in LA. I think of him in the passenger seat of my car. Playing croquet in my parents' backyard. Making me come in the bed I sleep in every night.

The pleasure grows, stoked like a fire finding fresh wood. I'm closer and closer, my breath coming faster and my heart racing as Oliver matches my urgency, his tongue swirling and his teeth nipping.

And then I'm flying, propelled by an invisible force that flings me into nothingness and then pieces me back together until I'm back on Oliver's desk, panting and relaxed as the aftershocks of my orgasm tremble through me. If we were *really* married, I'd beg him to do that to me every morning. Scream until I was hoarse.

A satisfied smile spreads across his face as he takes in my heaving chest and heavy eyelids.

I force myself to sit up, grabbing the cock that's turned an angry shade of purply red. Engorged and leaking, pulsing in my hand. I pump the tip, and he hisses.

"You have a condom?"

He's already pulling out his wallet. A piece of paper falls out when he grabs the foil packet. I don't realize what it is until I catch a glimpse of the writing on it before he carefully tucks it away.

"Seemed silly to actually burn it," Oliver mutters, grabbing the foil packet and ripping it open with his teeth.

I watch as he grips his dick and rolls the rubber on. Suck on my bottom lip, as the tip teases my entrance, sliding through the evidence of my arousal.

Oliver grunts as he starts to press inside of me, his fingers digging into my hips. My thighs tremble from the effort of holding open and the burn of him stretching me.

My breath comes in gasps and lurches, trying to acquaint myself with the sensation of him inside of me and also recognizing it's an impossible task.

Oliver's breathing is just as erratic, his abs clenching as he pushes in deeper. I can see each inch, watch as it disappears. Feel my inner muscles pulse around his thick length and notice the tendons in his arms tense, holding himself back.

I'm not sure if anything has felt better than the wet heat of his mouth tugging on one nipple, sucking it to a raised point as a fresh shock of electricity races through me.

Jagged pants spill out of my mouth as I rock against him, trying to erase all the distance between us and force more friction.

My breathing is loud and needy. All I can hear in the quiet space. I hiss his name, scrabbling at his back as I grip his shirt. It's too good—*too much.*

And then I'm flying, staring out at a dazzling view of the city.

Wondering how I'll be able to return to LA, after experiencing this.

CHAPTER TWENTY-TWO

OLIVER

My steps are sure as I approach his office, but the back of my neck is hot and itchy. It feels like every eye in this hallway is on me, wondering why I'm knocking on Crew's door.

"Come in," Crew calls out.

When I walk in, he's rubbing a temple and staring at a sheet of paper.

Crew looks up, spots me, and smiles. "Hey."

"Hey. You have a minute?"

He tosses the paper down and leans back in his chair. "Gladly. This fucking contract is driving me insane. I've reread the same page five times now."

I take a seat in one of the chairs facing his desk, glancing at one of the photos angled toward the computer. It's one I've never seen before, Crew and Scarlett smiling with the city of Paris spread behind them.

"When was that?" I ask, pointing to the frame.

Crew glances at the photo and smiles. "A couple of months after we got married. Scarlett went to Paris on a work trip, and I tagged along."

"Looks nice."

"It was," he replies. "If you ever went on social media, you'd know that I post a lot of travel pics."

"Is that what you do on your phone during meetings?"

Crew smirks. "Sometimes. You should try it sometime. Good brain break."

"Not sure what I would post."

He opens his mouth to say something, then closes it. Probably hearing the wistful note I didn't mean to let slip out. Because it's really only recently, since I've gone to Vegas and tried surfing and spent time in the city at other places beside my office and my penthouse, that I'm realizing how empty my *eat, sleep, work* lifestyle is. Like glimpsing light and then sitting in the dark.

Before I can decide how to transition from the lingering silence to the reason I'm here, there's a knock on Crew's door.

"Come in," he says.

Jeremy walks in, carrying a thick stack of papers under one arm. He halts when he sees me, glancing uncertainly between me and Crew.

Crew seems oblivious to the awkward energy humming in the air, taking a sip from the coffee mug on his desk. "Oliver, you know Jeremy, right?"

"Right." I flick a piece of invisible lint off my pants, attempting to appear unbothered about being stuck in a room with my divorce attorney and my brother, who has no idea I'm married. "Good to see you, Jeremy."

"You too," he responds. "I'll come back later."

"Does an hour work?" Crew asks. "I should be through this by then." He taps a pen on the papers piled on his desk. "We can get drinks after."

"Sounds good. See you then."

The door clicks shut behind Jeremy, and Crew glances to me.

"You're welcome to come too. Scarlett's parents are watching Lili tonight and she's going to a dinner, so I'm basically a bachelor for the night. Like old times."

"Have you ever regretted it?" I ask. "You could have told Dad you wouldn't do it."

"No," Crew replies, rubbing his jaw. "I've never regretted it. But that has everything to do with Scarlett, and nothing to do with Dad."

I nod. I knew that would be his answer. "I'm going to turn down his deal. It's not how I want CEO. And Quinn deserves someone who could make her happy. That's not me."

There's no change in Crew's face, his expression carefully controlled. "Date didn't go well?"

"That's what you got from what I just said?"

He shrugs. "It's your decision. And I'd rather see you happy than successful." I raise a brow, and he grins. "*More* successful."

I clear my throat. "Thanks."

"So…it didn't?"

"No." I sigh. "It didn't."

"I'm sorry." Crew's teasing tone turns sympathetic.

"I'm headed to meet with Quinn now. Let her know I'm not… it's not…you know."

Crew whistles. "Good luck. At least you know what you're going to say."

I roll my eyes, and he smirks. "If you need a drink after, offer stands."

"Thanks," I say, and mean it. The invitation matters to me, so I feel obligated to add, "But I, uh, have plans already." I pull in a deep breath. "And that's what I wanted to talk to you about."

Crew's eyebrows rise as he leans forward to grab his mug. "So asking me if I regret my marriage and telling me you're not taking Dad up on CEO was your version of small talk?"

I rub my hands on my slacks. "I guess so."

"Okay." He leans back and laughs. "Hit me with it."

"I'm bringing a date to Garrett's wedding tomorrow."

"Okay… Not Quinn, I'm assuming?"

"Her name is Hannah Garner."

I track every emotion that passes across Crew's face. Surprise. Uncertainty. Concern.

"Wow. I…I, uh, didn't realize you…" He grabs a pen off his desk, rolling it between two fingers. "I didn't realize you two knew each other."

"Likewise."

"How'd you find out?"

"She told me, after learning my last name."

He nods, still rolling the pen.

"I get it's awkward, Crew. If I'd known about the past when I met her…" *Married her*, I add silently. I clear my throat. "I like her."

"You like her." His voice sounds stunned.

Crew has always been better about sharing thoughts and feelings than I have been, especially since he met Scarlett. It's never been a strength of mine. I've considered it to be a weakness, actually.

But I feel like I owe him some explanation about Hannah, especially since it feels like our relationship has shifted since that night he showed up at my door drunk. I don't want this to become another wedge between us. To erase what little progress we've made. And it's nice, in an unexpected way, to finally have something—someone—meaningful to share, after years of hearing about Scarlett.

I nod. "Yeah. A lot."

His eyebrows creep a centimeter higher. "How long have you been seeing her?"

"A few weeks." Longer than most of my "relationships" have lasted, which Crew knows.

"Since before Dad went to you about Quinn?"

"Yes."

"Is she factoring into you saying no to Dad?"

Rather than respond, I reach out and grab the baseball off its holder on his desk. "Remember when you got this?"

Crew shrugs. "Sort of. You and Mom were out of town."

"She took me to the Houston Space Center because I told her I wanted to be an astronaut. Which pissed Dad off because she indulged me. So he brought you to a game while we were gone. And he did it because I'd been asking him to take me for weeks. I thought it was *my fault*, Crew, for ever saying something to Mom."

I rub my thumb along the baseball's stitching.

"I'm done with Dad thinking he can control whatever he wants, whenever he wants to. Everything that happened with Candace…maybe I needed to realize how destructive chasing his approval was. If I take his deal, that'll never end." I exhale. "And if I hadn't met Hannah, I probably would have given Quinn more of a chance. I might have talked myself into it, so I'm not alone and was *more successful*. But now…"

I continue to turn the baseball around in my hand for a few more seconds, then set it back in its holder.

When I look up, Crew's head is tilted as he studies me intently. I'm not sure what he's thinking. I'm dumping a lot on him at once. Years—decades—worth of hidden thoughts and secret feelings.

"I'll support you no matter what, Oliver," he says.

My throat feels tight and thick as I nod. "I—me, too. I'll support you, I mean."

One corner of Crew's mouth creases into a comma. "You okay? You're usually a little more eloquent."

I scoff as I glance at my watch, realizing I have to leave now if I'm going to meet Quinn on time. "I'm fine. Just tired."

"Do I wanna know why?"

He's smirking when I look up, and the knot of anxiety in my chest eases even more. I know Crew has moved on. He's happily married. Obsessed with Scarlett. But I was still nervous how he'd react to hearing about me and Hannah. If he'd see it as a betrayal or look at me with resentment. It never occurred to me he might tease me about her.

I shake my head and stand. "I've got to go, or I'll be late to meet Quinn. I'll see you tomorrow, at the wedding?"

Crew nods. "See you tomorrow."

I head for the door.

"Hey, Oliver?"

I turn back around. "Yeah?"

Crew leans forward, grabbing the baseball off his desk and tossing it to me. "Throw that away for me, will you?"

My palm stings, as my grip on the leather tightens. "That's not what I was …"

"We should go to a game sometime. I'll buy a new one."

I nod, the motion jerky and uneven as emotion clogs my throat again. "Sounds good."

I don't want to be responsible for marring Crew's relationship with our father any more than it already is. He's my younger brother, and there will always be some instinct to hide the ugliness in our family from him instead of revealing it. But I'm realizing doing so has come at the expense of *my* relationship with Crew, which isn't a sacrifice I want to make.

Once I'm back in my office, I rush through grabbing everything I need, say a hasty goodbye to Alicia, and then head for the elevators.

I give my driver the address for the coffee shop where I asked Quinn to meet me, and then pull my phone out of my pocket, scrolling through the list of contacts until I come across a name I've never called before.

Scarlett answers on the second ring. "Hello, Oliver."

"Hi." I clear my throat, caught off guard by the realization she has my phone number saved. It says a lot about our dynamic, none of which I'm particularly proud of. I learned a lot more from my father than just successful business practices. "How are you?"

"Fine." She sounds amused. "You?"

"Good. Thanks."

"So… Is this a social call, or should I be concerned?"

"Your subtle way of asking if I fucked up again?"

"Did you?" she asks.

"I'm bringing Hannah to Garrett's wedding tomorrow. I told Crew because I wanted him to have a head's up. Thought I owed you the same."

There's a ten-second pause before Scarlett responds. "Jeremy said you filed for divorce."

"I did."

"But you're also dating her?"

I stare out the window at the city, not really seeing any of the buildings or cars we're passing by. "Honestly, I don't know what the hell I'm doing."

"What about Arthur's offer?"

"I'm not taking it. I'm done jumping through his hoops."

"And you wouldn't have married Quinn, if you'd met *her* drunk in Vegas."

It's a statement, not a question, but I answer it anyway. "No. I wouldn't have."

Regardless of what addled my decision-making that night to the point of marriage, my memory of meeting Hannah in that bar is completely clear. There was an immediate spark—an interest—that wasn't there when I met Quinn. That's never been there with anyone else.

"I appreciate everything you did to help with the divorce, Scarlett. I hope you know that."

"I involved Jeremy because I thought a divorce was what *you* wanted, Oliver. If it's not, then…"

"A divorce is what's best."

"That's different from—" There's a sudden commotion on Scarlett's end of the line, followed from a sigh. "I'm sorry, Oliver. I've got to go handle something."

"It's fine. I'll see you tomorrow."

There's a pause, where it sounds like Scarlett might be considering saying something else. But all she adds is a goodbye before hanging up.

The car pulls up in front of the corner coffee shop a few minutes later.

I spot Quinn as soon as I step inside. There are plenty of open tables at this hour. I'm not sure if this was the best choice of venue for this conversation, but I didn't want to have it over the phone, and this was the best I could think of.

Quinn is sitting toward the back. Posture perfectly straight, her hands cupped around a mug.

She looks up and smiles as I cross the small coffee shop. "Hello, Oliver."

"Hi, Quinn."

I unbutton my jacket and take the seat across from her.

Her painted nails tap the side of the porcelain as she stares at me, bergamot-scented steam curling up from the cup of tea in front of her. "You're not getting anything?" she asks, tilting her head to the right.

"I can't stay long, unfortunately."

Quinn nods, something knowing growing in her gaze.

"Are you feeling more settled in the city?" I ask.

"I am, yes." She grabs the tag of her teabag and lifts it out of the mug, dropping it onto the saucer. I watch the brown liquid pool around the base of the cup. "There's a new Monet exhibit at the Met, have you heard about it?"

"No, I haven't."

"I have tickets for tomorrow morning. I was going to invite you, but I'm now realizing that would make this even more uncomfortable."

I exhale. "Quinn…"

"What's her name?"

"Sorry?"

Quinn smiles. "I know why my father arranged the dinner with yours, Oliver. Why you asked me out to dinner. We make sense. And from everything I've heard about you, you fall in line. But you're here because you're not going to. So…what's her name?"

"Quinn, I never meant to—"

She laughs, then leans forward. "Oliver, I barely know you. Maybe we would have worked out. Maybe we wouldn't have. You're exactly the kind of man I thought I would marry, so I wasn't opposed to finding out. But my parents got married because they made sense, and I saw how that worked out. I'm not interested in sentencing myself to that same fate. Or you."

My father turned Quinn into a bargaining chip. I looked at her and saw CEO. It's a relief to separate the two, to have made the decision that disqualifies me from the position.

"Me neither."

Quinn tilts her head, her expression curious. "Do you love her?"

Yes.

The answer comes to me immediately, unencumbered.

But then the doubts and second-guessing trickle in. The reality. I'm not sure if Hannah sees me as much more than a fling. She agreed to stay in New York through the weekend when I asked, but her life is still entirely in Los Angeles. There's nothing for her here except for me, maybe. And every relationship I've ever had has failed, at least in part, because of my inability to prioritize anything above work. I told Crew I couldn't make Quinn happy. I have the same fear about Hannah.

"It's complicated," I say.

Because we're married. Because she has history with my brother. Because I don't think Hannah's answer to that question would be *yes*.

Quinn blows on her tea, then takes a sip. "I had one of those."

"What happened?"

She raises a delicate shoulder, then lets it drop. "Nothing spectacular. I met him in university. Fell hard and fast. We were exciting and dramatic. The highs were high, and the lows were low. But eventually, it became exhausting. So I told him things had to change, or I would leave." She smiles, and it's a sad one. "Here I am."

"I'm sorry, Quinn."

"It wasn't meant to be, is all. Maybe yours is."

"Maybe."

I've always prioritized logic over emotion. Reason over instinct.

But I suddenly find myself hoping for fate.

The smoke alarm is blaring when I open the front door.

"Hannah?" I call out, dropping my briefcase in the entryway and sprinting toward the kitchen.

She's standing on the kitchen island barefoot, flapping a dish towel back and forth. A pan of charred contents sits on the top of the stove.

Suddenly, the smoke alarm stops. She sighs and swipes hair out of her face. Spins and spots me.

"Hi." Hannah drops down and slides off the side of the counter.

"What happened?" I ask as I walk over to her.

"I was trying to cook dinner. Got a work call, and…" She waves at the pan.

"Looks good."

Hannah scoffs, tossing the towel she's holding over the dish. "Rude."

I smirk, focusing on her instead of the burned food. "Good day?"

"It was okay." She blows out a long breath. "My dad brought up me getting certified again."

"You haven't said anything about architecture school?"

Hannah shakes her head. "I want to talk to him in person."

At that, I feel a stab of guilt. I asked her to stay in a spurt of selfishness, not thinking about how it might affect her life, just mine.

"How was your day?" she asks.

"It was good, actually."

"Good." Her head tilts back as I move closer. "Sorry for almost burning down your kitchen."

"There's a sprinkler system."

Hannah huffs a laugh as I press her against the counter. "You're home early."

"So are you."

Her fingers slide into my hair, nails gently grazing my scalp. I nearly groan, it feels so fucking good. She's wearing a dress, so there's no barrier keeping my hand from slipping beneath the fabric and up her thigh. The temptation to touch her is a relentless urge. No matter how many times I do, it's never satisfied.

"My last meeting was canceled, and that's when I decided to go grocery shopping. I wanted to make you my favorite meal, except—" She gasps, as my fingers pull her underwear to the side.

"Except you burned it?" I whisper, my lips moving to her neck.

"It just got overdone," she murmurs, her head tilting to the side so I have better access.

I laugh, stepping back just enough that I have room to free my cock from my slacks.

Since she temporarily moved in with me instead of keeping her hotel room, Hannah and I have had more sex than I've had in the past few years combined. I slid into her this morning before the sun even rose, both of us still half-asleep, then dragged myself out of bed for my daily workout. But despite how much action it's gotten lately, my dick is so hard it's painful.

Hannah tosses her underwear on the floor before she spreads her legs, granting me full access. Her ankles hook around my waist, pulling me closer.

"This isn't very sanitary."

I smirk. "It sounds like we'll be ordering takeout tonight anyway."

I grip the head of my cock and rub it around her entrance, making sure she's ready to take me. Both of us moan at the sensation. I push inside of her an inch, watching her pussy stretch around me. Feeling how slick she is for me…

"Fuck." I freeze.

"What's wrong?"

"I didn't—I don't have a condom on."

Hannah glances down. I've barely entered her, but the difference in sensation is noticeable.

She swallows, a small, barely noticeable bob to her throat.

I pull out, the end of my cock glistening with her arousal as a vein pulses angrily along the shaft. "I'll be right back."

Hannah catches my arm, then quickly drops it. "You don't have to wear one."

I freeze, just as stunned as I was when I realized I'd forgotten protection. I've never been inside a woman bare. My father couldn't care less if Crew and I slept around. But it was drilled into us that repercussions would ruin our lives and destroy the family name.

More than the fear of paying child support or enduring gossip, it's something I've never considered because I *like* the barrier. It's the same reason I prefer to have sex from a position where I won't see a woman's face. Even with women I've dated, I separated lust from feelings. Any connection was always independent from physical intimacy.

But that urge has never been there with Hannah.

I can't seem to get close *enough* where she's concerned.

The smoke alarm suddenly begins blaring again, making us both jump.

"Turn on the vent and open the patio doors," I say, not sure if

Hannah can even hear me over the racket. She must catch some of it, though, because she nods before slipping off the counter.

I force my erection back in my pants, gritting my teeth as my hard dick strains against the stiff fabric in protest. There's a stepladder in the hall closet. I haul it out, locating the button on the alarm and pressing it. Nothing happens. I jam it three more times before the ear-splitting shriek finally stops.

The silence that follows sounds louder than the screeching was.

Hannah is out on the patio now, staring out at the sweeping view of Central Park.

I stow the stepladder back in the closet, walk to the open door, then pause. "Should be all set now."

She glances back at me and nods, not moving from the railing. A cool breeze pulls some hair free from her ponytail, the blonde strands blowing across her face.

I'm not sure what else to say to her. *Sorry for freaking out a little, I'd love to stop wearing condoms?*

I've never had this conversation with a woman before. Maybe she's regretting the offer. Maybe it was the heat of a moment that's totally cooled, thanks to the smoke alarm.

And it's most definitely a bad idea, no matter how turned on I am by the thought. We're in the midst of divorce proceedings. I shouldn't be having sex with her at all, let alone with less protection.

I can retrace every decision that ended up here, but I can't figure out exactly how it happened. How what should have been the simplest of decisions—ending an accidental marriage to a stranger—somehow turned into this ball of dread in my stomach. I'm dreading our *divorce*, not panicking about our marriage.

I tug at my tie, the knot suddenly feeling too tight.

My phone rings in my pocket. I pull it out and glance at the screen.

It's work. It's *always* work.

"I need to take this," I say. "Shouldn't be long."

Maybe I'll have figured out what to say to her by then.

Hannah nods. She doesn't roll her eyes or sigh the way other women have done when I've taken work calls, and it's the first time I've wished someone would. Some sign she cares would be nice to see.

"Okay. I'll look through takeout menus."

"Sounds good." I turn away and answer the call. "Oliver Kensington."

"Hey, Oliver. I stopped by your office, but I must have just missed you."

I don't miss the surprise in Scott's voice, so I don't tell him I left the office an hour ago. Just like I shove away the voice that whispers that's where I should be.

"Zantech wants to talk. By the end of their day, so early morning for us. Are you available for a call at six?"

Tomorrow is Garrett's wedding. Up until the ceremony, I had an open schedule. And since Hannah's return flight to California is the following morning, I was hoping to spend the whole day with her. But we've been trying to woo this company for months. Chances are, Hannah will still be sleeping when the call ends. "That's fine. Set it up."

"Great. Will do. Have a good night, Oliver."

"You too, Scott."

I continue down the hallway, but don't stop at my office. I'm sure I have a hundred unread emails, but I'm not interested in dealing with any of it right now.

I head into the master bedroom, then walk straight into the attached bathroom. Both of my hands rest on the cold granite surrounding the sink as I take deep breaths, trying to sort the mess in my head out. It's getting harder and harder to suppress my feelings, to pretend fucking Hannah out of my system is accomplishing anything except her sinking deeper under my skin.

And I can't get the picture of her sitting with her legs spread on my counter out of my head.

With an annoyed huff, I jerk my pants back down and tug my cock free. If anyone had told me a year ago I'd be standing in my bathroom jerking off to the memory of my wife's wet pussy, I'd have told them they were insane. Yet here I am, because I can't decide what else to do and my erection isn't going anywhere.

I've stroked myself exactly once when the door opens and Hannah walks in. Her blue eyes widen the second she catches sight of me standing with my pants undone.

"I thought you were doing work in the office." She's not looking at me. Her gaze is focused on my hand, wrapped around my throbbing erection.

"I, uh, finished."

Hannah's lips quirk. "Doesn't look that way to me."

My grip tightens as my body reacts to her attention. Having Hannah here is way better than simply imagining she's here. She's still wearing her dress, the fabric around her waist extra wrinkled from being bunched by my hands.

"Want a hand?"

I raise both eyebrows, hating and loving the smirk on her face.

"Or my mouth?"

She takes a step closer, her hand replacing mine as she sinks to her knees.

And from the first swipe of her tongue, I know this will be the best damn blowjob I've ever received. I have to brace my hand against the counter, blood rushing south and reason leaving with it.

"You taste good," she tells me as she traces the tip and then sucks it into her mouth.

Hannah pulls back to blow on the damp skin, and my hips jerk forward. My balls are tight and aching, desperate for release even though she's barely started touching me.

She pulls back slightly, using her hand to jack me off as her tongue swirls the tip like she's licking an ice cream conc. And then she's sucking me deeper and deeper into her mouth, until she manages to take all of me.

Hannah swallows, and the muscles constrict around the sensitive tip as it rubs against the back of her throat. My dick throbs, thrilled with this turn of events. It's been a while since a woman was on her knees for me. And *never*, did she elicit the reaction Hannah does, even when I try to fight it.

Pleasure swims through me in devastating currents. I'm not worried about anything, but I'm not totally mindless either. I'm totally focused on Hannah, watching her head bob between my legs and knowing this will be a new fantasy when she's gone. Memorizing the sight of her pink lips spread around my erection.

I comb one hand through the blonde strands that have fallen out of her ponytail, wanting to see her face better. She licks along the length of me, her tongue wet and warm.

Then her mouth ventures lower, sucking one of my balls into her mouth and releasing it to tease the other. I moan her name. Her lips close around the ridged head of my dick, pulling me back inside of her mouth in a hot slide that has blood pounding in my ears.

"*Fuck*, Hannah," I groan, pumping my hips faster.

My hand tightens in her hair, and she moans, the vibration tingling along my shaft. Mixing with the sloppy, filthy sound of me fucking her mouth. Heat races down my spine, and I know I'm about to explode.

"I can't—I'm not—" I tug at her hair, trying to warn her.

Instead of moving away, she digs her fingernails into my ass. I growl as a powerful release crashes over me, filling her mouth. It goes on and on in a haze of pleasure as I lean back against the wall, letting it support my weight.

Hannah swallows again before she pulls away. Some of my cum spills out of her mouth, dripping down her chin. It's the most erotic sight I've ever seen. She's my wife, and it finally feels like I've marked her in some permanent way.

My cock twitches, satisfaction fleeing fast. It's *still* like this with her. It's *always* like this with her, it feels like.

I can't get enough.

And it's not just physical. There's an emotional attachment too. I can't help but think of how certain I was of the answer to Quinn's question.

Hannah stands and swipes at her face, missing the streak of cum entirely. I grab her waist and pull her to me, gently wiping the spot away with my thumb.

We're both breathing heavily.

There's too much I want to say, and nothing I can figure out how to articulate the right way. So I kiss her, realizing she tastes like *me*, trying to convey all the emotions ricocheting silently inside of me.

She just did that to please me, and it makes me feel inadequate. Unworthy.

I'm used to people trying to get in my good graces. But they always want something in exchange.

Hannah isn't asking for anything.

I want to give her everything.

"I've never not worn a condom, Hannah," I say, as soon as our lips separate.

The satisfaction disappears from her expression, shifting from sultry to serious.

"That's fine. Aren't there still some—"

"I want to. If you're sure."

She steps closer, surrounding me with the scent of grapefruit. "I'm sure."

I tug the hem of her dress up, tracing a trail up the inside of her thigh and into the wet heat between her legs.

She's dripping.

I tease her for a minute, before I drop my hand and wrap it around my hardening dick, using her arousal as lubrication. Her gaze is focused on my hand, watching me stroke myself. I slow my movements, torturing myself right along with her.

Hannah frowns at my throbbing erection. "Are you sure you're hard enough? I'm not sure if—"

I spin her around and slap her ass. "Get on the bed."

Hannah laughs but listens, pulling her dress over her head and walking out of the bathroom. By the time I pull off my clothes and join her, she's sprawled out on the comforter.

I arrange her until she's on her hands and knees in front of me, then line up my cock and shove inside of her, too impatient to tease.

This has always been my favorite position. I like the control of deciding how deep and how fast a woman takes me, and I also like the way I can't see her face. It's easier to focus on the physical gratification, which is usually the whole point of having sex.

And I know exactly why I'm choosing it now.

Because it's terrifying to take this step with Hannah, and it has nothing to do with risking pregnancy or transmitting diseases. She told me I could trust her, and this is me doing that. But I'm also doing this because I *love* her, and I'm not sure if we'll have much of—any—relationship past Sunday.

But it's not as satisfying, looking at the smooth lines of Hannah's back and her blonde hair.

I want to watch her react, to see her response to my touch.

So I pull out of her and lie back on the bed beside her. "Ride me."

Hannah's face turns so she's looking at me. Her hand lands on my chest, tracing down over the ridges of my abdomen and playing with the line of hair that leads down to my cock. But she doesn't go down that far. I groan, already missing being inside of her.

"Ask me nicely."

I smirk. "You want me to beg?"

"Would you?"

"I'll do any-fucking-thing in the world, if it means I get to watch you take my cock and play with your tits."

Hannah rolls her eyes, but her blue eyes are softer. And she moves, crawling over me so her body is suspended over mine.

I can't think of a better view.

"Are you tired?" She teases me, the heat of her pussy hovering just above the tip. Brushing against my cock and then pulling away before I can enter her. I grab her hips so I can grind up against her. She's slick enough I slip in easily, but I can feel her stretching around me, adjusting to the sudden intrusion. See her spread.

Hannah's breathing becomes heavy pants as our skin slaps together. Her blonde hair is a wild mess, her ponytail totally gone. The bedframe knocks against the wall. If I had any neighbors, they'd be able to hear how hard she's riding me.

"Oliver..." Hannah says my name like I've never heard it before, a raw, desperate sound that consumes me. She's hot and wet and tight and *perfect*, and I want this to last forever.

My grip on her hips tightens as I grind my pelvis into hers.

We're sweaty and messy and desperate, racing toward the peak together. My entire body tenses, refusing to orgasm until she does.

She rises until I totally slip out and then sinks down again. "We couldn't do this on the kitchen counter."

I groan. "Please tell me you're not cooking more food."

Hannah laughs and shakes her head, circling her hips. My hands wander over every inch of her skin I can reach, letting go of her hips and tracing her ribs until I reach her bouncing breasts. My mouth surrounds one nipple, sucking and biting. She moans, her inner muscles fluttering around me. She's so wet I can hear it. Feel it.

My fingers slip between our bodies, finding her clit and rubbing it. Her walls clench around me in a grip so tight it's almost painful. And she lifts her neck and kisses me, which I'm not expecting. The tangle of our tongues is just as filthy as the rest of us, an unorganized jumble of lips and mouths. Biting and sucking and tasting, as I fuck her through her orgasm. And then I find my own release, the foreign feeling of releasing inside of her pushing it longer and longer. Carnal and primal and possessive.

My mouth moves from her lips to her neck, nipping at the skin. Knowing I'm probably leaving marks and not caring at all.

Possessiveness isn't my thing.

It always seemed like a trait of insecure men. But according to a document filed in some office in Nevada, Hannah Garner is mine.

And I'm pleased by that fact.

Proud of it.

Possessive of it.

Hannah moves first, lifting off me and rolling onto the bed beside me. Her breathing is still rapid, but her eyes are hazy and satisfied. She exhales, running a hand through her hair. "I need a shower."

I lean down and kiss her forehead, the affection just as natural as fucking her. "I'll start dinner."

"You mean order takeout?"

"Do you have more of everything?"

"Well, yeah. But it will take a while to make and then cook, so…"

"Just tell me what to do first."

"The chicken has to be roasted. I already chopped the veggies. They're in the fridge."

"Okay." I roll off the bed, pulling on a pair of joggers.

Hannah stands too, and I catch a glimpse of the white liquid trickling down the inside of her thigh before she disappears into the bathroom. That same proud surge returns.

Immediately followed by dread.

If I love her, I should let her go.

We end up out on the patio after finishing dinner, which turned out better than either of us expected. The bar was low, after the charred pan.

This has become our nightly routine for the past few evenings, sitting on the outdoor couch looking up at the sky. Usually huddled under a blanket. Tonight, it's a little warmer. There's a hint of spring in the air.

I take a sip of whiskey as I stare at the skyline, savoring the smoky burn as it slides down my throat.

I'm a multi-billionaire. I could go anywhere. Buy everything. Experience anything. And there's nowhere else I'd rather be than exactly where I am right now.

"Want any?" I hold the glass out to Hannah.

"Whiskey?" Hannah makes a face but takes it anyway.

"I can get you something else. A martini, maybe?"

A quiet scoff is her response to my reference to the night we met. She hands me the glass back and drops her head down on my chest. "Do you think it was my idea?"

I don't have to ask what she's referring to. "It might have been mine."

It's not hard to imagine looking at Hannah and thinking that same thing: *Mine*.

"Can I ask you something?"

"Always."

"The thing with your stepmother. Was it just…physical? Was she hot?"

I rub the side of the tumbler with my thumb. Hannah has never asked about Candace, not since that night when I told her it happened. I don't know why she's asking now, and it wouldn't be my first choice of topic.

"She was…there. Crew was focused on his marriage to Scarlett. My dad basically forgot about me once Crew graduated business school, it felt like. There was some bitterness there, for sure. But mostly, I knew it was nothing anyone would expect from me. Crew would be photographed stumbling out of clubs with models and everyone would pat him on the back at work the next day. If I showed up two minutes late to a meeting, everyone would ask if traffic was bad."

"You wanted to be someone different."

"Yeah." I exhale. "Not that I wanted to be Crew. We're different. Always have been. He's happy being the center of attention; I hate it. He's naturally charming; I research the interests of every investor or client I work with, so we have something to talk about. He was patient with Scarlett; I would have just ignored her."

"And you felt different with Candace?"

"I felt like shit. The first time, I was so drunk I could barely get hard. And I never came after that, which pissed her off. She took it as some twisted challenge…" I shake my head. "It was toxic."

"Then why did you keep having sex with her?"

"She blackmailed me."

I feel Hannah's eyes on me, but I don't look over at her. I've never told anyone this before.

"The first time, I'd gone over to the house to give my father some documents. He wasn't home. He'd told Candace he was visiting the Miami office. We don't *have* a Miami office. It wasn't hard for either of us to piece together why he lied."

I take a sip of whiskey, staring out at the skyline.

"She begged me to stay with her. Said she was lonely and depressed and hated being alone in that big, empty house. It was the first time we'd ever been alone together. I'd always avoided her. It was strange—my father marrying a woman a few months younger than me. One he basically ignored and treated as a possession, just like he treated me and Crew like employees instead of family. At least we had each other, in some form. Candace had no one. Money and beauty, but no love or power."

I swirl the glass, watching the amber liquid slosh up and drip down.

"Cheating on Arthur Kensington with his son? Controlling me by threatening to tell my father what happened between us? It was a thrill for her. An obsession. All she had in her life. And I didn't see it until too late. I thought she just wanted a night to forget, which is what I was looking for. Crew was marrying Scarlett. I wouldn't be CEO. It felt like nothing was really important—like my whole life was reorganized in a split second. And every time my dad credited Crew with an account I'd worked on, and I sat silent, I knew I was getting back at him another way. But that was just for me. I didn't want him to know."

"She told him anyway?" Hannah asks.

"She told him she was pregnant. To get his attention, I think. To scare me because I was getting more and more fed up? I don't know. Regardless, my father had conveniently forgotten to tell his bride they wouldn't be having any children. He had a vasectomy after my mom died. So as soon as Candace told him, he knew she was cheating."

"What about you?"

I glance over. "What about me?"

"You can have kids, right?"

An unwilling smile tugs up one corner of my mouth. Because she's not looking at me with disgust or judgment, and I didn't realize how worried I was it might be there until I'm seeing it isn't. "As far as I know."

"What happened to the baby?"

"Never existed. As soon as my father told her the child couldn't be his, she folded. Told him about our affair, admitted to lying about the pregnancy. Their divorce was finalized a few months later. I haven't seen her since. Hopefully, I never will."

"She let you think…"

"Yes," my response is short, but I'm not annoyed with Hannah.

I'm irritated she's focused on the part of my past that has always bothered me the most. The few people who know about Candace and me are typically too caught up in the scandal and the torrid affair to comprehend there was a point when I thought I'd be a father.

"I'm sorry."

"I probably deserved it."

"You didn't." Hannah's voice is fiercer than I've ever heard it. "You *didn't*, Oliver."

"I told Crew about us. Not the marriage, but everything else."

"What did he say?"

"He was…surprised."

"I don't have to go tomorrow."

"I want you to."

She's silent for a minute. "I'm going dress-shopping in the morning. I asked my friend Savannah to help me pick something out, since I didn't bring anything to wear."

"I want you to go, Hannah. But you don't have to, if you don't want to. For any reason."

Another long pause, as she plays with the fringe of the blanket. "I don't do things I don't want to do, Oliver," she finally says.

She's talking about the wedding, I know.

But I can't help but wonder what else she might be referring to.

CHAPTER TWENTY-THREE

HANNAH

When I wake up, I'm alone in bed.

The surroundings are familiar. I've spent the past four nights sleeping in Oliver's penthouse, since I requested to work Thursday and Friday out of the New York office so I could stay here through the weekend.

Today is Oliver's friend Garrett's wedding.

And tomorrow, I'm returning to Los Angeles.

Returning to reality.

Oliver and I have spent the last few days acting like an actual married couple. We wake up together. Go to work. Eat dinner together. Lie out on his balcony together. Go to sleep together.

I'm waiting to get sick of it.

I thought I *would* be sick of it by now. But all I feel is disappointment, staring at the subtle indentation on the pillow next to mine and knowing I'll only see it for one more morning. That I'll soon be back in my bungalow, planning another renovation in an attempt to add some excitement to my life.

I climb out of bed and pad down the hall to Oliver's office. The door is half-closed, so I push it open slowly.

Oliver is sitting at his desk, unsurprisingly. He glances up from a pile of papers as the hinge squeaks, his expression distracted. It settles into a smile when he sees me.

"Morning." My voice is raspy from sleep.

"Morning. I tried not to wake you up. I have a call with Tokyo in three minutes."

"It's *six a.m.* on a *Saturday*, Oliver."

He sighs. "I know. They wanted to talk today, urgently. It's a deal we've been chasing for a while."

I take a few steps closer, emboldened when his attention remains on me. His eyes trail up and down my body as I walk toward him, and I return the favor.

A white t-shirt and dark gray joggers are a really good look on him, especially since the bulge below the waistband suggests he didn't bother putting on any boxers.

I surprise him—and myself—when I don't stop walking until I'm climbing into his lap, straddling his growing erection.

Oliver groans as his palms land on my bare thighs, the rasp of callouses and heat of his hands sending sparks across my skin. "Go back to bed. I'll be there as soon as I can."

My hips move back and forth, teasing the growing bulge.

I'm intensely aware of what's driving this urge. I'm leaving tomorrow, and after that there will be no trips to New York. The next time I see Oliver—*if* I see him again—we won't be married. And what is only a piece of paper has come to mean something to me. It's an invisible string, something tying us together that isn't shared by anyone else or affected by anything.

His breathing quickens, the tendons in his neck straining taut. "The rest of the day, I'm yours. I won't do any work."

"Do you promise?" I ignore the modifier.

He's mine—temporarily. He knows we're a ticking clock, just like me.

"I promise." Oliver groans, his fingers tightening on my hips as they continue moving. "Dammit, Hannah."

I giggle. The thrill of him responding to my touch the same way I react to his is a high. I'm not wearing any underwear, so all that's separating us is the thin material of his pants.

Oliver's hand inches higher and higher on my leg, until he's under the flimsy fabric of my negligee. His dick twitches when he discovers how wet I am, something primal and proud heating his gaze.

He glances at the phone, then the clock. "Sixty seconds, Hannah."

I don't realize what he means at first. His palm cups my breast, the touch gentle and teasing. His thumb barely brushes my nipple, but it floods me with need and want and feeds the addiction I've developed to Oliver Kensington.

I cry out when he suddenly pinches my nipple, the burst of pain reverberating throughout my entire body and heightening my lust.

"Fifty seconds."

He means it. If I don't come by then, Oliver will stop touching me.

And I could get myself off, but it wouldn't be as satisfying. He's what my body wants.

"*Oliver*." I love saying his name. Love the way his expression changes, some secret shift that's a response to my voice.

"What do you want, Hannah?" One finger pushes inside of me, curling against a spot that sends sparks of pleasure flying through me. "You want to fuck my hand and pretend it's my cock?"

I moan, pressing my face against his neck and inhaling deeply. The expensive scent of his cologne is familiar. Comforting and arousing, all at once. I'm used to the scent on his skin. On the sheets I sleep on. For the rest of my life, it will always remind me of him.

"Thirty-nine," he murmurs, amusement saturating his voice.

My hips rock faster, my entire body tight and aching with need. A second finger stretches me open. And then, finally, his thumb touches my clit. My entire body jerks, the zap of sensation pushing me higher as he rubs small circles around the swollen spot.

"Twenty, Hannah."

I grind against his hand, forcing more pressure and focusing on that one spot.

"Ten."

His fingers curl, hitting a sensitive spot inside of me. And then I'm coming, collapsing into him as shuddering pleasure crashes through me. The wild rhythm of my heart blocks out every other sound, gradually slowing until I can hear and think and *breathe* again.

Oliver is already on the phone. He watches me with a satisfied smile on his lips, slumped in his lap, as he listens to whatever is being said on the other end of the line and nods along.

I start to get up, but his arm tightens, trapping me in place against his chest. When I glance up, the line of his jaw is sharp and tensed. I give in, relaxing against his chest, and the muscle relaxes.

At some point, I fall asleep in his lap.

Savannah is already waiting when I climb out of the car Oliver insisted on calling for me. Her light brown hair is swept back in a neat chignon, a few strands blowing in the slight breeze. It's a perfect spring day, sunny and low humidity. And early enough on a Saturday that New York's normally bustling streets are mostly deserted.

"Hey, Savannah."

She spins, the front of her white trench coat blowing open with the motion.

I'm dressed casually, in jeans and an oversize *Yale* sweatshirt that belongs to Oliver. It was a shock to discover he owns comfortable clothing. And since I was only planning to stay in New York for three days, I'm short on clean clothes. And wedding guest attire, which is the reason for this outing.

"Hannah!" Heels clip against pavement as Savannah hurries over. She hugs me, then pulls back to survey my outfit.

She, of course, looks much more fashionable. Back when I visited New York more frequently, Savannah was the one who always styled me when we'd go out.

I brace for judgment, but all she does is raise an eyebrow. "You look happy," she says.

"Is that code for homeless?" I tease.

Savannah laughs. It's light and airy, like a tinkling bell. And I'm quickly reminded of why New York wasn't for me, how I always felt inadequate.

But I don't now. There's nothing I'd rather be wearing than my favorite jeans, a comfy sweatshirt, and sneakers, my natural waves pulled back in a messy bun. I'm cozy and warm, and I'm not wondering what strangers on the street think of my appearance.

"No. It's not what *I* would wear. But it works on you."

I smirk. "Thanks."

"Let's head to Fifth first."

"Sounds good."

I figured that would be our first stop based on our meeting

point and Savannah's expensive taste. Which is exactly what I need for today.

Garrett Anderson's wedding will be a who's who of New York's elite. I can only imagine the cost of some of the dresses that will be worn there. And I'm showing up with Oliver Kensington, which will draw attention.

Attention I'm worried about, honestly. Attention that I didn't think Oliver would want.

"Have you talked to Rosie lately?" Savannah asks as we walk along the sidewalk. She and Rosie know each other from growing up in the city, which is how I first met her. Unlike Rosie, Savannah never left Manhattan.

"Not for a few days," I answer. I've been avoiding it, knowing she'll have many questions about why I'm still in New York. "You?"

"For a few minutes yesterday. She was busy with Jude."

"He's nice. I met him on my last visit to Chicago."

"Well, he's lasted longer than most." Rosie tends to fall fast and hard, and then lose interest just as quickly. I've always envied her ability to be so willing to stumble. It's rare, I think, to be so consistently open. Of course, Rosie is usually the one ending things, which is an easier position to be in.

"What about you?" I ask. "Any guys?"

Savannah blows out a frustrated breath. "No. There aren't many straight men working in the fashion industry. And work has been so crazy and hectic, I've barely gone out. I didn't get home until almost midnight last night."

"Seriously?"

She nods. "No one leaves until Scarlett does."

My stomach twists at the mention of her name.

Savannah scored a coveted assistant editor position at Haute last fall, which she was ecstatic about. The one time we ran into

Scarlett and Crew at a restaurant, it was all she talked about for the entire meal. It made me wish I'd confessed my history with Crew to her back when our fling was taking place, but I never did. Rosie is the only person I told.

"I'm surprised she works that late," is all I say.

"She leaves at five and comes back at eight, usually. I don't know how she does it, honestly. She knows everything that happens at Haute, oversees *rouge*, and is a wife and mom. And rumor at the office is, she's pregnant again."

I wonder if Oliver knows, if it's true.

We don't discuss Scarlett and Crew, aside from when he mentioned them last night. In the few days I've been basically living with him, there's been no evidence of any communication, making me think that Oliver wasn't exaggerating the disconnect between him and his brother. Or maybe they only talk at the office.

"Okay!" Savannah claps her hands together once we reach the corner that intersects with Fifth Avenue, startling a nearby pigeon pecking at a hot dog wrapper. "What look are we going for?"

All I told her via text was I was in New York, needed a new dress for an event, and asked if she was free to go shopping.

"Wedding guest."

Savannah's eyebrows rise a half an inch. Every other time we've gone shopping, it's been for slinky club attire or professional workwear. "Okay…what's the dress code?"

"Black tie."

"Venue?"

"It's at the New York Public Library."

"Tonight?"

I nod.

She puts the pieces together immediately, which I'm expecting. Savannah follows New York society closely. "I didn't know you're friends with Sienna Talbot."

"I'm not. I've never met her. Or Garrett Anderson." I pull in a deep breath. "I'm going with Oliver Kensington."

Savannah abruptly stops walking. "You're *dating Oliver Kensington*?"

"No. I'm just going to a wedding with him." I shrug a shoulder, putting on a good show of indifference as we walk along the sidewalk.

"How-how did you meet him?"

I hesitate, knowing she'll mention this to Rosie the next time they talk. The main reason I texted her is I want to look good tonight, and that isn't what I should be concerned with.

"At a bar." I opt for some version of the truth. Rosie won't share the whole story with Savannah, knowing I want to keep the marriage a secret.

"Have you slept with him?"

"No," I lie. "Maybe tonight, after the reception."

"So he's not dating Quinn Branson?"

My head whips in Savannah's direction, my breakfast churning unpleasantly in my stomach.

"Who's that?" I don't keep up with New York society anymore, but I recognize the names of most power players.

"Leonardo Branson's daughter," Savannah replies. "She just moved back from London. She and Oliver were photographed at dinner together, with Garrett and Sienna, last week. Most people were assuming she'd be at the wedding with him."

She's the woman Oliver was out with on Friday night, I realize. The one he said he wouldn't be going out with again. The worries those words swept away so easily come back in full force. She's more real with a name, and it sharpens the realization

Oliver will move on with someone else, if not her. Forcing me to confront how much that idea bothers me.

Savannah is waiting, expectantly, for me to say something.

"He's never mentioned her," I tell Savannah. "We met, hit it off, and he invited me to the wedding."

"Huh." Savannah pauses, glances at the display in the front window of a store, and then continues walking. "Well, Oliver has always been different."

"What do you mean?"

"He's totally focused on Kensington Consolidated. If I was worth billions, I'd take a vacation every once in a while. But he doesn't party, never gets photographed with women. That's why everyone made such a fuss over the photos last weekend. Some people are speculating they're engaged, and that's why he was seen with her."

"Oh."

Savannah glances over, her expression creasing with concern in response to whatever look is on my face. "Leonardo Branson does business with Arthur Kensington. He probably asked Oliver to connect his daughter with the right people, now that's she's back in town."

I nod, my mind still a mess of thoughts. My family and Rosie know about my marriage, but I haven't confided in anyone about how real it seems. I have feelings for Oliver that go much deeper than lust or attraction, and no idea how to navigate them.

"Let's go in here."

Blindly, I follow Savannah inside a brightly lit store and over to a long rack of colorful dresses, trying to shake off the anxiety and second-guessing. The terror that I'm in so deep with Oliver that I won't be able to dig myself out. It never felt like this with Declan. With anyone else. Like falling, with nothing to hold on to. No way to stop myself.

"Any budget?" she asks.

"No." My voice comes out dull, so I clear my throat, trying to summon back some of my earlier excitement. "And I'll need shoes and a handbag too."

Oliver handed me a black credit card before I left. And since this is the last night we'll probably spend together, I fully intend to go all out.

Savannah grins at me, and I force an answering smile.

At least I'll look good on the outside, even if I'm a mess on the inside.

Oliver's standing in the kitchen when I walk into the penthouse, studying his tablet. I guess he reverted to his workaholic ways while I was gone.

He looks up, taking in all the bags I'm holding. When he sets down the tablet, I realize he was watching a baseball game, not staring at documents.

"I see you gave the card a good workout." He smirks at my overloaded hands.

I want to smile back. Want to walk over and kiss him.

But I've done too much of that lately. I need to remind myself what my life will be like starting tomorrow. That I'm an independent woman with goals and ambition, not a pampered princess in a fairytale.

I fish the credit card out of my jeans' pocket and toss it on the spotless countertop. "Consider it our divorce settlement."

His cheek twitches. A tiny reaction, but one I notice. Neither of us have mentioned our pending divorce in the past few days.

But I can't lose sight of the fact we're not an actual couple.

That Oliver doesn't want a wife and will soon be spending his limited breaks from work with other women, some of whom might have sophisticated British accents. I looked up the photos Savannah mentioned in the car ride back here. The woman he went out with was stunning. Quinn Branson looks like exactly the type of woman a successful billionaire would date. And maybe marry, if Oliver ever changes his view about it.

I never thought I'd have to remind myself to protect my heart. With every other guy, it's been my natural instinct. I've been *too* detached, according to most of them.

"Did you have fun with Savannah?" There's a hesitant note to Oliver's voice, as his gaze trails over my tensed posture.

He's obviously sensed the shift in my mood. I left here smiling. And he has the audacity to remember Savannah's name, even though I only mentioned it once. The thoughtfulness just pisses me off more. This would all be a lot easier, if he was as bad at relationships as he claims to be.

"Yeah, it was fun."

"You were gone for a while."

I lift a shoulder and drop it carelessly. "Nothing to do here."

This time, his jaw clenches. His only response is a stiff nod before he glances back down at his tablet. I can see him retreating, shutting down. Exactly what I was hoping for, but I also hate that it's happening.

"Car will be here in an hour."

"I'll be ready."

I grab my bags and leave the kitchen, walking down the hallway and into the guest bedroom for the first time.

Oliver's entire penthouse is professionally decorated, all matching furniture and coordinated shades. It's beautiful, but empty. It's obvious he doesn't spend much time here.

The guest room is all shades of blue. I drop my bags on the

navy comforter and then head across the hall to grab my bag of toiletries from Oliver's bathroom. Thankfully he's still in the kitchen, so I don't have to navigate another stilted encounter.

I rush back into the guest room, shutting the door and leaning against it with a sigh, acting like I just completed a perilous mission.

I exhale, trying to release the anxiety in the same rush. I thought I'd be able to handle this better.

All week, I knew this had an expiration date. I thought simply knowing that would protect me. That logic would soften the blow. That this would be a fun fling with a guy I'm intrigued by and attracted to. That's the problem, though. I'm *too* intrigued. *Too* attracted.

I just got into my dream school, hundreds of miles away from where Oliver lives and works. My past is entangled with his family in an awkward way. And most importantly, Oliver has never given me any clear indication he *wants* this to last.

We were never going to end any other way.

I never *thought* we'd end any other way.

But thinking about it won't stop stinging, like the invisible, persistent slice of a paper cut. I never thought inevitability would hurt this much.

I head into the bathroom with my bag of toiletries, stripping out of the jeans and sweatshirt and stepping into the shower. Everything in here is made of marble: the floor, the counters, even the walls. All the light fixtures and accents are black metal.

I don't register much of the luxurious surroundings beyond those contrasting colors, stepping behind the glass pane and turning on the shower head. It has ten different settings, because *of course* it does. I opt for rain.

Warm water falls in gentle pelts as I scrub and soap and shave. Reluctantly, I shut the shower off and grab one of the fluffy towels hanging on a hook, drying off and then wrapping it around my torso as I pad across the tile floor until I reach the vanity.

The mirror is covered with steam since I forgot to switch on the vent. I brush my teeth and comb my hair while I wait for it to clear.

I usually straighten my hair, so I decide to curl it for tonight. Thanks to the natural wave in the texture, I have to straighten and *then* curl it, which takes twice as long. Time I don't really have, since I delayed coming back here until the last possible minute. Once the last spiral falls, I comb through the curls, spray them, and then pull a few pieces back with bobby pins. Satisfied with my hair, I start on my makeup.

The dress Savannah talked me into purchasing is bolder than I was planning to wear. The last wedding I attended was for an older cousin. That one took place in Santa Monica, right by the beach. Most of the guests were barefoot for the ceremony and the reception. It was casual and bohemian and nothing like the chic events I've attended here.

My dress tonight is a brilliant teal, a departure from the navy or black gowns I usually wear to fancier events. There are ruffles gathered at the shoulders and capping the hem. It has a sweetheart neckline that's fairly modest, but the back is sheer lace, with a delicate column of fabric buttons running down the center.

I feel pretty with it on. It's beautiful armor.

Two minutes remain in my hour by the time my makeup is finished. I rush into the bedroom, still in a towel, pulling the matching clutch and silver heels out of their bags. The clutch is only big enough for my phone, credit card, and a tube of lip gloss. I shove it all in, praying I'm not forgetting anything.

There's a knock on the door. I spin, pulse pounding.

"Hannah?"

"Yeah?" My grip on the towel tightens.

"The car is here, and traffic is bad. Are you ready?"

"I'm naked." I say the first thing that comes to mind, then screw my eyes shut in an attempt to block out the words that feel like they're hovering in the air between us, gaining size and substance. "I'll, uh, I'll be right out. Just give me a minute."

There's a *long* pause.

This morning, he fingered me in his lap. Now, it feels like we're total strangers.

I don't know if Oliver is reacting to my coolness or deciding to pull away as well. The guy who carried me from the balcony to bed last night would burst in here and smirk as he watched me get dressed. But the girl who fell asleep on him would have left the door open. Wouldn't be getting ready in the guest room at all.

It's disconcerting how so much familiarity can disappear so quickly, like a popped balloon.

"Okay." Oliver finally responds. I listen to his quiet steps walk away, then release a deep breath.

I pull the dress out of its box and step into the center of the chiffon, pulling the fabric up and over my shoulders.

The exposed back makes it impossible to wear a bra, but the designer thoughtfully included a padded front that provides enough support. I fix the dress in place, reach around for a zipper, and freeze.

I can't zip up my dress. It's held together by dozens of tiny buttons that I can barely reach, much less attach. I thought nothing of it at the store. I was still trying to shake off Savannah's comment about Oliver's rumored girlfriend, and she helped me with every gown I tried on in the dressing suite, inspecting fabric and studying details.

My body is frozen in place, my mind racing.

I have nothing else to wear. I didn't buy a backup dress, and all I brought from LA was business attire, pajamas, and jeans.

I walk into the bathroom, my horrified expression clear as day in the mirror.

Without anything holding the back together the teal material is sagged forward, dipping so low over my cleavage it barely covers anything. There's absolutely no way I can wear it like this, even with a jacket over it.

I suck in a fortifying breath of oxygen, knowing what—who—my only option is.

I walk back into the bedroom. The silky fabric of the dress swishes against my skin as I walk, brushing it like an erotic whisper. And reminding me I forgot to grab underwear when I grabbed my toiletries from Oliver's room.

I step into the heels, grab my clutch with one hand, hold my dress with the other, and open the bedroom door.

Oliver is leaning against the opposite wall, waiting.

I suck in a sharp breath, my eyes trailing up from his black dress shoes to the tailored pants, stiff jacket, and ironed shirt of his tuxedo. He shaved, the line of his jaw sharp and defined. I can smell his aftershave from here, the scent woodsy and spicy.

It is *unfair* for him to look this good.

Since I'm focused on his throat, I see it bob as he swallows. My eyes make the rest of the journey up to his, something clenching deep in my stomach when our gazes connect.

His smile is slow, spreading across his face and lightening the harsh angles. He looks every inch the intimidating billionaire.

And…I realize with a start, he kind of looks like *mine*.

Because he's staring at me like I belong to *him*.

"What's wrong with your dress?"

"Uh." I blink rapidly. "I'm, um, there are buttons." I gesture toward the back of my dress vaguely, realizing too late why that's a bad idea. The lace and silk slip off one shoulder, and my right breast makes an appearance.

I scramble for the strap, but Oliver is faster. In one smooth motion, he captures the fabric, pulling it back into place.

My cheeks burn as his fingers graze my bare skin, leaving a warm, tingling sensation behind.

"Sorry for flashing you." I croak.

One corner of his mouth curves up. "Nothing I haven't seen before."

I swallow and nod.

"Turn around."

I comply, inhaling quickly when his fingers trail down the column of my back, tracing over every bump of my spine. Despite his words earlier, Oliver doesn't seem to be in any big rush to leave now.

Magically, the back of my dress begins to tighten. Oliver's fingers are deft and efficient, popping the buttons into place one by one.

"I like the dress," he says. "Even if the buttons are impractical."

"The compliment every woman dreams of."

"Sorry I couldn't offer you *more*." The edge to his tone makes it clear my *nothing to do here* comment struck a nerve.

"Don't apologize," I mumble.

Neither of us say anything else, until he steps back a few minutes later. "All set."

"Thanks."

I start down the hallway, toward the elevator that will take us downstairs. After a beat, I hear Oliver's footsteps behind me. Feel his eyes on my back.

Mine stay straight ahead.

CHAPTER TWENTY-FOUR

OLIVER

Hannah won't look at me.

And I can't stop staring at her.

I twist the cufflink in its hole above my wrist for the twentieth time, needing some outlet for all the nervous energy pinballing inside of me.

This was supposed to be a special evening. The wedding of one of the few people I consider a true friend, spent with the woman I can't seem to get enough of.

But ever since Hannah returned from her shopping trip, she's acted like my presence is an inconvenience, and I'm not sure how to handle it. What it means. All I know is I hate her sudden indifference. I feel like a toddler, sulking because I'm receiving less attention.

I've always felt like Hannah was either an instigator or a willing participant in this *thing* between us, which has no easy label. We're married, but we've never been a couple. We're in the midst of a divorce, but currently living together.

My thumb rubs against the rough surface of my cufflink. These are my favorite pair, one of few gifts from my father I actually like. Constructed from an ancient Rome inset, the center is a depiction of Julius Caesar, with *veni, vidi, vici* sketched around the rim.

I came, I saw, I conquered.

Doesn't seem fitting. I'm more defeated than victorious at the moment.

I steal another glance at Hannah. She's staring out the window, entirely motionless, with her hands folded neatly in her lap.

From this angle, the neckline of her dress gapes a little. I can see the curve of her left breast. My dick twitches in my tight pants, remembering how she looked standing in the hallway with one breast bared. The flush of scarlet that stole across her skin when she realized I was looking.

I stood outside the guest room for way too long earlier, listening to water rush through the pipes and staring at the shut door. Feeling like an interloper in my own home. Torn between honoring Hannah's obvious wish to be left alone and pounding on the door, demanding she tell me what changed in the few hours she was gone.

I ended up staring, trying to will away the coil of dread that appeared as soon as I realize she'd chosen to get ready in one of the guest rooms instead of my room. It's still there, sitting like a lead weight in my stomach.

If she sleeps in there tonight…

This shouldn't bother me. It grates that it does. There are a million other things I should be focused on and thinking about. But all I can see is her, wearing a blue-green dress that manages to cover everything but also be the sexiest thing I've ever seen.

"Is something wrong?" It's a relief to finally speak the words, after thinking them on a nonstop loop.

"No." Still, she won't look at me. And it *hurts*, aches like a punch to an existing bruise. I'd rather she yell and scream than ignore me. At least I would have some idea what she's thinking.

"One."

Finally, she faces me. I'm caught off guard by the eye contact.

My favorite look on Hannah is when she's barefaced with tangled waves, naked in my bed. But she looks devastatingly, heart-breakingly beautiful tonight, and I should have told her so earlier.

"What?" she asks.

"I'm counting the number of lies you've told me."

If she's told me others, they haven't been so obvious.

Her eyes narrow, but the blue is still intense and consuming. Overwhelming. And shifting. They remind me of the sky, where there's always something different to see. A cloud or a storm or a rainbow.

The car stops moving. I glance out at the stone lion that guards the entrance to the library. Thousands of candles have been placed on the steps leading from the sidewalk to the doors, flickering in the fading light. Once it's completely dark out, it will be a dazzling sight.

I open the limo door and step out, taking a deep breath as I adjust my cufflinks one final time. From here on out, I won't display any nervous habits. I can already feel attention turning this way, my shoulders tensing as I paste a fake smile on my face.

I walk around to the other door, shaking my head at the driver as he reaches for the handle. He steps back instantly, bowing his head a little.

Hannah wasn't expecting me to be the one opening her door. I watch the delicate column of her throat bob before she steels herself and grabs my hand, the silk of her dress exposing a flash of calf before it falls in a loose waterfall.

"Thank you," she says.

"You're welcome."

Hannah takes my elbow as we climb the stairs, her balance shaky on the uneven stone.

I can't help myself. "Maybe you should have worn flats."

"Maybe you should stop criticizing my outfit," she shoots back.

I bite the inside of my cheek to hide my smile.

Hundreds of people are milling about the massive lobby.

The first couple I see are my brother and sister-in-law.

And since we're Kensingtons, everyone is staring.

The muscles of my shoulders bunch beneath the tailored seams of my tuxedo.

"You good?" I murmur to Hannah.

"Fine."

"Oliver!"

I turn to see Chase Anderson approaching, a broad grin on his face as he shakes my hand and then claps me on the shoulder. His exuberance is contagious, relaxing a little of my stiff posture.

"How the hell are you, man?"

"Not bad," I reply. "I saw you clinched playoffs, congrats."

"Thanks. Gotta grab a flight back to Detroit tonight, but I couldn't miss Garrett's wedding." He glances at Hannah. "Hello, gorgeous. I don't think we've ever been introduced."

I glare at him, my hand automatically finding the small of Hannah's back. The heat of her skin burns my fingers, separated by only the thin layer of lace I buttoned up earlier.

"We haven't. But I helped negotiate Conor Hart's trade, so since he was the one who scored the overtime goal against Chicago, you're welcome for a chance to chase the Cup."

Chase blinks at Hannah, uncharacteristically speechless. "You're an agent?" he finally asks.

"Not exactly. I just work at a sports agency."

"Which one?"

"Garner Sports Agency."

"Damn." Chase whistles, looking impressed.

"Chase!" A middle-aged woman I recognize as Mrs. Anderson appears, her bracelets jangling as she waves her hands around. "You're supposed to be helping your brother get ready."

"He's a grown man, Mom. What am I supposed to do?"

She shakes her head. "*Not* be out here drinking and socializing. Go!"

Chase downs the glass of what I assumed was water but am now guessing is vodka, then holds it up in a *cheers* motion. "Good seeing you, Oliver. Lovely to meet you, Blondie."

Garrett's mother squeezes my arm, smiles at Hannah, and then follows her wayward son.

I glance to where Crew and Scarlett were standing before. They're still in the same spot, talking intently. Arguing, knowing them.

In the crowded lobby they're given a wide berth, everyone shooting them awed, surreptitious looks but not daring to approach the couple considered to be New York's king and queen.

Crew looks up and meets my gaze, giving me a nod of acknowledgment before his eyes slide to the woman standing next to me. Scarlett follows his attention, and then we're all staring at each other.

"We should say hi."

"We should," Hannah agrees.

My hand remains on Hannah's lower back as we navigate our way through the crowd toward my brother and sister-in-law.

Crew is wearing a tuxedo, same as me. Scarlett is wearing a bold red dress that hugs her torso and then flares out dramatically at the waist.

I open my mouth. But unexpectedly, Scarlett is the one who speaks first, addressing me. "You clean up nicely, Oliver."

"So do you." I drop my hand from Hannah's back so I can lean forward and kiss her cheek, then shake Crew's hand.

"Nice to see you, Hannah," he says, kissing her cheek the same way I greeted Scarlett.

There's a swell of relief and affection, watching their interaction. I don't know how I'd react if Crew had shown up to an event with a woman I had history with. It's an uncomfortable situation for everyone, and I appreciate my brother acting like it's not.

"Nice to see you too," Hannah replies. I watch her take a deep breath, then look at Scarlett. "Hello, Scarlett."

Scarlett inclines her head, her eyes flicking between Hannah and me like we're a puzzle she's trying to decode or a map she's trying to follow. "Hello, Hannah."

I rarely bring a date to events like this. Usually, I see them as a networking opportunity, which most women grow bored by or resentful of. So there's a different dynamic tonight that has nothing to do with Hannah. Crew and Scarlett have never interacted with a woman I was dating.

The lobby is beginning to clear, other guests filtering past into the central room where the ceremony is set to take place.

I grab Hannah's hand, squeezing it in a silent show of support. "We should go grab our seats. See you guys at the reception?"

I catch Crew's nod before we turn away, following the flow of traffic into a round room that's been decorated with hundreds of flowers. The altar is set up in the very center, with rows of seats surrounding it. It's not nearly as extravagant as Crew and Scarlett's wedding was. But their nuptials were intentionally planned out so they'd be impossible to top. No one does regency like royalty.

Lots of people greet me by name as we pass by, shooting

Hannah curious looks. She's poised as we walk down a middle row, chatting with Jennifer Robinson when she takes the seat on her other side.

I scan the program that was left on my seat. Since neither Sienna nor Garrett have bridal parties, it's just a description of the ceremony. Short, since it's a civil one.

All the surrounding chatter dies down when the familiar strains of Pachelbel's Cannon fill the huge space. Garrett steps onto the altar, staring down the constructed aisle.

Almost everyone turns to watch Sienna walk toward him. But I focus on Garrett, a close friend who's about to make a commitment that, technically, I've already made.

Whatever alcohol or drugs I consumed in Vegas wiped my memory of getting married completely clean. Or maybe I just don't *want* to remember. Maybe it's easier to pretend that someone else made that decision, totally separate from me.

But I glance at Hannah, and I can picture it perfectly. Can imagine her walking toward me wearing white, so clearly that I wonder if it's memory or something less substantive. Some hazy, dreamy state.

Sienna is beaming when she reaches Garrett. I don't register any details about her dress or veil, but I scrutinize her expression closely. Witness the happiness that appears genuine. Wonder what regrets she has. If she has any.

I have a long list, but Hannah isn't on it. I can't say I wouldn't change anything. All the stress and uncertainty of the past few weeks since I woke up married to a stranger has been unwelcome. But they also landed me sitting here, which doesn't feel like too high a price to pay.

Once the ceremony ends and the newlyweds have walked down the aisle together, everyone stands to head into the reception room. This space is long and rectangular, with multiple tables stretching from end to end, with a dance floor and stage set up in the very front.

Uniformed servers move silently through the space with appetizers, and bars have been set up in all four corners.

"Do you want a drink?" I ask Hannah, the first words we've exchanged since the end of the ceremony.

"Sure," she answers, looking around the cavernous space. The ceilings are tall, patterns of stained glass worked into them.

She's not looking at the flowers or other decorations, I realize. She's studying the architecture.

It's an unwelcome but necessary reminder. Hannah has a lot waiting for her. A whole new future spread out ahead. While my life will remain the same, working in a building that I love but am also realizing I hold a lot of resentment toward.

I'm dreading telling my father I'm not accepting his offer. Once I do, I have no clue how he'll react. It will be taken as a personal affront, no doubt. I'll be rejecting what he probably sees as a generous concession from my father *and* my boss.

For the first time, I seriously consider leaving Kensington Consolidated. It's a thought that's passed my mind now and again. It was more persistent after everything came out about Candace. But there's always been something stopping me, and it's still there now. It's a part of me. A piece that would hurt to lose. It's more than a paycheck to me, same as it is for my father.

But there *are* other paychecks. Other CEO positions.

And I think, glancing at Hannah as she orders a cocktail from the bartender, some of them are located in California.

"Finally left Kensington Consolidated, Oliver?"

I turn around to face Camden Crane.

He's an entitled prick I make a point to avoid as much as possible. But my disdain is nothing compared to Crew's, who supposedly punched him a couple of years ago. I only heard about the aftermath, since it was back when my father confided in me. He was furious Crew jeopardized a business relationship, and even angrier it was because of Scarlett. Crew wouldn't admit it was, but nothing else would have made him fly off the handle like he did.

"Do you even know where Crane Enterprise's offices are, Camden?"

He laughs like it was a joke. It wasn't. Sebastian Crane took a very different approach to his son's involvement in the family business than my own father did. Camden happily takes a portion of the profits, so he can party and drink his way around the world.

"Life's too short to spend it in a cubicle."

"I'm sure your stockholders would agree," I reply.

Camden chuckles again. He's always attempted to act buddy buddy with me, probably in an effort to annoy Crew. And I've usually tolerated it, because Crane Enterprises is a competitor of Kensington Consolidated and there's something to be said for the *keep your enemies close* adage.

But I'm not so accommodating now, partly because Crew deserves my loyalty more than the company does, and partly because Camden has noticed Hannah. His expression is lecherous as he watches her pick up a martini glass, and I completely understand Crew's compulsion to rearrange his face.

"I'll take a whiskey, neat," I tell the bartender when he turns to me next.

"I don't believe we've had the pleasure of being introduced," Camden says, holding a hand out to her. "I'm Camden Crane."

"Hannah Garner." She shakes his hand with her free one.

"Are you two…"

"Yes." My tone is short and clipped.

Camden isn't deterred. "Do you live in New York, Hannah?"

She toys with the olives in her martini as she shakes her head. "Los Angeles."

"Great city. If you need a tour guide while you're visiting, I could probably make myself available. Oliver has a reputation for being a very busy man."

"I prefer to date men with a work ethic, Camden. Now, if you'll excuse us…" Hannah walks away before Camden has a chance to respond.

I smile at Camden's stunned expression. "Nice to see you."

Then I follow Hannah toward our assigned table.

CHAPTER TWENTY-FIVE

HANNAH

Once I'm locked in the bathroom stall, I bang my head against the door. Unfortunately, these are fancy doors. Instead of plastic that absorbs sounds, they're constructed of some ancient wood that echoes the knock.

I blow out a long breath.

I just have to get through the rest of tonight. My flight is first thing tomorrow morning. I pee and flush, then grab the handle.

A cacophony of tapping heels echoes off the marble floor, accompanied by several female voices.

"…the blonde here with him?" one of them is saying.

My hand freezes, remaining still instead of opening the latch.

"She's pretty," another voice says. "He's probably just fucking her."

"Leonardo Branson told my father that Quinn will be a Kensington by the fall." A third voice joins the conversation, as I realize exactly who they're talking about.

"I didn't think Oliver would ever get married, honestly. Even when he was supposed to marry Scarlett. He's too…*serious*, you know?"

"Oliver still needs heirs," someone else adds. "Unless he wants Crew's kids to inherit everything. I heard Scarlett is pregnant again."

"Really? I'll never get off the *rouge* waiting list, at this rate."

Laughter echoes before the conversation changes to lipstick and mascara flakes while the group of women touch up their appearance. I lean against the door, listening to their voices bounce off the tiled walls before beginning to fade as they head back to the party.

I unlock the door and finally step out of the bathroom stall. No one else is in sight as I turn on the tap. Warm water starts to run, right as another stall door opens.

I freeze, watching in the mirror as Scarlett Kensington approaches the sink next to mine. She pulls a tube of lipstick out of her clutch, coating her lips in a fresh coat of red.

"People will say whatever shit they want about you," she says, capping it. "To you. Doesn't mean you should believe a word of it."

I don't miss the double meaning. *I've* said some shit.

Nerves ricochet around my stomach. My memory of exactly what I said to her in another fancy restroom isn't crystal clear. I was tipsy, and it was a couple of years ago. But I remember enough to know the flood of shame is warranted. And while I've wished for the opportunity to apologize, now that it's here I'm not sure exactly what to say. Scarlett is intimidating.

"So Oliver isn't supposed to marry Quinn Branson?"

"He was." Her diamond engagement ring glitters as she looks through her clutch for something. The purse is dyed to match the fabric of her dress exactly, just like mine. "He won't, though."

"Why?"

She turns toward me, her expression amused. "Kensingtons don't ask stupid questions, Hannah."

There's a fresh flood of anxiety as Scarlett stares at me. Her dark hair is piled on top of her head, a few ringlets cascading down in perfect spirals. She's stunning, the woman who captures attention anywhere she goes.

And *she knows*, I realize. Either Oliver told her or she found out some other way.

I swallow. "My last name is Garner."

"I remember. Hard to forget the last conversation we had."

I hold her gaze. "I didn't know who Oliver was when we met. Honestly, I hoped I'd never see you or Crew again."

Her lips quirk. *Almost* a smile. "I believe you about that. But I didn't think you were the type of woman to get married without asking for a guy's last name."

"I figured that was *exactly* the type of woman you thought I was, actually."

A ghost of a smile flitters across Scarlett's face. "I like your dress."

My hand wavers before shutting off the faucet, stunned by the compliment. "Th-thank you. Savannah picked it out. She works for you, at Haute."

She glances over. "There's a button open on the back. Bothered me through the whole ceremony. May I?"

"Um, sure."

Seconds later, there's a tug on the fabric. "All set."

"Thanks. I didn't think the back through."

"Fashion isn't meant to be convenient."

I don't think she's talking about fashion, though.

Scarlett heads for the door, her heels tapping out a quick pace.

"Scarlett."

It takes a few steps, but she pauses and glances back.

I pull in a deep breath, nerves making my palms sweat. I'll have to wash my hands again. "I'm really sorry. What I said to you—what I remember of it—is unforgiveable. I had a…different impression of what your marriage was like, but that's no excuse. If I could go back and keep my mouth shut, I would. And I'm happy for you and Crew. It's nice to know real love exists, for those of us who haven't found it yet."

Scarlett stares at me, unblinking. The *drip drip drip* of the leaky faucet is the only sound, for what feels like an eternity.

"Everyone makes mistakes. And if you haven't found love yet, you aren't looking very hard, Hannah."

She leaves in a swirl of red fabric and expensive perfume.

When I walk back into the reception a few minutes later, I find Oliver across the room immediately. He's shaking hands with a group of men, appearing to be saying goodbyes.

I feel my forehead wrinkle with confusion.

"Hi, Hannah."

I turn, hiding my surprise. I was expecting Crew and Scarlett to avoid me tonight. Ignore me.

"Hi, Crew."

"How've you been?" He tilts his head, studying me with a mixture of curiosity and uncertainty.

"Good."

"So…you and Oliver."

I nod, not sure what to say.

"You didn't mention it, in Los Angeles."

"At the time, I didn't think there was anything to say."

"And now?"

I shrug, reverting to nonverbal responses. I know Oliver's relationship with his brother is complicated. And I hate that I'm probably adding to it. Whatever Oliver wants to share—or not share—about us with Crew should be his call.

"You seem different," he tells me, tilting his head. "More…settled."

"You're the one with a wife and a kid."

He nods, a crease appearing in his cheek. "Soon to be two."

A rumor I've heard twice now but wasn't confirmed. "Wow. Congrats."

His blue eyes are back on me. Searching. "Oliver didn't mention it?"

I shake my head. "We don't… It's a little awkward, obviously. And Oliver and I aren't that serious."

Crew laughs, surprising me. "Bullshit, Hannah."

My lips thin. "Happy endings don't fall in everyone's lap, Crew."

"You think I don't know that? But I know Oliver. I know you well enough to tell you care about Oliver in a way you were never invested in me. And Oliver hasn't checked his email once since you guys arrived, which is about twenty times less than I normally see him on his phone. This was the first week in five years that Oliver wasn't the last one to leave the office. You're good for him, Hannah. He needs something to care about, besides the damn company." He glances away to where Oliver is still standing across the room. "What I'm trying to say is, don't let anything that happened between us affect you guys."

"You think pretty highly of yourself, huh?"

Crew raises one eyebrow. "You're the one who told my wife I think about you when I fuck her."

I wince and look away. Couples have started dancing, now that dinner has ended and the cake was cut. "I was drunk."

He smiles, then shrugs. "We all have moments in the past we wish we could change. Me. Oliver. Don't let them talk you out of taking risks."

"What are you, a therapist?"

He laughs, then glances past me. "Hi, big brother."

Oliver's eyes are on me, not Crew. Checking on my reaction.

I offer him a smile, more at ease than I've felt since we arrived. It feels like a boulder has been lifted off my chest now that I've apologized to Scarlett. Maybe some mistakes are resolvable. Some regrets reversible.

"I should go find Scarlett," Crew says. "She hates attending these events sober. Nice talking to you, Hannah."

"You too," I say, before he disappears.

"You okay?" Oliver asks as soon as Crew is gone.

"Yeah. We were just…catching up."

He nods, then sighs. "The company I talked to this morning wants to do another call. Now."

"On a Saturday night?"

"It's Sunday morning, for them."

"Doesn't sound much better."

He half-smiles. "No. It doesn't."

"So, you have to leave?"

Oliver's gaze is searching as he stares at me. I have no idea what he's looking for. "Do you want to stay?"

"Alone? No, thanks. Camden Crane might show up again."

"You handled him fine."

"Not the first time a guy has approached me at a bar."

"Yeah. I know." He holds my gaze, and there's a tangible pulse between us.

Somehow, I know he's recalling when we stood together at the bar in LA. When he insisted he wasn't jealous. "Well, if we're leaving I should—"

"Do you want to dance?"

Crew's words echo in my mind. *He needs something to care about, besides the damn company.*

"What about the call?"

"It can wait until Monday."

"Okay." I nod, the movement jerky. People are staring at us—staring at him—and I'm uncomfortable with the scrutiny.

Oliver leads me out onto the dance floor. The music is slow and sweeping, a waltz that evokes floating on water or spinning in circles.

"You look stunning, Hannah." His words rise inside me like a growing tide, spreading heat across my skin.

"Thank you," I manage to say.

Oliver's smile grows as our gazes connect; his attention totally focused on me. His attention is overwhelming, but I can't manage to look away. I wonder how I'll live without it. If the simple act of someone looking at me will ever feel this way again.

"The woman you went out with was Quinn Branson?" I can't keep the question contained. It spills out of me like an overflowing fountain.

Twin wrinkles appear between Oliver's eyes as my question registers. "Yes."

"And you were supposed to marry her?"

"Where did you hear that?"

"Does it matter?"

Oliver's hand tightens around mine. A muscle leaps in his jaw. "My father suggested it."

"Why aren't you?"

"I'm already married."

His voice is low, and I match it. "We're getting divorced."

"Won't change anything."

"It could." I'm not sure why I'm pushing it. After Oliver and I part ways, what he does with his life is none of my business. It's none of my business now, honestly.

"Did Crew say something to you?"

"No. Some women were talking about it in the bathroom. And Savannah mentioned the photos of you two."

"Is that why you've been acting this way since you got back?"

"No," I lie.

"Hannah, I—"

Whatever else Oliver was going to say is lost in a sudden flurry of activity, as a group of guys appear and surround us.

"Here you are!" The same man who approached Oliver when we first arrived slings an arm around his neck. "Come on, Garrett wants to do a group photo." He glances at me. "We'll have him right back."

I nod as they pull Oliver away, caught somewhere between relief and frustration about the interruption, before I head toward the bar, so I'm not left standing alone out here.

Oliver and I are both silent as the limo pulls away from the curb, headed uptown.

It's late, and I'm exhausted. I'm also very aware of how few hours remain of my time in New York. Oliver and I haven't had a chance to talk alone since our dance was interrupted. The rest of the night was spent conversing with what's become a blur of names and faces in my mind. For someone who claims to hate attending parties and socializing, he's awfully good at both.

I kick off my heels, stretching the arches of my feet. Oliver's head tilts in my direction, tracking the movement. I'm tipsy, and I think he's buzzed too. Every time I saw him standing in the center of a group of men who were hanging on to his every word, he had a glass in hand.

The limo rolls through the city streets slowly, the lanes crowded even at this late hour.

"I haven't been in a limo since senior prom."

When I glance over at Oliver, he's looking at me. "Who'd you go with?"

"A group of friends."

One eyebrow rises. "No guys asked you?"

"They did. I just didn't want to go with any of them."

"I should probably find those high standards flattering."

"Who'd *you* go to prom with?"

"I didn't go," he replies.

"Did a girl turn you down?"

He scoffs. "No. I didn't see the point in going."

If I ever meet Arthur Kensington, I would hand him a parenting book. He did a number on Oliver. On both his sons.

"The point is *fun*, Oliver."

"It only would have been *fun* if we'd gone to high school together."

I tuck my feet under the silk of my dress and roll my head toward him. These leather seats feel like sitting on a cloud. "You would have asked me?"

"Of course." He says it like there's no other possible answer, and for some reason I believe him.

Warmth unfurls in the center of my chest, flooding me with an intense affection I'm scared to name.

I don't drop his gaze, feeling around for the buckle of my seatbelt. The quiet *snap* of the belt releasing sounds loud, in the silence between us.

Shadows pass across his face as I crawl into his lap, the flashing lights of the cars and buildings we pass disappearing as quickly as they appear. Then the car stops, either at a red light or stuck in heavier traffic, and I can see Oliver's expression perfectly.

He's staring at me like he never wants to look at anything else.

All night, I saw him schmooze. Watched him be charming and intimidating and serious, all at once.

I knew it was a mask. I've seen past the polished tycoon act he portrayed all night. And it feels like even more of a privilege, after witnessing him in his world tonight. Knowing none of those people get to see his real smile or hear his real laugh or experience the potent sensation of his undivided attention.

His hands slip beneath the fabric of my dress that's fanning out around us, settling on my calves.

The car begins moving again. I shift on his lap, not prepared for the motion, and his grip on my legs tightens.

"Hannah…"

I rest my forehead against his, inhaling his scent. "Can you be quiet?" I whisper.

"Can you?"

I kiss him. It's messy and urgent and heady, sending pulses of arousal through my entire body. Oliver called himself boring, but I'm more daring around him than I've ever been with anyone else.

There's no hesitation as I shift away so I can pull his pants down to his thighs. I'm convinced there's no sexier sight in the world than Oliver Kensington in a tuxedo with ruffled hair and blazing eyes, his rigid erection proudly on display.

His hands slide up my legs, using the leverage to pull me against his body. They move higher and higher, until they rest on my hips.

"You're not wearing underwear?" The question comes out half-choked.

My face flames. "My suitcase was in your room, and I forgot to…*oh*."

I completely forget whatever I was saying, when his hard length rubs against my bare, wet center. Need pools low in my belly as our pelvises grind together, simulating sex. I slide back and forth along his shaft, and Oliver grunts a "Fuck," his fingers digging into my skin in response to the tantalizing friction.

I reach between our bodies, tracing the throbbing vein that runs the length of his cock before I fist him just beneath the flared head and guide him to my entrance.

He doesn't push in right away, and I don't sink down. We're suspended in a moment of anticipation, and we both know why.

This will be the last time we do this.

There's going to *be* a last time.

Oliver's jaw clenches. And then he pulls me down, forcing me to take him in one swift shove. I gasp, the sound too loud in the silent car, as I adjust to the sudden stretch.

I might have started this, but Oliver is in complete control now. His hands squeeze my hips as he lifts me and then pulls me back down again, filling me over and over again. Heat spreads through my entire body as my breathing picks up, the scent of his cologne mixing with the smell of sweat and sex.

I'm disoriented when he suddenly stops thrusting, glancing out the window and half-expecting to find we're already at his building. But the car is still rolling along an unfamiliar street.

Oliver lifts me off his lap like I weigh nothing, setting me down on the seat next to him. I blink at him, then open my mouth. "What—"

He silences me with a searing kiss.

I'm falling onto my back, lying on the soft cushions of the car. The seat is long, but not lengthy enough to accommodate Oliver's six-foot-something frame. He has one foot on the floor of the car as he leans over me. I inhale quickly when his mouth moves along my neck, then traces a path down my chest with his tongue.

"It's never enough," he says, sounding angry about it.

And I know exactly what he means. Calling this pull between

us *attraction* seems too tame. It's an enchantment. An addiction. A compulsion.

He pushes into me more slowly this time, a slow drag that electrifies every nerve ending. I moan, loudly, no longer caring that the driver might hear. Need eradicates any inhibitions. I'll scream his name for the whole damn city.

My fingers weave into the thick strands of his hair, mussing it even more as Oliver rocks his hips into mine. His lips find mine again, a deep, erotic possession that sneaks down my spine in rivulets of heat. The friction is indescribable, pleasure bubbling inside of me like a shaken bottle of champagne ready to explode. The thick invasion of his cock and the grind against my clit is all it takes for release to pulse through me. Oliver continues thrusting, and it goes on and on in endless, blissful waves.

I feel him swell, followed by the unfamiliar spill of heat as he comes inside of me.

Oliver doesn't move off me right away. When he does, it feels like a loss. He doesn't make any attempt to fix his hair or bowtie, just pulls up his pants and refastens his belt. I straighten my dress, pressing my thighs together beneath the fabric.

The car comes to a stop outside his building.

"You were wrong."

I look over, but Oliver is staring out the window. "About what?"

"Marrying you being on my list of regrets."

He opens his door and steps outside.

CHAPTER TWENTY-SIX

OLIVER

New York appears as sleepy as I feel, the streets nearly empty this early on a Sunday. Even amidst the skyscrapers that house the most profitable businesses in the country. In the world.

I cover a yawn as I step outside of the car, buttoning my coat against the morning chill. Walk past the manicured hedges and the trickling fountain, wondering what I'm headed toward.

The security guard nods his head as I approach, appearing unsurprised by my appearance.

I swipe my badge and head for the elevators, scanning it again before I press the button for the executive floor. My head pounds for multiple reasons, as it ascends toward the top of the building.

Once the elevator doors open, I head toward my father's office, passing thc familiar rows of empty, dark offices.

Crew is already waiting outside. I take a moment to appreciate the show of solidarity, nodding to him as I walk past and open the door to enter the largest office on this floor.

My father is seated behind his massive desk, scowling like he's the one being inconvenienced by this last minute, early morning meeting that *he* requested. The sun rises behind him, casting diluted light over the leather furnishings that match every office on this floor. His glower deepens when he catches sight of my outfit. Both my father and Crew are in suits. I'm wearing a sweatshirt and joggers.

"What the hell are you wearing, Oliver?"

"Clothes."

"You expect anyone to take you seriously when you dress like you've just left the gym?"

"Did you call me here to lecture me on what I wear into the office on a Sunday, Dad?"

My father's expression barely reacts, but I can tell he's taken off guard by my tone. I've spent years as his yes man, never challenging a single decision. I'm done.

"No. I want you to explain to me what the fuck happened last night. We lost Zantech, and I want to know why. How?"

"You're overreacting, Dad," Crew says from his spot in the corner. His tone is bored but his posture is tense.

As much as I appreciate his support, I wish he'd keep his mouth shut. There's nothing our father likes less than us presenting a united front.

Predictably, he disagrees with Crew's assessment of the situation. Red creeps up his neck beneath the collar of his blue button down. "*Overreacting?* You know exactly what that contract was worth, Crew. Gone, now. Covington won't let that deal slip away."

"Somehow, I think we'll manage to keep the lights on without it," Crew drawls.

"This is no joking matter, Crew. If your brother hadn't just managed to fuck up a hundred-million-dollar contract, I'd be tempted to reconsider you as my successor."

My molars grind as I forcibly tamp down any reaction.

Arthur Kensington is a master at emotional manipulation.

If I'd left the reception last night and locked down this deal, I'd have been shocked to receive a *good job*, much less a promotion.

But losing it? Of course, Kensington Consolidated is on the brink of financial ruin and I'm inept.

Only my mistakes are acknowledged.

"They called you?" I ask.

My father's sharp gaze shifts back to me. My phone begins buzzing in my pocket, but I ignore it.

"Emailed. They only talk on the phone with companies they do business with, apparently."

"I spoke to them on the phone yesterday morning, and he mentioned nothing about a later conversation. Or a pending decision. They've had weeks to agree to terms. And he suddenly decides to commit immediately, or he'll go elsewhere?"

"Your job was to get him to sign, Oliver! Whenever he decided to! A fucking intern could have handled it."

"Maybe you should have assigned one, then, instead of expecting me to handle the jobs of three employees."

My father's stare grows harder. Colder. I feel like a kid again, kicking myself for not doing better. For forgetting a chore or getting one B instead of straight A's.

But I'm an adult now, who realizes my father's standards are impossible to meet. That I need to stop trying to before I go insane.

"Offer is off the table, Oliver. You won't be the next CEO of Kensington Consolidated. You're obviously not willing to do what it takes."

He's expecting me to argue. React. I don't give him the satisfaction of either. I just nod. All I want to do is get out of here and back to my penthouse before Hannah has to leave.

"If you want this company to continue being run by a Kensington, he will be."

My father and I both look at Crew, who abandons his spot in the corner to walk over to the desk, pulling a piece of paper out of the inside pocket of his jacket and dropping it down on the varnished wood.

"For you, Dad."

His forehead wrinkles as he picks it up.

"My resignation letter," Crew adds.

"*What*?"

The twin exclamation is one of a few instances when my father and I have been on the same page at the same second. We both sound…stunned.

"This is my official notice."

"What the *fuck* do you think you're doing, Crew?" our father spits. "You're turning your back on your family?"

Crew meets his gaze, calm and unaffected. "I'm *choosing* my family. The woman I love. Our kids. Lili is getting older. I'll have a second child soon. You might have been fine letting nannies raise me and Oliver, but I'm not interested in replicating that childhood. I'm going to *know* my kids, Dad. So call a headhunter and tell them you need a future CEO picked out. Or give it to the son who was always meant to have it. I'm done. If you want to be my father, that's fine. But I'm done with you being my boss."

Crew turns and walks out without another word, and it's the one and only time I've seen my father truly speechless.

For all his posturing and manipulation, I'm positive he believed neither of us would ever walk away.

Crew just called his bluff.

There's nothing else for me to say, so I follow Crew out, leaving my father to stare at the repercussions of his choices.

The hallway is empty. I walk until I reach Crew's office, knocking once on the door.

"Come in."

I open it to find Crew standing with his hands in his pockets, staring out at the rising sun.

"That was a hell of an exit."

Crew turns. He attempts a grin, but it falls flat. "I'm sorry I didn't tell you first. I found out everything was finalized yesterday, and I hadn't decided how to go about it."

"Where are you going?"

"Royce Raymond made me an offer at my wedding. Said he wanted to hand his production company over to someone with decent business sense and some shred of integrity. I reached out to him after Scarlett told me about the pregnancy. It's better hours, more flexibility. The chance to be part of something that wasn't handed to me."

"You're partnering with him?"

Crew shakes his head. "Full ownership. Scarlett is already house hunting in Los Angeles. We'll split time, but I want to be out there at first. She was already working on remote plans for once she's farther along in her pregnancy."

"I—wow."

My father wasn't the only one who thought Crew would never leave this company. None of the reasons I've ever considered doing so apply to him. I'm proud of him for putting his family first and stepping into something new. But despite the strife it's caused, I'll miss having him here.

Default isn't how I wanted to inherit this company.

"You deserve to be CEO, Oliver. You know it. I know it. Dad knows it. But if you chose to walk away too, I wouldn't blame you."

"I don't want to walk away."

He nods. "I mean it, Oliver. You deserve it."

I shove my hands into the pockets of my pants before walking deeper into his office, looking out the windows. The sun is higher in the sky, casting brilliant light over the city.

"She lives in Los Angeles."

Crew turns to take in the same view, standing shoulder to shoulder with me.

"You could try working remotely."

"I basically live in this office. All the meetings and presentations and Alicia... I could do my job, but I couldn't do it as well."

"What about her job?"

I swallow. "I don't know."

Except, I do. Los Angeles School of Design doesn't have a New York campus.

"Ask her. See what she says." He makes it sound easy, and it's anything but.

It took me half an hour to undo all the buttons on Hannah's dress last night. Then we both collapsed into bed, too exhausted to talk. I didn't bring up anything that happened in the limo, and she didn't either. And I'm worried it means she *does* regret our marriage.

"I married her."

Crew makes a shocked, strangled sound. "*What?*"

"When I was in Vegas for Garrett's bachelor party. I met her in the hotel bar, asked her to meet me later, and woke up next to a marriage license."

"Holy shit."

I laugh. "Pretty much."

"Then what?"

"We're getting divorced. Papers were filed on Monday."

"Why?"

I glance over at him. "Because we didn't mean to get married."

"But you're in love with her."

I look away, quickly. "Doesn't matter."

"Have you told her?"

Silence answers for me.

"*Tell her*, Oliver."

"I'm just like him," I say.

"No, you're not. You're good at your job, and that's where the similarities end."

"I picked her over my job last night, and I'm pissed at myself about it. I did fuck up the Zantech deal. This job is who I am, and I can't expect her to accept that. No one else has."

"Why'd you stay last night?" Crew asks.

"I…wanted to."

He smiles. "I think you're less hopeless than you think."

"Thanks."

He holds out a hand. "Good luck."

I shock us both by pulling him into a hug. "I'm proud of you," I tell Crew after we step apart. "For standing up to Dad. Doing your own thing. Lili and baby number two are lucky to have you as a father."

Crew nods and looks down, the angles of his face harsh with emotion. For the first time, I realize my opinion might matter to him. It hasn't felt like he looked up to me for anything since we were little kids.

"I'll see you later," I tell him, then leave his office and head for the elevators.

My foot taps impatiently as I wait for one to arrive and again, as it descends at what feels like an impossibly slow pace.

Crew's right, I decide, watching the numbers slowly tick down. I don't want Hannah to leave without knowing exactly where I stand. The alternative is losing her for certain, and I know I'll regret that.

Once I'm back in the car driving toward my building, I pull my phone out of my pocket. And my stomach sinks when I see I have a missed call and a voicemail from Hannah.

Heart in my throat, I tap on her name and lift the phone to my ear.

"Hi. I'm sorry to do this over the phone, but I wanted to say goodbye. I—my sister called, and April went into labor. There are complications with the delivery. I don't know all the details. But the airline was able to switch me to an earlier flight, so I'm on my way to the airport now. I woke up, and you were gone, so I just.... I hope everything is all right. And if you just needed space, well, I get that. Thanks for...thanks. I'll sign whatever you send me. So...goodbye, Oliver."

Dammit, I think.

And then I dial the number for Kensington Consolidated's private pilot.

CHAPTER TWENTY-SEVEN

HANNAH

My dad is waiting next to the baggage claim with a dorky handwritten sign that reads *Favorite (Middle) Child.*

I smile, shedding some of the exhaustion and stress as his arms wrap around me. A barrage of texts was waiting when my plane landed, letting me know that April and Eddie now have a son named Ezra and that both baby and mom are happy and healthy.

"Hi, sweetheart."

"Hi, Grandpa."

He laughs. "That title will take a little getting used to."

"Everything is really okay?"

"Yep. Just a scare. He's a cute little thing, all wide eyes and tiny toes. Reminds me of when you were little, not extending work trips to spend time with a husband."

I cleared my trip extension with his assistant since I don't have a direct supervisor. And I should have known it would take less than a minute for him to mention my longer stay in New York.

"We're still getting divorced, Dad." I pull my sunglasses

down over my eyes as we walk out the automatic doors into the sunshine. It's at least ten degrees warmer than when I left New York.

My dad says nothing, which is worse than a lecture.

I'm a coward who left New York without telling Oliver how I feel about him. And I feel the echo of that weakness in each second of silence. In the fact none of the texts waiting when I landed were from him.

My dad is a rule-follower, so we trek across the hot asphalt to the parking lot where he left his car. I fill him in on the meetings with Tyler as we walk, even knowing he's already received reports. This is the part of my job I'll really miss, if I do leave Garner Sports Agency. Sharing it with my dad.

"I met with Logan Cassidy again last week," he says, once we're in the car zooming along the palm-tree lined road, the scenery so different from New York's concrete jungle.

"How did it go?"

"Good. I think there's a good chance he'll sign with us."

"That's good." I fiddle with the hem of my t-shirt. "I got into architecture school, Dad."

I realize while he's driving probably wasn't the best time to tell him *after* he drifts over the lane divider, setting off a series of honks. He quickly swerves back, correcting the car's path.

"I'm not sure if I'm going to go," I add, once I'm confident he has driving under control again.

"Why wouldn't you go?" he asks, which is not the first question I would have guessed he'd ask.

"I'm not sure it's what I want. If I applied because it was the right decision or because I was wanting something different."

"What school?"

"Los Angeles School of Design."

"Long way from New York."

I look away from him, out the window. "It is," I agree.

And I know it's a part of my indecision. Committing to school here is different from continuing my job here. Some hopeful part of me wants to leave possibilities open.

"I've loved having you at the agency, Hannah. You know that. But starting that company was my dream. I want you to follow yours, wherever that might lead. The offices could use a facelift, so it would be handy to have an architect in the family."

"Thanks, Dad," I whisper.

He turns on the stereo, stopping on an old Beach Boys song. It serves as our soundtrack to the hospital, where my mom and Rachel are waiting in the lobby. They both give me hugs before we head to April's room. Since I'm the only one who hasn't visited, I go in first.

April is sleepy and smiling when I enter the tiny hospital room. Eddie is standing beside the bed, beaming down at her and the little bundle in her arms.

Stranger than the realization I'm an aunt is the recognition my brother is a father. That his life changed irrevocably today.

When Eddie asks if I want to hold my nephew, I don't hesitate to say yes. He's wrapped in a striped blanket, even smaller than I'm expecting. I stare down at his miniature features, his eyes closed and expression peaceful. Sleeping like a baby.

"He's beautiful, you guys."

"Thanks, Hannah," April says. "I brought the duckling onesie in my hospital bag to take him home in."

I smile. "I got a more original gift too. I'll drop it off tomorrow."

April replies with "You didn't need to get us a second gift!" at the same time Eddie tells me "Thanks." They glance at each other, then laugh.

"I'm sure Ezra will love it," she says.

"I hope so."

Unfortunately, thinking about the lamb rocker only reminds me who suggested I buy it.

I pass Ezra back to Eddie after a few minutes, noticing how exhausted April looks. I hug them both goodbye, then head out into the hallway.

My parents both duck into the room to say goodbye as well, while Rachel grabs a snack from the vending machine. I stare at the infographic about the common cold while I wait for everyone else to be ready to depart.

Everyone is cheerful and excited once we're in the car. Everyone except me, but I try to fake it. My mom is gushing about Ezra. My dad gets a call about a new contract offer. Rachel chatters about her summer trip. She's settled on Greece.

"Will you come over for dinner tomorrow night, Hannah?" my mom asks as we turn onto my street. "I want to hear all about your New York trip."

Dread trickles through me, but I know I'll have to have this conversation eventually. Might as well get it over with. "Sure, Mom."

My dad pulls over in front of my bungalow, then climbs out to grab my suitcase from the back. I check to make sure nothing fell out of my bag into the footwell, then unclick my seatbelt.

"Oliver came back with you?"

I glance over at Rachel. "What?"

She points out the window. "Isn't that him?"

Rather than look, I climb out of the car. My dad has spotted him too, waving once he's set my suitcase on the sidewalk. "You got it from here, Han?"

"Yeah. Thanks, Dad."

He winks, squeezes my shoulder, and then climbs in the car.

I start up the front walk to my house, rolling my suitcase along the path.

Oliver stands as I approach, the porch swing rocking slightly as he walks over to the front steps. He's wearing joggers and a sweatshirt, looking rumpled and nothing like his usual polished self. His casual clothes make me smile, for some stupid reason. It feels like some part of myself I've left on him.

I abandon my suitcase a few feet from the stairs, racing up them and flinging myself into his arms. Oliver staggers back a half-step before regaining his balance.

I don't know why he's here. But he came, and that matters to me. He wasn't too busy to notice I'd left. His arms tighten around my back, and I exhale for what feels like the first time since I left New York.

"Is April okay?"

I pull back so I can see his face. "She's great. I have a nephew. Ezra. He's really cute. So tiny, I was nervous to hold him."

Oliver smiles. Then, very seriously, asks, "Do you want kids?"

"I, um, I…" I'm completely thrown, is what I am. That's he's here, and that *that's* the second question he asked. "I don't know. Do you?"

"I didn't think so. But I would be open to it, if my wife did."

I study his face, trying to determine if he's using wife in a general sense or if he's referring to *me*.

"I thought you didn't want to ever get married."

"Yeah. I thought that too. Then I realized I don't want a divorce, either."

"You don't?" Something that feels a lot like hope spreads through me.

"No. I meant what I said last night, Hannah. I don't regret

marrying you. It was the best damn thing that's ever happened to me."

Happiness expands in my chest, bright and fizzy.

"I'm selfish, Hannah. Set in my ways and I spend way too much time focused on a company that doesn't spare a thought for me. But it's who I am, Hannah. I'll never be able to change, not all the way. I need you to know that. Just like I need you to know… I love you. I'm *in love* with you. I'm not sure when it happened, when it started, but it's gone nowhere. It's this part of me now."

I don't realize I'm crying until he gently swipes a tear away.

"Sorry." I sniff, wiping the rest with the back of my hand. "It's been a day."

"I know."

I step closer to him, inhaling his familiar scent. It feels like home, more than the house we're standing in front of. "I'm in love with you too."

Oliver visibly swallows, and I wonder if anyone has ever said that to him. If he's ever said it to anyone. So I say it again, in even simpler terms.

"I love you, Oliver."

He tugs me against his body and kisses me. It's slower than most of the ones we've shared. Savoring and sweet. Like the first of many, instead of possibly the last.

Oliver brushes some hair out of my face, tucking it behind my ear. "My dad called me in for a meeting early this morning. I thought I'd be back before you woke up."

"What did he want?" I ask.

"He was pissed about a deal that went sour. But the real surprise was Crew handed in a resignation letter. He's leaving the company. Moving here, actually, part-time."

That's why he was here a few weeks ago, I realize.

"So, you'll be the next CEO."

"If I stay."

"What do you mean, if you stay? You've dedicated your whole career to the company. You *want* CEO."

He doesn't disagree. "The headquarters are in New York. It's where I'd have to work."

"They have architecture schools in New York."

Oliver's jaw clenches. "I don't want you to have to give up on—"

"I'm not giving up on anything. I promise."

His green gaze simmers with emotions. "I love you."

I rise up on my tippytoes, wrapping my arms around his neck and fusing our mouths together. His hands land on my ass, pulling me into his growing erection.

"How long can you stay?" I ask, when his mouth moves to my neck, nipping and sucking at the sensitive skin. I literally melt against him, giving up on holding myself upright.

"Couple of days. I took the jet, but my dad can't do shit unless he wants to hand the company over to a stranger."

"If he *really* can't do shit, you should stay for a week."

I feel his chest reverberate with a chuckle. "You could probably convince me."

"How?" I ask, feigning confusion.

Oliver laughs again, and I savor the sound. He pulls away to grab my suitcase from the spot where I abandoned it, while I unlock my front door.

And then we walk inside.

Together.

CHAPTER TWENTY-EIGHT

OLIVER

There's a knock on the door. "Come in," I call out.

I'm expecting Crew.

Instead, my father steps inside.

My fingers freeze halfway through the buttons of my shirt.

I'm not surprised he came. Appearances matter to my father, if nothing else. Attending the wedding of his son isn't an event he could miss without raising a lot of eyebrows. As far as most people know, my father is far more affectionate with me and Crew than he ever has been in private. Been with me, at least.

"Hi, Dad."

"Oliver."

Crew officially left Kensington Consolidated two months ago, right before Scarlett gave birth to their second child. He and my father had a long conversation at the hospital when he came to see the baby, while I sat in the room with Scarlett and Hannah. As far as I know, that was the first time they talked outside the office since Crew told him he was leaving the company.

This is the first time *I'm* talking to my father outside of the office. We discuss work and nothing else, adjusting to the new dynamic of no Crew. It's not really better or worse. Just…different.

"You never RSVP'd."

One dark eyebrow rises, like a slash. "You thought I wouldn't come?"

"I wasn't sure."

There's a flash of emotion across his face, something that almost looks like sadness. It disappears too quickly for me to tell for sure.

"Nice church."

Turns out, when it's unrelated to golf or business or expensive alcohol, my father is terrible at small talk.

I clear my throat, finishing buttoning my shirt and straightening the collar. "It's where Hannah's parents got married."

He nods. "Met them outside. Nice couple. Dean has done well for himself."

"Yes. Thank God the woman I'm marrying isn't penniless. Her father isn't a billionaire, but she should inherit *something*." Sarcasm drips from my voice.

My father clears his throat. "She seems like a nice girl, Oliver. I hope you're happy together."

"Thanks."

"I know I've been a shitty father." He drops the blunt declaration on me with no warning whatsoever.

I blink rapidly, trying to decide how to respond to the candor. "I've been a shitty son." No matter what, Candace will always be a regret I can't reverse.

"I only wanted the best for you boys. I was…proud. Of the men you were becoming. The legacy I was leaving. And then…it was hard to know when to stop pushing. I always wanted you to accomplish more." He clears his throat, the closest to uncomfortable I've seen in a long time. Then holds out an envelope. "A wedding gift."

I take the envelope from him and pull out the sheets of paper. It takes a minute, to digest the legalese. "You're stepping down *next month*?"

"You've earned it." That's all he says, before turning and leaving me reeling.

Typical of my father, to never linger. To hand me what matters most in the world to him like it's a lukewarm cup of coffee and give me no chance to respond.

Eventually, I realize I've been standing here too long and need to finish getting ready. I've just finished the buttons on my shirt when there's another knock on the door.

"Yeah?"

This time, it is Crew who walks in. His newborn son, Christopher, is strapped to his chest.

Christopher *Oliver* Kensington.

I'd be lying if I said I didn't get choked up when I first heard his full name.

"You're not ready?" he asks, looking at the hanging jacket I've yet to put on.

I hold the papers out to him. "Dad stopped by."

Crew absorbs the contents faster than I did. He whistles, long and low. "Wow. Congratulations."

"I wasn't sure if he'd ever step down. Let alone in a few weeks. I've barely adjusted to you being gone. Now…it's a lot."

"Well, Dad never cared much for good timing. Business doesn't wait, and all that."

I nod, tucking the papers back into the envelope carefully. Now that the shock is wearing off, there are other emotions. Excitement. Anticipation.

Today, I'm gaining the two things I always thought would be

discordant. I thought I'd have to choose between becoming CEO and marrying for love. Between success and happiness. Gaining both is unsettling in the best way.

Garrett and Asher walk in as I'm finishing getting ready.

"Reporting for baby duty," Asher says, holding out his hands for Christopher.

Crew is serving as my best man, and Hannah's sister Rachel is her maid of honor.

"Make sure that you—" Crew starts.

"I got a twenty-minute spiel from Scarlett," Asher says. "I can handle carrying the kid from here into the church. Promise."

Reluctantly, Crew lets his son go.

"Good luck," Garrett tells me, punching me lightly in the arm.

As far as he knows—as far as most people attending our wedding know—Hannah and I aren't married yet. But we halted the divorce before it was finalized, so we legally are. It's easy to pretend this is our first wedding, though, since neither of us remember it.

"Thanks," I reply.

"You ready to do this?" Crew asks. "Sober?"

I roll my eyes, but smile. "Yeah."

I walk side by side with my brother, toward the church where I'm marrying Hannah Garner for a second time.

HANNAH

My mom cries when I hug her goodbye. "My God, you look so beautiful, sweetheart."

"Thanks, Mom."

"Call me when you land, all right?"

I nod. "I will."

My dad kisses my cheek. "I love you, sweetheart."

"I love you too."

Rachel is next, bouncing on her toes with excitement until she has the chance to throw her arms around me. "Thank you for marrying a guy with tons of hot, rich, single friends. You're my favorite sister."

I shake my head and laugh before hugging Eddie. He tells me to travel safely as I hug April and kiss Ezra's forehead.

Then, I reach Oliver's family, which is infinitely more awkward.

Scarlett is first.

"Thank you again for the dress," I tell her.

Much to the envy of brides everywhere, I'm wearing a *rouge* original. They don't even have a bridal line.

I was stunned when Scarlett offered. And it's everything I imagined and more, mostly since it signifies the wedge between Scarlett and me might not be permanent.

"We'll get dinner, next time you're in New York?"

She nods, glancing at Crew, who's attempting to console a crying Lili with a sleeping Christopher strapped to his chest. "I'll leave Crew at home with the kids. Oliver can help him babysit."

"I heard that," Crew says, pulling a fruit bar out of his pocket and handing it to his daughter. The waterworks stop immediately.

"Bribery, really?" Scarlett asks.

"Did you have a better idea?" Crew asks, straightening. He leans forward for a one-armed hug. I squeeze his arm, careful not to crush Christopher between our bodies. "I'm happy for you, Hannah," he says.

"Thanks, Crew."

We share a smile.

And then, I'm face to face with Arthur Kensington in person. I've split my time between LA and New York leading up to the wedding, but none of the time I've spent in Manhattan has been around Oliver's father. I wasn't even sure if he'd be here.

When I asked Oliver if his father was attending, his response was "Probably."

The picture I had in my head was a villain, some gnarled monster with dead eyes and an icy heart. But I'm staring at what Oliver will look like in thirty years. The resemblance between him and his father is uncanny. Same eyes, same jawline, same proud stance.

"Hello, Hannah."

"Hi, Mr. Kensington."

His expression is shrewd as he studies me intently. I resist the urge to shift under his scrutiny. Undoubtedly, he's thinking about all the ways I'm lacking. In comparison to his other daughter-in-law, I'm contributing nothing to the Kensington name.

"We're family. You're welcome to call me Arthur." His smile is warm, and I can't tell if that's genuine or feigned. I should have guessed he'd be charming.

"I didn't think you treated your family different from anyone else, Mr. Kensington."

Arthur's smile tightens. "You're wrong. I treat them worse."

I'm taken totally off guard by his response. In my experience, narcissists are rarely self-aware.

He reaches into the pocket of his navy suit, extracting a rectangular velvet box. "These belonged to my late wife, Elizabeth. She'd want Oliver's bride to have something of hers."

"Thank you," I say automatically, flipping the lid open. A pair of diamond earrings twinkle in their settings, the jewels almost blinding in the sunshine. There's a central diamond surrounded by a halo of smaller ones. The design matches the engagement ring Scarlett is wearing. "Wow. They're stunning."

"I had them custom-made to match her ring," Arthur says. "Gave them to her on our wedding day."

There's a softer note to his voice, but any emotion is carefully shuttered away by the time I look up.

"You should stow those for safekeeping. They're worth a small fortune."

He doesn't want anyone else to see them, I realize. Nodding, I slip the jewelry into my bag for the plane, hiding the thoughtful gesture. Wondering how much else Arthur hides behind.

After we say the rest of our goodbyes, a car takes me and Oliver straight from our reception to the airport. It's a short drive, about twenty minutes in total.

I regret not changing out of my wedding dress after about five. I wanted to savor wearing it, since this is the only occasion where I will. But the yards of fabric take up most of the backseat, bunching around my waist and around my legs.

Oliver casts me an amused smile but doesn't comment. He carefully helps me out of the backseat once we arrive at the tarmac. We're taking Kensington Consolidated's private plane, which I've only been on once before.

Uniformed attendants rush around, loading up the plane with our luggage and doing last-minute safety checks. I climb the four steps that lead inside the plane, surveying the luxurious surroundings.

I drop my bag on the couch and walk over to a window seat, kicking off my heels and peering outside. Oliver has refused to tell me where he's taking me for my honeymoon, so I had to guess about what to pack. That's reflected in the four suitcases that are being carted from the car.

Oliver climbs onto the plane a few minutes later. "We should be leaving in a couple of minutes."

"Can you hand me my phone?" I ask, pointing to my bag. "I want to take photos of the plane."

"Why?" Oliver asks, looking amused as he grabs my purse and starts to dig through it.

"Have you *seen* it?" I ask, digging my toes into the soft carpet.

"What's this?"

I glance over to find him holding the small velvet box I slipped into my bag before leaving our reception. I bite my bottom lip, not sure how he'll react. "Your dad gave them to me as we were leaving. They were your mom's."

He opens the box, then quickly shuts it. "Yeah, I recognize them."

"I don't have to wear them…"

"No, you should. She would want you to."

I don't tell Oliver that's exactly what his father said. I watch the emotions war on his face as he turns the box over and over in his hands before carefully setting it back inside my purse.

"Maybe he has regrets too," I whisper.

Oliver shrugs, but the motion is stiff. He walks over and hands my phone to me, then takes the opposite seat and looks out the window. We're beginning to move, turning toward the airstrip.

I don't bother unlocking my phone or snapping any photos. There's a melancholy surrounding Oliver that I'm guessing has everything to do with his parents. I've never appreciated my own mom and dad more than I do right now. They were both at my wedding. Both supportive, even knowing how our relationship began. Oliver didn't have that today. Hasn't had it for a long time, if ever.

"Are you going to tell me where we're going now?"

I'm relieved to see him smile, before glancing toward me. "It has impressive architecture," he tells me.

I roll my eyes, then watch out the window as the plane takes off. Once we've leveled out, I stand. "I'm going to change."

The only other time I've been on the jet was to accompany Oliver on a work trip to Chicago. Asher and another Kensington Consolidated employee, Scott, were with us, and it was a short flight. I looked in the back bedroom but didn't spend any time in here.

The rear of the plane contains a king-sized bed, centered with windows on either side and decorated with cream and gold accents. If not for the occasional swoop in my stomach and the cloud cover through the windows, I'd have no idea this bedroom is airborne.

I struggle with the back of my wedding dress for about thirty seconds before calling Oliver in for help. He'll probably grumble about it, but I don't want to risk ripping the fabric.

A few seconds later, I hear him walk in the bedroom.

"What do you have against dresses with zippers?" he asks, his hands finding the buttons holding the back of my dress together.

"I didn't design the dress. Ask Scarlett."

I don't tell him, but it took Rosie, Rachel, and April a half hour to get me into this dress. I should have had them help me out of it too, but I liked the idea of leaving in my wedding dress. I wasn't opposed to having sex in it either, but that's looking unlikely.

Oliver's silent, as my dress loosens bit by bit.

"Are you happy?" I ask.

His hands stop moving, and then a few seconds later I'm spun around to face him. He looks torn between bewilderment and incredulity. "*Of course* I am. It's our wedding day."

"You've barely said anything since we left the reception."

He exhales. "I'm sorry, Han. My dad decided to hand me the

company today. He's retiring next month, and it caught me off guard."

I gape at him, stunned. "You're going to be CEO *next month*?"

Oliver nods. "Yeah. I knew it was coming. But I didn't think it would be this soon."

"Wow. Congratulations. That's…wow."

I knew it was coming too. But it's still a big moment. A big moment Oliver has spent years—decades—working toward.

He smiles, then pulls me closer. "I'm happy, Hannah. So fucking happy. Seeing my dad just… I wish my mom could have been there today. Wish things were different with him. It's just harder, some days."

I slide a hand beneath his tuxedo jacket, until I find the steady thump of his heart. "You have me," I whisper. "You'll always have me."

He kisses me, and it's so intense, so consuming, that I don't even realize he's moving me toward the bed until I'm falling onto the mattress.

Awareness crackles between us like electricity as we continue kissing. I grew accustomed to the idea of being married to Oliver a while ago. But this feels different—me in a wedding dress and him in a tux. It feels real and permanent and lasting, all of those forever ideals marriage is meant to represent.

I wriggle against the comforter, the fabric of my dress forming its own blanket around me. "Can you please get me out of this?"

Oliver grins. "I only made it through ten buttons."

"Out of…"

"A hundred?"

I sigh. "Can you keep going? There's no way I can sleep in this tonight."

"Who said you'll be sleeping?" His smile turns wicked. "*Wife.*"

I can't see his hands. But I feel them, lifting and shifting the fabric of the dress until my legs are exposed. White silk blocks my view from his shoulders down, but I have an idea what he's intending when the thong I'm wearing gets pulled down my legs.

My hips jerk when I feel his tongue trace my slit, the sudden sensation electrifying. He licks me until I'm shuddering and gasping, then replaces his tongue with his dick.

"This what you want?"

I'm too busy moaning to form actual words. There's no worry. No second-guessing. I can just sink into the pleasure, knowing he'll be there to keep me from drowning.

No one but Oliver has been able to push me so far, so quickly. I can feel a second orgasm cresting, even though I just came. The addiction only he can feed racing to the surface. He rubs my clit and I tighten around him, holding him, even though we're permanently fused in other ways.

His strokes are deeper. Harder. Like he knows exactly what I need. And then he's kissing me, possessing my mouth the same way he's controlling the rest of my body. I come in a shuddering wave, feeling his release fill me with warmth.

"It will never be enough," he whispers. "But it'll be a hell of a lot of times."

EPILOGUE
OLIVER

Sweat dribbles down my back in steady streams, the sun relentless in its beams. The group ahead of us finally moves ahead to the next hole, so we can stop standing around, baking in the heat.

"Easy angle," my father says, carefully selecting a club and walking over to the waiting ball. But he surveys the course intently, not taking the shot immediately.

Crew groans, lifting his club and pressing it against the back of his neck as he looks up at the blue sky. "Just hit the damn ball, Dad."

It's crowded and hot, and our dad refuses to take anything less than a perfect shot.

Golf has never been Crew's thing. My dad and I have played together a lot, but that was usually with possible clients. Never just the two of us.

But this outing was his idea, so here the three of us are, attempting to look past years of animosity and resentment and mistakes over the course of eighteen holes.

"Working in Hollywood has made you impatient."

Crew rolls his eyes, then grabs a bottle of water from the golf cart. I stare at the motionless leaves on the palm tree until they begin to sway, the breeze off the water finally moving this way. The air is too warm to offer much relief, but it's something. And despite the heat, the surroundings are beautiful. The lush green of the resort's golf course stretches right up to one of the white beaches, with the turquoise water continuing into the horizon.

My dad finally takes his shot, rolling it close enough to the hole, he'll probably make it on the next hit. Then, it's Crew's turn. His swing is weak, barely moving the ball. He scowls at my dad, who doesn't offer a criticism, shockingly. My ball lands between theirs, not as close as my dad's but not as far as Crew's.

By the time we finish two more holes, my back is completely drenched with sweat. Crew and I exchange glances, and it's like we're kids again. Neither willing to break first.

Surprisingly, our father is the one who calls it first, suggesting we finish the course tomorrow. Crew and I quickly agree; Crew even more eagerly after our dad offers to take his kids for ice cream.

They drop me off at mine and Hannah's private villa, after making plans to meet for dinner at six.

A gust of cold air greets me as I step inside the small house, the air conditioning raising goosebumps on my damp skin. There's no sign of Hannah in the living room. I step into the bedroom, which is also empty, stripping off my sweaty polo and tossing it in a corner. I head toward the bathroom, where I left my swim trunks to dry last night.

To my surprise, the handle doesn't move. It's locked.

I knock. "Hannah?"

There's a delay before she responds. "I thought you were out golfing."

"It was crowded and hot, so we cut the trip short."

And Crew started speeding after our dad offered to take Lili and Christopher to get ice cream. I'm certain how he's hoping to spend his alone time with Scarlett, and I was thinking something similar with Hannah once I wash the sweat off in the pool or ocean.

"What's wrong? Are you sick?"

The door opens so suddenly, I almost fall forward.

"Not currently, but I will be." Hannah presses a piece of plastic against my chest, then walks past me into the bedroom and flops down on the bed.

I blink down at the pregnancy test. The *positive* pregnancy test.

"Wow."

Hannah scoffs, then covers her eyes with her elbow. "My reaction was a little more extreme than that."

I set the test down on the dresser and crawl onto the bed next to her. The bed faces the turquoise water, a private pool and patio the only thing separating the private villa from the sea. The view from our penthouse is nice but doesn't beat this one.

Hannah rolls over, hooking a leg with mine. I run a hand up and down her arm.

"I didn't think it would happen," she says.

"I know."

We tried to get pregnant about a year after our wedding. The timing seemed right, since she'd just stopped working at Garner Sports Agency in favor of starting an administrative job at an architecture firm, trying to decide if going back to school was what she really wanted.

After two years of unprotected sex, I think we both assumed we'd need to explore other avenues to parenthood. Something we've been too busy to discuss, let alone act on. Hannah just started her second year of architecture school. And I've been the

CEO of Kensington Consolidated for nearly four years, which hasn't decreased the number of hours I have to spend in the office by any stretch.

"You're late?"

"Yeah. And I've felt nauseous for the past few days. I thought it was just jet lag and living above the ocean, but then I decided to take a test. It could be wrong, obviously. I don't know how accurate they are."

"Your boobs feel bigger," I say, running my hand up her arm and across her chest to cup one breast. She's wearing a flimsy bikini beneath her tank top. I feel her nipple pebble, reacting to my touch.

"That's helpful, thanks."

I chuckle, rolling so I'm hovering over her and can see her expression better. Balancing my weight on one elbow, I brush the hair away from her face.

"I hope it's right. If it's not, we can keep trying."

Hannah chews her bottom lip. "I could never tell how disappointed you were…"

I exhale, knowing this is something we probably should have talked about more. We both assumed this moment would have happened a while ago. Then got used to it never appearing.

"I didn't know either, honestly. But I'm happy, Han."

"I'm terrified," she says, bluntly. "I have no clue how to raise a kid."

"At least you had good role models. I barely remember my mom. And you know how my dad is."

He's better, I'll admit. Coming on this vacation was a big step forward. He's way more relaxed around Lili and Christopher than he's ever been with me and Crew. Maybe it's because he won't be responsible for who they become.

For better or worse, I know Crew and I would have turned out very differently if he'd been a more indulgent father. We might have been spoiled and entitled. Definitely less hard-working.

"So basically, we're fucked?"

I smile. "Crew and Scarlett seemed to figure it out."

"Their children are terrors."

"They're both stubborn and demanding. Of course their kids are mini dictators."

"*You're* stubborn and demanding, Oliver."

"Thank God you're so sweet and mellow, then." I steal a kiss.

Hannah rolls her eyes, then shoves at my chest. "Get off. You're all sweaty."

I roll onto my back, watching her head into the bathroom. "I was going to swim. Want to come?"

"I'm supposed to go over to Scarlett and Crew's to borrow a dress for dinner. I got distracted, after buying the test."

"My dad took their kids to get ice cream. So now probably isn't the best time to go over there," I say, rolling off the bed.

"Okay, fine. I just need to put more sunscreen on."

But when I walk into the bathroom, she's not applying sunscreen. She's standing with her shirt lifted, staring at her flat stomach in the mirror's reflection.

I step out of my khaki shorts and pull on my swim trunks, before walking up behind her. My head bends, kissing just above her collarbone before my hands land on her belly.

I rest my chin on the top of her head. "Any regrets?" I ask her. It's our version of *you okay?*, since that's all we were supposed to be. Regrets.

Even if I wasn't staring at her face, I'd hear the smile in her answer. "Nope. You?"

"None."

My arms tighten around her.

Hannah makes a sound of contentment deep in the back of her throat.

Her head tilts to the side, just enough for me to capture her lips with mine. It's slow and certain. The languid kind of kiss you only share with someone when you're certain they're the person you'll be kissing for the rest of your life.

It's everything I thought I'd never have.

And…it's *real.*

THE END

ACKNOWLEDGMENTS

This book was, by far, my most challenging to write. Hannah and Oliver are two complex characters who experience a lot of growth between *Fake Empire* and the end of this book, and I struggled a lot to make sure that was conveyed on page. I'm so happy with how this book turned out and so grateful to my amazing team for helping shape it into the best possible version.

Kim, thank you for this incredible cover. It matches *Fake Empire*'s perfectly and I couldn't love it any more. You always make the cover design process efficient and enjoyable, and I couldn't be more grateful.

Mel, thank you for taking the extra time and effort to help me ensure everything I intended came through as clearly as possible. Your insight and input on this manuscript were invaluable.

Tiffany, you went above and beyond and *beyond* on this book. Thank you for being a cheerleader in addition to an amazing editor. I'm so grateful for your friendship and support.

Alison, thank you for an incredible proofing job. It's always a pleasure to work with you and I hope to do so on many more books!

Autumn and the whole crew at Wordsmith Publicity, thank you for everything you did to ensure this book reached as many people as possible!

And finally, thank YOU for reading. I was blown away by the love Crew and Scarlett received, and I hope you enjoyed Oliver and Hannah's story just as much!

ABOUT THE AUTHOR

C.W. Farnsworth is the author of numerous adult and young adult romance novels featuring sports, strong female leads, and happy endings.

Charlotte lives in Rhode Island and when she isn't writing spends her free time reading, at the beach, or snuggling with her Australian Shepherd.

Find her on Facebook (@cwfarnsworth), Twitter (@cw_farnsworth), Instagram (@authorcwfarnsworth) and check out her website www.authorcwfarnsworth.com for news about upcoming releases!

ALSO BY C.W. FARNSWORTH

Four Months, Three Words

Kiss Now, Lie Later

First Flight, Final Fall

Come Break My Heart Again

Famous Last Words

Winning Mr. Wrong

Back Where We Began

Like I Never Said

Fly Bye

Serve

Fake Empire

Heartbreak for Two

For Now, Not Forever

Friday Night Lies

Tuesday Night Truths

Pretty Ugly Promises

Six Summers to Fall

Left Field Love

Printed in Great Britain
by Amazon

42418325R00219